At The End of Magic

MARY PETRIE

ISBN: 1499194013
ISBN-13: 978-1499194012

DEDICATION

For John, Stryker, Scarlett, and Merrick.

CONTENTS

ACKNOWLEDGMENTS

For years, I've enjoyed the friendship, encouragement, and critique of fellow writers Brian Felland, Marianne Herrmann and Ann Browning Zerby who not only read early drafts of this book, but every bit of fiction I've written: thank you! My husband, John, has been steadfast in faith and love; his presence in my life has made all its goodness possible. It's a privilege to be a parent when you land children like this: Stryker, Scarlett, and Merrick. Thank you for cheering me on and for the fabulous adventures of your lives! This book would not be here without Stryker, who surreptitiously acquired the manuscript and painstakingly shouldered every element of publication: thank you for taking your mother's dreams off the shelf and turning them into this book. Tessa Portuese's cover design is not only beautiful on its own but also perfectly matches my vision. It's an honor to have her gifts and intuition shaping this book. Of course, any missteps in plot, character, tone and sentence are entirely my own.

1
DELPHI

The little girl has curly, red-blonde hair. I'm guessing she's four or five. Can't be three, not with that vocabulary—unless she's a genius. See, there I go. Reasoning like a sane person, except the thing I'm trying to analyze doesn't exist. When Professor Gaines spits out platitudes, the rest of my classmates sit up and listen, obviously unaware of Molly or Heidi or Heather, or whatever her name is. She stares out the window and sets the beakers that line the shelves spinning. The kid keeps a sly, indirect eye on me. She explores an empty desk before walking up the aisles to study my more tangible companions. Gaines drones on about the Tao of science. Give me a break. This is Physics for Poets, not a trip to East. However, far as I can tell, he has my so-called peers in the palm of his hand.

I can't quite *hear* the girl. Instead, I spend the precious minutes that might actually let me pass this class trying to field the odd ideas that pop into my head. I seem to be thinking somebody else's thoughts. Random, baby fragments about blue Popsicles, plastic hats at Bennie's birthday party, and painting patio chairs. Whoever heard of painting chairs, just for fun? Yet I look at this girl in a yellow flowered dress—always the same—and am immediately reminded of hauling a white plastic patio chair onto the driveway. I sweep streaks of purple across the back, pink along the legs, and neon green on the seat. The art chair, I call it. This is a memory. I've never painted a chair in my life.

I'm seriously considering a psychiatrist. Soliciting help, and fast, would be the logical action to take, and I sure could use some proof of my level-headedness. However, implicating myself as imbalanced would immediately occupy all my time—shrinks and pills and meetings with my father. Graduation is in ten short weeks: I'm too busy to become a patient.

Honestly, her presence feels natural, not nutty. When she first appeared, I was barely surprised, mostly curious. I might even enjoy her hanging around if I didn't get weepy by the end of class. She's sad! Not normal kid-sad, as if she'd lost a doll or missed the circus. Her mood is fundamental. Even though there's a particular problem—something she lost that she's worried about—this child wasn't happy long before. Can a person be born yearning?

She pirouettes in the corner, staring solemnly at the swoops her arms make.

I watch her dance. Is feeling comfortable with your delusion a symptom of schizophrenia? There must be a book on the topic.

"Delphi?" Professor Gaines taps on his table and bellows. "Sorry to interrupt. I'm requesting input on paper topics." He chuckles as if he knows my type—one more woman lost within the subtleties of science. "You wouldn't happen to have an idea. Would you?"

If only this lout understood that he poses the sole threat to my 4.0, a grade point average earned, in part, by avoiding all subjects remotely scientific. Unfortunately, this otherwise cushy liberal arts system demands a moderate dose of atoms, numbers and similar muck that flies against the grain of my otherwise well-functioning brain.

My solution to the requirement is Physics for Poets, a course with a cruelly deceptive title. Turns out, overly stimulated science freaks can't get their fixes the regular way; they sign up for sections reserved for the ill-equipped. Even worse, half the guys take this class to meet women. I'm stuck, ogled by the very people I was trying to avoid. How are all the artsy students fulfilling their science requirements? You'd think at least one of those clay-streaked slackers who smoke behind the art building would've ended up here.

"Delphi?"

I wish I'd been paying attention, if only to whip out a response worthy of wiping the bored look off Gaines' face. Being assigned to this class must have been some departmental punishment.

Alas, I have no pithy reply. I'm contrite. "No, sorry. I don't have a topic to contribute."

"Fine, then." Expectations met, he moves to the man behind me without pausing. The interaction gives me an instant headache. Nothing major, a small painful slice behind my left eye.

The girl has hoisted herself onto the ledge by the window. She folds her legs into the yellow dress, sets her pointed chin on her knees, and smiles at me.

Not a single other person turns in her direction. The football player type right across the aisle gazes out over the parking lot without indicating anything unusual is afoot. I blink and stare again.

She's still there. God, I wish somebody would stand up and point: who is that kid!

Mr. Football annoys Gaines as much as women. He pounces on him for a topic.

"I like the consciousness thing," offers Football.

Gaines raises his eyebrows. "You and half the class." He sighs heavily and leans against the table. "Shall we make this official? How many here would like the physics of consciousness as a term paper topic?"

Nearly every hand shoots up. Wow. I missed that whole debate. I might be the only person in the room who has no idea what the topic even means.

Professor Gaines beams at us condescendingly. "Well, well. Once again, I'll be reading thirty essays on brain waves—or lack thereof."

As if he wasn't the one who mandated a group topic—a requirement obviously reserved for the slow-witted, since I've never stumbled onto the concept before. I do see the advantages, even without Gaines' commentary on the historical significance of scientific communities. Great—sharing information has served humanity well. Let's hope the practice serves me well, too. I hope to glean enough info off others' ideas to come up with a few thoughts of my own.

I check on the kid—still sitting and staring. I wince into the sunlight, headache intensifying. Great.

Gaines shuffles us into pairs. "Brainstorm," he says dryly, as if there aren't enough cells in the room to pose a real danger of that happening.

I land the guy behind me, Ian somebody or other. He's tall

and skinny, all glasses and pale face that scream: I've been locked up in a lab all summer!

"The physics of consciousness—that has great potential, don't you think?" He beams, so gung ho I feel sorry for him. This is probably the closest he'll get to a humanities topic all quarter.

Me, I lack enthusiasm for anything except relief from the suddenly escalating pain behind my eye, now spiraling through my forehead. "Yeah, great idea. What are you going to write about?" The more he talks, the less I have to. I press two fingers to my skull and smile encouragingly through the haze, not registering a word.

The pain is unbearable. I must find a bathroom or get a drink of water. The throbbing destroys my ability to think. The room starts to blur and white flashes ripple the corner of my vision. This is exactly how Dad describes the auras that herald his migraines. I swear, genetics have never treated me well—now this!

The little girl stops dancing to wave at me. She hops up and down, excited.

Oh God, the room is white! I can't make out Ian's face. People and desks around me dissolve into rows of waves, weaving in rhythm with my headache. I'm gripped with panic: must get out!

"Excuse me." I lurch up, unsteady. "I think I'm getting a migraine."

Ian stares a split second before leaping to his feet, hand outstretched. Suddenly, I'm steady. I stand still, listening into the light. I can't see her anymore, although I know she's here. The waves settle into a still clear pool. No longer boxed in and afraid, finding her is all I care about.

"Will you, will you?" Such a tiny voice, sweet and clear! A

person could love this voice.

The room stops shimmering. She's gone, and my headache is, too—that quickly.

My physical equilibrium is restored. My psyche is another matter. I now appear to be *fond* of my hallucinations, which have begun to speak as well.

"Delphi?" says Ian. "Are you okay?"

I turn to assure him—and myself— that everything is fine. The second I look at him, everything is worse, a million times worse.

A flood of impressions and emotions and judgments rush through me, hitting me hard on so many levels that I have to sit back down. In a single sudden moment, I look at Ian and *know* him. He's the most generous person I'll ever meet. He gleams— literally. There's pink around him. Now his face won't come into focus. Is he old, as in ancient? A wrinkled old man sits before me, someone who seen his share of sorrow and has carried other people's pain. Here's Ian again. I put my head in my hands, which are shaking. I may throw up.

I turn my head to escape from Ian and catch the eye of a woman a few feet over. She's pretty, in a carefully planned sort of way. But lonely! The space around her is gray, the air ice. Her need claws a path toward anyone who can distract her—from what? When her face starts to change, I turn away. This is a future I don't want to see.

I hold my stomach and shut my lips. Bile rises. I *am* crazy after all, have never been this disoriented. I should run to the nearest psych ward before somebody else carts me off.

"I'm sorry—this headache is making me sick. I think I should go home." Strained and unreal, my words break across Ian's stunned face.

Ian touches my arm. "Did you drive?"

Looking at him feels like a violation.

I practically push the poor guy over to get out that door. Ian doesn't follow. Bet he can't wait to see me leave. Some partner I turned out to be. I race to the restroom and lock myself in a stall. Sweat rings my hair. I hold onto the walls and wait for complete psychosis to take over.

Instead, relief slowly sinks in: I am thinking my own thoughts. No visions dance nearby. Faces are not morphing out of the metal walls. Nobody drops from the ceiling. No strange sensations, nothing. Still, my hands don't stop shaking. All I want is to go home. I let shock propel me to my car and blanket my brain, afraid to do as much as look over a shoulder, lest I trigger another mental collapse.

Ordinarily, the drama of firing up my 1986 Century Buick is a moment to fear. Today, the routine is soothing. Four times, I turn the key and pump the gas steadily. I vow into the steering wheel: "You'll never be scrap metal, okay? Strictly museum material." Pound the dashboard to placate the temperamental.

Please, please let the damn thing start.

She does. All rust and rumble, we roar away. Let's ignore the fact that I've been talking to a car for the past three years. Another strike against sanity—perhaps I shouldn't keep track.

Oh, let us not focus on the unpleasant. Let us crank the windows for cold air and blast the radio. Meaningless noise overwhelms the synapses. Crazy, crazy, crazy, croons the music.

Distance between the Macalester campus and my car centers

me. I'm calm enough to think through my situation: I must be suffering some kind of psychosis. What else could be happening? Here I've been proud of my mental agility all these years. Aren't the smart ones those that crash and burn?

The image of insanity solidifies. Old movies strike the most fear. Jessica Lange deteriorating in *Frances*. Some girl groping and muttering mumbo jumbo in *I Never Promised You a Rose Garden*. Could things get worse? *One Flew Over the Cuckoo's Nest*. My future takes on a terrifying new shape. Is this how those school shootings begin, the collapse of a quiet mind? Just as panic descends, one possible—no, let's say highly probable—alternative pops into my mind. I leap and grab, weak with relief. I am having an allergic reaction!

My breakdown could be environmentally induced. Perhaps a chemical in the room—there are dozens—triggers hallucinations! I'm environmentally sensitive? Possible. You read about that sort of problem these days. Could be that my vulnerability isn't a single solvent, but a malignant combination: think of the explosive possibilities in all those beakers, ready to combust with the perfume and antiperspirant and hair care products that circulate each class session.

The more I mull over how astoundingly toxic the earth has become, the better I feel. This must be the answer! By the time I'm downtown, my hands have even stopped shaking. Benzine, ether, hydrochloric acid: that chemical-laden room is the culprit. Who knows what Gaines stores on those shelves? Imagine the mix—ammonia, alcohol, ethanol. I'm nearly giddy—this close to the brink of institutionalization, pulled away so neatly! I'll withdraw from the class, transfer, or do whatever it takes to get away from the poisons.

I'm breathing normally again now. At least, as normally as anyone can in this industrial wasteland. Isn't St. Paul sixty miles from a nuclear power plant? God only knows what is leaching into the soil. Don't forget those air quality alerts we had last summer. I'm not crazy. I'm polluted!

Downtown traffic is a breeze if you know the less used routes. In a matter of minutes, I'm sliding the rustmobile into a conveniently long parking space a mere block from home. Before opening the car door, I gulp air and hold my breath until safely inside the hulking warehouse. More winded than one would expect, I trudge to the third floor (elevators here are hopeless), round four corners, and turn the key to the huge wooden door of our loft.

Dad is making soba noodles and broccoli for dinner. Comfort food. He must've had a hard day. The magic works on me: I take in the garlic and sesame and the lingering incense, feel the cool wood beneath bare feet, and am nearly convinced that my own day was fairly routine. Late afternoon light filters in the banks of huge windows that line the walls. Dad has set a slim silver vase of flowers on the table.

Buoyed by beauty and calm, I promise myself an evening of hearty repression. Any inkling of insanity and I'll deny, deny, deny. I know Freud would come in handy, even if it's trendy to say he's passé.

"How was school?" Dad nips at the end of a noodle, straight from the pot, and lets the rest flop back in.

I've told him a million times how much I hate that. Really, he might be a blood relative but do I need his germs, too? "I'm dropping physics," I say, heatedly. "The professor is a pig. He hates

9

women."

"Good grief! Misogyny that bad in the academy these days?"

Immediately, I realize my mistake. Dad's all ears. He's going to want all the details of whatever 'ism' is afoot and then will happily expound all evening—but in a forgiving, accepting sort of way. He occasionally has a hard time reconciling his life as a Zen priest with the go-for-the-jugular instincts he honed as a graduate student. A priest for over fifteen years, he hasn't shaken off all sarcasm and disdain, thank God. Those are my favorite qualities.

"Please don't start. This problem is one person, not entire institutional structures. Gaines has no clue. He does the subtle stuff—talks to the top of my head while he'll look a guy in the eye, calls on men first. Nothing to officially complain about; I simply don't see why I should subject myself to that treatment."

"I see why." Dad pours tea. We sit down for the *gate* that's blessed our meals since I was a baby:

Earth, water, air and fire combined to make this food.
Numberless beings have died and labored that we may eat.
May we be nourished that we may nourish life.

The words normally pour past me like air. Tonight, I appreciate the soothing sound of my father's voice, one note in my life that remains steady.

Dad slides bread and butter across the table to me. "Science requirement. Ring a bell? Penultimate procrastination."

"I'll find another class."

"Three weeks into your last semester? Lie low. Ignore the unpleasant aspects of Professor Gaines. Notice his better ones.

Maybe he is supposed to learn from you. Ever think of that?"

"Certain people are not embraceable, okay?" Damn! He's right—could be too late to switch classes. The possibility jump starts my anxiety. Repress, repress, repress.

"Let's focus on your day, dear father. Bad one, huh?"

He laughs. "Am I that readable?"

"Noodles."

I half listen to the latest drama at Moon on Mountain, the Zen Center where Dad serves as priest and administrator. Dad's conflicted about charging high admission fees to popular lectures. Tonight, a famous Zen psychologist is speaking at the *sangha*; several of the students are complaining that there should be a sliding fee.

"They're right. That's what troubles me, Delphi. Of course, we all know they're right. The question is how to reconcile philosophy with the bills. We're broke." He sips his tea and stares out the window. "An earthquake split open the Center today, too. Gorilla escaped from the zoo and lumbered into my office. All sorts of Biblical mayhem fell upon me: floods and famine. The earth broke apart. Twice."

"That's nice."

He keeps looking at clouds. "Want to tell me what's wrong?"

I'm instantly alert, defense mechanisms mobilized: no need to drag Dad into a drama that's almost over. I stand up to signal disinterest. "Oh, end of college nerves. Maybe I'm afraid I won't pass physics."

"Maybe." He considers my comment before checking his watch. "I'm truly sorry to do this to you again tonight. I have to go. I want a few minutes to sit with Dr. Stiller before the speech. Let's continue this conversation tomorrow, okay? Remember to--"

"Please leave a note if you go out, even if you are twenty-two," I finish. We both smile.

Dad slips on sandals. We live in a loft above the Moon, smack in the middle of downtown in an old warehouse turned trendy: coffee houses, art galleries, artists' apartments. He taps the tall thin table by the front door. "Letter." He's off.

Mommy! Once a month, I get mail postmarked Bombay, her main base since I was a baby. The letters have come every month of my life. I take the pale green envelope to my bedroom and pull out its sisters—247 squares and rectangles of different colors that I keep in the black lacquer box hidden under my bed. Not that Dad would violate my privacy. I just need to hide them. The box is lined with blue velvet and has peach-colored Japanese characters on top. Once Dad asked if I wanted him to translate and I said no. I've never read him any of my letters, not a line. He and Mom had an agreement: he saved the ones from the early years, unopened, until I could read them myself.

Dad gave me the letters when I was seven. The first hundred plus are simple, a child's picture book version of one woman's life: my house is yellow; I take photographs to sell in my store; I ride a bike around the city. I wrote back right away, and can still remember those first lines: Hi Mommy! Yellow is my best color, too.

As I got older, her letters became more complex. So did my replies—and I memorized everything I told her. After mailing a particularly long letter when I was ten, I discovered that I couldn't remember, with certainty, what I had said. I was so miserable that I skipped school to reconstruct my words. After that, I started writing two letters: one to send and one to save. I never, ever use a computer to write to my mother, but now know the value of a copy machine.

Getting a letter after such a rotten day feels like an omen. Even though I hate myself every time—I mean really hate myself for being such a slow learner—I rip the envelope and immediately scan the lines to see if she finally asks me to visit or accepts my standing invitation. My heart always beats a bit faster until the end, the inevitable end that never hints of a meeting. She always says the same thing: listen! Listen, she writes, and you'll find me at your side. All my love, Mom.

You would think I'd get used to such disappointment. Of course, I go through angry streaks. The worst was when I was eleven. The real story of my parents' break-up replaced the watered-down, happier version that managed to link Mom's wanderlust to love for me. I was named after the city in which I was conceived, ruins rich with mysteries of tragedy and love. When I was young, Dad claimed my name reflected Mom's passion for the exotic, her need for myth and magic. These desires intertwined with love for Dad to produce the greatest gift of all: me. My mother's yearnings eventually led her on a spiritual journey to India, with an itinerary too weighty for a child. That's the tale I was spoon-fed: Mommy is on a mission.

In reality, mother's flight to India was not so lofty. When we were in Nepal—I was two—she ran off with the interpreter. Those are the facts, flat and raw, without a trace of myth's magic. Dad schlepped me around the subcontinent for another year, waiting, then took me back to the States. The interpreter ditched Mom a few months later. She didn't come back to us. Formally nomadic, my wounded father saw travel as the origin of evil. He settled with a vengeance. What could be more staid than the Midwest?

When I found out about the interpreter, I didn't write to my mother for six months. Her letters kept coming—steady, informative, chatty. She refused to acknowledge my silence. I finally broke down and replied. Telling her about myself was a need. See me! The impulse of a two-year old, I suppose. Maybe that's how old I'll always feel in her presence. I couldn't take the risk that she'd give up if she didn't get something back. That thought was—is—unbearable.

Her framed picture stands on my dresser. Early on, I would take new friends in to see the photograph. I loved to hear, one more time, how much alike we look. We have the same good skin, wild dark hair and bold features. I wish I knew her height. I've always felt myself two inches too tall.

At fourteen, Wendy Katz and I stood in front of her photo. "I knew you were Jewish," she told me, triumphantly.

Of course, I was already marked: a Buddhist. Guess who loses out at Christmas, both ways around?

"She is—I mean, she used to be," I answered.

"Then you are, too," she insisted.

As I got older, I'd debate the theological implications of bloodlines with my friends, who were always enamored with the contradictions that swirled around my very existence. I never took up the topic with my parents. Buddhists believe in neither a separate self nor God. My father has another distinction: he doesn't believe in race, except as an example of hatred—a cultural construct, he'll proclaim. Mom is a yogi—not that American kind, stretching at the YMCA or toning up tummies at an upscale studio—no, she's into the whole Hindu tradition, complete with deities and a deranged system of third-century science. However, that's not why I don't ask her. I'm afraid she'll fall into Dad's camp and deny this bind. Having so little of her, I'm not willing to risk losing more.

Now I curl on the bed to savor the bits and pieces of her life. Nothing spectacular—she's preparing for a show at her gallery this summer, photographing food for an upcoming cookbook (and enjoying the task of tasting, she adds), and preparing for her annual two weeks in London next month. She fills me in on the idiosyncrasies of her conservative Indian neighbors, who (Mom thinks) try to set her up with each single American man they encounter because her behavior doesn't behoove a woman living alone. They think that a man would settle her down, or at least move her to his home, preferably in another neighborhood. She asks me about school and demands a better explanation for my break-up with Brent, who Mom liked as much as you can like a person from a letter.

I read and reread her latest words. The worst part of a letter is the ending.

Eventually, I slip Mom's letter into the box—always the most recent on top—pick up my sociology textbook and dive right in. Smooth transition into the woes of class struggle, a final review for the essay I need to compose. No room for missing Mom, not a moment to fret over the day's events. One does learn about quieting the mind after years of Zen training, although I'm as leery of my father's religion as Methodist ministers' kids are of theirs.

When Dad comes home, he cracks open the door to wish me

a nice night. Respectful of study, he doesn't linger. By eleven, I'm close to completing the essay's startling conclusion—being poor sucks in a million different ways. Bet that earth-shattering news will earn me an A. Why do I bother with college at all? Oh yes, there is the life of genteel poverty my father's chosen, a path to be avoided above all. I want a real house, instead of an apartment door with a number. Nothing like a good sociology text to reinforce what I already know.

Minutes before midnight, I climb into bed and click off the lamp. I am instantly afraid.

I sit up straight and survey the shadows. I *knew* this would happen—the day's horrors return full force. The toxin theory rattles, weak, in the darkness. The girl is here. Delusion, ghost, or chemical vapor, she's on the edge of my consciousness. What did she say—will you? Will I what? I cover my eyes. Breath heats my hands. Everything I touch—my face, arms, belly, legs—is solid. I do not feel delusional. I feel strong. I lay back down, protected by the hard ball my body makes.

I used to call the time before sleep a waking dream. I would make up stories, sometimes about Mom. Mostly, I would dream about people I didn't know, made-up characters in colorful tales that ushered me into night. The people that popped into my head fascinated and inspired me, like the imaginary friends I had as a child. Sometimes I imagined my life, the future. I love a waking dream.

Lately, I've resorted to tricks like counting sheep and repeating nursery rhymes. My constant companion and comfort, imagination extraordinaire, has abandoned me. Worse, I wake up anxious every morning as if I've had horrible dreams I don't remember.

Aren't sleep disturbances a sign of lead poisoning? If only I'd listened to Gaines when he listed the goodies stored on his shelves. Could he possibly have radon in that room or is that the chemical that hides in houses to kill you? Who knows what is infiltrating my poor skull at this very minute! Last I heard, though, dread can't be chemically induced. Maybe I should be hustling to that psychiatrist after all.

What's happening to me? I'm supposed to be the precocious child, ten years ahead of my time. A meditative upbringing made me a mini-adult by ten, I've been told. Think I would have conquered that fear-of-the-dark thing by now.

I turn on the light to make sure I'm alone.

I lean over and pull out the box of letters. There: a lifetime of my mother's words at my side. Warmer without trying, I can enjoy the tuck of the blanket from the tips of my toes to my nose.

What did my mother's mother say to her before sleep? Something in Hebrew, I'm sure. A night prayer: May my family be perfect in Your sight. Grant me light, lest I sleep the sleep of death. It is You that gives light to the eyes. *Sheynah.* Sleep.

I shape myself around the box. Listen. Feel her, smiling and smoothing hair. Comforted, my heart quiets and skin softens. Safe, I let the worry stop and believe what every mother dreams and demands: you are fine, my darling, fine. Mom prays for me with a song, a *niggun*, wordless and hypnotic. I am fine. Tomorrow we'll find a way out, together. I'm able to turn off the light, certain who waits for me now. Listen again—just like my old nights! Here's Mom. She sings all the songs I missed as a child. Look into the dark, unafraid, and float into sleep on her whisper.

2
LEILANI

Leilani dreams. She's in a coffin. The hearse weaves through a gray network of freeway. Pools of acid line the road. The city is a wasteland, a mass of garbage heaps and smokestacks. Even locked in the dark, she can see the outline of decay. Stop! She screams and pounds. Her husband chats calmly with her mother in the front seat. The procession follows, headlights flashing like flares. So many people loved her. They need to know that they're not too late! The cemetery floats in an old chemical landfill. The stench of sulfur and burning metal make her gag. She claws at the box's silk lining and screams as she's lowered into the ground. This is a mistake—a terrible, terrible mistake. The worst kind of terror grips her. Black earth thuds on the casket. The smells become less definable, less tolerable.

Leilani sits up with a small scream, panicked. Hands to eyes, chin, throat—a regular cotton t-shirt! A dream! Moving toward reality, terror lingers, tangible—what could be wrong? Memory jabs a slim finger and pushes her forward. She is in the bedroom she slept in as a teenager, long since reassembled into antique-filled quarters for company. The door actually locks. What she would have given for that at fifteen! She smiles at the thought of herself, so young!

Fully awake, she remembers.

Every time she wakes up—every day—she's forced to relive the discovery. This predawn morning, she covers her mouth to quiet the reflexive moan. The weight of their absence flattens her back into bed. How can she stand up, pull open the curtains and watch the neighbors take out the garbage, as if the world hasn't stopped spinning? Leilani lies in bed until dim, barely discernible light lines the window.

Suddenly, the house is abhorrent. This window is intolerable. The curtain and the happy people beyond, unacceptable. Purpose allows her to rise and turn on a lamp. She assembles an outfit that signifies composure and rustles through drawers for other things she may need. With each movement, dullness expands through her body. She grows thick and placid. Must leave before anyone else wakes! Doors and floors creak despite her best efforts. She tiptoes downstairs.

The smell of coffee and her mother's disappointed voice hit her simultaneously.

"Lani! I'd hoped you were finally getting a good night's sleep."

There isn't a single person alive that Leilani doesn't hate. She gets a glass of orange juice, which she carries pointedly into the living room.

Margaret sighs and surveys the small bundle of Leilani's possessions: thin suitcase and battered tan leather briefcase. Margaret remembers buying that briefcase. Her daughter had been happy. The roles of new wife and assistant professor suited and excited her. You're the only one, Margaret had always told each of her children, who can make your dreams come true. Seemed then as if all three were on the right track, were people you could be proud of. She stares at Leilani's rigid back and thinks: a foreign country has fallen into my house.

Leilani and Margaret talk from their separate rooms. "I'm going for a drive," announces the daughter.

"At 5:30 in the morning? With luggage?"

Leilani dreads going into the kitchen for her bags. She closes her eyes and narrows herself into something steely: I will not look at her, I will not cry, I will not explain. So fortified, she breezes in to retrieve her things. A few feet away, Margaret watches.

"Honey," she holds out a hand.

Leilani's gone. Every morning, she makes a similar exit, as if this is the last. Every night brings her return.

Margaret stands in the center of the kitchen, more alone than before. She allows herself to consider crying. She imagines a complete collapse: fall against the table and weep into the tall ceilings and oiled wood floors, a house unnaturally quiet. The gingerbread house, Holly used to say. This is true. Margaret needs color. Every nook and cranny is jeweled and vibrant: a scarlet staircase, emerald bedrooms, ripe melon kitchen. The back entryway is purple with gold trim. Margaret once seriously debated sketching stars on the ceiling. Magic, cried her granddaughter! Magic in Grandma's house.

The thought of Holly galvanizes: one must never sit down and give in. Margaret picks up the telephone. "Seamus," she commands into the yawn on the other end, "you should come home."

Leilani is strangely euphoric. The Honda flies past the few others on the freeway, windows down and sharp air stinging the face, numbing hands. Each curve in the road is another chance to accelerate, to prove that she can keep her hands firmly on the wheel.

Can she close her eyes? She squints them into a slit, trying for instinct, and barely slows down in time. The car skids to the side of the road next to the guardrail—only slightly bent now, evidence that disaster can be patched up and welded away. Fully awake—alive, even—Leilani takes off her coat and opens the door to her new home, the scraped and blackened patch of grass beyond the guardrail.

Leilani sits in the center of the earth where they bled—where metal shot through her daughter's chest, where Holly screamed as she took ten horrible minutes to die, they said. Mama! When Leilani hears her daughter's last word, she imagines a whimper—Holly too weak to yell one more time what every emergency worker, every passerby, and every cop regretfully, reluctantly confirmed: yes, she asked for you. Mama. The single defining moment in which her child had needed her most, had begged for comfort, Leilani had been sitting in a billowy leather chair at a meeting, wondering if the last remaining pastry was blueberry or plain butter.

The makeshift memorial has been taken down. The flowers are gone and she feels the grass beginning to repair itself underneath the frost. She will remain rooted, unchanged.

"Ma'am? You're going to get killed too, sitting here, five feet from the freeway. Rush hour soon, you know." Frowning against the low sun, a worried face extends a hand. "Please. Get up."

Leilani huddles in and shakes her head.

"I can't leave you like this," frets the man.

It goes against human nature to walk away from the dead, to leave them unattended. They both stay.

All Leilani wants to do is lie down alone where her daughter died, and listen. In stillness—in the private wide space of silence, she can reach through the earth to feel Holly's life again. She is convinced of this with the same animal instinct of birth, a mother's blind drive toward a child. Leilani laughs out loud at cruelty's cool perfection: mother and daughter both doomed to the noisy chaos of traffic, longing for the impossible—each other. She can't stop giggling.

The man winces. He drives this route daily. He remembers the tall wooden cross and half-acre of flowers, up for several weeks. Read about the tragedy in the paper and saw the child's face on TV: father and four-year old die in collision. There was another car—drunk driver? Witnesses who saw the red pick-up veer into the wrong lane long enough to send other cars spinning before careening wildly away. Nobody got the plates although a small crowd witnessed the aftermath. Plenty of people ready for their moment of fame. Plenty of people ready to recount, with barely concealed glee, their connection to calamity that is unspeakable for real victims. He always turned the channel. They should be ashamed.

A kind man, with a brand-new second marriage and eight grandchildren between them, he puts his arm around Leilani.

Driving by daily, he has noticed her throughout the months since the accident, always early in the morning, standing too close to traffic. Today, she sat down. Something about her, low and dark against the ground, alarmed him.

"Your family?" he asks.

She lets herself fall into the blackness with a stranger. He sits with her while she cries. Tonight, he will go home and call his children, every single one.

Margaret is doing just that, this very minute. Finished with Seamus, Anna gets a turn.

"Mother, I can't talk. I'm barely awake, the kids are screaming, Martin's in New York again and the nanny won't be here till eight. I have a deposition scheduled for eight-thirty. I can't believe you called Seamus. It's two hours earlier in San Diego."

"I'm not asking you to drop everything and rush over. I am simply alerting everyone: a family emergency is underway. Your sister is not going to pick herself up and be fine."

Barely six a.m. and Anna's neck begins to ache already. The baby wails in his crib; books crash in two-year old Ben's room. She'll have to review notes for the deposition in the car. She thinks longingly of her office, a clean and quiet castle. "I'm hanging up, Mom. I'll call you from work."

Anna sets the receiver firmly in the hook.

Still, Margaret is satisfied, certain that progress has been set in motion. Only one more person to wake up. She heads upstairs to her husband.

Leilani has made her way to another home, the one they shared. She hasn't entered the house once since the accident. Anna searched for the paperwork—insurance information, certificates for birth and marriage—proof that these were Leilani's people. Her sister spent hours here selecting funeral clothes for all three of them. She watered the plants and arranged for the mail to be forwarded. She even took their dog, Daisy.

Nearly six months, and Leilani still cannot walk into the

house. The next-door neighbor, Rocco, keeps the plants alive and shovels the sidewalk. Nobody asked him to take on these tasks. One day, Leilani drove by and there he was, packing in new snow along the edges of the driveway. She sat in the car and watched until he came over.

"I can care for the inside, too," he'd offered. "Plants, hot water heater, furnace, that sort of thing."

Leilani had Will's keys in her purse. She handed them over. "Thank you."

Unlike the others, Rocco never bothered with questions about returning home, going back to work—becoming normal. When his wife died two years ago, Leilani had measured the event: sad, but not tragic. Cecile had gotten sixty-three good years, most of them with a man she loved. Rocco had seemed similarly affected. He carried on as usual, fussing over his lush Italian-inspired garden through three seasons and ice-fishing in the winter. Only now is Leilani struck by the fact that she hasn't been inside Rocco's house since Cecile died. She can't remember the last time anyone else entered, either.

Other houses begin to come to life. Pulled shades glow, isolated orange and yellow bulbs. A few curtains are already open: quick figures move across kitchens and bend over beds. A dog barks and a car creaks by; freshly delivered papers sit on doorsteps.

Will loved these people. He was the one who selected the house on a run-down street, a little too reminiscent of her blue-collar childhood for Leilani's tastes. But he fell hard for the West Side, a neighborhood smack in the center of the city, where block-clubs weren't social events but necessary strategy sessions. The year before they moved in, a fifteen-year-old boy was shot to death in what would become their front yard. Upwardly mobile friends joked about their selection. Bring a gun, one laughed. This house had been their first significant disagreement and one of just two times that Leilani had lost a major battle within her marriage. The other had been the decision to have Holly.

Will had good instincts. He saw beyond the pit bulls and Rottweilers, the junked yards, and cranked-up cars screaming with angry young men and their music. Will pointed out the newly renovated houses, the burgeoning anti-crime efforts, the generations of families holding their ground and new ones flocking toward low cost housing. Walk one block, he marveled, and you get five conversations. Men put down rakes to shake your hand; the young mothers swung toddlers on hips and spoke of schools and babysitting co-ops. Will saw significance in the family from Mexico living next door to the one from Laos, the Polish Catholic church offering a Mass in Spanish. The coffee shop around the corner, he proclaimed, makes the best kolaches in the city.

Ultimately, the people weren't enough to pull Leilani. The river swayed her. Although she'd lived her entire life in St. Paul—a city that spun, web-like, out of the water's defining pulse—she had never understood the lore surrounding the Mississippi until she stood, yards from their prospective doorstep, along the sheer bluff above the river. A step away from stumbling into the tops of trees that climb the cliff, she thought: I could easily fall, or jump. The idea drew her—not actually jumping, but the nervous thrill of the idea itself.

Leilani had opened her palms to the wind. She shut her eyes. Perhaps everyone gets one such moment of unexpected joy, carried for a blind moment on air, water, and earth. She could feel the caves half a mile underfoot, vibrating. Now, of course, she understands this moment was foolish—wishful thinking, to weep and believe what is elemental holds spirit—but then, she felt herself standing in the center of her life, the center of something beyond defining. Sacred was how Rocco described this land. She experienced herself in that word.

She'd returned to Will, and said simply, "Let's do it." The look on his face! The way he tried to toss her in the air, how he understood the emotion behind three simple words! That unbound life and all the hope he held, gone.

Leilani's knuckles are white from gripping the steering wheel. Her hands hurt. She sighs—keep this up, and she will never get inside the house to find the forms for the realtor. The neighbor kids, Carlos and Evalina, wait at the corner for the school bus. Eight-thirty? How does that happen, time escaping this way?

Rocco is discreet. He knows to stand a few feet back from the window and direct his gaze through the gap between the curtains. Yesterday she sat there for six hours, barely under five the day before. He is not as patient or as wise as reputation holds, a reputation that has less to do with Rocco himself than with the American movie version of Italian men over sixty. Largely, Rocco is disappointed. He has always recognized similar disappointment in Leilani and is now witnessing its drive for dominion. Cecile would say: not on my watch. He is too tired for that kind of fight. Rocco sucks in the stale air of his undusted, unkempt home and is glad Cecile isn't here to see his cowardice. Anyone can shovel.

Shortly after noon, Leilani starts the car. Today doesn't feel right. Maybe tomorrow, if she can get into position early enough, before the well-wishers walk by and stare. See that crazy woman in the car? Pitiful creature. Children are already frightened. They creep by on their way to school. The smaller ones cast anxious faces at the steamed car windows before they run, run away from the death that still gives them nightmares. The girls continue to ask their mothers: tell me one more time, where is Holly? Her daughter was part of a tiny tight ringlet of three—Holly, Isabel, and Miranda. They called one another "honey baby" and "sweetie love." Each had an alias and each was a sister. Sisters Sally, Samantha, and Sarah were the ones tripping over pink tutus and squirreling away snacks in hideouts.

Leilani is ferociously glad that Will is dead. Just punishment, she thinks, for killing our daughter.

Somehow, she's at Carver Community College, climbing up steps and waltzing into the English Department.

"Lani! We're so glad to have you back! How are you doing?" Mary Beth, the office secretary, hurries to offer a nervous hug. The student office worker freezes at the copy machine. A colleague at the door stops himself from entering and slides away, unseen.

Leilani smiles calmly into the beginning of the echo: She's back! How is she, what do you say, how can she bear it?

"I'm doing well, actually. Quite well." She pats Mary Beth reassuringly.

"I'm so happy to see you," says Mary Beth, tears ready. "We can only imagine what a terrible time this has been. If there's anything else I can do, you'll tell me?"

"Of course." Leilani pulls a small silver box from her briefcase. "Thank you for corresponding with all the students, taking on the extra work. Open this later. Holly would like knowing that a fellow dog lover has this."

As expected, the sound of Holly's name—not to mention a gift of something precious—renders Mary Beth speechless. This is Leilani's well-plotted chance to leave. She cannot endure significant conversation. "I'll be in my office. Really, I can't thank you enough." She flees.

Lielani unlocks her office door and reviews the scene, content with the perfect pained-yet-comforting tone she'd managed, the sentiment of the gift. How will that play after I die, she wonders? Mary Beth will hold out the statue of Toto for all to see, with a sigh: kind woman! Always thought of others, rose above her own pain. What a tragedy, to lose her too.

The pain in her lower belly sharpens as she opens her desk. Leilani is fairly certain she has ovarian cancer. She spent an hour studying the subject last night and the symptoms correspond with all her aches. Unfortunately, the day before she was convinced of leukemia. Last week, she spent an hour sitting outside the emergency room, waiting to see if the headache was indeed a stroke.

Suicide would be more efficient, but she is profoundly afraid of dying. A real mother would want to be with her daughter above all else. Another failing. Just like the so-called career in a windowless office in a third-rate Midwestern community college populated by students who can't make the cut anywhere else. Homeless, to boot, now too. Her only hope is disease. She takes three Tylenol, one more than recommended, and wonders if Sergeant Garcia has any news about the pick-up truck.

When there's a knock at the door, Leilani answers briskly.

"Professor O'Brien? The registrar said I needed a referral for your Women's Literature class. Could I talk to you about that for a minute?"

"Please, sit down." She smiles competently and arranges papers, mind groping toward the beautiful, malignant possibilities buried within the John Hopkins Family Health Book that she has tucked into her suitcase.

Outside her office door, the echo does indeed fly: did you see, how does she seem, can you believe—she looks good, maybe tired. Relief rides along the whispers. Most of us can only see the great gifts of our own lives in the mirror suffering holds.

3
DELPHI

I can't drop physics. The sour woman behind the Registrar's desk is only too happy to stick to the party line: no canceling classes this late in the semester. Bail, and I get an F and still have to meet my science requirement. My only hope for an independent study is out, too, since Professor Wilcox—the one humane scientist on campus—is on sabbatical. Ms. Sour almost bursts with joy, watching me bump up against reality. You have to wonder how little control she has in her own life, the satisfaction she gets from being the army ant of institutional power.

A definite setback: graduation requires my return to that toxic room. Onto Plan B, then: assessment and strategy, a day of library toil. I'll gather data on the three most logical scenarios—insanity, environmental sensitivities, and supernatural visits. Once the origin of my crisis has been ascertained, all I'll need is the right professional. Shouldn't be too tough. After all, Catholics still believe in Exorcism and if memory serves, some people actually make a living busting ghosts. You can find ten shrinks per block downtown and there's no shortage of New Age doctors prepared to battle dioxins. I'll be fine. I can roll with any punch doled in my direction.

Three hours into my library stint, and my optimism is sorely tested. I do not roll well, after all. Every time I peruse a new class of mental illness, my stomach cramps with the task of self-diagnosis. My hands sweat at schizophrenia, summed up in Introduction to Psychology as disordered thinking, delusions, and hallucinations. One particular sentence sinks my spirits completely: a schizophrenic sees and hears things that do not exist for others. The truly well-endowed wacko cannot distinguish reality from the movie reel in his head. Lovely—a perfect description of yesterday.

The section on signs and laboratory findings is more encouraging. Disorganized speech, grandiosity, paranoia, chaotic appearance—I don't fit the bill, Dad's opinions on my fashion sensibilities aside. I easily rule out all the personality disorders, although some of the symptoms are vague enough that I could commit half my friends, and certainly my father. Ordinary Americans do not become Zen Priests. I photocopy definitions of schizophrenia, since those hit a bit too close to home for comfort. How to broach the topic of hereditary disposition with my parents and not arouse suspicion?

As for the environment—well, those woes alone warrant an entire week. A mere forty minutes and I'm despairing: one more paragraph and I will never eat from an estrogen-laced can again. Forget breathing. Minnesota is home to dozens of coal-fired power plants; I might as well sign up for my oxygen tank right now. Poor Dad, tossing out the mercury thermometers for digitals. Meanwhile, one profitable power company spews out enough of the stuff to turn fishies a new shade of silver. Another cheery discovery—half of our bathroom supplies could be carcinogens. We should be scrubbing the toilet with organic, all natural products instead of the dollar-durable Comet. My last straw is a gruesome article about a woman whose allergies isolate her to a sterile cabin in Utah. I give up. Pollution will kill me, regardless.

My plan to get a handle on the ghost angle is dealt a lethal blow by the realization that ghosts and poltergeists do not rank high on the priority list for college collections. There's not a thing—just one lousy book on paranormal psychology. I'm too embarrassed to ask the librarian for help. Excuse me, where's the spirit world section? The security guard would escort me to the door. I decide to pack up and head home for the Internet, where I'm sure to find plenty of web sites devoted to UFOs and all things other-worldly.

To add insult to injury, I stumble across Ian, sole witness to my burgeoning career as mental patient. He stands by the exit, beaming, backpack full of books. My heart clenches for a split-second. I don't see pink. Nobody's face peels and folds. Maybe yesterday was a fluke. Maybe the room, not me, is indeed the issue.

"Hey, Delphi! Finishing up?" He holds open the door for me.

How gallant. What century does he think this is? "Ian. Yes, I'm on my way out. Sort of a busy day. You rushing off somewhere?"

"The opposite, actually." He is amazingly undeterred by hostile body language and a quick pace. "Wanna grab a cup of coffee? I'm headed for The Pitt."

The favored hangout for Macalester college students is a two-story bungalow near campus that was converted into a coffee house several years ago. Campus sprawl, cried the neighbors, sad to see solid citizens replaced by a thirty-something Brad Pitt look-alike who popped in with a commercial restaurant license and general indifference to decency. The place reeks of cigarette smoke, the couches are ripped, and newspapers that fall on the floor stay there for weeks. Don't even dream of using the bathroom. The establishment's official name is Red Dog Café. Even the owner, a purported womanizer flattered by at least one connotation, calls his place The Pitt. Alas, the coffee's great and so is the food. None of that organic whole grain fare—we're talking sugar and preservatives. My newfound fear of toxins fades in the face of hunger. Breakfast with Dad consisted of green tea and amaranth cereal swimming in soy milk; barely ten a.m. and I'm starving.

"Come on!" Ian reads temptation.

Maybe I'm taking the wrong approach. Why not go through a test run? After all, Ian's implicated in the very problem I'm supposed to be solving. I'll have coffee—remain distant, yet polite enough to satisfy—and see if the impressions remain at bay. If all goes well, I'm that much closer to confirming that my imbalance is isolated to the physics lab. Then, I'm free to head home for wacky spirit world research on-line before Dad returns. I look at my watch as if I have a full schedule to consider. I'm really thinking croissants and cappuccino.

"All right," I smile, despite my better judgment, and clarify my commitment. "I don't have much time. I have to go to work." A half-lie, since I do, only not until six.

We walk toward The Pitt. The unusually warm spring has seduced the hardier tulips to push out, has greened lawns three week early. The day is glorious. Global warming has an upside. Ian asks about my job.

"I work part-time, receptionist at a downtown art gallery, Suzanne Strauss." Seeing his blank look, I add, "You wouldn't recognize the name unless you're into the St. Paul art scene. Suzanne's fabulous, although the gallery mostly shows other people's stuff these days. Suzanne's pushing seventy, plus she has lots of commissioned work."

"You an artist?" Ian looks excited. Oh yeah, walk into The Pitt with a hip art chick on your arm.

"Not a creative bone in my body. And you?"

"Depends on your definition. Can't a vocation be an art form? You know, a calling—painter, carpenter, astronomer. Maybe if you're good at anything, you're an artist."

"And what are you good at?"

His smile disappears instantly. "I don't know yet."

Well, the look on his face is a conversation stopper, thank you. Yet I hear myself sigh, "Me neither." Wait one minute—I said distant. No need to get wrapped up in this. I point to The Pitt.

"Oh goodie. Casanova himself. With a broom! We should call the papers."

Perhaps The Pitt had one too many littering tickets; the owner himself is finally stooping to the task of swiping aside debris. He sees us coming and flicks—yes, a flick, oh so calculated—his dark blonde hair out of his eyes and lasers in on me. He leans against the broom to give me his full attention.

"Good morning," he smiles.

I return the smile, expecting a specific sort of engagement: guy's greeting to girl is more than casual; girl's reply reflects her degree of receptivity. The whole exchange is highly effective and surprisingly routine—at least when you're under thirty and single.

Forget the routine. When I meet his eyes, one part of my mind freezes and another flies to life.

"Oh my God, you're gay." I blurt out, shocked.

I cover my mouth, horrified. How could I say such a thing!

Ian laughs nervously. "Whoa—you two have a bad date?"

"Bitch," hisses Pitt. He casts me the worst, I mean the most evil, look I've ever received.

He is gay.

The newly alive part of my brain overtakes all else, just like yesterday. He's afraid—why, why, in this day and age? Seems every other parent you meet is gay, not to mention the most interesting guys. And Wendy, who came out in eighth grade, which was like the smallest shock you could ever have, a total nonevent. But this guy! What—he went through one of those boot camps, a Bible Belt thing where they beat emotion out of you. His Dad's idea. God, he believes the shit they told him. Every day—one unmonitored thought—can confirm his conviction that he's evil and headed for hell. That's why the hyper hetero act! He is consumed with women! Must constantly protect against real desire, a trick someone taught him. His father again. I am ice cold and starting to fall over, want to run—hide, pretend you're not breathing! Never be awake when he comes home. The cruelty isn't sexual, another physical punishment from a man who needs to see someone weaker than he is suffer.

"Delphi!" Ian has dropped his backpack to shake me, hands on my shoulders. "Jesus Christ! What's the matter with you?" He picks up our stuff and pushes me to the sidewalk. "Let's get out of here."

The formerly glorious day is now painfully bright. My legs

wobble. I struggle to get my bearings: here, this sidewalk, safely at school. Pitt! He's nowhere to be seen—inside, I suppose. I regret what I said to him more than anything in my entire life. I know precisely how lethal my words were.

Ian's a wreck. He babbles, arms flailing. "This is your idea of casual conversation, followed by a repeat of yesterday's blank act? I'm not sure if you belong on a stage or if you're plain cruel. Was that a performance evaluation or do you enjoy public commentary on which side of the aisle guys walk?"

Poor even-keeled Ian. He really is worried—mostly because he likes me, but partly because he's afraid for himself. Who wants to be friends with someone so unpredictable? See, there I go again. I know what he feels. The recognition isn't the huge flash I got during physics, but I know.

My life is impossible. Yesterday's panic resurfaces. I stop walking, put my hands over my face and cry.

This reaction does not help Ian. He puts a hand on my shoulder. "Hey, I'm sorry. I didn't mean to be rough. I was shocked—what you said and the way that guy went off. Don't cry, please, Delphi."

He is incredibly nice. I should go home and lock the door behind me. Why ruin his day, too? As soon as I can catch my breath, I will wish him a good life and leave.

When I'm finally able to speak again—Ian patting me on the back while I collect myself—I have my pithy departure line all prepared. I peek through my fingers at his kind face.

"I'm so scared," is what comes out of my mouth. I feel much, much better.

He stares into my face. Whatever he sees moves him forward.

"Let's go sit down somewhere. You're shivering. Then you tell me what's happening—and I'll help you."

I swear this is the nineteenth century. I let a man I barely know adopt the age-old protective stance, leading away the damsel in distress. If I weren't so miserable, I'd laugh. The last time I was this demure was when I had my appendix out; I held Daddy's hand and demanded that he sleep in a cot next to me. I was fifteen, for heaven's sake. Maybe that moment marked the beginning of my psychosis.

Ian stops next to a maroon mini-van.

"This is what you drive?" Now I do laugh.

"I'm only the chauffeur," he explains as we climb in. He starts the engine and cranks the heat. "My Mom remarried a few years ago. Combined, Mom and Bill have five kids. We do the home shuffle—you know, my brother, sister, and I have rooms at our Dad's place, too. Bill's kids—two little guys, six-year old twins, they're the greatest—split their time between our house and their mom's. I dropped the twins off. After dinner, I hit a dance studio to retrieve my sister, Kate."

"Sounds complicated."

He laughs. "It is. How about you—brothers or sisters?"

"Not that I know of," I joke. "I live with my Dad and haven't seen my mother since I was a baby. She lives in India."

To his credit, Ian doesn't ask if I'm Indian or comment on the fact that I don't look Indian or tell me how much he's always wanted to see India or make any stupid India remark at all. He doesn't say a thing. I can't remember the last time I sat next to a guy from school who didn't knock himself out with banal prattle. Ian turns on the radio. We warm up for a few minutes, quiet.

I stare out the fogging windows, marveling at my newfound capacity for getting into strange situations. Wasn't I complimenting myself on my linear, problem-free life a few days ago, all smug underneath my great big well-functioning brain?

"Why are you scared?" Ian asks eventually, quietly.

Could confession make things any weirder? Probably not. I decide to tell him the whole story, starting with the girl in physics who popped up last week. I try to downplay the part where, as of yesterday, I seem to know stuff about other people. That seems rude: by the way, I saw your soul, Ian. I can see the book title now—How to Meet New People and Frighten Them Away. I think of Pitt. Even worse—Meet New People and Rip Out Their Hearts. Oh, I'll be fun at parties.

Ian does not appear the least bit shaken. He listens seriously, chin in hand. When I've finished, he smiles. "You're not crazy."

He makes a declarative statement on my sanity this soon? I was expecting some company in despair over my demise, minimum. Here he seemed so sympathetic.

"And you're an authority on mental health?" I ask, surprisingly irritated.

"Think of this as instinct—a judgment call. Be honest. Do you really think you're crazy?"

"Does anyone?" I ask sharply. "Isn't that sort of the hallmark of insanity, blasting through the world, confident that your delusions are real?"

"Somehow I don't think so," he muses, unfazed. I watch him closely. He stares at the dashboard, lost in thought, my anger unregistered.

Excuse me? My life is falls apart and I get bland attitude?

"Here's the problem," he says. "I don't believe in physic stuff—visions, voices, all that." His voice cracks, falsetto. "Call Fatima at 1-800. Dump that guy because he's cheating and his love child's on the way." He laughs. "Sign me up for Jerry Springer."

Now I'm furious, and strangely insulted. "That's the problem? Your world view? I don't care what you believe! I want to know what's happening to me!"

"I'm sorry. Can't help myself. But," he gets serious, "this could be fun. What if I'm wrong? What if there is another plane of reality we can't see, a different type of logic? What if you are psychic, the real deal? Then my whole belief system is shot. Could be exciting."

I hang on the very self-assurance that I found irritating. "You're certain I'm not crazy?"

He laughs. "Sure."

"What about the chemical combustion theory? I swear, my physiology changes the second I walk into that room."

"Possible, but unlikely. Gaines runs a tight ship. There's nothing leaking, I can guarantee that. As for general environmental sensitivity, isn't that pretty rare?"

"More like uncommon—and rapidly increasing."

"Still, I say we explore the psychic angle first. Seems to be the easiest and cheapest. If we eliminate that option, then you'll have to shell out the big bucks for a diagnosis, blood work and that sort of thing. Beyond my scope."

"You're willing to go down this psychic path without further psychiatric exploration? Certain enough to put your whole belief system on the line?"

"Let's can the crazy talk, okay? You're probably a little

wacko—don't look at me that way—wacko in a normal, off-the-beaten-path style. Otherwise I wouldn't instantly like you. As for laying my belief system on the line, I'm definitely not prepared to sacrifice reason. But plenty of people believe in this psychic stuff, including my Mom. She's a real devotee. My problem's always been lack of evidence. If we can prove that you know things you shouldn't logically know or that you're seeing someone who's dead—well, that would be something," he sighs.

"Is being off the so-called beaten path something you routinely look for in friends?"

"Only the female ones." He smiles and starts the car.

Otherwise I wouldn't like you, he said. How much would that be, Ian? Why not test your theory right now? If I am psychic, I should be able to bore right into that bony little brain of yours and find out. I squeeze my eyes shut and focus. Ian, Ian, Ian. I drum up every single meditation trick I learned during years of sazen. All I get is a sore forehead from scrunching my eyes too hard. I open them. We're on the freeway. Who said I wanted to travel?

"Were you reading my mind?" Ian asks, enthusiastically. "Did you get anything? I was sending you a specific message."

Am I that incredibly lame? Not only unable to read his mind, I didn't even know this was a joint experiment. "You're more psychic than I am," I say miserably. "This is ridiculous."

He shakes his head. "We need more information."

"On what?"

"Psychic skills. We're going to this bookstore, The Curtain. There should be some sort of primer, Wacky Witch World 101 or whatever, that outlines your basic seer characteristics, principles—something. We move on from there, matching what you do to what the book outlines."

"You're enjoying this, aren't you?"

"I love a good problem—something with import and consequence, an issue complex enough to sink your teeth into."

"Sounds great in theory. Except, speaking as the problem, it's more fun to be the scientist—outside, looking in."

"Wrong! That's the great myth science itself is disproving. A scientist doesn't exist separately from what he studies. Once you set the guidelines for the experiment, draw the parameters of your vision—boom, you're already in the experiment."

"Scientist and subject of study are mutually dependent?"

"Exactly." He slams the steering wheel. Here is a man easily thrilled.

I look at him sharply, assessing. "What's your major?"

"Biology." Instantly sober. Obviously a bad topic. I am now compelled to pursue.

"Mine's sociology. What's with the attitude shift?"

"I love biology. I hate my options for the future." Off the freeway, Ian navigates the busier streets of Uptown—perfect excuse to shift his attention away from the conversation. "I don't want to go to graduate school and can't imagine myself in a white coat with a corporate logo. That leaves independent labs and an indentured servant's salary. Or worse, same salary for teaching in a public high school—there's torture for you. Speaking of eating—which I wouldn't be able to do with that income—ever been there?"

He points to a beautifully lit Mexican restaurant where they serve football size burritos. I love the place for the dark orange tiled roof and fried corn tortillas. Who hasn't eaten there? You don't have to read minds to know that he's changing the subject. Let's see: continue torture or change topic? Usually, I really enjoy this kind of dilemma, however predictable the outcome. See someone squirm and I rarely give up. Yet something about the slope of Ian's shoulders and his hang-dog face sways me.

"Love the place," I offer perfunctorily.

"Me too." His voice equals my enthusiasm.

Neither of us cares about tacos. We stop talking. I watch people out the window. If you have money to burn, Uptown is the place—full of expensive clothing stores, trendy restaurants, and people who consider themselves hip. In Minnesota, the words 'wine bar' were first uttered along this strip. The Scandinavians probably scrambled for cover, and with good reason. Fashion marched through the Minneapolis and found its home here. Perfectly coiffed blondes push four-hundred dollar strollers and tug at the edge of their Capri pants, unaccustomed to exposed skin. These are the wives who live in the million-dollar mansions that line the Minneapolis lakes. Then there are the drunks, the punks, the slackers, the hip-hops, the artists, the Dead-heads and the hippies (the latter two interchangeable, at least in a commercial sense), and the nondescript workers in need of decent rent and a bus route. These are the people who live in the wide ring of apartments surrounding the mansions.

A woman about my age struggles to control a lunging black lab. The unsuspecting target, a petulant looking preschooler, lags behind his mother, waving a large cookie at dog-eye level. The lab strains and sniffs. The woman pulls, laughing. Her green hair matches her slip dress—and her eyes, I imagine—perfectly. Half a dozen rings line her jawbone, and when she does look in my direction, I see I was right about the eyes. For some reason, she looks right at me and smiles, beautiful and happy. She pulls a jean jacket more securely over her dress and walks on with the disappointed pet.

Something about the exchange depresses me profoundly. "Have any piercings?" I say out loud.

"Maybe your sanity does need evaluation: imagine the germs." He arches an eyebrow. "You? Didn't think you were the type."

I lift up my shirt and we both survey the tiny silver post in my navel. "I'm not. I wanted to see if the needle would hurt," I say softly.

"Did it?"

"More than I expected."

Ian nods sadly, as if he understood.

He stops the van in front of a shoddy storefront, its crooked red awning a stark contrast to the slick, streamlined windows of the coffee shop next door. My inexplicable melancholy deepens. There has to be a pill for this. Screw diagnoses—I need to be medicated. I must become a more serious alcohol drinker.

Ian's half out of the van, apologizing for the fact that he even knows about the store's existence. His mother used to frequent The Curtain when she was in her Tarot phase, an era that coincided with the days she stayed home with three children and a bad marriage. I feel a surge of sympathy: my idea of Hell, if I believed in such a place. Divination—oh, cards, how do I survive diapers and depression past lunchtime—seems reasonable.

The Curtain is as much haunted house as used bookstore, with low lights, eerie New Age music and beads cascading from the doorways. I smell incense. The place is tiny and jam-packed, complete with a rolling ladder to access floor to ceiling bookshelves. Every flat surface is stacked; the floor space a maze of counters and tables, most covered with deep purple cloth. I peer under a mound of black velvet and find a crystal ball. Runes, Ouija boards, potent herbs and spell books line one counter. Need advice on channeling, meditation, or honing your intuition? The CD selection is endless.

The entire set-up is an ode to marketing. I should've stuck to my original plan and holed up with my computer.

Ian grills the peaked middle-aged man behind the counter. His pudgy pocked face and dyed black hair give me the creeps. He seems to be just the ticket for Ian, who happily loads up on battered old books and pays the bill. Ian hoists the bulging bag. Do I hear the clink of commission? God, am I crabby. The familiar low-grade ache settles between my eyes.

"Mission accomplished!" Ian spins his plastic bag full of books. His good mood sets us miles apart, which he either chooses not to notice or ignores.

I can't wait to walk out that door and see the sun. Dracula wiggles his fingers good-bye from beyond the counter. Clearly, part of the spook show.

New concerns over particulate particles aside, I savor a long, relieved breath on the sidewalk. A well-dressed man and two women breeze past us. Probably comparing stock market tips. The idea of people making money and worrying about where to go to dinner or how the new baby sitter will work out lifts my spirits. Normal life is possible: I need to figure out a way there. The crisp coffee shop next door calls me. Time to wash my hands and have someone wait on me in a dust-free environment.

"I'm hypoglycemic," I announce. "If I don't eat now, I may faint."

Ian snaps to attention. "God, why didn't you tell me? Let's go." He practically falls over himself, trying to open the door while monitoring my upright position.

I am amazed at the new person I'm creating—and how much I enjoy being the focal point for action. Here I thought I was primarily sidekick material. Note to self: reevaluate friendship with Queen Wendy.

A genuine hypoglycemic would be weak from plummeting sugars. I slump into a seat and try to look wan. Ian is at the high art steel counter top, pointing at me in a failed attempt to hurry along the older woman at the counter—a woman with unbelievable hair, a thick white blonde mass piled high on top of her head and secured with a pencil, the fortunate type that grays a decade late. The small woman underneath the mound moves meticulously, unruffled by the imminent collapse of a patron.

I am truly, undeniably starving. Barely polite, I break off an enormous piece of the moist orange and ginger muffin that Ian hands me. The act of eating soothes and strengthens. Tension begins to drain from my shoulders. Ian and I appreciate the café's eclectic use of citrus—he's eating a cocoa and tangerine scone—and banter about the decidedly upscale décor and clientele. Something close to normalcy descends, as long as I keep my eyes off that bag of books.

Until Blondie strides back to our table, wiping delicate pale hands on an apron. To my horror—I am truly too tired to socialize with the help—she pulls up a chair. Can't complain about lack of personalized service, I guess. Everything about her cascades from her hair—ice blue eyes, crepe paper skin and pointed chin. Although probably pushing sixty, she radiates translucence and health. Despite myself, I sit up straighter. Her presence commands attention.

"I don't think the problem's low blood sugar," she says carefully. "There's actually an excess in your system—some sort of anxiety. You know that, though, don't you?" She points to the bag from The Curtain. "And you don't need to read those, although I imagine you will. A little reading won't hurt, as long as you don't take the stuff too seriously. Your best education will come in the field, or from a good teacher." She arches her eyebrows—a dare—and smiles.

Ian's mouth is unappealingly open. I hate this woman.

"My name's Evelyn," she says, extending a hand I don't take. "And I am very pleased to meet you."

4
LEILANI

The Macalester campus blooms around her, its beauty further proof that she exists separately from the living. Spring-wet lawns are vivid green, bordered by early flowering bushes. Vines dotted by frail purple buds wind up majestic stone buildings. A student weaves through the lawn to catch up with friends, baby's breath braided through her fine hair. Youth pours past Leilani with expansive faces and eyes to the sun. They reach for one another. They wear weather-inappropriate clothing, all skin and cotton and pale summer colors. Women in their late teens and early twenties hold hands, still girlish in each other's presence. They laugh and link smooth arms; long legs taper off into painted toes. For all their posturing, the men lose no opportunity to poke, punch, or grab. Couples slink along, intertwined. Even the odd pairings—the gangly boy struggling against the pace of a steely, stunning woman—aren't immune. His fingers graze her elbow, wistful.

Leilani lets her eyes close. The landscape is unbearably bright. Hopeful. Not that she wishes she could return to her own years of freedom. She simply regrets not appreciating those days more. If only she had known! If only there is a way to know, when you're twenty, the brevity of youth and the staying power of despair. Her eyes burn with exhaustion. She's not afraid of the nightmares. Waking terrifies. Better to never sleep, than to open your eyes to memory arched above, waiting. Lids half cracked, she limits vision to the movement of feet. She senses the impersonality of the library ahead, cool marble floors and steep lobbies. Only inside can she afford eyes wide open, at home in the natural melancholy of the old building.

Leilani is amazed at how many dark corners and synchronistic twists one can find in any situation, if only you know where to peer. Imagine—here she is, eagerly stomping down stairs at the one academic institution she swore never to step foot in again, the place that summarily rejected her job application on the first round. Not even a personal note! Her query warranted only the slimmest, most impersonal form letter. She channeled her deep disappointment into witty party dialogue about the shortcomings of Macalester faculty (and she knew a few details) and the pseudo-radical stance of the students.

Transported to campus in parents' Mercedes, these so-called rebels shed clean clothes in favor of torn t-shirts and bandanas. The defiant accumulate dreadlocks, armbands, and tattoos in solidarity with this cause or that race or the emerging vogue in oppression. They protest in comfort: full-size refrigerators stocked with organic greens and a pricey local micro-brew; Palm Pilots safely inside grimy rucksacks; and two-hundred dollar sandals on feet prepared to meet the marching demands of any demonstration.

What better place to host an exhibit of U.S. Army art?

There were the requisite outcries. The exhibit opened to students chanting against the evils of war and the perils of militia, generally. One group waved signs about the World Bank and globalization, unable to resist an opportunity and eager to make the intellectual connections for anyone who inquired. Another faction—the most sympathetically received by their elders—focused on the Middle East. Signs decried various wars throughout the world, some of which Leilani had no idea were being waged.

But the exhibit promised World War II combat art. However vigorous, the protests didn't capture the imagination of ordinary St. Paulites, already and always wrapped up in the unforgettable drama of the last good war, and eager for new images. Leilani was part of the crowd on that first day, wholly comfortable to stand in front of those brutal, beautiful paintings and weep alongside everyone else.

The crowds thinned over time; Leilani returns often. She spends hours in the cool dim center of the building, surrounded by battle: the agony of boys who die with guns in their hands; the hazy impressionistic reds of naval rockets against the black-blue bob of boat on sea; the thready sketch of women raped and murdered, the inevitable victims of every war. Pain miraculously transformed into beauty.

Leilani is equally flattened by the irony and ambition that sent painters to the front lines in the first place. Governments of the western world offered up their artists to war. In 1942, the United States implored her most promising to paint, draw, bleed, and bring back what they could, if they survived its production. The army's pitch to prospective recruits is posted as part of the exhibit. Leilani judges that letter the greatest masterpiece of all. The call to duty is sublime. What ideal-driven soul could resist such an entreaty? Artists were asked to capture the "courage, cowardice, cruelty, boredom of war . . . express if you can, realistically or symbolically the essence of spirit of war. You may be guided by Blake's mysticism, by Goya's cynicism and savagery, by Delacroix's romanticism, by Daumier's humanity and tenderness; or better still follow your own inevitable star."

Were these young men seduced or duped? Leilani isn't sure. They brought back over 12,000 pieces of art, now stored in military warehouses, hanging in tiny museums and obscure universities, or hiding in the homes and souls of the aging artists themselves. She is acutely aware that these young men were sacrificed so that she, and others like her, could stand in front of the broken bodies and torn landscapes and undergo their own transformations.

Today, Leilani stares into Three Dead Chinese Soldiers. Three gold bodies float at the mouth of a jeweled hole, as if to spin toward some journey: rotund cubist bodies shine; thick lips and eyes are blissful. The painting has a vaguely embryonic quality—moist colors and circles and fish limbs—and Leilani allows herself (for one tiny, unprotected moment) to imagine Holly, buoyed in a new womb, moving toward a different future.

Anna eyes her sister from the doorway. She casts a calculating look at the work on the walls—singularly depressing and to be avoided at all costs. Typical of Leilani to become mired in this muck, she thinks. Clutching her Prada briefcase like a weapon, Anna strides toward Three Dead Chinese Soldiers, peach Richard Tyler shift rippling as sails of ship in battle. Several people in the spare basement turn to look. Anna is a tribute to the persuasive power of hundred-dollar haircuts, aerobically managed bodies, and flawless grooming. She has sculpted herself into the image of success.

"Tough love, tough love," mutters Anna, an attempt to

bolster herself against the inertia ahead. "Lani!"

Disoriented, Leilani visibly startles at the sight of her sister.

"Oh my God," sighs Anna, efficiently whisking Leilani toward the door, "can't somebody prescribe you some Valium?"

A large man, supported by a cane, immediately takes Leilani's place in front of the painting. What, he wonders, held that woman so – gave her such a face? He stares into the dark canvas.

"The Commandant sent you?" inquires Leilani coolly, not sounding nearly as comatose as expected. The crisp tone and accurate observation annoy Anna equally.

"I wish you'd stop calling her that. How would you feel if your child called you—oh Lani, baby. I'm sorry. Christ." Anna stands still and covers her face with her long fingers.

Leilani notices Anna's new ring—a gorgeous magenta stone, undoubtedly real, whatever it is. She's pleased to witness Anna in such an obvious state of psychological distress. Over the past few months, Leilani had begun to wonder if Anna experienced discomfort in any form, at all.

Remorse floods Anna, who hates herself for such carelessness, hates Leilani for needing such care, and hates her mother the most for putting her in this position. Her own hostility also pains her. Anna prefers to think of herself as gracious and capable in a crisis. Aiming toward that end, she commands the core of her body to calm. Hands move off eyes. She effectively funnels internal conflict into a familiar, free-floating, low-grade rage.

"Let's get some fresh air. Start over." She smiles serenely.

Outside, Leilani lights a cigarette and sucks as hard as possible, hoping to dispense tar and nicotine smack into the cellular structure of her lungs. Yes! Carcinogens flood the blood stream. The drug hits her. Hope is hers for the moment. She wobbles.

"You're such a novice," laughs Anna. She grabs the cigarette for one loving drag. "Why must this be poison? The worst part of pregnancy was quitting. Then once Bennie was here—well, the stakes seemed too high."

Leilani takes back the cigarette. "I know what you mean."

Anna rolls her eyes and says dryly, "We've all gotten that message loud and clear: Leilani's life is over, no reason to live, can't go on, blah, blah, blah. Start smoking and we can all see that you no longer care about your own life. Frankly, I thought you had more potential—not necessarily rebound potential, but an ability to fall apart with more aplomb."

"Perhaps my creative juices have dried up with the rest of me."

"Not the sister I know, the one who turned every facet of life into performance art: the purple hair, the drama over each boyfriend, grabbing the lead in every school play and reliving each role at home. You were the only one of us screaming and hurling lamps through the hormonal teenage years. Jesus! Now you're going to waste away in library basements? I expected more: shave your head, become a nun, travel the world."

Anna's enthusiasm grows as Leilani's correct collapse solidifies in her mind. "I expected exotic dancing or a barn-size sculpture. Throw yourself into a cause." She flails—what example, what do-gooder liberal thing? Oh, everybody's favorite! "Save the earth! Look at that girl who lived in a tree for a year to make a point about, what, rainforests and giant bugs and such—think of the possibilities! Become the president of Women Against Military

Madness, some feminist thing. As we speak, people are strapping themselves onto endangered bats or wild dogs or God-knows-what, lying in front of bulldozers, picketing pharmaceutical companies—that's what I expect of you!"

Anna, who has repossessed the cigarette, smiles happily.

"Why pharmaceutical companies?" muses Leilani.

"They're always to blame. Get to the bottom of a scandal, and boom—drug company fuels the whole thing. Watch the weekly news shows regularly, you'll see."

Leilani files away the fact: pharmaceuticals at fault.

Anna looks at her watch. "Listen, you're right. Mom asked me to talk to you. She's desperate. You get in your car before dawn and drive aimlessly. She thinks you're stopping at work or maybe at the house? Because you're not talking, she doesn't know." Anna gasps in mock horror, eyes wide. "God, maybe you are interesting, after all. Let's see—you're running guns or you've started a homeless shelter! Wait, I know." She leans forward, conspiratorially, "You're actually doing nothing for hours and hours on end. How clever! Bet nobody in America has ever done that before."

"Spare me the editorial. What does Mother want me to do?"

"See a psychiatrist."

"Fine. I'll go." Easy, the way lies fall.

Agreement was all Margaret asked of Anna; follow-through is another story. She knows Leilani will never make the appointment.

"Thank God," she says blandly. "Mom will be so relieved." She stands and smoothes her silk. "I'm half an hour behind, sweetie. Are you going to be all right, sitting here alone?"

"Please don't be any more insulting than you naturally are."

Reflexively poised for attack, Anna pauses, reconsiders, and allows herself a tightly reigned smile. "Don't be touchy. I worry about you, that's all." She gives Leilani an efficient hug, pulls out her cell phone, and hurries away. Leilani forces herself to light another cigarette. Anna rounds a corner of daffodils and disappears, a blitzkrieg.

For an instant, Leilani is sorry for Anna, who interprets all inactivity as a personal affront. Then again, she may be doing her younger sister a favor. Anna barely bothers to conceal her distaste for the family, a sentiment shared (or initiated, Leilani can never tell) by Martin. Leilani rationalizes: her current bad behavior compliments Anna's needs nicely, offering rather spectacular current proof of familial dysfunction and historical inability to excel. Leilani's failings alone could justify the psychological distance Anna maintains from the rest of the family. Until the accident dragged her back in, that is. Martin and Anna even postponed their move to New York, headquarters of Martin's law firm—and of legitimate humanity, if you ask Martin. A Manhattan native, Martin routinely confuses his laundry list of detestable Minnesota personality traits with party conversation.

A complex constellation of hostility and love structures Leilani's family.

Inside her blue Volvo wagon, Anna flips off the phone and congratulates herself on a clean escape. Then she makes a single mistake: she remembers Holly.

Not Holly-as-current-problem, but Holly trimming Ben's baby hair. She was wearing her favorite dress, the yellow one with bold red flowers. Anna was so angry—the first haircut is special, she yelled! She had planned to put the pieces in a locket or press them in wax paper—the instructions were in some master baby behavior book purchased for precisely such a question. Anna yelled and pointed at the mess on the floor, at Ben's crooked scalp. Oh, how Holly cried! She was filled with remorse. She frantically swooped up the stray blonde hair, searching for wisps under the table, chest heaving and face red. Anna felt herself a giant, cruel and stern, against the two wailing children at her feet.

"Can you use this? Please?" Holly had asked her aunt, holding up handfuls of wet hair.

Anna falls against the steering wheel and sobs as if she'd just gotten the news. Try as she might to forget, she had loved Holly.

Lielani makes her way back to the basement. The paintings pull her, beautiful underbelly of American art. On the stairs, a muscular, graying man smiles politely as he passes, moving up. He has the look of a runner, weathered and lean. She's forty-three years old. Has her time run out? Do you walk up to a man and ask: want to be a father? Even the thought is heretical—there's no replacing Holly. Every parent succumbs to the fantasy of fear: illness, accident, and pain. Even in her darkest dreams, Leilani had never imagined herself utterly alone. She lost a man that she'd talked to or touched every day for fifteen years, someone who once loved her completely. What had she given in return? Will was another gift she had taken for granted—wasted well before he had started the car that morning.

She stays at the exhibit longer than planned, requiring fortification for the trip home. Kerr Eby's soldiers do the trick. The men are desolate and strong, often depicted at the moment of their own destruction – which isn't the same as death. In Jungle, they march without faces, a line of bowed helmets and sagging shoulders. The foliage is exotic and ominous, black ropy vines that bind and follow the silent men. Leilani appreciates the downward impulse of the painting, the way each plant and every face falls toward the dirt.

She envies Eby's demise. His moral standards killed him. A soldier in World War I, Eby's etchings of that slaughter were eventually published in his anti-war pictorial, War. The world didn't heed his message. Compelled to capture the torn heart of battle again, Eby tried to enlist in the next war, only to be told he was too old. He found his way to the South Pacific as a civilian and planted himself in the center of destruction. When the war ended, he took home the tropical disease that eventually killed him. He left much work incomplete.

Leilani is inspired by the thought of all Eby left behind, the pictures half-drawn. He was no different than anyone else. Imagine his home on the day of death – laundry not yet folded, paint brushes to be cleaned, browning bananas a day beyond eating. He would've set a coffee cup in front of a window, forgotten as he took a last look at the sky. Where are the unfinished etchings? Leilani resolves to research tropical diseases. Which one killed Kerr? She envisions herself on a plane to the rainforest, without vaccines or good shoes. Maybe Anna is onto something.

Time to drive. She has the loop down to a science, hitting each exit and flying back on to circle the accident site over and again. Leave the windows open for the roar, the wind that gives the nightly earache. Never buckle a belt. Unlock poorly shut doors. Sit too close to the air bag. Leave a cigarette burning on the seat. Leilani soars past other cars, aware that her speed may endanger another daughter. Don't forgive me, she says out loud. Later, she screams into the noise of the freeway: I am evil. Nobody ever calls the police. She can never understand, how you can get away with murder—murder—and not one person will call to stop the accident waiting to happen, to alert the police to the drunk or the crazy tailgating some innocent and her family. Every evening she tests her theory—chaos rules—and every evening is proven right. Tonight the speedometer hits 100 even, a pure number.

She finds herself, finally, at home. The pink tulips Will planted along the front sidewalk are nowhere in sight. Not enough sun, but that's where he'd wanted them. She can see the blue walls inside the screened porch. The slate wood floor is painted green; there are red chairs (a slouching fifties style) and a wicker table in the corner. They ate on the porch every evening in the summer. Holly sat in front of peas and mashed potatoes, yelling dinner invitations at neighbors. Half the time Isabel or Miranda ended up at the table with them. Leilani sneaks a look, a block down in either direction, half-expecting to see the girls run over.

Holly hated daycare. As a baby, she turned herself over to other people without protest. Compliance evaporated a few short months later. She screamed until her face was blotchy red and eyes swollen. Every morning, she clung and clawed at her parents, her only hope against the gallows ahead. Both hated to see her suffer; Will made the sacrifice. He would write his dissertation evenings and weekends. He'd teach on the same schedule, if at all. Why hurry, he reasoned? They had both meandered this far, taking decades for doctorates that others whipped out in four years. Their lives had been largely unprofessional patches of odd jobs, activism, and long afternoons in coffee shops.

Holly's existence slowed Will down even further. He wanted

to savor every second, he said. Leilani, on the other hand, sensed urgency for the first time. She needed to finish that dissertation, write articles, land a job, sign the dotted line on some institution's health insurance plan. If Holly ate cookie crumbs off the kitchen floor, Leilani was overcome with the urge to scrub floors; Will's instincts were to scoop their daughter in his arms and find a fresh cookie.

Too late, Will and Leilani discovered that daycare wasn't Holly's issue—leaving Leilani was. Their own home became the medieval torture chamber, echoing Holly's desperate screams every time Leilani closed a door. Leilani learned to reserve exits for the necessities of work. She left to teach classes, for late night library research; she locked the sunroom door and holed up with the computer, headed to interviews and eventually, to her every day, real life job at Carver, where an adjunct gig miraculously turned into the real thing.

The greater Holly's anguish over separation, the more Leilani longed to run. She craved time alone (espresso and the paper, once!) and the convenience of dashing to the grocery store without a toddler. She allowed herself neither. Holly sat on the bathroom floor and sang while Leilani brushed her own teeth and used the toilet. Holly helped hand Leilani her clothes and sat on her lap for breakfast. Holly followed her mother upstairs and down, into every room and closet and shelf; she hovered at an elbow while Leilani talked on the phone. By the time Leilani left for work, she was exhausted and claustrophobic. Always initially happy to see Holly at the end of a workday, within an hour she would've paid good money to use the bathroom without an audience.

Will—the only one in the family to read Mothering magazine

from cover to cover—promised Leilani that this too would pass. Eventually, Holly would become less clingy, more confident. Till then, the family rode the wave of need—for well over a year. Holly was a solid three before capable of a calm good-bye and a chair at the dinner table that wasn't pushed up against her mother's. The change barely mattered to Leilani, whose established emotional rhythms vibrated between an urge to flee and a desire to sustain inseparability.

Leilani looks up from the dashboard. Two blocks ahead, the sky over the bluff begins to change color. She leaves the car and walks to the river, fearful that someone—particularly Carmen or Linda or any of the mothers who live along the street—will open a door and shout. Not tonight. She walks the short distance from the old house to the bluff, untouched and heavy with remorse.

For every time she gracefully met Holly's needs, Leilani can find several—dozens—that she did not. Did she stoop and smile and ease every transition? Half the morning flights to work were a slamming door and a scream, from both of them. Leilani was happy to get in that car! She stayed at work later than necessary, sometimes grabbing an illicit bite to eat without telling Will. Leilani occasionally snuck in the back door as Holly watched from front windows, buying twenty minutes to undress and read the paper. Leilani made sarcastic comments while Holly stood outside the shower, towel in hand. She studiously and creatively avoided her daughter. Indeed, brainstorming ways around Holly's watchful eye occupied no small amount of her mental energy.

Now Leilani relives every crushed look and each disappointment. Why do you hide from me? Holly had asked her the question. Leilani can't remember what lie she preferred at that moment. The truth: Holly didn't have to beg for Daddy. He was there, without question or plea. Mama was the person she wanted and the one who walked away, happily, every day.

She reaches the highest point above the river—beautiful! Sit on the bluff at sunset, and you're forced to remember that this is a planet. Leilani watches her small rim of the earth redden as the darker hood of orbit descends. Ever since she was a child, she has been horrified by the fact that human life—her life—hurtles constantly through the dangers of space, dependent on the laws of science and gravity and such, and on chance. Leilani marvels, once again, at how living on a planet can be both such an abstraction and so concrete. She has no idea what the larger universe actually is, yet she is a part of it.

Her feet, independent entities, move inches, then an inch, now a half, to the edge of the bluff. The drop isn't straight. A rocky, tree-laden terrain extends below. One might fall into a bush or something, quite anti-climactic. Her eyes close. She sways, pretending wind is at fault. She expects to be greeted with some kind of vision, but all the mind reveals is a seventh-grade rendition of the solar system—nine colorful orbs on a black background, a dusting of stars in between. Sway harder. There's almost certainly a breeze.

"Plan to keep me company?" Rocco stands next to her, shoulder to shoulder.

"I hadn't." Eyes still shut, she feels his arm brush against hers and isn't surprised.

"I could use some help. I need to borrow bricks from Ricardo's—hard to lift into the pick-up when my knees are bothering me. I am a senior citizen, after all."

Leilani shoots him a quick look. He's watching the skyline. "That's called stealing."

He turns his face to her and takes a step toward the sidewalk. "I've been borrowing for decades. They can have their old stones back after I'm gone. Coming?"

Conviction drains from Leilani. Her body is putty again, eyes leaden. Only her feet remain certain. Soon, soon, soon! The river is a siren song, a promise.

"What are you building now?" She relents. The air recycles itself around her, ever so slightly. The song still hangs in the river valley, timeless and patient.

"A new path—runs along the south side of the house." Rocco is already climbing toward his truck.

She follows.

They work for the last remaining minutes of light. Leilani has done this before, helped Rocco load bricks from behind the large warehouse on the bank of the river. He's right—the bricks are company cast-offs. Half the West Side builds patios from this quarry; still, Leilani knows it's wrong. When Rocco has what he needs, they drive the two blocks to the bottom of the cliff. An enormous green metal staircase winds from the cliff's base on Wabasha Street to the peak of the bluff above, where Leilani and Rocco's houses sit. The stairs begin at an entrance to the maze of caves that sprawl underneath their neighborhood. Gangsters' old homes, goes the legend. Hit men hid in the dark recesses while inept police searched the riverbanks and nearby bars.

Now the doors are a well-marked tourist attraction, the patterns and paths inside mapped and plotted and maintained. Neither Rocco nor Leilani have ever paid to take the tour—a fact they're both proud of. At this flat base below their houses, Rocco rolls out the chunk of limestone he spotted from the truck, a large piece fallen from the cliff. Leilani helps him lift. He appreciates stone, not the exotic kind, only local.

They complete their evening in the dark, lounging on chairs in Rocco's idyllic backyard. Will used to tease him about the landscaping, the tasteful lawn set, the sparkling white lights: you're a Martha Stewart protégé.

Rocco brings out a tray with two small glasses. "To timing." He tosses the liquid with a single swallow.

Leilani mimics the motion but ends up gagging. "Good God, what is this?"

"Something strong. I'll make you an espresso in awhile, unless you're watching caffeine these days?"

"Hardly."

The bitterness of her voice stops him from saying anything else. Under the pretty glow of his roof of white lights, he can see the rage settle. The lines of her face have changed permanently. He has seen some of his own creases deepen over the years, while other channels—lighter lines of smiles and easy hearts—have disappeared.

"I have a son," he tells her.

Leilani's heart lurches. She'd never once heard either Cecile or Rocco mention children.

"If he's alive, he's about your age—forty now. We haven't heard from him in a decade. Last phone call was from Holland. He wanted to wish Cecile a happy birthday. He loved his mother and was sorry for hurting her, leaving her that way. Didn't have much to say to me."

"Do you have any idea where he could be? You've tried to find him, of course!" Somebody's child is out in this world, lost, and nobody, at least at this minute, appears to be looking!

"Drugs." His son's entire life unfolds like a movie in that word. "Cecile swore he had straightened up. He's ashamed to come home, afraid, she said. She believed he would ring that doorbell someday."

"What do you believe?"

"He's dead. I feel him, same as I feel Cecile." Rocco's voice shakes.

Leilani puts a hand on Rocco's arm, dangerously close to the abyss, muscles taut with the effort to stay alert and dry-eyed. She closes one gap between them. "What was his name?"

"Victor." His emphasis on the vowels draws the word out, poetry.

"Gorgeous," she whispers.

They sit silently for a long time, warm from the new moon and the sweet scent of spring. Rocco's chest aches from all the good-byes he has said in his long life—and not only those he's mentioned to Leilani. He's afraid to speak. Leilani, on the other hand, smiles, fueled by a new sense of purpose.

5
DELPHI

Evelyn sits with hands on lap, smiling at us both. She is a blue ice sprite, tiny and pale and persistent. I never was a fan of fairy tales, even as a child.

"You're in shock, I suppose?" she smiles.

Embarrassingly giddy, Ian grins. One afternoon—oh, try one hour— and all his theories pay off. He's hit the proverbial jackpot, what with his rational world blown apart. He'll be happily reconfiguring logic all summer. As for me? Yes, Tinkerbell, I'm shocked—and highly suspicious.

"Excuse me if I'm not dashing off to pursue my new career." My heart beats loudly. Really, I am far more agitated than the situation warrants. "You sit down, uninvited, and announce that I'm some sort of genie—"

"Psychic," interrupts Ian.

"An unusually gifted psychic," corrects Evelyn. "And I was invited. Just not by you."

"Oh, pardon me. Another miscalculation on my part—a Higher Power led you to me. I'm the new Psychic Superstar. How could I forget? You're my teacher since leading the blind is your great gift—although you're psychic yourself, too. Pretty darn convenient. Otherwise, how would you recognize me? Have I accurately summed up the sixty seconds we've known each other?"

"Perfectly," smiles the sprite.

"Great. Thanks for the lesson." I stand up and turn to Ian. "Let's get out of here. This is ridiculous."

"Now you are acting crazy, Delph," declares Ian. "Twenty minutes ago you were dying to find out why your brain malfunctioned. Here's your chance. You must admit this is pretty amazingly coincidental." He beams.

Evelyn grabs my hand! I loathe that touchy-feely quality in people.

"Listen to the voice in yourself, the one you ignore. What if this is true? What if someone is here to point you toward your destiny and you walk away? People pray for definitive moments. Isn't the rest of your life worth ten minutes of listening?" There's no mistaking her urgency.

"Delphi, don't be an idiot," says Ian, calmly.

While not too sophisticated, Ian's idiot argument is the most convincing, if only because I've known him three hours longer than this over-rated cashier here. He's also earned a tad bit of trust in that time, devoting himself to my cause. Note to Delphi: find out if Ian does have own life.

I can't stand the way Evelyn lunges at me. However, I am curious. I'm tempted. I don't know. We should leave.

"Your name is Delphi," says Evelyn. "Right?"

I sit down, shocked into compliance.

"Wow—yes, it is!" grins Ian. "Do you know mine?"

Evelyn shakes her head apologetically. "I'm sorry to say I

don't. Your presence here isn't accidental, I can tell you that. Delphi needs a good friend."

"Ian." He holds out a hand.

"Well, Ian, I'm pleased to meet you too."

Slightly recovered from the name trick, I groan. They're practically lifelong buddies. What happened to Mr. Scientist's skepticism?

Evelyn flutters and clasps her hands together. "Good Heavens, I'm excited! I don't quite know how to begin. You think I would've planned a conversation, waiting." She turns to the glass door as a man in a business suit, peers in, debating. "I better shut up shop," she whispers conspiratorially, and darts off, slamming the closed sign in front of the poor guy's face. He rolls his eyes and moves on, resigned. Evelyn scuttles back to her chair. Ian and I arch eyebrows at one another.

She sighs and shakes her head sympathetically. "He has consistent bad timing. Could use a good Reiki session, too. Now, would you like me to talk about how we should proceed—training-wise—or do you need the part where I convince you that you're psychic and that this isn't some wacko's babble?"

Clearly nervous, Evelyn has just referred to herself as a wacko. Not a strong start.

I'm a long way away from considering an upcoming schedule of events. "I need convincing. A lot," I say, firmly.

"I was afraid so. Just because something is right, doesn't mean it's easy."

I look pointedly at my watch. "You get those ten minutes. No more."

"Okay." Flying hands and eyes instantly settle, all business.

"You do your part, too. Uncross your arms and legs. We're all more receptive if we're not hunched up, guarding."

Surprised, I survey my twisted limbs. The shock shows. Usually my posture is stellar. I reposition myself on the chair: legs straight, arms unfolded, spine drawn long. Good old Ian unwinds, too. He's a trooper.

"I've been dreaming about a student for a year or so, now. She's pretty, with hair you notice. I thought she was Greek—the dark eyes and complexion. Then—," she breaks off to qualify, "I'm talking impressions now, not who you actually are."

I nod.

"All right. I understood that her existence has been inordinately defined by religion. However, far from embracing a spiritual life, she was resisting that path. I got the sense of her as a hostage. I started thinking fundamentalism—not Christian, too ordinary. A Sikh?" Here she pauses to look at me, wondering.

"Buddhist."

"Yes. Something foreign. That was important." She glosses right over the hostage part, which I'm not quite done discussing! "You are an outsider. The capacity in which you serve as an outsider will change. The general stance is yours for the keeping. Don't worry." She shoots me a kind look. "You'll get more comfortable with that."

She thought I was an imprisoned Muslim. I'd say Evelyn's been watching too much anti-Arab garbage on TV. I look at my watch. Eight minutes left.

"Time. Yes." She inhales slowly, thinking. "More on the future later. We need the past."

She wastes nearly forty-five seconds with her eyes closed,

silent. Oh yeah, I'm really impressed—like I haven't seen that glazed over look my whole life.

When her eyes pop open, they're harder. "Your greatest connection is to your mother. She doesn't feel the same. That distance—emotional or physical, can't tell—shapes your sense of self. You shouldn't let her wield so much power. You think you know her. You don't."

My throat burns, holding back a response. Since when do you argue your case by hurting someone's feelings?

She digs in. "You enjoy food that's both sweet and salty. You're lucky to have a strong physical presence, be comfortably embodied: a lot of gifted psychics live pretty ethereally, you know. Give yourself a chance and you'd enjoy hiking and surfing, that sort of thing. Spend some time in the mountains. That will be your favorite place. You were born a wanderer. Don't always travel alone. You're by yourself way too much. More isolated than you were meant to be. Put that gregarious streak to use. Fear stops you from making stronger friendships. Reach across generations. You're old for your age for a reason."

Ian politely studies his teacup. Great—I'm supposed to be the psychic and my interior life is the one revealed. Could he possibly think that he understands me, based on what she says?

Time to end to this. I lean forward. "Generalizations. Stretch your statements and they apply to anyone. I'm not convinced. Time's almost up."

She shrugs. "You're right—I'll never convince you. You already know."

To my enormous surprise—and against my intellectual disdain for the whole process—something about her comment triggers a flare of recognition, as if you see someone familiar out of the corner of your eye, hear a phrase that taps a dormant memory.

"Explain that," I say cautiously.

"Calling yourself psychic, or not, doesn't change who you are. Using the word 'psychic' simply gives you a label for the way your mind has always worked. Return to yourself as a child: you've always known what other people have not. You followed a different logic."

In Buddhism, they say you realize the dharma. What is the dharma? Dictionaries speak of comprehending the cosmic order or understanding absolute truth. You can't know the dharma on an intellectual level, the way you'd figure out a multiplication problem or peruse an encyclopedia entry. Realization is a visceral knowing—body, mind, and emotion come together to dramatically and simultaneously register that Truth has been heard. Realization reverberates through the whole self. Realization reorganizes the world.

In the flash of Evelyn's words, I realize the truth.

She knows victory. She reaches for my hand again.

This time I don't flinch. I bend my head and try to pull myself together.

Ian is alarmed. "What happened?"

Evelyn silently rubs my wrist. A minute or two passes before I can talk normally. I smile. A great gift dangles in front me. Now that I see the shine, I want it.

"Feel relieved, thrilled, astounded—still slightly skeptical—all at once?" asks Evelyn. I nod.

"Thank God. Right on target." She is an elf: she actually bounces on the chair.

"A little help here," complains Ian brightly.

I try. "When I was five, stop lights sent me messages. I'd think: if the light turns yellow, we're having spaghetti for dinner; if green goes on, I get a burger. Ping—yellow appears and later, spaghetti."

"And this explains what?" he demands.

"My childhood was full of signs and stories nobody else saw. Pat a dog and my head ran a movie about Fido's family—kids, parents, whose bed the dog slept on. If I was riding my bike, I'd ask the clouds if I should drag along the lock: sometimes yes and sometimes no. My bike never got stolen. I had three imaginary friends, girls who told me who to trust and what to expect. Wasn't interested in other kids—only the girls. Dad freaked. He brought in a psychologist, who pronounced me sane—and wildly imaginative. Maybe a child who wanted sisters, she said. After that, Dad claimed me the most creative child on the planet. They were both wrong! I wasn't creating a thing—I was paying attention."

How I loved the girls! How secure they made me feel, confident! Do other people lose their grip at eleven? That's how old I was on the horrible day I realized that the real world—the one with school and Daddy and people I could touch—wouldn't tolerate the girls. I eventually said good-bye. Jane was the name of the one who spoke most. The other two weren't big talkers.

"The girls were real, weren't they? They were something!"

Evelyn wags a finger. "I always tell parents not to discount invisible friends! You never know when you've got a ghost or a guide floating about."

If only I hadn't been talked out of believing. Maybe they'll return? Maybe they already have?

"Have you ever interviewed for a job you didn't get, Delphi?" asks Evelyn quietly.

I rack my brain: "No."

"Ever end up in a horrible relationship? Date the guy from Hell or get dumped?"

"I've had good luck. No jerks."

"Often in the right place at the right time?"

"Daddy jokes that if he needs to go someplace important, I'm the designated driver. He swears that nobody hits the green lights and misses the backlogs the way I do. When I show up, free samples appear at the bakery. I know how to hit a sale rack. Does that sort of thing count?"

"Isn't that dumb luck?" asks Ian.

"Plenty of people would say so—they'd be wrong. Delphi's tapped into what we might call the randomness of events; she can unconsciously anticipate and navigate that field better than most of us."

"Does this happen to all psychics?" I wonder. Where would I find some other psychics, by the way? Are they listed in a master registry? Is there a standardized exam?

Evelyn shakes her head, "I wish! We all have our weaknesses, usually related to life lessons we need to learn. I have radar honed into Mr. Wrong, among other things. However, I can see some of your strengths, Delphi. Navigating space and time is one of them. Friendships will be, too—you're learning now. Lest you get content—not a good quality, in general—understand that you have more than your fair share of blind spots! You'll navigate your life lessons on faith the way the rest of us do. Some things even the most gifted psychic can't see, even when they're right under her nose."

I have so many questions! Where to begin: does this mean I pick the winning lottery numbers on Saturday?

Ian half raises his hand. "How did you know her name?"

Fully relaxed at this point, Evelyn pours fresh tea from the pot on the table. "Popped into my head when I saw her. Funny how little control one really has, hmmm? Now I understand the Greek bent better. Glad to find out I'm not too far off. I have a tendency to get half the picture," she sighs.

"Do you make a living as a psychic?" asks Ian.

"Too much pressure. You'll see. Seriously, I tried until something more lucrative dropped in my lap." Her laugh shimmers into the wide circles her hands make. "Real estate! Saw an ad for the training and knew I'd found my meal ticket. I don't take on many clients anymore but keep my license active so I can invest without a middleman."

I study her with new interest. A psychic entrepreneur?

She continues. "Of course, I had an uncanny knack for knowing the day, sometimes the hour, that a hot property would come on the market. I knew what house the buyer really wanted, when to offer over asking price or put in a lowball bid. About ten years ago, I bought The Curtain. Last year I added this place, Crystal's, to my list. Rock bottom prices," she adds, smugly.

Ian and I talk at the same time.

"Isn't that cheating?"

"The café and The Curtain couldn't be less alike—two different worlds!"

"No and yes—I wanted The Curtain and Crystal's to be distinct. They balance each other out. As for cheating, in general, psychic abilities can only be applied toward the greater good. That doesn't mean the gift won't help you—wise use will make your life richer in all ways, although never to the detriment of others. Tricky terrain. You'll have to sort out the beneficiary rules for yourself."

"If I did win the lottery," I protest, "I'd give half to the sangha or Feed the Children. Wouldn't that be for the greater good?"

Evelyn stands up to clear our table. "Instead of worrying about cashing in, I'd wonder why money is first thing on your mind. Could be one of those life-lessons under your nose?"

"Please don't tell me I'll never live among the idle rich," I moan in mock horror. I'm only half-joking.

"Okay, I won't," she says cryptically. "Excuse me, kids. I need to re-open. My late afternoon regulars are on their way."

Time's up? She can't send me packing! What do I do now, start making predictions? Evelyn carries cups to the counter. The whole past half hour becomes ridiculous. Did this conversation happen?

Ian leans in for a gentle tease. "Who knew? You're going to be famous. What's a sangha? A cult or something related to the hostage thing?"

Damn. I forgot to have the "Daddy is a Zen Priest" conversation, a topic dense enough without the newly discovered psychic angle. I can now officially bill myself as a complete—even multi-faceted—freak show.

"My Dad's a Zen Priest. A sangha is a Buddhist community. Sort of a long story, Ian. Can we do Buddhism 101 later?"

"Sure," he says simply. Once again, he bats a thousand by keeping the comments to himself and sitting tight. Suspiciously good-natured. Wish I could read minds.

Evelyn returns. She takes my hands. Yup, the touchy-feely type. "Don't doubt yourself. Promise?"

Who does she see when she looks at me? I wish I could sense what she does, have such confidence in myself. I promise, although now I understand the real meaning of transience—ten minutes outside my own awakening and doubt begins.

"We'll see each other once or twice a week, here. When can you come?"

"Monday?" I say. "Afternoon?"

She hands me the bag from The Curtain. "Promise me one more thing: do not believe everything you read. Check the sources."

I give another vague yes. She stands up and we follow her to the door. She's practically shoving us out! I'm not ready.

"Lovely," she turns to Ian. "So was meeting you, young man. You're an old man at heart, you know. See you again soon, too."

Well trained, Ian shakes her hand warmly, as if she'd only commented on the color of his sweater or eyes or something. "Really great to meet you, Evelyn."

"Wait!" Now I'm the one who's urgent, the one grabbing Evelyn's arm. "The girl! She started this whole thing—I've been seeing a little girl. I thought I might be hallucinating. Maybe she is some kind of ghost or guide?"

Evelyn puts a finger to her lips and looks at the ceiling for a few seconds, thinking. "My initial impression is that she recently died. I'd have to spend time with the image to know more." She looks straight at me. "Think your mystery girl and this meeting are isolated events?"

Before I can answer, she shoos us out with the familiarity of intimate friends. "Get a late lunch or early dinner. Grab a beer. You should celebrate. This is exciting!"

An energetic looking mother pushing twins smiles her way past us into Crystal's. Evelyn greets her by name and walks her to the counter, waving us a happy good-bye. Was this woman yesterday's major psychic find? Sure, I had a few confident minutes back there. However, wouldn't altering my entire sense of self require more than a flash of clarity and a stranger's declaration?

Ian and I remain planted on the sidewalk, blinking adjustment. Which is the surreal—pale and pointed Evelyn with her box-like and contained café, or the sidewalk of strolling shoppers and brisk business people? I'm lost.

"Should we buy that beer?" repeats Ian.

"Maybe several."

We laugh tentatively, treading strange ground.

"Ever go to Liquor Lyle's?" I ask. "They have huge appetizers, cheap."

"All the time. I saw you there—once," he adds quickly. "You were with a girl, lots of hair and unusual taste in clothing."

Wendy's into vintage and varying shades of hair. We turn and walk toward Lyle's. "I didn't see you," I fret.

"Strengths and weaknesses, remember? Possible we both have good timing, only my vision may be better." He laughs, lighter in the promise of the unspent afternoon, the upbeat swell of the street and hint of the first warm night in a northern climate.

I feel the energy and soften a bit myself. "Can we assume Fate? You saw me. We register for the same class, end up partners. You show up at the library the day I do."

"Where's my free will?" jokes Ian. "Now we're getting food, as Evelyn commanded. Hey!" He points upward. "Hey You! Untie those ropes from thy puppet, Master." He whistles a surprisingly good version of the Twilight Zone theme.

The combination of the day's drama and scant food make me a light-headed. My fragility intensifies as we walk into Lyle's. Grow up in a family of non-drinkers and you don't typically traipse into bars at four in the afternoon. Even this early, the high-backed booths are nearly full. Several young men line the long red bar, sharing free goods from the popcorn machine. They look so normal, breaking away from jobs or skipping a class. I can't imagine that they have any problems. Mine seem unduly weighty.

I make the conscious decision to step outside of myself and fade into the blur of the warm bar and its people. You can lose yourself in a mood, can't you? Ian and I find a booth. At first we talk about nothing in particular. We order greasy baskets of chicken wings and fries. I venture beyond that single beer into the tipsier world of two. The conversation becomes denser. We could be on a date: we find out we're on the same political page (left side of the book); Ian's mother is a conflicted Catholic who makes her offspring attend Mass; he likes Sting and Macy Gray, whereas I have a fondness for the old seventies feminist tracks, thanks to a retro phase that relied heavily on Cris Williamson and Tret Furie. Neither of us has strong opinions on fraternities, and we both agree that our elders have thoroughly destroyed the earth. We're uncertain if we're up to the job of recouping the planet.

Ian offers me a third drink. He's looking a little cuter: warning sign. Stop drinking.

I wave the glass away. "I have zero tolerance."

He sets the pitcher aside. "And I'm driving. Is the minimal drinking a religious imperative?"

"Not for me. I dislike the toddler-like motor skills that come with being drunk. Ugh. Some people in our sangha drink. The serious students don't. Buddhists have precepts, similar to your Commandments. One precept prohibits intoxicants. I've never seen my father drink."

"Would you describe yourself as a serious Buddhist?"

"You answer the same question as a Catholic!" We laugh.

Ian shakes his head resignedly. "The minute I move out of the house I plan to officially lapse. Lapsed Catholics never go to Mass. Yet we'll scream for a priest on our deathbeds and make the sign of the Cross in a crisis. That's me."

"Do lapsed Catholics doubt the existence of God?" I wonder.

"This one will."

"I do. That's my problem. Buddhists don't believe in an identifiable entity called God. Sometimes I think I do. One thing's for sure: I won't be chanting in front of a shrine once I'm in my own apartment. Same time, the fundamental principles are sort of in my bloodstream."

Ian nods, sympathetic. "Probably harder to bail because of your Dad. Big letdown for him. What will he think about Evelyn? Do Buddhists believe in psychic phenomenon?"

"Do Catholics?" I ask back. "Who knows?" Dad's cosmology has been set in stone for decades. Last I heard, ghosts weren't part of the picture. Individuality among the living is suspect, let alone a distinct person lingering after death. Should I keep this a secret? An hour away from Evelyn's explanatory grip, and a list of new questions begins.

"Aren't we getting a bit serious for bar conversation?" I ask lightly, hoping for a clean escape from myself for the rest of the evening.

Ian persists. "Serious discussion is what we're supposed to be doing. Youth and all—haven't you heard? College is the one time you get for far-flung existential analysis. After that, you're a drone, a worker."

"That myth applies only to sophomores and juniors," I scoff. "Freshman year is confusion and pretense. The middle years you have real friends and get to gab and ponder life's greater meanings. Senior year—especially the last half—is precisely about embracing dronehood. You must learn to become truly impassioned about the weather and baseball and other dribble."

He shakes his head. "Hardly seems to describe either of us."

"You're wrong: that was me a few days ago."

"Then thank God you went crazy."

We both laugh, and I have chills: he's right.

I turn my head in time to see the woman from the street, the black lab's owner. Still the green slip dress, same sparkling jaw line and smile. Her muscular arm tucked comfortably around a man's back, she lingers next to the door before stepping out into the street with her boyfriend.

The coincidence gives me an idea.

"Is experimenting on other people ethical?" I ask Ian.

"Psychic experimentation?"

"Yeah—I pick someone and see what information I can get. Remember what happened with Pitt?"

"Try me! We can confirm your accuracy, plus, I get a chance to ask questions about my post-graduation plans—or lack thereof."

"I can't." Reading Ian again feels like a breach of our friendship.

"Why not?" He's indignant. "You have my permission."

"I'm not ready. Besides, what happened to your skepticism?"

"Let's say I'm suspending my disbelief."

"Clarify, please."

"Skip the drama requirement?"

"I said clarify, not define. I want to understand exactly where you're coming from."

"Pretend you believe and you might. I'm not on board with the voodoo club, yet happy to entertain the possibility and see where I end up."

My resolves solidifies. "Gotcha. Still, I don't want to know stuff about you that you don't tell me first."

He leans back into the booth, a man assessing. "Okay. You call the shots. I'll play along—nothing to lose, since you're the best thing that's happened to me all day."

Possibilities stretch out between us.

I change the subject by taking command. "You pick the person."

We sit up and scan the room, excited. My stomach starts to quake a bit, as if I'm sneaking a look at a blonde's darker roots: does she or doesn't she?

Ian leans low across the tables to point and whisper. "There."

A guy, about our age, sits by himself at the bar. Every hair is sprayed stiffly into place, clothes meticulously stylish without much flair. He's over-dressed for Lyle's; the dress code for this place is a barely a notch above nudity. The target has an untouched bowl of peanuts next to a drink. Vodka with lemonade? Make mine a double, I hear him say. His shoulders are rounded, resigned. Obviously, he's lonely.

"Too easy," I complain. "Anyone skilled in the ordinary art of people watching can tell he's unhappy."

"Not me," disagrees Ian. "I see a guy with a good pick-up line. He's dressed to kill. Notice how he scopes the room? Targets in on the three women in the corner? The sunglasses on the stool next to him look brand new and pricey. This is not a tragic figure."

"See? You know more than I do." I'm annoyed by the discrepancies between our interpretations.

"You haven't even tried," goads Ian.

I don't bother to reply. I study our stranger. Maybe the beer relaxes me. I don't feel the need for effort. As I watch, he blends into the backdrop of an entire scene. I take in the red shirt of the waitress standing next to him. She reaches for her order, tired. The couple across the bar is silent, one stirring her drink with venom and the other frowning into the wall. The man I was watching turns gray. The back of his neck blackens. Stone heavy, he sits as the rest of the room dances and screams. The noise! Minutiae are magnified—a woman whispers the secret she swore she'd keep. She tells the wrong person. Someone's bitter disappointment cuts a line through the crowd, and the sweet high note of romance—the authentic kind, rooted in honesty and hope—arcs above all the rest. A circus. Impossible to track what happens where—the room rocks with the needs of the body and heart. There he sits, unmovable and dense, in the midst of the chaos, a thickening dark center to a beautiful day.

The little girl in the yellow dress plops on the empty stool beside him. She puts on his sunglasses and smirks, silly, before more seriously assessing her affect in the bar's mirror. Satisfied, she returns the glasses and stops to study the man's gray face. Fingers spread, she almost touches him. Then she turns to me and shrugs, face lit. Maybe? I don't hear the word, but feel it. More urgent, she asks me to help her: will you, will you, please? I was right—she has lost something. Nothing is more important. Loss roots her here and expands sorrow into the universe. Her pain is primal.

Mama. Other strangers heard the whispers and lived its desperation. They were powerless against time: a phone call, frantic police, the paramedic who held her hand and wept openly while he sang to her, instruments useless. I am the one she's now asking: Mama. This child left a wide wake of despair. Touch her death, and you're changed.

Her presence intensifies and breaks apart from the rest of the room, need so great that she becomes a beacon of light, of pain. She stands next to the crumpling man, watching me. Too terrible! I snap my eyes open, unnerved. My guy at the bar is no longer mottled. He finishes his drink and flips through a wallet, departs with a couple of bills on the counter.

My hands are ice cold. "Something bad is going to happen to him," I choke. "Horrible."

Ian is pale. "Omigod. Should we tell him?"

Instead, we watch the guy walk out the door.

I shake my head. "Wouldn't matter. He's sick. I think he knows. I can't tell you anymore than the problem's serious. He could be dying. His body turned black."

Ian pours us both another beer. I don't argue. We sip in silence, scared and excited in our different ways.

He shakes his head. "I shouldn't have let you do this."

"Free will," I remind him. "I wanted to test out Evleyn's theories."

The significance of the past ten minutes hits me. Satisfaction spreads through my entire system. "I can do this," I announce, elated. "Evelyn's right."

"You're convinced?"

"At the moment. As convinced as I can be of the impossible. Whatever I did back there felt good. Natural. I enjoyed the whole scene—mostly." I tell him about the little girl's devastating face and the need for her mother. "We have to be quick."

For the first time, Ian balks. "I'm not sure," he admits, arms folded.

"The minute I'm on board, you're ready to bail? I don't believe this!"

"Between us, this is a game—we're playing Psychic Quest or Guess that Ghost. Dragging in somebody else means the stakes are real. What do you do: tap some woman on the shoulder and tell her you've made extrasensory contact with her dead kid? We'd be handing her grief, especially if ghosts don't fall into her world order. You'd be a crazy, salt in the wound. Worse yet, she's a believer. Then what? She wants you at her side 24/7. Only way she gets her daughter back. Not to mention finding this woman! Got any ideas for tracking her down? The kid could've been dead decades or days. If she exists, that is. Got a continent pinpointed? You haven't mentioned a name, either. Can't start a search without a name," he finishes, heatedly.

"Thanks for the vote of confidence," I say, hurt, standing. "I'll call a cab."

I expect him to leap and grab me. He stays put. "So you're a bolter. Call that cab. Or you can calm down enough to listen. I'm not bailing."

I sit, pouting. One more thing I hate to admit: I need him to believe this is all happening, or I'll be lost.

"That's better." He's still stern. "There are issues to iron out, that's all. We don't want to do more damage than good. We can't run around telling strangers that you commune with dead relatives."

"Unless we're very, very sure that these are the right strangers," I interrupt, warming instantly.

"And that they'd be receptive to ghosts," he clarifies.

"Assuming we can find the mother in the first place. You've got a point about the name—and continent." I'll give him that.

"We need a major strategy session, and not in a bar," Ian concludes. "Let's start over tomorrow, minus the temper. In the meantime, we each try to figure out the practical hurdles ahead."

"First hurdle: real life," I moan. "I have three classes in the morning and the gallery all afternoon."

"Similar issues here," he grins. "You never asked me about my job. I work for my mother. I'm on duty tomorrow, too."

"Your mother? What do you do?"

"Call me a personal assistant. Remember—it's complicated. She's a one-woman corporation that changes logos every month. Mostly, I act as unofficial nanny to the twins and format her newsletter. Let's meet at my house when you're done at the gallery. You'll see. We can ask her advice, too. She'll be totally into the seer scene. We may have to fend her off with a spell or something. You'll like her."

We exchange official information (phone numbers, address,

last names even!) and walk to the car in front of The Curtain. Evening has slipped over the city, Wall Street types replaced by couples and groups of men and women. Ian's arm grazes mine. In front of Crystal's, I peer into the pretty pink-paned window at the nice crowd, tables full of people sipping tea and talking. Evelyn is nowhere in sight, and I wonder what she's doing. Does a psychic-store-owning-realtor do her own dishes?

The night is still young when Ian deposits me at the warehouse.

"Cool!" He whistles at the massive brick building, scans the rows of enormous windows shooting seven floors up.

Easy to say when your digs are in Crocus Hill, rich boy. I fold up the paper he gave me and promise to meet him tomorrow, keeping my opinions about Ian's very expensive address to myself. When I thank him, however, I mean it with my whole heart. Ian has 'Mr. Dependability' plastered on his forehead, a most attractive quality at this juncture.

Thankfully, Dad's downstairs in Moon, as usual. I do not want to say a word to another person tonight. However, Dad's nothing but respectful of my space. He never barges into my bedroom or demands conversation. One note requesting privacy, and he won't even knock to say goodnight. He'll make popcorn (stove top with oil, never microwave), finish the morning paper, and scope out reality TV, a guilty pleasure.

I tape the note to the fridge and glide into my bedroom. Not in the mood for the seventies, I crank Alanis Morissette. I spend a full three hours on my letter to Mommy, rewriting and revising every last detail, from the dead girl to Evelyn to Ian and the bar. When my hand hurts, I turn on my tiny TV in case network programming has shaped up in the past 24 hours. I reread the draft. I want this to be a confident report: I'm psychic, isn't that great! The letter reads more like a plea for help, which won't do at all. When I hear Dad prepare for bed, I decide to return to Mom in the morning, when I'm fresher.

Only when I finally, gratefully ease into bed—where for once, I fall asleep quickly—do I allow myself to cry for a few minutes. The day hits me. I don't want to search for somebody's mother. The weight of a little girl, lost, is too much to bear. My own loss wells in the darkness: one week ago, life was simple. Gainful employment was my only stress. Ask me then, and I didn't believe in ghosts or clairvoyance. What happens after death was an issue I'd planned to worry about eight decades out, not this weekend. There's no going back. Step through a door where you see something different, where new truth unfolds and shines before you, and there is no going back—not if you're honest. You can never fool yourself into forgetting again.

6

LEILANI

She has no shortage of symptoms: sleeplessness; aching eyes; sore joints; fatigue; back pain (stabbing and throbbing); the occasional rash; peeling skin; strange tingling in fingertips; cracking knees; ringing ears; jaw tension while chewing; difficulty swallowing; chest tightness; shortness of breath; abdominal pain; thinning hair; bouts of acne; and digestive difficulties that extend beyond the stomach to elimination.

Signs of specific diseases ebb and flow. The hair loss, fortunately, appears to have stabilized. Die she must. Who can fault her for wanting to go with a full head of hair? The rashes and pimples flare and fade. The bottom of her heels peel since she stopped buying moisturizer. If she forgoes greasy doughnuts—and she doesn't—the ulcer-like grinding in her stomach subsides.

Fatigue remains constant. Fatigue is her favorite symptom, leading her to no less than fifty-seven potentially fatal diseases, including plague. Not only is fatigue fabulously fruitful, it is inducible. Leilani checks the clock, to be certain. Nearly forty hours without sleep—a personal best that brings on a dizzy, dreamy state, as if she had two glasses of wine too many. The mind loops and body wobbles behind.

She slaps her cheeks to snap back into a studious state, wiggles into a longer line on the floor next to the bed, and refocuses on the John Hopkins' Family Health Book. If the bathroom scale is right—Anna reconfigures the baseline each time she visits—the book weighs ten pounds. Yellow post-it notes flutter from a third of the pages; pencil scrawls make the case for affliction next to the most hideous diseases.

She was onto something about the tropics. Kerr Eby could teach her a thing or two about a painful death. Viruses are lethal, yet the possibilities discouragingly remote: leishmaniasis, typhoid, cholera, hanta—even rabies. All hard to come by. Worms may be a better route. Whipworms breed without symptoms; the young grow and reproduce at a mad pace, clinging to the walls of the colon until the intestines are alive. The abdomen teems with colonies of the two-inch parasites. The host continues to eat, drink, and sleep as if nothing were amiss, sustaining the secret universe he or she carries. Maybe there's a bellyache or slight distension before fever sets in, before the bowels become compacted and the body, overcome.

Yet no matter how painstakingly she maps out illness, parasite, or accident—no matter how exquisitely certain she is that this is the solution, the body inevitably wins: not strong enough to withstand sleep and too strong to succumb forever. She always falls, always wakes. The car doesn't crash. Fever won't set in.

If she worked harder, death could be convinced to stampede at full speed ahead. However Leilani may long for such expediency, she lacks the commitment that this path would require. In her former life, she acquired habits. Change would require effort: seek out partially dehydrogenated vegetable oils; begin a sun bathing regime; wield the hairdryer recklessly while in the bathtub; eat mercury-laden fish (one benefit of living in the Great Lakes region); increase salt intake; start hormone replacement therapy; and figure out which cholesterol is good and which is bad and how to achieve their imbalance. She does not have the energy.

Latent disasters are her best hope. Worms might be too ordinary. She turns the pages to waldenstrom's macroglobulinemia, not as glamorous as Eby's but more interesting than pinworm. Fatigue is the first symptom. Weight loss? Could be, ask Anna. Reading by flashlight to increase eyestrain, she sits up unsteadily to shine the beam into the mirror and check her pallor. Definitely ashen. Vertigo, nausea, visual disturbances? Sure. Mild lethargy and stupor—assuredly. Blood is always the stumbling block. To be the definitive marker of death, blood must appear in the wrong places. She ignores the inconvenient absence of red from her own stool or saliva. Indeed, her bones are being infiltrated—at this very moment—by abnormal plasmacytic lymphocytes. Her instantly enlarging spleen gorges vessels with blood, which develops rapid viscosity and immunoglobulin M parraproteins. Although her blood remains woefully invisible, at least it is lethal: abnormal proteins seep into her internal organs and connective tissues.

She closes her eyes in a form of reverse visualization, picturing the cells of her body as malignant, willing them to malfunction and reproduce. Her blood does feel coarser, less comforting. Perhaps the pressure is increasing, too, an unanticipated benefit? She can sense the veins of her arms bulging. Waldenstrom's macroglobulinemia is a slow disease; she'll have time to suffer. Oh no—once shut, her eyes are cement, pulling the body down.

The creak of a door thunders, given the hour and her physiology. Startled, she jumps into a squat, eyes glued to the changing line of light beneath the door. Her father's distinctive tread crosses the floor. The bathroom lamp throws shadows. He's the one who should be worried, peeing every two hours all night long. She puts the flashlight's face on the floor as footsteps stop on the other side of her closed door. They both hold their breath: Leilani straining to become smaller, George swelling to listen. He shuffles back to bed. Leilani's turn to listen, taking in the tenor of her parents' whispered consult, if not the specific words. No matter. She can guess.

Waldenstrom's won't do. A slow death is exactly what she's trying to avoid. Isn't that what we're all suffering through anyway, from the minute we set foot on the planet? Myeloid metaplasia's attractive description ("deranged proliferation of red blood cells") catches her eye, although pace is a problem. The disease can be "managed effectively" for a few years. She flips through pages. Most cancers are far too curable. Think of the lymphomas, decidedly standard fare, with an outcome that's guardedly optimistic.

Finally, both tone and outlook suit: chronic myelogenous leukemia. The prognosis is grim; the authors shy away from the word 'fatal,' yet in the interest of honesty, are forced to convey that meaning nonetheless. Symptoms initially appear benign. Who isn't tired and pale upon occasion? By the time diagnosis is made, death within days is possible.

Encouraged, Leilani finds the strength to heave her body to a chair in front of the computer. On-line, reward is heaped upon her: personal web page after page of tragedy and loss, all chalked up to the marvels of myelogenous leukemia. Electronic images of angels and Christ fly across the screen. This illness means business. The time lapse is lovely. One poor man died three days after the doctors made their proclamation. That's efficiency.

Without making an actual decision, she plugs the name Victor Crea into a search engine. In 13.8 seconds, over 15,000 options flash invitations. A year ago, Leilani would've groaned at the number; tonight, she's giddy. Here's a project. Here's a time-consuming task! If her daughter were missing—no body, no death certificate, no irrefutable proof—she would open every last link. She would search each continent for the tiniest, hairline connection to her child. One cannot rest in the presence of a missing person. One does not line the patio with stolen bricks, while away weekends ice fishing, and find time for the Monday night movie on TV! A lost child is all-consuming. Her respect for Rocco is shaken. You hear about these things, the shortcomings of parents. She gets to witness such negligence firsthand.

But 15,090 entries! She laughs a little loudly and covers her mouth with a nervous glance toward the door. Not to worry—her parents are probably asleep. No one can outlast her at night. She scrolls the list, assessing. Lots of links in Spanish, highlighted for 'crea,' far more popular than a surname warrants: a word with its own meaning.

She wishes she had studied Spanish, a usable language. Instead, she learned German in graduate school and had actually minored in Chinese in college, a totally worthless combination. Perhaps, even then, she was unconsciously aiming for dispensability. Sometimes she hears the lilt of Mandarin in a grocery store, at a museum, near the park. A young mother explains some American idiosyncrasy to a small child or two (never more). However tempting it may be to dredge out her rusty salutation—ni hao—she remains quiet. Memory has left her with random words and ideas, not a conversation: I'm hungry, this is the littlest sister, which way to the University? Worthless.

She'll have to sneak into the den and search out the old Spanish/English Dictionary, if Seamus didn't spirit the book to San Diego. She won't begrudge him that. Seamus has never taken a thing from this house—or family—that he didn't need. If standing up weren't so burdensome, she would slink downstairs while no one else is awake. Movement, however, proves impossible. The humming computer is hypnotic. Her finger is barely plugged into the wall of sleep, a dam threatening to flood her slim defenses any minute. She can't disrupt the precise weight of her body. Leilani squints into the hazy pink screen, a spectacularly convenient color—Holly's favorite, and a pale, peaked backdrop that taxes the eyes ever further. Yesterday she added tiny white background dots to heighten the effect.

Lots of links are related to Victor Hugo. Why such interest in a melodramatic old man, long dead? Broadway! The star-struck assemble elaborate electronic shrines to their favorite Fantines and Jean Valjeans. No matter—she will browse each! She will beat the odds! Somewhere, some stout woman in support hose tinkers with her web design and chuckles: folks, I loved the play and now have the man, a real Victor. That could be her Victor Crea—visible by a thin, blue line of language, if only she looks down every last hole. Or the woman is svelte and lush, full lips and high cheekbones, hiding a reference to Mr. Crea from Minnesota in one of the thousands of links containing the highlighted name. Leilani frowns into the screen. Is crea a verb?

She enters site after site in Spanish, vaguely ascertaining that crea is some kind of high-end cotton product, and indeed, a verb. Her eyes water and burn, the lids flutter. Cells scream for oxygen; she bites her cheek to stifle a yawn. Her fingers thud on the keyboard, each click a resounding knife-bite into night's stillness. If the eyes never close, one would go blind: corneas require the moist ooze from the meaty blanket of lid, a shield that protects and renews. Leilani makes an O out of her mouth to widen the whites and pull her lids apart as long as possible. She clicks the next link. Another genealogy, the wrong Victor vain enough to think his family line matters. There is such a thing as eyelid cancer. She keeps blinking to a minimum.

Leilani slumps onto the desk. Isn't there a hereditary disease that rendered an entire family sleepless? She vaguely remembers the PBS documentary. She and Will sat on the couch, holding hands in horror at the suffering these people endured. Very rare—a quarter of the people in this clan (more Italians, she thinks) stopped sleeping sometime in middle age. They died horrible, hallucinogenic deaths as both body and brain malfunctioned and fried. People approaching forty knew their fate and stopped enjoying life early, in anticipation. Unaware, their dark and beautiful children played happily, doomed. There's a death for me, she grins: relatively speedy (a matter of weeks, the tiny snatches of sleep here and there ever decreasing), yet slow enough for significant suffering.

Such an appealing possibility distracts her from the Victors. She should be able to move the mouse up the tool bar to conduct another search. Her limbs should carry her toward the John

Hopkins' home horror industry, open on her bed. She imagines herself standing. The leap between idea and movement is too great. Astounding, how many children this particular Victor begot. Except they don't use that word anymore, do they? Just as the demands of the body win and sleep takes over, Will smiles. Remember me, he insists. She does not want to—he's the last person she plans to take with her. It is physically possible, as Leilani does, to fall asleep while crying in protest: please, no.

Do seconds pass? Hours? Light floods the room. Leilani jolts upright from a dreamless sleep, gasping. Did she miss a lecture or class? Where is the daytime noise? Will should have woken her. She stumbles forward from the chair and takes in the flat computer screen and last night's notes and within seconds (the entire process, the toehold of normalcy and her return to nothingness is a whirlwind; you blink twice to pass that much time), her head is back on the desk, immersed anew and again. Leilani is defeated before she can push back a chair and find her footing. Amazing, how time can pass and mean nothing. She takes up last night's ruminations after missing a single beat, memory's waking gasp.

A long laugh startles her into an awareness of life outside her room. Seamus? She tiptoes to the door, the guilty teenager, listening. Margaret's military voice: set suitcase there, wipe feet here, do not sleep in a room half painted. Seamus! She hears his mock protest. She imagines him popping a characteristic kiss on Margaret's forehead, wrinkled from years of strategic planning. His very presence, undoubtedly, is a direct result of her current skirmish.

Even the tenor of her father's voice is relaxed, as if he had all the time in the world. George is the least available man Leilani has ever known. You don't write the rags to riches story by wasting time, he would remind his waiting children, emphasis on the word 'write.' Not satisfied to live out that wildly popular and largely elusive cultural narrative—no, he must lay claim to its creation. After barely scraping through high school, George made a fortune destroying trees and shrubs. Nobody in the Twin Cities has been better at stripping root structures and cleaning up after Dutch elm disease. He has the four-story Victorian in historic Crocus Hill and the stock portfolio to prove it. Hundred-foot tree endangering power lines and spawning a block of roots? Parasite threatening the shadiest section of the city? Even semi-retired, George remains the expert, fielding calls and questions year-round, routinely donning the hard hat again to examine someone else's problematic bark or dig.

Seamus bounds up the stairs. Leilani scrambles to the desk, licking hands to smooth hair and clothes into some semblance of order. Yes, I've been awake for hours, she'll say. I woke early to research an academic article. Better yet, a book. I'm writing a book, practices Leilani with a whisper, on the use of wallpaper imagery in eighteenth-century women's literature. That will certainly stop further inquiry, possibly even from the ever enthusiastic Seamus. She hurriedly clicks off last night's genealogy and randomly opens a document, screws something resembling focus onto her face.

Seamus doesn't knock. He stands in the hallway and sings— poorly. Worse, his selection is a mock hula, featuring a falsetto "aloha."

Leilani used to laugh; today she opens the door, grimly. "Hello, Seamus," she says without welcome, arms folded.

"What?" Seamus pulls out all the stops. He has an Irish

brogue. "No kiss for the wayward laddie?"

"Please don't do this," hisses Leilani, fiercely, pulling her brother into the room. "Don't try so hard."

Seamus obediently collapses onto an exquisitely recovered crimson chair, effort evaporating. "Thank God," he smiles. "Some of your kick is left."

Even though she can't smile back, she can almost remember the peace his presence brought her.

"Maybe your routine has just lost its charm," she says.

For decades, Leilani and Seamus have mocked the names that marked them as playground fodder. Newly married and therefore a woman (all of 18 years), Margaret dreamt of travel she couldn't afford. She bestowed those dreams upon her children, plucking their names from her desired destinations: Hawaii, Ireland, and Russia, in that order. If she hadn't been exhausted by then (three children in four years; she stopped caring what the Pope said and got the prescription), she was fully prepared to head toward China. As adults, Leilani and Seamus have come to enjoy this particular dream they inherited. Address Anna as Anastasia (or worse, the nickname she chose as a child, Stacy), and she bats her eyes and says, "Who?"

"That's good," says Seamus without missing a beat, "because I've lost my touch for the vodka voice. Speaking of which, how is she?"

"Richer than last week, I'm sure. She and Martin are very busy achieving. We peasants are to remain appropriately envious. I 'ooh' and 'ah' on command."

"Ouch. I can hardly wait to hear how you describe me."

"I generally don't."

Seamus surveys the scene: his sister's unreadable face, the tightly closed windows and rigidly clean room—with the exception of one carefully contained desk corner depository for papers, half-full glasses, coffee mugs, and several cans of Coke. He pretends to pass over the computer screen, but gazes quickly: a two-year old letter complaining about a faulty garbage disposal? He's been in this room a thousand times; now, Leilani has managed to turn the space into a hotel. Her suitcase is open on the floor by the bed. Closet is ajar, nothing hanging. He bets the drawers are half empty. She's been living here six months. Not one photograph or memento. Not a piece of wrinkled clothing, not an earring or tissue dropped on the dresser.

He stands up. "Let's get breakfast somewhere."

"Can't." She grabs her purse from the top of the suitcase. So she wears this shirt another day. Who's counting? "I have plans."

"That's not what I hear."

Everyone loves Seamus. His happiness is torch and lure. Leilani adores him because he loves her back.

How to deal with unexpected temptation, with Seamus? She might try truth, which Leilani has always felt to be a highly overrated concept. By nature, she is not prone to full disclosure. However, lately she's been experimenting with the practice. People don't trust what she says. They chalk up truth to grief: she's lost touch. She hasn't come to terms, is alienating herself from loved ones. She's in denial. There has been no closure. She hates the strained, professional language of loss, every syrupy word. With Seamus, honesty isn't a ploy or marker of morality or therapeutic goal. Maybe he, of all people, will simply believe her.

Hand already on door, she tells him: "I'm going to drive to

the house and then go on the freeway for awhile."

Seamus considers and nods. "What about the cemetery?"

"Never."

"Work?"

"I sit in the office sometimes. They assigned me a class for the fall. I asked."

"Plan on actually teaching?"

"Not really. I have to get going."

"Wait!" He holds her wrist, lightly. "Do you ever see Carmen? How about Nora and Jose? Any of the old crew?"

The names are foggy, a wet map of a world she used to visit. "Not that I recall. I need to leave now, Shay."

At least he gets the nickname. "Your reprieve is temporary, sweetie. I'm staying for a while and my plans include you."

Neither of them smile, wills locked. Even allies are capable of battle.

Leilani gets as far as the hallway when Seamus lobs his first big gun. "How's Daisy?"

The dog. God damn him. Daisy slept on the furniture and master bed. When they had hamburgers, Will fried an extra for the dog. Overcome with yearning for a fist of smelly fur, the scratchy pad of paws, Leilani proves that she's stronger than desire, again.

"No idea. Ask Anna." Flip. Perfect. She's on the first step.

"Been inside the house lately?"

Leilani stands at the top of the stairs, stopped by the disappointing realization that she does have what could be called progress to report. "I sat in Rocco's backyard yesterday."

Tell this to Margaret and approval would've rained upon her. Margaret would wag her head in wild affirmation, a beacon pointing her daughter in the right direction. Just like she had a two-year old in the house again. Yes! Sat in backyard. Good girl.

Seamus only asks if she can be here for dinner—please.

"I'll try." Leilani flies past her mother, late for visiting the house and probably facing yards full of children.

Margaret is on the stairs before the door shuts tightly. "You let her go? After a five minute conversation?"

As long as Seamus can remember, his mother's resolve—her sheer will to make something happen and her astounding success rate—has been equally infuriating and inspirational. Considering the circumstances, he is currently inspired and therefore, patient.

"Isn't that five minutes more than you've been able to talk to her?"

His mother allows herself to momentarily lean against the stairwell. Hard to admit you need someone else's strength. Seamus has always been her favorite—everyone's, actually. He holds them together, deflecting tension and mirroring back their best qualities. Where did such a gift come from, the way Seamus loves life? Margaret still marvels.

She stands up, ready. "I don't care if it's April. I'm making pumpkin pie. Then you and I are going shopping."

He slips down the stairs, already comfortable in her rhythm. "Jim needs a new bathrobe. Thank God this city finally has a Neiman Marcus."

"Snob," says Margaret fondly. They go into the kitchen.

Safely inside the locked car, Leilani watches her old house. She counts four children darting between backyards. Worse, she sees Isabel skip out of her front door toward the garage. Her mother, Carmen, fumbles with keys and reads from a piece of paper as she walks. She is oblivious to the miracle of following a daughter, a day of errands. Leilani ducks below the dashboard until she hears a vehicle creep by. She senses Carmen's laser gaze of pity.

Leilani has seen too much. The lightness of Isabel's step, the high knees and happy gait are a betrayal.

She knows her death will hurt Seamus, perhaps irrevocably. Since he's come to save her (no one has to tell her; Seamus does all the saving), he'll be the target later. Jim will try to convince him otherwise and Seamus' own sensible side will concur. Nonetheless, he'll be guilty. Perhaps failure will tarnish his status as golden child. He may never be completely confident again. He remains happy now, less sidetracked (although no less affected) by the loss of Holly and Will than the others.

Just over a year apart, Leilani and Seamus each fell in love, hard, for the first time when they were at the University of Minnesota, a senior and a junior. Anna was a freshman. All three still living at home and driving to campus in one car: no use throwing away money simply because you have some, proclaimed their father. Leilani loved a lanky, slope-eyed boy named Matthew, after the saint. Seamus fell for a harder body, a track star with crisp dark hair and blue eyes, Eric.

The only surprised person was their father. Leilani used to argue that George was too busy to see the signs; Seamus laughed that his father didn't know what the signs were. Margaret, on the other hand, never wasted energy on lost causes. As soon as she got wind of the first affair (the late night phone calls, Seamus' giddy goodwill toward the world, the ardent and unexpected interest in high bars and sprints), she hustled him off to the University's counseling office for a session or two on gay identity. Then she informed her husband the following evening after their offspring were shuttled out of the house. She didn't leave a minute of announcement or aftermath unplanned. A dazed George sat in the same counseling office the next day, taking in all kinds of information he never dreamt existed.

As pragmatic as his wife (they were a good, and largely content, couple), George only took a few weeks to come round. He had had hopes for this son that included grandchildren and a certain way of life that he believed were snatched from him in a single hour. However, he had a deep respect for the tenacity of nature. A majestic, hundred-year old pine could be destroyed by a single stroke of lightening—he'd sawed the charred branches, ground the stump and sold the needles for mulching. Consider buckthorn: wrench out roots with a bulldozer and the damn thing still grows back. Leave a single seed and the bush springs to life again; a few red berries lost on the ground and the sparrows replant an entire hedge. Nature, not God, metes out fate.

Leilani scans what she can of Rocco's quiet back yard. Maybe he's off shoplifting little-used planters from some sidewalk café. A small strain of distaste—frail, an aftertaste—for Rocco's choices trickles through her. He's let someone down; she thought he was different. She forces herself to look at Miranda's house. No movement there, either. If memory serves, Miranda would be at her grandmother's, sitting out her parents' annual Boundary Waters canoe trip. Boats tip, muses Leilani. Nobody ever caught her wasting a week in a canoe. She wonders whatever became of Eric, a person she hadn't thought of in years. Good old Seamus: he used to keep in touch and offer updates to Leilani, his first confidante.

She slides lower in the seat, sullen from memory. Such

exuberance. Nature treks and love affairs. She refocuses on her own front door, insurmountable. Are there ghosts inside? Does the refrigerator smell and has the incremental drip in the upstairs tub caused the floor to cave? Something is rotting, she's sure. Perhaps the decay is plumbing or electrical, deep tissue problems of the home—the very infrastructure malignant. The image is comforting.

Lists also soothe Leilani. Today, she tallies up people she wishes dead. Inventing their endings is a bonus. For people with faith in God or belief in karma—or even those with a sense of goodwill—such fantasies carry the weight of conscience. Leilani, on the other hand, no longer operates under such moral compunction. She can, and does, indulge. Generally, she begins with Anna (whose autopsy makes modern science by finding a causative link between a burst blood vessel and whole-hearted embrace of consumer culture). Work colleagues follow. The grand finale is the successful crew from graduate school. Today, for no very good reason, she starts with Eric. Haven't heard from a gay man in years? Dead! AIDS is the simplistic and stereotypical answer. Transportation accident is much more likely. The dangers of Amtrak trains seem to Leilani to be wildly underestimated. Every time you pick up the paper, one more has derailed or rear-ended another. Then there's air travel. Only a fool feels safe in a plane anymore. Random terror aside, consider the annual statistics. Sure, cars are safer. Not by much, if you read the fine print.

She chants a ditty from childhood: "A boy was sitting on the railroads tracks and did not hear the bell. I'd like to give you the rest of the story, but it's too sad to tell." Which child to place in harm's way? Satisfaction won't be in the death, but subsequent parental suffering. People always swear they wouldn't wish their tragedies upon others: Leilani does, daily. She hums the ditty. Her brains rolls, Rolodex style, through families she knows.

"Leilani? Lani!" The voice is unmistakable, Puerto Rican accent a breeze after three decades north. Always an insistent presence, Carmen is indomitable from the leathered height of a shining new silver SUV.

Leilani forces herself to strain upward, tiny and insignificant in the low-slung ancient Honda. Wasn't Carmen the one rallying the troops for electronic cars and cautious oil consumption, mocking suburban mothers famous for their gas-guzzling monstrosities? How quickly people turn!

"Oh, Carmen. Isabel." Her voice is cracked and dry with the names she hasn't spoken in months. A securely strapped Isabel waves cautiously from the backseat, trying to boost herself to see out the window. Her older brother, Hank, is lost in a Spiderman comic.

"My God, how are you? We are all worried sick," cries Carmen. Her sincerity stabs Leilani's aching chest. Carmen opens her window all the way to lean out. "Would you come over for awhile? Chuck made banana bread last night. I can put on a pot of coffee. Please."

Is this an Encounter, wonders Leilani? She writes the script: Encounter left the woman unfettered. What a wonderful word— unfettered. People don't use that enough.

Perhaps Carmen hasn't been here long enough to qualify as an Encounter. No, this is a scrape. A sigh, a twinge: proof that she is indeed unable to communicate effectively with others, a landmark heralding real decline in the grief industry. Here is proof that she does hate all the happy people. She hasn't come across this character flaw in the literature; common sense suggests such negativity signals trouble. Why, thinks Leilani, I might even despise Seamus. He's unacceptably happy. Without question, Carmen is evil.

Carmen is also crying. "I wish you'd talk to me, at least. I wish you'd return my calls—all those messages. Jesus, I know your mother better than I know you now."

Their friendship has been trundled and locked in the darkest corner of Leilani's memory, space reserved for all the varied love that entered her life through Holly. That's how she and Carmen met—strolling equally fussy babies around endless blocks, delighted to find they had much more in common, shared so many dreams and complaints.

Leilani struggles to think of something to say, anything, to end the Encounter. Time has passed. Long stretches of silence, even. The event is official. Unable to dredge up a single sound without betraying her internal state, Leilani starts to shake. She bites the corner of her lip. She refuses to join the crying jag.

"Please talk to me," Carmen begs. "Look at me."

Leilani listens to Margaret's phone conversations. Along with other friends and well-wishers, Carmen has received her instructions: leave my daughter alone. Let her sit in the car, wait her out, give her space to heal. In the past months, Margaret has evolved into a bereavement industry. Shelves in the den had to be rearranged to accommodate the books—not only pop psychology, but tomes, Freud and Rank rubbing back jackets with Elizabeth Kubler Ross; the latest journal articles ordered and filed; dense theory packaged for academics lying, half-read and thickly underlined, on the kitchen counter. Margaret hollows out a cavern around every crisis, a protective bubble of information. When Anna came down with mononucleosis in high school, Margaret had her hour on the phone with the Center for Disease Control in Atlanta. Family myth holds that she spoke with the Director Himself. Who knew there was a Hernia Institute (in Florida) until George required surgery? Preoccupied with all the labor, however, Margaret generally forgets to return to the heart of the issue, the person generating need in the first place.

Leilani realizes that Carmen has been talking—a lot. Her cheeks are bright red, deep brown eyes wet and open. Will once called her beautiful. That didn't bother Leilani; she was proud to have such a friend. Wait. Once again she's lost time and focus. What has been going on?

Jekyll and Hyde-like, Leilani suddenly determines the Encounter must not end—no, not before she hears Isabel speak. She is consumed with masochist desire. How does a little girl's voice sound, six months later?

"Isabel," she inquires brightly. "How are you?"

"I'm five now," Isabel says, solemnly. The same! Low for a child's, husky.

"Mama gave me Princess Barbie for my birthday. She said I wore her down and let that be a lesson in begging."

Isabel smiles, her feminist home no longer a Barbie-free zone. Will went belly up in that battle early—what does a doll matter, he had asked. A snapshot of her daughter, joyful and alive, flashes through Leilani's thickening skull: Holly as a happy whirl of Barbie-pink sequins and silver blonde hair, dancing through the house with a new doll.

The sledgehammer descends: Isabel is a year older.

"Five!" Leilani chokes. She starts the car, frantic. How could she be so stupid, so careless! To forget a fundamental fact: birthdays!

She jerks the wheel, desperate to find a way around the silver giant. In the midst of the motion and the din of Carmen yelling, Leilani steals a quick, critical look. Isabel is different. Let's be honest: there's been a haircut, a slight maturing of the cheeks, a tauter pull to the collarbone. Nervous under scrutiny, Isabel waves and gives a tentative smile. Isabel offers a truce with Holly's mother. Leilani can't forgive her.

The Honda squeals and spins, vicious. She's free, racing around the first corner and down the huge hill that leads first to the river flats, the anonymity of downtown, and finally, the freeway. What may be a milestone for Carmen and her children will forever mark loss for Leilani.

Isabel was a spring baby, Miranda early summer. They get to grow older. Holly will be four forever. If her rotten luck holds, Leilani will die at ninety, wrinkled and runny-nosed, the only prune with a four-year old. The next few years unfold. She must suffer through Isabel and Miranda's newfound height and leaner bodies, witness first days of school and mastery of two-wheelers. Her daughter's best friends will grow up, these first four years a whisper. They will forget Holly. She can never forgive that, not even—especially—in another child.

No time for sitting at the site today. She has an agenda. Calls to make from the office, deadlines and time constraints. The void of driving will have to do. She figures she can squeeze half a dozen swings around the stretch of freeway and still be at her desk by nine. The Honda edges toward eighty, horns and fists raised in her wake. She slows down—abruptly—to thirty miles an hour, for the ten-foot stretch where Will's car skidded.

She swerves around a boxy red Jetta. Her heart jolts in surprised recognition. Will? The long face and hair more red than blonde! She stares at the man behind the wheel. He wears glasses. Of course, this is not her husband. Maybe ten pounds too heavy, he throws a frightened look her way as her car wobbles, unsteady, within inches.

She is never tricked into thinking she sees Holly. Will haunts her. That last year they'd lived like college roommates, buddies who occasionally get on each other's nerves and even more rarely, fall into bed for lack of better chances. Nobody had said divorce. However, the "what happened" conversation was a regularly scheduled event. They rehashed major disappointments: Lielani with the doctorate and job, Will's dissertation tossed into the garbage the day the University's clock ran out; Will the parent Holly presented with finger-paintings and puppet shows, Leilani the parent who induced screaming. Will had the nerve to present those dynamics in terms of nurture and personality, rather than the logistics of employment. Leilani never forgave him for that accurate observation.

Then, Will seemed happier. She suspected he was falling in love. The early, unconsummated stages, she'd guessed. Snooping had been on her 'to do' list before the accident. Maybe a clue in drawers or pockets, something subtle: ticket stubs for the children's theatre or zoo, play dates with the same child (and mother) over and again. Who? She'd begun looking at neighborhood women suspiciously. Certainly, Carmen was the most attractive, yet in love with her own husband. She possessed principles, as well—or so Leilani thought until the SUV.

Leilani scouted the peripheries of their social circle. While insulted, naturally, relief was her overriding emotion—wild, hopeful relief that an easy ending was in sight. She would even get to be the one slighted! She would rack up the social sympathy points.

Her primary concern was Holly. Leilani had vaguely mapped out a joint custody discussion the morning of the accident, construing the ideal schedule. As the mother, she'd rightfully claim more time with Holly than Will. Even so, she would have hours to herself again—uninterrupted weekends, leisurely evenings, days to work late if she chose, the freedom to sit and read the Sunday paper without someone asking for a cookie or swiping the Arts. Time! Solitude! The dream lit up her body and pressed another inch between her and marriage. She half-listened to the department chair outline budget cuts and staff changes. For the first time, she thought, perhaps, that the 'what happened' conversation was ready to morph into something more definitive, a question with an answer. Distracted by a direct question from a colleague, she answered, got a second cup of coffee, and debated a pastry. Then Mary Beth opened the conference room door and gingerly pulled Leilani into the hallway.

Nobody wanted to tell her that Holly had died. The hospital chaplain who met her in the emergency room broke the news about Will first. Leilani spontaneously, unthinkingly, gave into the relief: problem solved, decision made! Every day since, that moment taunts her, proves her inhumanity. In the later days of their marriage, Will claimed that she didn't have a nurturing personality: too self-absorbed, he protested. More similar to Anna and your mother than you think, he'd observed. Dying, he proved his point. Will is a brick wall that she hits every hour with remorse and anger. Holly is the raw wound.

Stillness startles Leilani into more complete attention to the world outside of her mind. The car now sits in Carver's faculty lot. As usual, of course, she has the misfortune to survive her sprint on the freeway.

At the office, she swirls in the sticky vinyl chair and picks up the telephone. Leilani interrupts the operator's voice with a weak, dry cough—practicing tuberculosis. Feigning phlegm will be a problem. Finding the appropriate notch in the Dutch bureaucracy takes forever. Aiming for Amsterdam, nadir of European heroin addiction, turns out to be her sole time saving decision. Otherwise, she weaves through desk after desk, official after official, her story polished with each retelling. Finally, she finds the equivalent of the county courthouse, the person holed up in Holland with the records.

"Death certificates," shouts Leilani into the phone, connection unstable. "Can you check a name?"

The crackling male voice on the other end is happy to help the anxious Ms. Crea. "What a trial, finding you have a brother and not to know where he is! I am happy to help, happy." The man making promises introduces himself as a Mr. Van Eyck.

He warns that addicts generally die without names. Their friends—the ones who wrap a vein, share a needle, and then steal the stash—often don't get surnames, either. There's a strong intimacy that supersedes such details, he lectures, a trait of the heroin community. Administrator Van Eyck requires different details: color of Victor's hair, scars or surgeries, exact age, and dental work done? Perhaps he can piece together Victor's defining qualities and match them to paperwork that follows each corpse? Does Ms. Crea have a more specific time line? Ten years is a lot of ground to cover, Mr. Van Eyck reminds her.

By the time she hangs up, Leilani is satisfied that her afternoon talking overseas has cost the English department a pretty penny. Since when did heroin addicts qualify as a community, she wonders? Leilani walks down the nearly deserted hallway with purpose. She must collect her mail! A termination notice could come any day, she thinks, delighted. Maybe she's been accused of plagiarism or conducting herself in a manner unworthy of her profession. One would actually have to engage with the profession to reap those benefits, however. Again, too much effort.

Friday afternoon: the office is already vacated and locked for the weekend. She enters and grimaces into the usual mail—newsletters and calls for papers, announcements of colleagues chalking up honors. More successful people to kill. She'll have to probe Rocco for details on Victor, the kind to which a sister has access. What color was his hair, she wonders. Did he break an arm as a boy or chip a tooth? She smiles, fond of him already.

Leilani knocks over something leaning against the student worker's desk. She stoops to pick up the fallen object: bulky, flat and square. Excited, Leilani examines her prize—a large portfolio, the kind of case art students use to transport paintings from class to home and back. She slips out the rather bad sketches inside—three uninspired pencil drawings—and places them against the desk. Habit of guilt, rather than genuine sentiment, forces her to check ceiling corners for surveillance cameras she knows aren't actually there. Nobody will accuse a professor of theft. Some student will be targeted. Perhaps she should leave a clue? In the end, she shrugs off responsibility to chance, which will win, regardless.

As usual, traffic parts and scrambles to accommodate Leilani's dangerous barrel down the freeway. The portfolio sits next to her. She hopes the case is large enough. She checks the clock. If the defensive driving around her continues, she may actually make that family dinner. For the first time in months, the thought of tomorrow makes her smile, slightly: what time to arrive at the college, how to be utterly inconspicuous, what to do if the gallery is crowded? Most importantly: should she take Three Dead Chinese Soldiers or a Kerr Eby?

7
DELPHI

After waking in a full sweat at 4:00 a.m., I hear Dad prepare for morning zazen. Not for the first time, I'm grateful to have a parent with bizarre office hours. He's gone before five. How those students haul themselves to Moon for morning meditation is beyond me. I write Dad a lame note about an appointment and hustle out. Two letters taped to the fridge in a 24-hour period: I never flat out lie to Daddy; I avoid the truth. However, the fact that I'm out of the loft by 7:00 will probably raise his alarm bells anyway.

I skip classes in favor of a sterile suburban coffee shop where nobody knows me, lost in a favorite escape: Redbook, People, InStyle, Good Housekeeping, Vogue, Glamour and Soap Opera Digest. I cram in as much as I can, never skipping an article or line. My head's full of vital info. Cheese Whiz works on stains, nail polish stays fresh in the fridge, heart disease kills women, and the cords on mini-blinds can strangle a toddler. By the time I'm slated to start work, I'm as dopey as I desired. What day of the week is it, anyway? Gotta love those magazines.

Work is the best place in the world when I'm in a funk,

especially since Yang's show started. Despite high ceilings and generous square footage, the Suzanne Struass Gallery is welcoming. The imperious space is offset by buttery brown walls, rich red rugs, and welcoming corner clusters of comfortable furniture. According to Suzanne, coziness equates sound business in Minnesota. When she first opened thirty years ago, her colleagues shook their heads condescendingly: everyone knew art demanded no distractions, white walls and a minimalist décor.

Suzanne put down her own stubborn foot: people want warmth in this climate, she claimed, not another cold wall. She began the gallery when the wreckage of her second marriage left her with cash and resolve: time for her dreams. That's the way Suzanne tells the story, although I heard a different version from ex number three, the final spouse and the only one to cope with Suzanne's eccentricities for more than two years. Not many people are gifted sculptors and entrepreneurs; that kind of drive tends to scare people away.

Nearly seventy, Suzanne is now a regional force in the art world. Her gallery competes financially with those in Chicago, and the draw isn't the campy over-stuffed armchairs, bottomless pots of Earl Gray and bowls of plain Nabisco vanilla wafers—although what other gallery allows patrons to read the Sunday paper as if they're in a coffee shop? I spend half my time here restocking cookies and tending to tea. However homey Suzanne did manage to make the place, atmosphere isn't the ultimate attraction. People come for the art.

Even after six weeks of Yang Lee's show, the work still gives me goose bumps—and I see these paintings three times a week. I'm no expert, but even the desk help is required to read the reviews. Word is that Yang took a page from styles that emerged during the Harlem Renaissance and broke open the world of traditional Hmong art. The critic from the StarTribune called the show "more than breathtaking art: social commentary that pairs protest with hope." Suzanne and Yang giggled over the column's language; they popped champagne when the critic from the Times called and the East Coast dealers booked flights. As far as I'm concerned, Suzanne and Yang are both geniuses, which is why they're so buddy-buddy. Hard to find a peer when you're the best. Nobody writes reviews about Suzanne's work anymore; they talk about her life in Sunday feature articles instead. She doesn't do shows. Her sculptures sell, privately, for tens of thousands of dollars apiece.

For a few gorgeous minutes before the gallery opens, Yang's vision is mine alone. I find strength in these paintings, so beautiful they hurt—the high contrast of pale hues against black backgrounds, thick-lined drawings, and dark jeweled sheets of color mined by slender pinks and whites. Yang has placed a child in every frame. Their round, perfect faces are half the exhibit's appeal—children where they shouldn't be (as they often are), reflecting the agonies and joys of the world. Even the critics stand, agape, in front of Yang's children.

The gallery hasn't been empty since the show opened. Yes, I'm thrilled for Yang and Suzanne—mostly Yang since Suzanne's loaded and he's barely older than me—although today I'd prefer the old pace. The minute those doors open, the tourists will start to ooh and ah, or worse, roll out their high school level art history for my benefit. I'm too tired to feign animation for the next five hours.

Of course, that's exactly what happens: within an hour of

turning the bolt, I'm melting the masses with my haughty art smile (I swear, half the crowd comes only for attitude) and fielding gossip from the regulars. The writers and artists who live upstairs stop by regularly. Having lived among this crowd most of my life, I know who's wasting time and who is taking a quick break.

When the door opens very slowly, I cringe—this would be someone carrying coffee, probably two cups and probably Edgar. He works like a maniac for four fourteen-hour days (and actually makes a decent living in fine iron art) and starts his weekend respite around noon on Friday. Although he's harmless, four days locked up with hot metal and a torch makes him a little too eager for female companionship. Guess who's the captive target.

I brace myself—except the person bearing beverages is my father. In fact, he has an entire tray. At the sight of him, the atmosphere in the front of the gallery immediately disintegrates into nervous tics, spontaneous fidgeting, and a few impulsive bows. Dad has that effect on people. The appearance of a six foot four, 220-plus pound man with flowing gray robes, bare feet, and a shining bald scalp generally commands attention. Seas part for him.

"Coming through," he sings out, balancing the steaming mugs. He nods and bobs his way through the patrons, who either pretend not to give him special notice or who stare awkwardly. He sets the tray on the aged maple counter and pulls up the spare stool.

"Surprise!" He gestures: strong coffee, cinnamon mochi, and sesame honey bars. Dad hates making the bars; the process is unpredictable and time-consuming. They're my favorite.

"What's the matter?" I ask suspiciously. Dad generally just opens the gallery door and yells hi.

He pauses, pulling apart a piece of mochi—sweet baked rice. "What a coincidence. I was going to ask you the same question."

"Oh," I falter and scan the crowd. Doesn't somebody require a price rundown or my pithy Yang Lee lecture? I sip coffee, the last thing my bladder wants. Where is Edgar when you actually need him?

"Can't remember the last time you left the house before sunrise." He smiles. "You've hardly been home for two days, which wouldn't be unusual if you were with Wendy. She left two messages yesterday and one this morning. Urgent. A matter of the heart. Elizabeth called—Natalie, too. Your fans await."

"Thanks Dad. I'll call. I wouldn't worry about Wendy—another break-up with Jennifer, I'd guess," I shrug, oozing nonchalance. I read those messages this morning and set them aside. Guilt catches up with me: I promise myself an afternoon of phone calls.

"That would be three splits for the happy couple this year, right?" He plays along.

"At least."

We nibble silently. Finally, relief—a frumpy polyester-clad woman asks how much Frogtown Sunday costs. As if she had the taste! Normally, I'd eek out a disgruntled answer. Today, I engage her in satisfying conversation: not only do I avoid Dad for six minutes, I confirm my assessment of both her income and aesthetic sensibilities. The frame alone probably outstrips her mortgage, from the look on her face when I explain the pricing. She hobbles off, forty pounds overweight. Can't we institute some law against these people?

Dad stares at me.

"What?"

"That was mean," he says, surprised. "Is that your public demeanor?"

Ashamed, I want to hide under the counter. "Not really," I say, quietly.

"I certainly hope not." Disappointed, he studies his coffee cup, thinking.

"I'm tired," I protest. "And stressed, graduation and all."

"Strange way to handle stress. If I remember correctly, you had classes this morning. Did you go?"

Why do I crumple around him? Aren't I an adult, after all? "No," I say firmly. "I can skip a class here and there, you know."

He nods, "Sure. I'm not worried about your attendance record. I can tell something's bothering you. Wish you'd let me help."

"Nothing is wrong! Honestly. The pressure gets to me, planning for the future. You know, the big job hunt ahead? Beginning the next phase of life?" This is all totally true, just not perfectly representative of specific events and issues.

"Sure sounds logical," he says gently, "and I have to respect what you tell me. However, if something else should come up—another source of stress, say—I'd be open to figuring out solutions with you."

Neither of us says a word.

Finally! Here's Edgar when you need him! He sweeps through the door, carrying the predictable coffee from Spar. "Roshi!"

He and Dad shake hands. Only Edgar calls Dad Roshi, a Japanese term for teacher or master. Everyone else—except Grandma, who says she christened a Jeff and that's who she'll bury—calls him by his Zen name, Kokyoku.

Edgar is one of the few non-Buddhists completely comfortable around my father. On the surface, the two are pretty different— my father a hulking well-scrubbed teddy, and Edgar a hulking oily ogre. What they share is a zeal for politics. Set the two down in a stable environment and they will comb through each international conflict, nation by nation. Even better, they have the same radical bent. They spend happy hours reinforcing each other's righteousness, dismantling the current state of capitalism (they disagree on the fundamental morality of the system, Dad a firm no and Edgar a tentative believer), and working themselves into a mutual frenzy over the worldwide trampling of human rights.

Edgar slaps the counter. "Can I steal him, Delphi?"

Daddy shakes his head. "I only have half an hour. Never-ending computer woes—my assistant and I are meeting to crunch numbers. We need to upgrade into the realm of reliability."

"Impossible," shouts Edgar. A couple of people stare. This is not your typical art gallery. "Those damn computers will be our ruin. We're deforming our bones, all the typing instead of talking! You know that novelist in 308, Amad? Lost an entire year's work to a computer crash. Media's finally exposing the bloody truth— even the local TV rats ran the story about computer games triggering seizures. Misfired brain cells! That's the least of our worries! I hate the damn things."

Dad and I smile at each other. Let loose after a week of work, Edgar is a force of nature. The topic doesn't matter—it's intensity he seeks. He's not the easiest person to tame into gallery decorum.

In ways large and small, Dad never fails to come to my rescue. "Let's not waste that half hour, then," he says. "I bet there's a table at Spar."

Edgar makes a not-so-acceptable but complimentary (in his view) gesture behind the back of a woman standing a few feet from him. Dad feigns a shocked face and hustles him out, leaving me with the sesame bars and a smile.

"Dinner tonight or continuing psychological space?" he asks from the doorway.

Answering on the spot this way kills me: forced to confirm his suspicions or commit to a dinner devoted to probing.

"Space," I say, weakly. Where's my wit? My resolve? I wish I were faster on my feet in front of him, all witty responses and quick comebacks.

He looks at me knowingly and leaves. Why can't the one parent I get be normal?

The afternoon creeps by. After Dad's dour face, I can't get into the appropriate gallery mood. I fret about skipping physics (Ian will kill me and I'll never pass the damn class) and debate the wisdom of spilling my guts to Mom. Am I grabbing the first pipe dream somebody tosses my way? I'll be a sucker for scams my whole life, mail-ordering genealogies that link me to some fake royal line or believing (like a few people I live among) that I'm the next great artiste or singer or diamond in the rough, waiting to be discovered. Even the belief that you possess extraordinary powers qualifies as mental disturbance in and of itself. Wouldn't calling myself psychic qualify as magical thinking or delusions of grandiosity?

I take Mom's letter out of my purse and rip the paper into tiny shreds.

Ian will have more objectivity on the topic of me than I do. If the light of a new day confirms our gullibility for him, I'll agree we were duped. Eager to hear his assessment, I bolt the instant Amanda replaces me as mannequin on duty. Wendy and crew will have to wait. Haven't I held Wendy's hand over this particular relationship all year? She'll be fine. In fact, she could do better. Time my friend faces that harsh reality.

I rationalize my way right to Crocus Hill, where reality slaps me in the face well before winding its way to Wendy. Ian's street is a stunning spread of enormous oaks and historic homes. Most of the rambling houses are spindly, towered Victorians, others are majestic stone or brick with a couple of sun-washed stuccos tossed in. Nothing begs for a paint job. The front yards are spacious banks of chemical green; a maverick or two favor elaborate gardens instead, complete with fishponds, fountains, and tiny streams. There are barely any cars on the street. Must be parked in the triple stall garages along the alley—right next to the carriage house that appears standard issue. Always noisy, the Buick's rattle strikes a particularly gruesome chord.

When I spot Ian's address, I'm very, very glad that I didn't exchange my gallery clothes for the tattered jeans crumpled in my closet. Even on a regal block, the house stands out: double corner lot, towering trees, and an unusual, tangled garden that starts along the side of the house and winds to the back. The house itself is a stone masterpiece that appears to have three inhabitable floors. Dense vines travel across walls to the wooden awning that bridges garage and house. I can imagine owners of another era alighting from carriages and then cars, confident that not one raindrop would touch their ruffled silk. Ian doesn't have to worry about mud on his Doc Martens, either. Even though I sternly berate myself for caring, I preen and rearrange in the rearview mirror. This is the same old Ian I was prepared to run from or dump one day ago, I remind myself.

The doorbell is neither gong nor elaborate song as expected, simply a single chord. Please don't let a maid greet me.

A dark-haired boy with no front teeth opens the door and—in a glass-shattering display of six-year old lung power—screams in my face: SOMEBODY'S HEEEEEERE!

"Hi," I whisper, making a totally useless point.

He flashes a smile and peels away, choosing to deliver his message Paul Revere style. I stand in the open doorway. Invitation to enter or is the kid warning the clan of an intruder? Maybe I should've wished for a maid.

Ian appears. The boy, and another exactly like him, flop, puppy-style, around Ian's legs. "Hey! How'd you survive your first night as the anointed one? Exciting, huh?"

The cue: he believes. My knees give a little, relieved.

"Barely survived the night. These the twins?" I state the obvious. Noise radiates from the jumpy boys.

Ian presents each. "Eli. Noah."

After adorable grins, they lurch away, screeching. Ian was right. In a glance you can tell they're great: cute and crazed at the same time.

"Welcome," intones Ian grandly, sweeping an arm, " to the humble home."

"You didn't tell me you lived in a museum."

The foyer is twice as large as our living room. A wide staircase circles up on one side, and several large rooms spawn off an upcoming hallway. Looks like a kitchen straight ahead at the hallway's end.

"Took me a full year to get used to this," he says. "Bill's loaded. He's a partner in a public relations firm his father founded. You've heard the name—Minehart and Meltzer. They did those gubernatorial ads with the dachshund and the Volkswagen. Remember? Anyway, Bill bought this house for the tribe, as he puts it, when he and Mom got married four years ago."

"The driving dachshund? Who could forget that ugly snout." I'm impressed. Those ads made the evening news. The firm remains the subject of media focus. "Four years," I whisper. "Aren't the twins six? That marriage went by the wayside pretty quickly."

Ian checks the wings before talking. "Complicated, remember? Bill and Mom had a thing for years, an under-the-table attraction that surfaced when the twins were babies. Really, really bad timing. Believe me, the whole mess sucked for a long time— not too much on our side, because my parents were already divorced. But Bill's ex can turn a birthday party into a blood bath. We're way better now, although we still have our moments. Maybe I can spend holidays with you," he jokes.

I feel sorry for the nameless ex-wife: saddled with twins (and probably ten new pounds around the hips) only to find out that hubbie's jumped ship for trimmer, less sleep-deprived shores. Now she's the evil ex, harping? On feminist principles alone, I don't plan on liking this Bill guy much.

"Sorry," I say lightly, "we fall short in the holiday department. We do Thanksgiving in a big way. Otherwise, Dad and I exchange Valentine's Day cards and pass out treats on Halloween. Unless you count Buddhist events, none of which include presents to children, alas."

"Okay, other way around. You come here. We celebrate everything—Rosh Hashanah, Christmas, Easter, Hanukkah and everything in between. Bill and the boys are Jewish. Mom's raising her kids Catholic. Nobody's jumped camp yet and there are plenty of presents."

"You're right—complicated," I say, momentarily happy with my singleton status. "Do I get a tour?"

I do. The palace is incredible, as expected, with huge rooms and plentiful windows. Whoever did the decorating (Ian's mom, Meredith, I learn) has the understated expensive scene down. Plus, she can surprise you: a couple of rooms feature beaten-up furniture and funky colors, a nod to her former low-brow life seamlessly worked in. Even with five kids, there are enough bedrooms to go around and two to spare. Meredith and Bill both have offices—to be distinguished, of course, from the library downstairs. All three floors are in full use. Plants and flowers grow everywhere—in hallways, curling along window seats and sills, in the bathrooms. If I'm lucky enough to own a home someday, I'd enjoy hearty green growing all around me.

We conclude with a kitchen that spans the back of the house. Meredith's office is tucked to one side. The wide eating area opens to a covered deck and backyard on the other. The rooms are structured solarium style: walls are actually tall windows that open to the outdoor gardens. I take in the plants and gleaming wood and orange paint and colorful cookware and give in to about forty seconds of unbridled jealousy. Tough life, Ian.

At least he has the good grace to acknowledge the obvious. "Amazing, huh?" he understates. "Mom redid the kitchen last summer. Speaking of which, here she is. Brace yourself," he hisses, theatrically.

Ian's mother bursts in, trailed by a pack of early teens. The room is sudden chaos. Hard to tell what's really happening because of the junior high din. Meredith appears to be simultaneously unloading groceries on Ian, calling out the back door for the dog, commanding kids, and finally engaging in some conversation that probably includes me. She yells 'Nice to meet you' above the fray.

Everyone under twenty disappears with snacks and instructions. The noise level drops dramatically. Meredith unpacks a bag while grilling Ian about his foray with the twins to their piano lessons and progress on a newsletter's database. She slams the refrigerator door shut and snaps open a ginger soda. "Want one?" she gestures to each of us. "Did the contractor call with a date for the garage?"

"Sorry."

"Contractors are as tough to book as the Pope. You'd think repairing a lousy garage wouldn't be such an ordeal. Hope we don't have to rip out that oak tree in the process." She rifles through a stack of envelopes on the counter. "Schools: money or conference time. Please, don't tell me March is over?" She grimaces, tosses the letters aside, and leans across the wide counter to me. "Delphi! I'd be honored to be your first client!"

Meredith is standard Minnesotan fare—Norwegian blonde, blue eyes, average height and build. She's pretty, although not enough to bowl you over. There's something slightly slanted about her nose. Her eyes might be too narrow. I see some of Ian in the longish face. Height, he must've gotten from his father. She moves with more energy than any task actually requires. The soda is thumped solidly onto the counter, grocery bags fly instead of float into the cupboard, and conversation is beamed like a force field. From the look of those triceps, she's the jock type.

Despite my standing distaste for upscale motherhood (if I hear the phrase 'soccer mom' one more time, I'll scream), I like her instantly.

Ian taps my arm, "Oh, by the way – I told her the whole story last night."

Nobody requested food. Meredith slams apples slices and chocolate cookies on the counter. She hands us each the ginger soda we passed on a minute ago. "I take all blame. I routinely coerce my children into confessing recent activities and secrets. Otherwise, I'd never know what kind of people they were becoming, would I?"

Ian scrambles to his own defense. "She thinks she tricks us. I spilled my guts because Mom can help. She dabbles. She already has ideas."

"You believe in this stuff, then?" I ask, incredulously.

"Absolutely," she says adamantly. "Throughout the history of the world there have been mystics, seers, magicians, witches— people with special skills. Why should today be any different? The problem is sifting through the hacks. In my experience, very few people claiming to be psychic are actually more gifted than anybody else."

"Your experience?"

She sighs self-deprecatingly. "I did go through a phase."

"A huge, embarrassing phase," chortles Ian. He's the reason there's food. Half the cookies are gone. We should market that metabolism.

Meredith laughs. "Okay, I was a nut. For a while, I scheduled weekly Tarot and palm readings. Tried every new psychic in town, hit the astrology page in the papers. My first marriage was crumbling and the kids were barely in school; I was desperate to make some sense of the situation."

"Did you?" I wonder. "Through the psychics, I mean?"

"Oh, I got answers, all right." Her face loses some focus, softening back to that time. "Not the ones I wanted. I kept trying new methods of divination, hoping to hear something different. Never did," she finishes brightly.

I'm unexpectedly sad. She was the one hurt most in that first marriage! My clarity gives me a surge of adrenaline and an idea. What better place to play out Evelyn's claim than in front of a friendly   audience?

"You were ready to give things a second chance, and a third," I venture. "He wasn't."

She looks at me sharply. "That's right."

"I'm glad he left," I say impulsively. "You would've hung in there forever, even though nobody was happy. That would've been horrible, for everyone, especially the--,"

Children. I was going to say children. That's the required comment: such and such is hard on the children. We're doing this and that for the children's sake, ad nauseum. A picture of Ian's brother flashes through my mind, insistent. I don't know his name. Did I see him in the earlier passel? He's moodier by temperament than the rest of the family. Lack of love between his parents hurt him. The other two could've survived that marriage, unscathed. The father's not a bad guy, only a loner, not made for family life.

I try not to appear overeager. "Your son, not Ian. He's sort of delicate. He's much happier this way—you did the right thing," I add quickly.

"And my former husband? How's he these days?"

"Orderly! He has his schedule and don't interrupt it, either," is what comes out of my mouth without thinking.

Ian howls. "You have no idea! No idea how right you are. Man, you gotta burn your toast according to his itinerary."

"Well," comments Meredith, wryly. "You may be allotting him too much flexibility. One is simply not allowed to burn the toast."

They both laugh, although not unkindly.

Meredith smiles at me. "You're batting a thousand, my dear."

"I can't believe this." I sink into a tall stool and a swift tailspin. "The whole scene is too freaky. I say what pops into my head and I'm psychic? Seems too easy."

I haven't worked up a psychological sweat or exerted significant energy. Thoughts, impressions, and feelings pop into my head with less effort than counting out exact change requires. The only time my brain strains is when the kid appears.

Ian and I both look to his mother.

"Beginner's luck. Happens all the time and I don't think the area of expertise matters. I'm guessing, the stakes haven't been all that high yet? Nobody's put you on the spot, insisted accuracy that matters."

Ian counters. "You tell me that talent comes naturally. Feels good, follow the dream and all. If Delphi's seer gig is effortless, isn't that a sign she's found her calling?"

The way they look at each other, I get the feeling that this conversation is about more than me.

"Let me clarify. Delphi may be in the honeymoon phase of a new endeavor. Later stages bring over-analysis, self-doubt, or fear that the gift goes away or isn't sufficient. Sound familiar?"

"Nope," he says, stubbornly.

"Well, I've had such experiences. You must be luckier than I am."

"What experiences?" I ask encouragingly.

Ian is equally eager to redirect the conversation. "Do we mention the line of baby clothes first or the pottery?"

Meredith takes her cue and eases into a less toxic topic. She fakes a small scream and covers her head. "I'm a failure!"

He explains, "We go through careers the way other families eat ice cream. One year, she's creating a line of pricey hand-sewn baby clothes—because yes, Meredith threads a mean needle! Next year, she designs greeting cards. The year after, we peddle pottery or quilts. We're currently into the intangible world of consulting: life coach or interior design?" He curls his finger and looks at the ceiling. "Only the spirits know what's next."

Meredith enjoys the conversation, even at her own expense. "You forgot the part where I'm racked with guilt and self-doubt, and the enterprise fails." She shakes her finger, scolding. "The failure of each business is the moral: I quit when the going gets too tough or things fly along too well. Either way, I have a pivotal existential moment in which my true place in the universe is revealed to me: in some kitchen." She throws up her hands, helpless.

Ian rolls his eyes. "The kitchen where three replacement businesses are brewing. Don't listen to her, Delphi. She has a zillion things going on and fifty people pounding at the door. Ask her who the Red Cross calls to coordinate volunteers. Who organizes neighborhood-wide garage sales and fund raisers for entire school districts?"

"That's different," declares Meredith. "I'm talking about my creative dreams. That's where I stumble and where I think, hope, my real talents are."

"Don't you dare include cooking in your list of gifts," booms a voice from the doorway. A good-looking man—another athlete in the family, although this one has considerable gray—strides in the room, tosses a briefcase on the counter and aims a kiss on Meredith's cheek.

Are these people related to the Adams family or the Cleavers? Maybe I watch too much Nickelodeon, either way: Ian's family is too good to be true or else the pathology's buried, deep. A visit to Wendy's—or any other friend's, for that matter—is never so chummy. Where's the dysfunction? The fight?

Right on cue, screams of rage erupt from somewhere in the far wings, where the wild things play.

"I've got it," Meredith pops up in a sprint.

Ian does the introductions. "This is my stepfather, Bill. This is Delphi."

Bill throws out a hand to shake. We Buddhists place our hands together and bow. Outside of school, my childhood was spent at a Zen Center. Even as a preschooler, I was bowing the way other people say hello. Hundreds of times a week: you bow before the hug or the story or by the bathroom door. The handshake ritual was thrust upon me. I'm still adjusting. My grip is tentative and the process feels slightly foreign. I see the same hesitation and subtle stiffness in the bows of even long-time Zen practitioners.

Bill appraises me. He doesn't strike me as a subtle sort of guy. "I feel as if I know you already. Ian sang your praises last night, Delphi. What an unusual name," he observes. "Lovely name. What's your last one?"

Are you Jewish, is what he means. I've been on the receiving end of this line of questioning before: you can look Jewish, yet appearances can deceive and assumptions can be dangerous.

"My father's last name is Sandquist. My mother's name is Weisman. Lisa Weisman."

Hard to get guarantees on anything these days but the name is usually good enough for most people. He's no exception. He nods and places me in his world order.

"Which do you use?" he says, nicely.

"Sandquist. Weisman is my middle name." Two twenty-year old graduate students turned mystics wandering through Nepal did not rush to the American embassy to fill out paperwork when their baby was born. I didn't get a birth certificate until I was two. Since no legalities were mapped out while my parents were still a couple, Dad gave me both last names, allotting his own higher preference.

I'm half right about Bill. The man doesn't have a single subtle brain cell. Despite my resolve, I like him as much as I do Ian's mother. Casual conversation with Bill morphs into a meander through life's greater questions. We tour religion, family, and one's earning potential as a psychic. Grim, is his assessment. He'd urge me toward PR or law. Jew or Buddhist or both? Direct and gracious: he lets me change the topic without a good answer. Ian gets his fair share of attention. The topic of his post-college plans is not new to this kitchen table. He has a totally noncommittal, and nearly disinterested, stance. Catch up on sleep and fossilize beetles, he jokes. Meredith and Bill exchange glances.

Children come and go; the phone rings; I'm introduced to elusive younger brother and sister, Joshua and Kate. Meredith slices vegetables, which I gather is where her culinary talents end. Bill is the chef. I expected a speedy hello and skulking off to Ian's room. Here the whole family shuffles through or sits, engaged in debate that includes me, and my future. I love every minute.

Without too much prodding, I stay for dinner. Eight people make for a full table. The lights are set low and candles along the buffet soften the cherry red walls. Meredith stands, long matches in hand, above the row of hand-dipped candles that run down the center of the table.

"She's going to bless the lights," says Ian, stage whisper style.

I already know. I've read about Shabbat in handbooks on Jewish family life. I've seen the hostilities in Wendy's family lift for a few short moments of prayer on Friday nights. This is different: reverence and love is here. You see the difference on the faces of the twins, engaged in ritual. They sing Shalom Aleichem, invoking the presence of angels. You see the difference in the older children, content to be with family for dinner. The difference is Bill and Meredith, who take their turns in prayer before handing themselves, wholly, over to their children. Light, wine, and bread are blessed. Everyone is.

I hate to see the meal end. Dessert draws the experience out: chocolate raspberry torte Bill bought on his way home. The twins opt for vanilla ice cream instead. After that, the end is inarguably in sight. Joshua is headed to the movies. At fifteen, he still requires transport, which Bill offers—as well as a grocery run with the twins. Kate is expecting a friend for an overnight. The end of the day proves as chaotic as the beginning. Everyone must say good-bye to the guest. Meredith directs traffic: jackets for the boys; a whispered consult with Joshua; admonishments to Kate about the condition of her room.

Doors close all around us. Meredith smiles at Ian and me, the three of us alone in the enormous, cluttered dining room.

"Let's clean up this mess," she whispers, smiling mysteriously. "And find that little girl's mother."

I'd almost forgotten.

8
LEILANI

Before Leilani can enter, Anna steps out of their parents' house and shuts the front door, five-month old Luke a hard bundle of strapped metal and canvas on her chest. He has eggshell blue socks on his tiny feet. One rounding fist is wedged solidly in his mouth; the other claws and curls in the air, reaching.

Leilani recoils. "What?" she hisses, flattening against the house to get away from the baby, annoyed at being blindsided.

"Listen," commands Anna. "Shay came across the country to see you. Mom slaved over pies and a pot roast all day." She aims a finger at her sister's face. "For once—just once—act normal."

"Weren't you ordering me to be more eccentric yesterday? Why the sudden shift in radar?"

Luke smiles. He draws hand from mouth. A long line of drool folds over his fingers and falls to the ground. He was a Thanksgiving baby, born a few hours before the official festivities began. Holly had been dead thirty-nine days, gone a mere sixteen days into her fourth year.

Today is April 27th, a crisp spring Friday evening before mosquito season and humidity arrive. The air is still thin, although a wet breeze hints of warmer weather ahead; the few clouds are pure puffs of white against blue, a wallpaper print for a baby's bedroom. Holly has been dead 195 days. In two days, Holly would've been four years and seven months old, exactly—or, Leilani has calculated, she would've been four years and 207 days old. The magic number of days allotted to Holly on this earth is 1476. Leilani tallies her daughter's life and death in months, too, and when truly ambitious, in hours—Holly got 35,428. Leilani figures she can go on, indefinitely, keeping track of the days and hours that now separate them.

Anna follows Leilani's mournful gaze. She redirects her finger for Luke to grab, and exhales slowly. Her yoga teacher's placid intonation fills her head: cleansing breath, calm heart, cleansing breath, calm heart. Since the day Holly died—no, make that the minute—she has felt herself the penultimate reminder of pain. Eight months pregnant, she symbolized what Leilani lost. At the funerals, she used a coat to cover her belly; she and Martin barely mentioned the baby after his birth, the entire family forgoing the fuss that accompanies a new arrival.

Around her sister, Anna feels obscene. She oozes maternity. One peep from a child (any child, not only hers), a kitten's whimper on TV, or even a tender thought and milk hardens her breasts. Uncontrollable sprays erupt from her nipples, spoiling blouses and once, interrupting a meeting with a client. Curbing the flux requires steeling herself from sympathy, willing the body to neutrality she does not feel. She feels tired, an easy target. Eyes and brain burn from lack of sleep; her limbs are leaden by early evening.

Since Luke's birth, she's had neither free arm nor moment.

She holds or nurses (endless, even succumbing to daytime TV during maternity leave) or changes the baby—until Ben demands to be picked up, held, carried, read to and otherwise coddled, regardless of whatever task to which she's already attending. She embodies everyone's desire. She alone possesses the power to fulfill the needs of each person in her family (including Martin's), except her own. Some women thrive in this role; Anna has put on a stranger's skin. She carries a secret image of other, better mothers. These women stand in the midst of need with open hands. Better women bend to the clawing men and children, and offer themselves up for the taking. Anna will never be one of these women.

She hates the way Luke and Ben wail for her in unison, while Martin can read the paper two feet away, unnoticed. She hates the hormones—decidedly not postpartum, although that was a wretched era, too. No, new hormones are the source of her current ire, extending beyond the telltale acne to slick home medical tests and the subtle change in the quality of exhaustion. She has been betrayed by her body's resilience, its ability to reproduce without pause. Considering the scarcity of sex in her marriage, Anna is fairly certain of the day she conceived. She hasn't decided whether to tell Martin or take matters into her own hands. Maybe she'll have a miscarriage and be off the hook.

And here stands Leilani, archetype of despair. Rage and pity distort even Anna's simplest interactions with her sister. She longs for the return of her former self, the tighter life and psyche. Between Holly's death and Luke's birth, the past months had already reduced her to a fog of shock and fatigue. She's supposed to supply the lifeblood for yet another human being? She cannot shoulder more weight, not a single ounce.

"Leilani," she says with exaggerated patience. "All I'm asking is that you politely complete dinner. Don't disappear halfway through or pretend you've forgotten how to speak. Okay?"

Leilani mimics her tone. "Am I allowed to enter yet?"

Anna swings the door open. Leilani breezes past without another word.

In the family room (formerly neon blue, now a more discreet shade, thanks to the 24-hour period in which George made his point with Ray-Bans), Martin leans against a bookshelf, drink in hand, professorial. He lectures to Margaret and George, rigidly listening from a shared couch. Only Seamus and Bennie are relaxed. The toddler dissects an old Matchbox truck, with Seamus sprawled on the floor beside him.

"I have yet to see evidence of a truly vibrant culture in this state," Martin bellows. "There's no nightlife, no creative tension. Minnesota Nice? You mean Minnesota ice—takes a decade to chip into a social circle here. Ice! A total lack of vibrant community."

Seamus looks vaguely troubled. "Define vibrant," he insists. "I can't follow your argument."

Martin pauses to sort through his choices. "Vibrant: dynamic, alive, compelling. Vibrating! You know—vibrating energy. That's what I'm missing."

"Key word—missing. Perhaps you're simply overlooking a quality that does indeed exist," speculates Seamus, propping himself higher on an elbow.

"I don't think so," laughs Martin.

"Impossible?"

"I've lived here five years. I've been to a thousand barbecues and potlucks. I've sat my patient ass in dozens of bars listening to what's supposedly the best music in the city and made a point of taking my coffee in every quaint, friendly setting. Without exception, there's a monotone quality to every social interaction I've ever had—we're living among a million flat lines."

Seamus is insistent. "Monotone. Again, another confusing term. Even if we share a vague sense of how you're using the word, could you be participating in the creation of this monotone quality?"

Martin is thoroughly enjoying himself. "My creation? You're implying that the defining characteristics of an entire state that the rest of the nation mocks—you do remember Fargo, not to mention the whole Garrison Keillor Lake Woebegone thing—are a creation of my imagination?"

"Or perspective," offers Leilani from the doorway. "You forget. Who solved the murders in Fargo? Underneath the bluster, whose small town heart doesn't Garrison reveal to be simply quivering with sensitivity?"

Anna rolls her eyes, bored. Can't somebody else hold this baby? She tips slightly forward to pull at the front of her shirt; heat radiates from the space between Luke's carrier and her chest. She can script the next twenty minutes: someone challenges, Martin wins. Two years ago, she still enjoyed this particular topic. The previous decade spent in New York and Boston distanced her from her Midwestern sense of self. Laying claim to the East Coast gave her a social and intellectual edge. However, the newly blurred edges of her body and brain have softened the line she drew between her life, and the lives she'd left behind.

Margaret is annoyed at Martin and her own inertia. Years,

she's been sitting politely with her mild protestations. She should rise up and defend her people. Her unwillingness to do so confuses her and makes matters worse. Margaret is acutely aware that her attitude helps prove Martin's point. As for George, he understands that turning on the television would be rude, yet he will soon do so anyway.

Seamus is overjoyed by the possibility of a good fight with Mr. Homophobe himself. Martin makes the right remarks. He'll be the first to jump up and slap Jim on the back when he arrives. Yet he's constantly surveying them, too—keeping a few feet away, discreetly disapproving—and vaguely voyeuristic. Seamus is the only one (aside from Anna, who has heard plenty from Martin in private) to notice Martin's discomfort. Seamus has theories about this edginess that would be extremely unpopular. Then again, he has theories about nearly all straight men, especially those married to his sisters.

"Precisely my point," bellows Martin.

"What point?" asks Leilani.

"Garrison's down-home folk bumble their way to a deeper meaning. Sure, the girl cop gets the bad guys and the dumpy farmer cries at his son's graduation, or whatever. So, 'Art' tells us that even a dullard among dullards is capable of feeling. Emotion is elemental. Dig under the ice and there's a beating heart. Big deal. Ben here has emotions, Luke too. Does that mean they're open-minded? Intellectually alive? Does possessing repressed emotion make someone an engaging conversationalist?"

Now it's Seamus's turn to laugh. "I wouldn't say that belittling your relatives, friends, and their entire state makes you an engaging conversationalist."

"He's right," pipes in Anna, to everyone's surprise. "You're being combative."

Martin raises his eyebrows at her. "Thank you for your support," he says grimly.

She shrugs. "You're misinterpreting me. If you're not combative—I mean if you don't shake things up," and here she glares her way around the entire room, "nothing productive can happen."

Martin appears placated, if a bit off his footing. "True," he affirms.

"Since you opened the can of worms on Martin's demeanor," says Seamus, pleasantly, "I'd ask us to consider what purpose combativeness serves—if we're all on board with Martin and the combativeness thing? We are, aren't we?"

Seamus pauses for objections. Everybody knows that someone should object. Nobody takes the leap.

"Okay!" He continues, upbeat. "Here's a theory on combative behavior. Think vicious cycle: one engages in combat out of an unconscious need for an opponent and therefore, a relationship defined by distance and hostility. Soon, one becomes—as desired—isolated and hostile. Blame for subsequent unhappiness can be laid upon the opponent. One can be disappointed in the shortcomings of others, rather than in one's self. Hypothetically speaking, that is."

"Is this what they mean by queer theory?" asks Martin, all stealth and venom.

Seamus lifts a wrist, weakly. "Owie," he squeals. "You tell me."

"Fuck you, Shay," offers Anna half-heartedly. Seamus cowers behind a pillow.

Margaret stands up. This is her territory, children feuding. They've given her the upper hand, once again. Forty years old, and these three would probably pull hair, she thinks happily.

"Enough," she announces. "I don't know about the rest of you, but my tepid constitution," she looks significantly at Martin, "requires food every four hours. I'm overdue."

Martin groans temporary defeat. "Okay, okay. I would not describe anything about you as tepid," he acquiesces dramatically enough that everyone knows his statement is hyperbole. The women of the Midwest, no matter how flamboyant, have nothing on his New Yorkers.

George seizes his chance to turn on the television. When Anna spins out of the room, Bennie peels after her. Martin squeezes Margaret's arm, a gesture of reconciliation, before following.

Leilani sits next to Seamus. "Too bad," she says, patting his knee. "I know you were looking forward to more."

"Can't fulfill all your dreams in one day, I guess," he jokes. "Does he grate simply on in-law status alone? Are we that cloistered?"

"Everybody loves Jim," she reminds him.

"True," he reflects. "Everybody loved Will."

Except me, speculates Leilani. She turns to Seamus with some benign comment designed to derail that undesirable train of thought. Her brother is lost to her, face soft with memory. Leilani has seen, and had, that look: you are brought back to a moment—a comment, touch, or smile—that defines what you have lost. Seamus is missing Will. The two were closer than most in-laws. They were friends.

Leilani understands.

"Excuse me," chokes Seamus. He leaps up and out a doorway.

Every time somebody alights where she now lives, the land of grief, they are torn to shreds, that quickly. Even Seamus. Yet she's supposed to have the strength to pull herself together and move on? Hypocrisy may be what finally kills her.

George stares at the TV, oblivious to major emotional upheaval. Since nobody screamed or stomped, Leilani assumes he missed the whole interaction, much as he missed the subtleties of their childhoods. He snorts at a newscaster's comments. She wishes he would forget CNN and tune into some nature show. As a child, she remembers watching rhinos spear one another. Giraffes drowned in quicksand and lionesses ripped baby gazelles to shreds. Weren't there pygmies upon occasion, a focus on the bizarre piercing habits of natives? That would hold her attention. She stares at George's forehead, hoping to relay her desire without the effort of speaking: National Geographic. Think public TV, Daddy.

George turns away from the screen. Some celebrity update comes on; he could not care less. He feels his daughter's gaze boring into his skull and can't stop thinking about the hair in his ears. An unpleasant consequence of aging, the way hair has taken off in undesirable places and thinned everywhere else. He rubs his nose, another prime breeding ground. Can't she stare at something else?

"When are you going to sell that house?" he asks evenly.

"I don't know."

He rubs his pant legs, anticipating. "Well, I'd like to rip out that hedge by the garage. If you're going to sell the place, a nice white picket fence would show much better."

Buckthorn. George sees the scourge as his personal calling: a non-native, invasive plant popular in the fifties as a high shrub with pretty berries. He dreams about the root work, a virus underneath the city, crowding out plants and flowers that belong. Soon the whole river bluff will erode and sink downward. He can see the end coming.

Leilani considers. He's been after her about the hedge since before they bought the house. Will had brought George in for advice on their potential purchase. George took one look at the landscaping and said: disaster. They'd followed all of his suggestions except this one, as a courtesy to Rocco. The buckthorn ran along the back of his property, too.

Will had asked him about removal a few times: the shrubbery is non-native, he'd explained.

Well I am too, maintained Rocco. Is that a reason to uproot something that's been alive longer than you have?

They left the plant.

"Sure." Leilani thinks out loud. "Let's get rid of the buckthorn. Old habits."

"All right then," states George. "Out the thing goes." He picks up the remote and starts clicking though options, satisfied. After all this time: a yes. He can almost feel the dirt drying on his knuckles, smell the decay of the vine. Finally, he will be allowed to take action on his daughter's behalf.

Having made one family member happy, Leilani wonders if she should call it a day while things look good. She goes into the kitchen, rubbing the front of her throat vigorously. The thyroid! An internal organ that even the uninitiated can manipulate. She palpates the butterfly-shaped gland above her windpipe and rests against the wall, wondering why she feels repulsed by pies. Margaret peers into the hot oven to inspect her fruit and cream creations. The very thought of pie—of oven mitts decorated with kitties or flowers or spoon collections on greasy kitchen walls— makes Leilani nauseous.

Could Anna be feeling the same way, wonders Leilani? Her sister stares out the window at a backyard whose best days are long over, the frenetic activity and clutter of their younger days replaced by staid square patches of well-tamed shrubs. Bennie is probably out there, thinks Leilani, barreling across grass that nobody else touches anymore.

She smiles, genuinely optimistic about the thyroid. Underrated, this gland affects every cell in the body—every cell! Such potential gives her goose bumps. Maul the thing enough, feed it massive amounts of iodine (another bonus for blood pressure) and she may succeed in becoming hyperthyroid. She is focused on the big guns: thyroid storm! Blood pressure skyrockets, the pulse races, every single hormone—estrogen, progesterone, testosterone—exceeds every known limit. Cells and blood vessels and nerves are pushed beyond their limits. The heart explodes. Death by overload! The book specifically cautioned against touching: excess stimulation can contribute to the onset of woes.

Back from a foray to the bathroom, Seamus is morose. He slices bread, hard. The first potentially healing moment, and what does he do but well up and hide? Off his game, playing into Martin's hands. He wishes Jim had been able to slip away from work on the front side, instead of flying in mid-week. Maybe they'll sit next to Martin on the couch and grope—better yet if they can all be out in public, sharing a city bench perhaps. Seamus chops and smiles, as much at himself as at Martin's potential discomfort. Thirteen years, two houses, seven jobs (between them), four parakeets, two couches and one dog all with the same man: they rarely reach for one another the way they used to, have slipped into something stodgier and unimaginably more satisfying.

"Sore throat?" Eye on Leilani, Margaret opens a drawer for inspection. "If you're in the mood for the medicinal, I have Sucrets, Ludens and generic lemon discs. There's organic slippery elm tea, honey, and tea tree oil lozenges in the pantry, third shelf up." Her mother surveys another drawer as if that could hold the cure. "What about salt water? Sea salt or regular."

Leilani smiles apologetically. "Sore neck, not a throat. Rubbing seems to soften the muscles—don't mind me."

"Let's hope she doesn't sneeze or break a toenail. We'll have to purchase a medical supply store." Anna pulls herself away from the window and starts to assemble platters of food, radiating such hostility that Leilani wonders what horrible mistake she made, again, without knowing.

Luke screams from the dining room. Leilani waits. The noise doesn't end. Martin is in there; she hears his ministrations. Still, the baby screams. Martin yells to be heard: where's that high chair? As if he hasn't pulled the plastic frame out of the hall closet a hundred times. Anna's face tightens and focuses on her task.

Seamus slices the bread to smithereens, smiling all the while.

What's the time in Holland, she wonders? Perhaps Mr. Van Eyck is in his office.

"I'm going upstairs to rest," she decides out loud.

"You have got to be kidding," snaps Anna. "Get back in here."

Leilani leaves. She sits in the upstairs hallway, listening to worry and outrage below. Sounds of desperation come from the dining room. Martin sings to Luke and shouts encouragement at Ben, who must be occupying himself quietly. Good job Bennie, creaks Martin. Drive the truck under the table one more time. Six hours ahead in Holland? Van Eyck is in bed, Saturday morning.

Nobody here had a traumatic childhood. They didn't suffer through divorce, abuse, alcoholism, or neglect. The worst anyone could say is that children were seen as soldiers or underbrush: crisply ordered about and shuttled through various stages of growth. Weeds, George used to say—they get bigger and bigger, regardless. His style was to sit back and let nature take its course. Margaret stepped in to provide structure that nature did not. Young psyches received little attention, unless a temper tantrum interfered with piano lessons or a sullen attitude soured one's grades. Then the culprit received a stern talking-to, perhaps a punishment, and was quickly declared cured. All in all, uneventful: standard upbringing by Depression-era parents whose hopes for their children were measured largely by economics. On those terms, George and Margaret were a reasonable success.

Was she ever happy? Repeat the word over and over: hahpee, a nonsense sound, without meaning. She recalls a melancholy adolescence. Who doesn't? She never had goals beyond college (a parental requirement). After a few unimportant jobs, she drifted to graduate school for a degree in English Literature, her main qualifications being decent undergraduate grades and an ability to speed-read. Her graduate career was consistent if uninspired, as was the rest of her life. Events and people appeared and she responded, taking little initiative.

When Will showed up, he made the overtures and she responded—favorably, for the most part. Not that she lacked passion or opinion, simply that her strengths were in the minutiae and abstract. Which nursery school, what type car, how to insulate the attic, where for the cheaper dry cleaners? Shopping for the sake of conspicuous consumption didn't appeal to them; an ethical and ecological approach to money did. Obedient academics, she and Will believed that politics, above all, shaped their daily lives. They shouldered global crises. Need someone to sign a petition against war (any of them), picket a polluting ethanol plant, or leaflet the neighborhood on behalf of the Green Party? They were your couple.

They were busy. They were engaged with their community. They enjoyed their daily lives, careful possessions and political perspectives. Beyond that, they saw little, not quite realizing there was anything else to be seen. She mistakenly thought big ideas gave a bite to her life, the causes and campaigns and commitments to ideals that extended far beyond the scope of her own, tiny heart.

Instead, Leilani's marriage—like her childhood—became a calamity of trivia. That's how she now sees the ideologies that sustained her—clutter that distracted her from her daughter, staved off growing dissatisfaction with Will. Perhaps she shouldn't ridicule Anna for her obsessive accumulation, the expensive home and clothing and cars. Leilani did the same—except she collected aspirations that truly belonged in some other camp, generally halfway across the world. Served the same purpose.

Enticing smells, hot butter and bread, waft up the stairs to flirt with her aching stomach. As urgently as she needed to leave, she needs food. Initially, she made a stab at malnutrition, but quickly abandoned that tactic. She disliked the uncontrollable focus on food. Starvation reshapes the structure of the brain: one is obsessed with eating, with survival. Rolling with the punches, she toyed and debated: anorexia, then? But that seemed far too complex, all the psychological twists and turns the textbooks required. She eventually caved in to the rhythm of her appetites.

So guided—and ravenous—she pads downstairs to the table. Conversation lifts and freezes over her entry, then drops back in place, soft and steady swirl around her chair. Holly's favorite chair—the only one with arms and a deep purple cushion Margaret made by hand—stands alone in the corner, untouched. Margaret put the chair there and won't move it. She actually slapped Bennie's hand once, when he reached for the legs. When nobody else is around, Margaret sits there, comforted that Holly's spirit has a resting place in her house.

Leilani hates the chair's macabre presence, looming large and empty. She never acknowledged her mother's gesture.

Margaret nudges vanilla wafers at Bennie; Seamus summarizes the current goings-on in San Diego, where he's a city planner.

"Sprawl," George grunts between mouthfuls. "That's a national problem." He intuitively grasps the full import of any issue with a parallel in root structures.

Leilani fills her plate: slightly pink roast beef; sourdough bread gooped with butter; creamed corn meant for children; a baked potato topped with sour cream; three scoops of curried asparagus and tomato salad (Seamus or Anna's touch, as Margaret wrinkles her nose each time the dish passes); a generous handful of olives and pickles; and a good portion of the bag of Fritos, also meant for children. She rolls a chunk of meat into the flesh of potato and pops the gooey ball into her mouth.

Ben stares and screeches, delighted to find a dinner companion suited for his sensibilities. He slams a fist into his mashed potatoes and licks the mess from his fingers.

Anna frowns at both of them. "Hungry?" she asks archly.

Leilani stirs creamy corn and mashed potato into a single pool of dip for other foods. She grabs a carrot and slurps the stuff off.

Margaret rattles a spoon too loudly. In a voice they all recognize from childhood parables, she announces: "Your sister is starving herself half to death. She subsists on coffee and stale crackers. If I leave oatmeal on the counter sometimes she eats that. Nothing else."

"Not entirely true," offers George. "She eats. Take out from some foreign place, mostly, and enough to feed a family of four. Look, she's eating now. I don't think she's starving."

"Foreign place," queries Martin. "Has anyone besides us tried the Afghani restaurant on St. Clair Avenue? Cyber Pass? Always wanted to go but then thought I should, if you know what I mean."

"Supportive political statement," offers Anna. "After all, those people aren't to blame."

"Those people," echoes Seamus, still testy. He remembers the enthusiasm with which Martin and Anna had embraced the concept of Gay Pride, showing up at parades and fundraisers. The minute they had Bennie, they dropped from sight. The drag queens would frighten small children, Anna explained. Seamus thinks their fickle political sensibilities reflect trends, rather than heartfelt convictions. He can just hear Martin commenting on suspicions— or declarations—that so and so within the law firm is gay: we have one in the family, he'd say, smugly. He's a New Yorker, after all.

Why shouldn't he symbolize diversity to the great unwashed? Seamus takes an irritable, heartfelt swig from his wine glass.

"No," George shakes his head. "Thai food. I think she eats Thai. Lani?"

Anna answers. "Thai has always been my favorite food, not Leilani's. She likes Italian."

"If you look at her," interrupts Margaret, "you can see that whatever she eats isn't enough. She's skin and bones."

Methodically, almost meditatively, Leilani continues to eat. She slips olives into her mouth, lovingly, the tip of her tongue rolling into the open center of each.

"What happened to Vietnamese, Anna? Yesterday you were dying for egg rolls from the Lotus." Martin is disturbed. "Vietnamese is your favorite."

"Not in a long time," insists Anna. "I don't even know how you could be saying this. Where do you think we've eaten once a week for the past two years, Thai or Vietnamese?"

"Still jogging, Martin?" asks Seamus, pushing back from the table to survey Martin's slightly expanded waist.

George shakes his head soberly. "Where did American food go? There's one place on Grand Avenue for a decent steak and thirty for noodles—a shame."

Margaret puts her head in her hands and wonders, loudly. "Is it normal to starve yourself for two weeks and then gorge?"

"Maybe she's bulimic," offers Anna, bright with sarcasm.

Suddenly dizzy, Seamus feels himself propelled apart from the rest of the room. The people around him chatter away, each unheard. The empty chair is magnet and reminder: what matters? Holly was a somber girl. Her face—the pointed chin and focused eyes—reminded him of the child he once was. Was she as much like him as he imagined? He always believed that she knew far more about adults than most children, and that in her wisdom, she maintained her distance. Or maybe he's describing how he felt, nostalgic for company he never had? He looks a little more carefully at the faces around him, guarded by pain. His uncharitable mood dissipates.

"Martin," he offers congenially, "have you set a date for the move to the Big Apple?"

Anna groans and reassembles Luke on her lap. "Let's not discuss this now."

"I can't imagine a better time," says Martin. He slaps down his napkin and shrugs at Anna. "Seamus is here. We can let the whole family know at once, start making plans."

"Since you've pretty much gone ahead and told everyone by this point, finish the job," snaps Anna.

Leilani pours gravy on a second helping of creamed corn and breaks Fritos into the mixture for crunch.

Margaret sighs. She knows what's coming and had hoped the news would arrive much farther down the road—too soon to say good-bye to these grandbabies! Of course, there will be visits and vacations. However, relationships that rely upon airplanes rather than a drive across town are not her idea of family. A year ago, she was anticipating Luke's arrival—all those children regularly in the house! How different life looks today.

"I've put a new date on the transfer," enunciates Martin. "Three months."

"Great!" Seamus beams encouragement at other family members. "I know how much you're looking forward to going back home. Anna? Excited?"

"About schlepping a toddler and infant cross-country—not to mention a truckload of household goods, one dog," she glares at Leilani, who sips milk, "and a four-foot aquarium. Oh, lest I forget—there's that hard-fought career to consider, the one I disrupted to have babies and will have to retool in a more competitive city. Whoopee. I'm excited." She lifts a wineglass.

Leilani contemplates the slight flush in Anna's cheeks, hollow pockets under her eyes. She experiences an unexpected emotion: jealousy. Her sister does not look well. Always strained, Anna has slid into a thoroughly peaked state. Goddamn her. She probably has ovarian cancer. Some people naturally have all the luck; Anna makes hers. Leilani knows her sister well. Not one cell shakes or quivers without Anna's say so. She slowly slurps milk, stomach distended. She can feel liquid pooling at the base of her throat, blocked from further descent.

"Won't be the same without you two," says George, firmly. "Anna's been running this family so long, we'll probably be chasing our tails, trying to figure out which way's up."

"Or who to vote for," quips Seamus.

"Ha," snorts Anna. "As if you ever read farther than 'Democrat' on any ballot. Daddy and I are the only ones with any political sense."

"Hey, I've expanded my horizons," laughs Seamus. He leans forward to announce theatrically, "Once I voted Socialist."

Martin looks puzzled. "You're kidding, right? Or you wasted a vote."

Seamus leans back, pleased to see more familiar, comfortable ripples between them. "Not kidding—and not wasted. The

Democrats are going to lose people to third parties, a repeat of 2000, if they don't develop a radical agenda for social justice."

"God, you sound like Leilani," laughs Anna, relaxed for the first time all evening. "You said radical, not me." Seeking her father's conspiratorial grin, she catches the slide in Margaret's expression. So much for guarding her mother's good spirits. "Mom?"

Leilani has little interest in the conversation or self-defense. Were there elections after Holly died? She can't remember. In order to escape, she will have to stand up. She wishes she'd eaten a tiny bit less. Movement seems highly unlikely.

"I wish you weren't going," says Margaret simply. "I'm going to miss Luke and Ben."

"Bad luck comes in threes," George says comfortingly. "I've been alive long enough to see the truth in those old wives tales. If this has to be our second hit, I'll take it. One to go."

Martin clears his throat, "I wouldn't call this bad luck. New York is a stellar career move. I'm primed for partner; the move simply seals the deal."

"Daddy, don't be superstitious. We're leaving a little earlier than we discussed—before." Anna hesitates to pinpoint the grim weeks after Holly and Will's deaths, when their plans were remade. "Martin's right. This is good luck, not bad."

The city planner in Seamus calculates. "Hope you're quadrupling your income. We're talking major changes in cost of living—not to mention trickier transportation. Will you live in the city?"

Leilani stands up, finished. Her stomach hurts. "Well, good night," she says calmly.

"You're leaving?" Anna sits up straight, caught off guard.

"So?"

"Aren't you going to at least acknowledge the discussion—the fact that Martin and I are moving across the damn country? Can't you feign interest in somebody other than yourself?"

Sitting back down seems the reasonable response. Besides, her stomach is too tight to stand yet. Leilani falls back into the chair and closes her eyes, stuffed and slightly sick.

"Anna," sighs Seamus. "Stop."

"No, Shay, I'm serious. You haven't been here enough to know. She mopes around like a zombie, completely unable to function. Doesn't give a damn about anything other than whatever goes on in her head. You call that living? I for one am sick of walking on eggshells, pretending that my family died along with hers. Six months! That's not grief, that's ego."

Familiar with Anna's temper, each person at the table hesitates, trying to hone in on either wound or solution. George doesn't bother analyzing. He looks at his wife for a clue to Anna's behavior.

Margaret knows that everyone expects her to step in and stop the escalation: no fighting at the dinner table! They can hit and bite, for all she cares. Some good her rules were, all that intervention and labor—hard, hard work to keep three children alive and out of trouble.

Fear that's licked Margaret's heels since Holly died ignites, hollowing her out, that fast: no mother truly protects her babies, even when she thinks she has every angle covered. Her children, and theirs, are one doctor visit or car ride away from disappearing. They always have been. They've lived this long because of what:

luck or God? Not her. Let them fight.

Seamus waits two beats before continuing. He's soothing. "I wouldn't call missing your child and husband egotistical. Maybe we can all calm down enough to talk productively?"

Martin makes a small skeptical noise. George is attuned to his wife, uncharacteristically slumping over her silverware. Margaret has rules for posture.

Anna has the final word. "The prodigal son wishes us to lead us into therapeutic discourse. No thank you." She lurches up with a sleeping Luke. "Martin, will you wipe at least a quarter of that gravy off Ben so he won't complete the car seat's ruin tonight? The boys are pooped and I am too. Time to go."

"Come on, big guy." Martin unbuckles Ben from the chair and brings him to the bathroom.

George studies Margaret. She's not paying attention. He wishes he were sitting beside her. He would tap her hand. Across the table, his fingers move involuntarily. At that moment, she looks at him, bereft. When Margaret gets up and takes her plate into the kitchen, George follows. The rarely used galley door shuts behind them.

"Can't we have a normal conversation without losing half the room?" moans Seamus, heart sinking along with the door's swing.

"Wake up. We've never had significant discourse and probably never will," proclaims Anna, stuffing toys and sippy cups and bibs into a sleek black diaper bag. "Face the hard facts, Shay: we've never much gotten along or liked one another. That's not going to change because somebody died."

The word ricochets. Anna wants to slap each cheek in the room: dead, dead, dead! My sister's baby died. Rub their faces in that fact one more time, and maybe she can force pent-up agony out in the open. Yet the room remains the same, her siblings unreadable.

Leilani wonders if throwing up would be helpful, to herself or the general dynamic. Vomiting at the dinner table might reinforce Anna's bulimic theory. She'd rather not give her sister credibility or ammunition. Of course, Anna's right about the talking thing. She burps.

Stricken, Seamus hones in on another facet. "Never liked one another? Good God, Anna, what house did you grow up in?" He turns to Leilani. "Lani, help me out here, please!"

Me, thinks Leilani—somebody's asking me direct question? Oh, I've got bad news for you, little brother. Here's another chance to play with truth and watch the fallout. "Nobody was as miserable as Anna. The best word to describe how I felt would be disconnected—except from you, I guess."

Disconnected. Seamus frantically rewinds memory for clues he obviously missed.

Anna stands, waiting for Martin to reappear with a cleaned-up Bennie, uncertain if she should be grateful for validation or suspicious of Leilani's apt use of the word miserable. Anna was miserable, largely because she felt—continues to feel—ignored, a weak shadow trailing brother and sister. She stares at Seamus's serious, sad face, startled to realize that he honestly doesn't know, has never been aware that the entire family revolves around him— the son. Another example of the gifts he's been given: ignorance. Despite her fury, desire to hurt him with the truth wavers. Anna is not immune to the long time rules: Seamus shapes your position within the family. Hurt him, and the rest of them will hate her—

more than they do now, if that's possible, forever.

Leilani lives with the same dynamics, yet no longer cares what she loses. "Shay, you were their favorite. So you became our favorite—Anna's and mine."

Martin bellows from the front hallway. "We're ready!"

Seamus can't deny what he's always suspected. However, he had no idea that such a rift existed between his experience and his sisters'.

Anna's parting shot is an observation she's been saving for decades. "You could get away with anything," she announces. "Even the gay thing. Me, I had to knock myself out with the Miss America act just to get a pat on the head." She storms from the room.

Seamus and Leilani sit silently for a moment, stunned. Then, Seamus starts to laugh, hugely grateful: Anna will be Anna. There are some dynamics he had no part in creating.

Leilani can't help smiling back. "The gay thing," she giggles. "Guess you really pulled one off, huh?"

She has one, free happy moment with her brother, laughing at Anna's expense. Some changes don't come in a heartbeat.

9
DELPHI

Fire transforms the dining room into a cave, lush, eerily lit and lonely. Meredith believes in atmosphere. She instructs Ian and me in the art. The sheer red curtains are drawn. Rows of candles— squat, tall, thin, decorative and plain—top every surface. Some monastic-sounding choir benefits from a sound system that probably cost as much as our loft. Incense won't do: Meredith burns sage to sanctify the space. She puts curls of lavender in dried milk weed pods that Kate saved. The dining room table is cleared and cleaned; an old lace cloth runs along the center and a lone white candle burns near the end where we'll sit. We refresh glasses of wine and tea. Ian adds a silver tray of thin mint wafers to the otherwise esoteric layout. If consulting is her bag, let's hope the topic is indeed décor. Meredith is a natural.

"Ready," she announces, beautiful and newly mysterious in the flickering light.

When they both look at me expectantly—as if I know what's next—I realize how unprepared for this moment I actually am.

I groan. "I have no idea what to do! Anybody else?"

Of course, Meredith has ideas. She thinks I should make

myself comfortable at the end of the table. She thinks the candle should be place directly in front of me. Meredith thinks a lavender pod would go nicely near my right hand.

"Instinct?" she laughs quietly. "Can't hurt and the smell is nice, subtle."

We situate ourselves. Women chant in the background, velvety and dark. The walls glow. Meredith whispers. "I'm trying to remember what I read about mediums. Why am I nervous? Guess we've never invited a ghost into our home before."

Ghost? Is this really how I'm spending a Friday night? The whole scene is surreal, and I grew up among people who shave their heads and swear by reincarnation.

Meredith continues, "I think all you have to do is relax. If she wants to, she'll show up? Wish I could be more helpful, sweetie. I've always been a spectator in these events, never an organizer."

"Invite her," says Ian. "You should welcome her, Delphi. Ask her to talk to you. Say please."

"How do you know?" I ask, not needing to say what we all instantly realize—he's right.

He grins sheepishly. "One of us has been doing his homework. I kept a couple books from The Curtain for myself." He raises his eyebrows knowingly. "I suggest you take a spin through The Art of Channeling. Very interesting stuff."

"Good for you," Meredith says optimistically. She nudges Ian, teasing him. "I feel totally prepared—Ian's on task Seriously, do what he says, Delphi. Invite her."

Only what—two days into life as a psychic—and already I've learned an invaluable lesson. At some point, nobody helps me. Hand the mind over to the unknown. What enters that space—a common space, I think, meant to be shared—is not up to me. One aims and hopes for the best, relinquishing dreams of control.

My eyes shut. I sense Meredith and Ian ready. The energy in the room is poised. Help me, I think, addressing the plea to nobody in particular. Please help me. A definitely inappropriate urge to giggle interrupts my concentration. I give myself a stern lecture. Get a grip, young lady. Return to the curtain of closed eyelids, familiar territory. Zen life may have actually prepared me for a career as a psychic.

I cast my request for help physically, looking into the far left corners of my closed eyes, as if might find answers in the darkness. Help me. The thought rests and listens for a reply. Move the idea, the words to the center, nearly on my nose: help? The cry drops lower, to the cheekbone.

I'm warm. My chest aches; goose bumps erupt. Here! I sink into the feeling that greets me—without form or word, a pool into which I can easily drop. Again, not unfamiliar: I've had those rare moments, successful meditation when you do indeed bump, unaware, into something other than the self. But this required so little effort! Ha—tell that to all those aching apprentices, sitting in a half-lotus until each leg prickles and screams. Pleased with my easier success, I smile. In that split-second of contentment, I hear voices, loud and clear. Voices!

My heart leaps, shocked. So much for sustaining a smug attitude. If I weren't afraid of losing the momentum, I'd open my eyes to see if Meredith and Ian were playing a gigantic trick. The voices offer one word: yes. Three times I see hear the chorus, men and women, maybe four or five of them? Yes. By the final round, I'm certain this is a sound my hosts could never replicate. These voices originate inside my head, yet are so distinct from my psyche—my self—that it's impossible to mistake those people, or whatever they are, for me.

Self-conscious, I can't resist. I slit open an eyelid. There sit Meredith and Ian, all dutifully closed eyes and patient faces. Thank God. I'm certain I look like a total freak. Could some creature possibly take over my body, forcing me to moan and dissolve into goo? Aliens. Maybe there's truth to the wackos waiting in fields with binoculars. After all, could anyone possibly call what I'm doing normal?

Far from breaking my concentration, this shift in attention propels me forward. Half of me wrinkles, serious, with critique and takes on the role of reviewer. Hey you! Nodules in my brain congeal strangely to form a High Court. The Hague. The justices steer me in a new direction. Stop screwing around and get busy: people depend on you!

The rest of my brain cells are less confident and more polite. This section of the brain, lax and floppy (what I fear appearing) lopes in the direction of the voices, walks to the yes.

I'm in a movie! Meta-brain lets me analyze, while the other cells participate in the scene. The girl is wearing that same sleeveless dress. Oh, I see! We're in August, the best time of year for her. She loves the vibrant end-of-summer colors, the wet warmth. The High Court nudges me along: slow down and listen! Well, telepathy or whatever isn't that simple, thank you. However, I try harder. With the girl, I don't actually hear words. I sense them as if they were my own, which makes the distinctions between us less clear.

The High Court strains and prods; the rest of me remains in

the movie. Boy, would I would love to tell Meredith and Ian about this. However, my limbs feel oddly immobile. Great. Let us now assume that I look officially stupid. Integrity consoles me: neither will peek. They're too honest. Doesn't feel as if I'm drooling. Ian was right: I should've read one of those books from The Curtain instead of Vogue and Soap Opera Digest. Perhaps there's a psychic etiquette—helpful hints to maintain outward appearances while in an official stupor? Kelly Ripa's tips for applying eyeliner strike me as singularly unhelpful in this situation.

The High Court hollers. I return: the girl plays in a yard of wispy bushes and wildflowers. I like the garden's well-planned simplicity, the spindly selection of greens. Whoever held the hoe had an eye for beauty. I try to talk to the kid, to wrench out facts about her mother. My communication skills—at least the ones I've relied upon for the past twenty-some years—are suddenly non-existent. That's lovely; I get to regress, too? No. The Justices wave a collective finger: you get to observe.

The loopier brain cells fly toward the child's green-flecked eyes, her straight face. Genuine curiosity takes hold: what makes this kid tick? She's so damn serious! My image of the average four-to-five-year old has the kid screeching and squirming. This girl is focused. When I ask myself (or her, it's so confusing), who are you, I'm querying on a level that dives beyond date and names—even beyond temperament, to a quality I can't articulate. If I believed in souls, that's what I'd be looking for.

She's moved to a kitchen, with her mother! Can't make out a face: I'm bizarrely in the picture, yet far away, too. The only detail I can make out is hair: mom is a dark dishwater blonde, not the red coppery kind. She's no spring chicken. Yet she's the mother. I can see this through the little girl's love. Details, random and unimportant, flood my awareness: their house is white, on a hill; use the oven and a hall fire alarm goes off; the basement floods in a hard rain; and nobody in this house much enjoys cooking. The light is perfect—sun pours through southern windows. Mother and daughter appreciate that light. They dance in the late afternoon. Barefoot, they follow sun spots on the floor.

The High Court disappears. I do too. For a few dizzying seconds, the girl opens herself and I walk in. Her life is mine.

We dance on beams of light with Mama. This kitchen is the most magical place on earth. Safe. In a mother's arms, we are the same person. Laughing, laughing! We never want the song to end. Maybe the sun will beat through the window forever. There is no night to fall. We plummet through the wave of memory until a heavy wall hits our chest—a horrible, hot ripple against the lungs, belly. Breath turns into bubbles, liquid and slow. The nice man is here. His hands are warm and sweet. He sings and tries hard not to cry. But he does. He makes everything better until Daddy can come. We see Daddy! He tells the nice man thank you and holds out his hands. Run to him, safe forever. Night never falls. We were right.

I'm crying. My body tells me I've returned—every muscle and each cell feel as if they've been tossed and spun and spit back out. I am too afraid to open my eyes, too afraid to breath normally. The High Court smiles: quick study, my girl. Excuse me? Whoever signed me up to actually go through somebody else's trauma? My own problems are sufficient, thank you. What an ordeal—living and dying in five seconds!

However, I do allow myself one small smile of success: I

know her! Okay, I don't have a name or address. On the soul thing—I'm certain. I think of a mother's hands in mine, laughing in the late afternoon. We should've been making dinner! Unexpected bitterness laps the edges of memory that doesn't truly belong to me—a memory I've always longed for. My attention wanders to the paramedic. Here's someone deserving! That afternoon took a toll on him. Holly clung to his kind good heart; he allowed her to die with love.

Exhausted, I cast off a final query into the darkness of closed eyes: any more takers, anything else to tell? A series of images speed through my head, fast-forward style: a dog, men in army fatigues and a larger city—complete with skyscrapers and hot dog stands and a good museum. If I'd paid attention in geography, maybe the landscape would ring a bell instead of appearing completely foreign. Then I slip. My concentration deteriorates into Yang's children, the other tragic tales that currently color my life. Maybe my unconscious connects the girl to these kids? Or, I've repressed guilt at dumping all weekend shifts onto Amanda's shoulders.

I smell something. Sulfur or burning tar? The scent is dense and acidic. An urge to slip out of sight grips me. Okay, I have an official case of the heebie-jeebies. Some runty shadow slithers into the corner of my psyche—a totally pathetic excuse for a ghost, let alone a human being. Ugh. As he starts to come into focus, I change my mind: why would I set myself in front of someone so ugly—and I'm not talking hair and complexion. Here is one wretched creature, full of mistakes and rage.

My mind's eye snaps shut to save me. My eyes—the real ones, thank God, are working. I'm here again.

Ian sits placidly, lips curled in contemplation, lids lightly closed. At least my new (let's not forget, male) friend wasn't watching the Delphi freak show. Meredith's hand is on mine. I didn't notice. She stares openly, face intent and concerned. Much to my surprise, her scrutiny doesn't bother me. I'm sort of grateful.

"I wanted to shake you," she says, worriedly. "You didn't appear to be enjoying yourself."

Impulsively, I rub my eyes. They're wet, puffy, and painful to touch. I must've been a spigot. Ian opens his eyes, groggy.

"What happened?" he asks.

"You first." I get to exercise some control over my life, don't I? I will admit to a tiny bit of embarrassment over the sob scene, even if my audience was Meredith.

"Well, I figured that the only way to participate was to send support, if that makes sense." Ian laughs at himself. "I radiated, okay. Tried to radiate goodwill, the kind of thing that would make Mom happy and would kill, just kill, my chemistry professor."

Meredith is interested. "How did that feel, sweetie?"

I love how she calls everyone sweetie.

He shrugs. "Good, I guess. Almost like napping."

I should send Ian to Daddy—he's cut out for meditation. I can't tell you how many times snoring cuts through the silence of zazen.

Meredith is genuinely excited. "Ian, I felt your energy! Amazing! At first, I focused on the girl, thinking maybe I'd get lucky and see her. Of course, what came to mind were neighborhood children, all still quite alive thank God. I gave up, fell into listing chores, thinking about Joshua's concert, wondering if Bill will get tickets to the hockey game, that sort of thing. That's when I felt you Ian—hard to explain, other than as instinct that comes from years of living with somebody. You have a characteristic calm that spread through the room. Made me proud to be your mother, as usual." She smiles at him.

Ian accepts the compliment easily. "Freaky, how you knew that was me, huh? Do I get to tell the other two that I'm your favorite?"

They laugh, not far from their own truth, I bet.

Ian's ready for the verdict. "Did you see her?"

Meredith nods for me. After all, she watched the whole thing. She squeezes my hand to acknowledge that reliving the experience may be difficult. It is. I review the snapshot images with relative ease. Describing her mother, my throat aches and swells. Language is an impossible barrier. What words exist for slipping into another person's life and death! I must remember to ask Evelyn if there's a way to avoid taking on trauma that belongs to somebody else.

"I got a terrible feeling about her parents," I conclude. "Her father's dead. I can't tell when, only that he's with her. Her mother's alive, although in terrible shape. She may be dying? There's no energy or life left, nothing. I couldn't tell if she's sad or really sick."

Meredith is stricken. "Can you imagine," she whispers, "losing both your daughter and the child's father? That's quite a loss." Her own imagination must be good; her voice quakes.

"I forgot something," I say. "Hospital was her favorite game. She was the patient. Her friends took care of her. Other little girls, they used M&Ms and Skittles for pills and piled baby blankets on her. Really elaborate set-up these kids had going, complete with colored water in medicine bottles, thermometers—the works. Either the game is what I'm supposed to remember or the other kids. They were important to her."

"The center of attention," muses Meredith. "Now, maybe her mother is sick. What could that mean?"

"You're right about the attention," I agree.

Our exchange frustrates Ian. "Games are only important if we find the mother—proof you're not some freak, that you really know something about her daughter. What matters now is finding real people—and we're a long way from picking up the phone."

Meredith and I agree. Where to begin? The search is overwhelming, especially after we assemble the bits and pieces of information I've received. Not one obvious lead! Nobody can think of a single thread linking army men, skyscrapers, and dancing. We spend over an hour dredging up every detail, from the moment the visions began. Is the cityscape New York? Was her grandfather killed in some war or was her father in a spookier operation, the type nobody hears about? Did she die in the summer, in a yellow dress?

"The dress," says Meredith, suddenly. "Describe the dress again."

For the hundredth time, I think wearily. "Yellow, with large red flowers that sort of explode, fireworks style. There are pockets in front. She loved tiny objects: teeny plastic figurines, beads, and rings."

"You two probably aren't up on trends in children's clothes. I can tell you with certainty that it's the rare little girl running around in tight ruffled clothes anymore. Girls wear longer, loose clothing designed to let them move better. The yellow and red combination makes me think the dress is recent, maybe a designer thing?"

The smallest bit of hope buds. "You're right. The dress was new. I bet I've seen the style a thousand times on kids and barely noticed."

Ian presses further. "I don't understand why you can't just tell if she recently died or if she's been dead a long, long time."

"Believe me, I wish I could choose what I know. I can tell you how she felt, who she loved, that sort of thing. Figure out how, and I bet I can come up with the names of her friends and that dog. I think the dog was hers. The big facts are missing—the year, her parents' names, her address."

"She's four or five," clarifies Meredith. "Maybe she doesn't know her address."

"Once you're dead, don't you know everything—even if you died as a baby? Ghosts transcend earth age, wouldn't you think?" queries Ian.

Once again, they both turn to the only one in the room actually seeing dead people.

"Don't look at me," I protest, "I have no over arching theory. All I get are fragments."

"Leave the big picture questions for your Evelyn," suggests Meredith. "All I'm saying is that maybe—speculation here—maybe we know only what a child is able to convey. That's why you saw the dancing, as opposed to a picture of her mother entering an office building, conveniently complete with corporate logo and telephone number. We're getting a bird's-eye view, a child's perspective."

"Maybe I should rethink the type of questions I'm asking—redirect on a four-year old level."

Ian puts his hands his head and fakes a scream of frustration. "Please do not go down that road."

"What?" I say, surprised.

"Remember who among us is seven years older than the next sibling in line. Have you talked to a twelve-year old lately, let alone a four? If we try to wade through her world, we'll spend the first year just figuring out the logic to her language."

"She's all we have. What else can I do?" I'm equally frustrated—also exhausted and guilty. I stifle an urge to yawn. Don't even show me a clock. I forgot to call Daddy, who probably gave up on me hours ago.

"We. We are going to become adept at obituaries and death records." He looks determined, and surprisingly capable.

"Great idea!" Meredith claps her hands. "Check the past couple, three years."

"I'll start locally. There's a reason she contacted you and not some psychic in Anchorage. Her mother has to be close."

I'm annoyed that I didn't think of the obvious. So immersed in the visions and wacky-woo element of the past few days, I left my beloved left brain behind.

"I'm such an idiot," I cry. "I'm supposed to be thinking about the visions, as much as feeling them, if that makes sense."

"Balance," says Meredith simply. "You need rationality as well as intuition."

"Exactly," I agree.

"That's encouraging," jokes Ian. "We're all nothing if not rational people, sitting in the dark worrying about ghosts and the most logical way to locate their living relatives."

The absurdity of the situation takes the edge off the urgency we each feel, at least a little.

Meredith consults her watch. Bill has been on family duty: we've heard him shuttling the twins back in the house and to bed, and attending to the whimsical needs of Kate and her friend.

"Nearly midnight. Josh will be home within a few minutes—if he values his freedom for the rest of the week, that is," she quips. "I have a radical suggestion, Delphi. Why don't you spend the night? I'm too wound up to sleep. There's half a chocolate torte and more tea than you can imagine in that kitchen. We can have a final round of dessert and fall into bed; nobody has to step out into the cold."

Nothing is less appealing than facing the still black night by myself. Did I lock the Buick? Doesn't matter. That dilapidated boat is the last thing a thief in this neighborhood would steal.

"I'm sold," I grin.

Meredith commandeers Ian as kitchen aide and points me to a telephone. "Call your father," she demands.

I dread making contact, which is strange—we've had dozens of late night check-ins. I've called much later, middle of the night, to report that the evening out has turned into a weekend road trip, or whatever evolves. Tonight, I'm guilty. Spending the night feels like a transgression.

Thankfully, the machine picks up. Gotta love this century. I manage to get my message recorded in less time than Daddy could get out of bed and hustle down the hallway. Hanging up, however, I almost wish I'd talked slower. I could've used reassurance: yes, spending the night is fine, your decisions good, and your life on track! I love you. Nothing like having my whole sense of self turned upside down to make me want—and run from—Daddy.

Joshua must value his freedom. He's in the kitchen when I walk in. The chocolate torte is on the table; tea and cocoa steam. The four of us sit in the more casual, well-lit kitchen and relive our evenings. Joshua tells us—more or less, considering he is fifteen— about the movie and what they did afterward. Meredith, mostly, fills him in on our spirit quest.

Of course, he's intrigued. In my very limited experience as a psychic thus far, I seem to be batting a thousand: people welcome the adventure. You're psychic? Wow! Being a star seems easy.

Maybe the frightening finale to my meditation will dampen everyone's enthusiasm? I describe what happened and how spooked I was. Maybe Ian, avid reader, can shed some light on the event.

"I hate to use the word evil," I say slowly, "except that's what I felt. The thing's presence was menacing."

"Cool," breathes Josh. "Maybe you landed on the ghost of a serial killer—or even better, a real live demon."

"Real live nothing," retorts Ian. "We have no idea what we're actually talking about—none of this stuff is real, except through Delphi. I wish I knew who Mr. Creep was. Maybe you bumped into some sulky geezer wanting a way back to this hemisphere? I don't believe in demons anyway," he finishes, firmly.

I'm beginning to understand Ian better. He's a complete optimist. I know the type.

Meredith is uncertain. "Again, I defer to Evelyn. Follow her advice. We don't want you doing anything dangerous."

Ian has a final question. "Why not evil? You said you hate to use the word."

"I'm not sure evil exists. According to Dad—speaking as

priest—what we call evil is actually an absence of qualities like love or compassion. Nobody possesses innate malevolence. Some people miss the boat on the better stuff."

Joshua vigorously disagrees. "Are you crazy? Look around you—there's a new gruesome murder in the paper every day. Evil is everywhere."

Meredith is more diplomatic. "Your father has an awfully generous perspective, one that I wish I could share."

"Interesting," reflects Ian. "I've always thought of evil as intention—willing harm. I like your Dad's definition better."

Yes, Ian is the eternal optimist. Oddly, I find myself feeling fuzzily fond of the quality.

"What about your mother, Delphi? Ian tells me she's in India." Meredith appears genuinely curious—and sympathetic, without that pitying look we semi-motherless tend to foster—that I do something unusual. I tell them the truth.

I talk about when Mom left and why. I describe her photography studio in Bombay, her devotion to Himalayan yoga, the art dealer she used to date in London, and the letters we write each month. Maybe the psychic thing is honing other instincts as well: the second the story's out, I'm glad. I trust them. Strange, considering I can tally the slim hours of our acquaintance.

"What does she say about your newfound sensory skills? Maybe there's a good explanation for this in Hindu theology, or it's an inherited yogic trait," says Ian.

Meredith shakes her head. "Not yoga. Of course we'd find commonalities in Hinduism. Look beyond the basics of any religion and you find lore regarding the dead. I'm no expert, but I've had my flirtations with different types of Christianity and now

Judaism. The dead talk to us, regardless of religious tradition. As for inheritance," here, Meredith turns to me, finger raised, excited, "that's a compelling thought. What if you've inherited this gift? Maybe what your mother could tell you is if there's a legacy in her family."

"Or your dad, for that matter," interrupts Ian. "What do they say, Delph?"

I cover my face. "Oh God, I haven't told either of them!"

This is a family prone to full disclosure. They're horrified.

Meredith grabs my arm. "Oh, sweetie! You ought to tell your parents, right away. They can help you like nobody else—not to mention that they would want to know what you're going through!"

"We could be racking our brains for nothing. Maybe Delphi's Mom is psychic, too. She could help us out," offers Ian.

"If she was psychic, wouldn't she call or something," asks Josh.

Obviously, he missed the defining—and possibly stickiest—characteristics of our relationship: we don't call. That's tough for outsiders to understand. People wonder why we don't communicate like the rest of the world, with telephones and email. Of course, when I was little, Mom set the tone. I didn't think to question. By the time I wondered about the letters, I knew that nothing about our situation was normal. Why rock the boat? Guess I've felt that way ever since. She always breezes past any invitation to visit. Why would a request for a phone call be any different?

"Believe me," I say firmly, "she's not psychic—I'm the mystic of the moment and I know."

Meredith backs me up. "I have to agree. Something tells me that Delphi's Mom isn't the answer to our dilemma." She stops there. I can fill in her blanks: what kind of intuition allows a woman to trade in her two-year old for travel and a transient affair?

"Okay, if not Delphi's Mom, maybe an aunt or grandmother," insists Ian. "One more reason Delphi should spill her guts, and now. We need all the info we can get if we're going to maximize this psychic thing and find that kid's mother."

Meredith laughs. "Maximize? Since when did you become so goal-oriented?"

Ian shakes his head, unfazed. "All I can think about is that poor woman. We're supposed to find her."

Nobody argues. We sip tea. Meredith licks her spoon and sighs before returning us to matters more mundane, and perhaps more manageable.

"Ian," she asks, a tad gingerly. "Are you going to work on interview material tomorrow?"

He is instantly, completely uncomfortable. "Totally spaced that. I made plans—basketball with Chris in the morning and there's a party at Todd's. In between, I thought one of us should make some headway on that physics project." He looks meaningfully at me.

"Does this mean you're not doing the interview?"

"Interview?" I ask cheerily. How nice! Spotlight on Mr. Dependable for a change.

"With Bill's firm," offers Josh, equally upbeat. Obviously, there are a whole set of family dynamics here to which I'm not completely privy. "Ian's settling."

"I am not," snaps Ian. "I'm not settling. I'm exploring my

options."

This is a topic I'm not going to touch with a ten-foot pole, at least not in front of Meredith. One could wonder what a PR firm sees in a biology major, and vice versa. Unless, of course, your stepfather owns the joint.

Meredith smooths the waters. "Let's not raise our blood pressures at this late hours, guys. I just wanted to remind you, Ian. Hoped you've been working on some drawings, that's all," she finishes, lightly.

"Drawings?"

"I tinker in pencil and charcoal," he mutters.

"He's great," says Josh, unexpectedly. That's the kind of comment I'd expect from Meredith. She's clearly making a decision to sit this one out. Another artist cluttering my life. My karma must be loaded in favor of these sensitive types.

"More on my non-profit interests later, okay? I have to be dribbling by ten. Time to say good-night. Don't you have early swim practice, Josh? I remember doing laps for Schmidt with three hours of sleep under my belt. Ouch." Mr. Diplomat stands up.

We all follow suit. Meredith directs me to nightwear and an appropriate bedroom.

Before long, I'm wearing real silk pajamas and opening a new, boxed toothbrush, standing in front of the antique bathroom sink. Appears that guests are not uncommon in this house. Meredith has prepared for us all. The hall closet and medicine chest are full of unopened, pretty toiletries.

She waits for me outside the door to my room, wrapped in a yellow terrycloth robe and holding an over-stuffed pillow.

"I hope you don't think this is too silly," she confides. "I'd rather you weren't entirely alone. I thought I'd use the other guest room—across the hall—and leave the door open." She rests a hand on my arm, apologetically. "Not that I'm trying to be pushy. I wouldn't want you to be uncomfortable, considering what you're going through and being in a rather large, strange house. God knows I was nervous the entire first six months I slept here, wondering what lurked in every closet—and I wasn't even talking to little dead girls."

How did she know that company was exactly what I wanted?

"Sure," I shrug, smiling. "That might not be a horrible idea."

We say good night and, without making a big deal about it, I leave my door open a tiny bit, too. A thin line of light falls between our two rooms, as if she had a low lamp on, reading. The image is comforting. The guest bed is about as luxurious as I had hoped for—everything I touch screams big money, cushy inches of organic cotton and down and linen. For the second night in a row, I fall asleep quickly, without problem—only this time I don't need my imagination to make me feel as if I'm not alone.

10

LEILANI

The telephone holds new fascination for Leilani. What other ancient invention has steadily increased in importance, rather than faded the way of albums or eight tracks? Ten-year olds carry cell phones. Adults use them like pocket pens. Holed up in a bedroom—two days running—cordless at her side, she's digits away from any product or country. Then there's the Internet. In her previous incarnation—in which she had naively believed to know the way the world should work—she'd been suspicious of students who turned to computers for facts formerly found in encyclopedias. Chat rooms replaced dorm room conversations. Her social scientist colleagues cited studies showing the brain adapts to the computer's patterns, as much as the other way around: the machines were shaping personalities! She shuddered and considered science fiction (a second-rate genre within the University) with fresh eyes.

Leilani now calls herself a convert. She not only comprehends, she appreciates the ability to create a stronger self on-line or over the phone, a fully informed, invisible self whose options appear limitless. She marvels at the ease with which she's able to discuss the dead with a stranger in Holland, her Mr. Van Eyck. Initially, she feared he would offer his first name. Such an overture of intimacy would have to be rejected. Fortunately, he remains gorgeously formal, while expending extraordinary energy on Ms. Crea's painful, protracted search for her brother.

She's forced to elaborate on her initial story without the benefit of real facts. Declaring both parents dead, Leilani sidesteps the tricky issue of access to information that Mr. Van Eyck desires, details a mother or father have. Poor Ms. Crea, the sister, is Victor's one relative. Her memory is woefully inadequate: indeed, an inability to remember all but the barest facts of her brother's life (he was significantly older) might even be called a coping mechanism. Traumatized by Victor's disappearance, her parents called him a cousin; she recently learned the truth, a last-minute confession by their dying mother.

She tries the story on Mr. Van Eyck. He clucks in appreciation or sympathy, she can't tell. Regardless, his noises are affirming. His actions are kind. He goes to the office on a weekend to search an entire decade with nothing beyond a name, estimated year of birth, and gender. An email dialogue is quickly established for routine details. A phone call signifies real development. The time variable between countries is not a barrier; she's awake throughout the night. Insomnia, she explains to Mr. Van Eyck. He expresses concern for her sleeping habits, brought on by anxiety over Victor. The transatlantic cluck, cluck she hears is indeed sympathetic.

The definitive call comes. She hasn't had to leave the bedroom, except to use the toilet down the hall.

"Ms. Crea, I'm afraid we must acknowledge defeat," Mr. Van Eyck announces, soberly.

"Excuse me?" she says, unprepared.

"I have gone through ten years of death records. Horrible, how many people we were unable to identify! Even if we had more information—history of teeth or bone being most accurate—I doubt we could be certain. There are too many. Too much time has passed. I found an entire six-month period in which records were barely kept: if he died between March and August of 1994, we wouldn't even have an age. Whoever entered data had a tendency to skip fields on the left side of the keyboard. Looks as if somebody had a bad habit, hitting the tab button too soon." He sighs.

Leilani reconfigures her assessment of Holland from a neat, almost fanatically organized nation to a cluttered mess of incompetents. Indeed, who in their right mind would roost under water? Fools, every last one, from the beginning of time to the present, culminating in the hapless Van Eyck.

The persona she's created is entirely sympathetic and she feels a deep obligation to Ms. Crea's integrity. She forces herself to remain polite. "What about men around my brother's age? How many deaths have there been in that category, if we can become more specific?"

He takes a breath. "My calculations give me sixteen deaths that could possibly be your brother. All white men, probably born between 1961 and '63, without any striking characteristics: simply noted as deceased white male."

"Sixteen," she sighs. "Poor babies."

"Two deaths occurred within the past eighteen months. Otherwise, they left us long ago." He pauses, entering a delicate arena. "We cremate the bodies, Ms. Crea. All other avenues of investigation are closed. I have the paperwork, which tells us nothing."

A long silence ensues. Leilani feels her character's despair: what will she tell Rocco? Every parent deserves an answer. Process is a hype, means nothing. Outcomes matter. Final destinations.

Mr. Van Eyck changes tactics. "If you're certain he lived in Amsterdam, perhaps your best recourse would be to travel here or hire an investigator to track other information?"

"Perhaps," she replies, reflectively.

"Maybe he had a credit card," Mr. Van Eyck offers weakly. They both know that if heroin did indeed kill Victor, credit cards and bank accounts and signatures on leases went by the wayside years before his death. Truthfully, teeth probably did, too. Mr. Van Eyck is too polite to mention this. "A good investigator could infiltrate the drug community, locate your brother's friends and contacts? Perhaps my news is good? He's alive, yes?"

"Alive, yes. Maybe," she agrees, vacantly. Leilani has already leapt beyond Mr. Van Eyck to more viable options. Amsterdam was a bad choice. Victor returned to the States. Maybe he rebuilt a life in Nevada or New England. The problem with this scenario is Victor's silence. Alive and well, wouldn't he have contacted his father? Reasonable people do not disappear from the face of the earth. Victor is dead, deranged, or drug-addled beyond assistance. Or, Victor bears a grudge, legitimate or not, that keeps him from his father.

Mr. Van Eyck struggles through some semblance of a good-bye speech, expressing concern for her and a desire to be informed of her endeavor's outcome. He will keep an eye out, indefinitely, he maintains.

An eye out! Someone else, a cohort across the Atlantic, hopes to save Victor, too. Those Dutch may not be so wretched after all. She thanks him profusely and promises to call if she stumbles across any facts.

"If you don't hear from me, I'm still searching. I may be too overwhelmed to get back in touch," she says, urgently. "This could take years. Don't give up."

"Never!" Conviction rings through the wires. "I will always remember you, always remember your brother."

When they hang up, Leilani is less alone than she was ten minutes ago. Mr. Van Eyck will never forget. She won't either. There's Rocco. Anyone else? Victor Crea will soon slip into eternal anonymity. The three people who know his name will die. Victor's memory—or the slim concept of Victor Crea, as far as Mr. Van Eyck and Leilani go—will die go with them. Within fifty years, Rocco's son will be wiped from the most intimate record of the planet: memory.

She calculates her own extinction. Recent evidence aside, common sense suggests that Luke and Ben are her best hopes. Optimistically, one will mention their bereaved aunt and lost cousin to his own children. Even more optimistically (yet possible), one of those children is taken with the tragedy and will occasionally think of her great-aunt and distant cousin who never had a chance. Leilani is too much of a realist to think that she could possibly continue beyond a generation. She gives her fantasy detail and longevity: Luke lives to be one hundred, conveniently conceives a child at fifty, and that child—the girl with the heart for a sad story—lives to be one hundred. Life expectancy is on the increase, after all. Leilani Michelle O'Brien is officially forgotten sometime in the year 2152, not far, in the scheme of things. The world will tip forward as if she had never touched a blade of grass.

She is already disappearing. She has minimal contact with humanity, isn't the proud creator of any intellectual, artistic, or physical product. There are some credit card charges. There's a bulging bank account, thanks to the life insurance that she was compelled to buy—anticipating payout to her daughter, above all. She has some impact on the lives of her family, a regrettable and unavoidable state of affairs. Otherwise, she has left no stamp on the world. As for Holly, nobody can do justice to her daughter's memory. Perhaps the most desirable ending is that Holly disappears with Leilani, rather than linger, distorted, in some relative's memory.

Not for the first time, Leilani entertains the idea of destroying all evidence of Holly's life. She keeps returning to fire: that wretched house would be taken care of, as well as the possessions inside. No realtor wants another's family's fate. She tried to sell the contents, en masse, once on the Internet: clothes, photos, furniture, toys. She created a web site geared toward her own erasure. Amazing how many buyers leapt up! People willing, even eager, to take on the treasures and debris for the right price. In the end, she couldn't go through with the deal she struck. The couple lived in Oklahoma. They were willing to drive up with a truck and claim each last thing as their own, every hairbrush, towel, and sock. Then they failed the quiz.

She had posed the question carefully, offering adequate preface in the hope that they were capable of subtext and its demands.

"Holly had a large collection of dolls. I have to warn you—

they're not valuable. They're mostly Barbies and dollhouse miniatures, odds and ends from garage sales. But—."

A careful listener would've heard the catch, a mother's steadying pause.

"Holly swore the dolls were real. They were alive for her. She would want the girls in the right hands, the best hands. She never called them dolls; they were her girls."

She waited for them to jump in with a yes. Yes! We will dress the cold girls in their finest. We will find matching shoes and put the head back on the one with the movable hands. Yes! We will wash their naked plastic bodies. We will love them in her absence. Your daughter will be in every fixed eye and painted smile. Yes! We will cherish the games and the giggles—the trappings of little girls.

Instead, she could hear them both breathing and making other ordinary, small noises from the two phones, upstairs and down, in their split-level Tulsa home.

"What would you do with the girls?" she asked flatly.

The woman answered. "Well, of course, we'd find a home for the dolls—girls. We live on a block full of five-year olds who love dolls." The gentle voice seemed the product of a good education—accent evident in the cadence of her sentences, rather than a long vowel drawl.

"I can think of a dozen kids, right off the top of my head," offered the husband, eagerly, his smoother voice a hint of pudding and boarding school and news anchor diction.

"I'm sorry," said Leilani. "I've changed my mind."

No dummies, the Tulsa two knew what thin ground they were treading on from the get-go—a strange sort of business, trafficking in loss and longing. They held their breath a beat. The woman ventured: "If you want us to, we'll keep the dolls."

"I don't think so," smiled Leilani, relieved that thousands of miles separated them. She tried not to be rude. "I'm so sorry to put you through trouble for nothing. Please don't call me back." She hung up.

Who were these people, offering to find the girls a home! What did they think Leilani had been doing those past weeks, sorting through the psychopaths who answered her ad until the harmless, if offbeat, remained. They were the girls' destination. Leilani destroyed the web site within the hour.

Further destruction may be the solution. Her mind's eye ignites the fire. Flames start in the basement's north corner, in a pile of boxes Will saved for their sturdiness. A dollop of gas, a match, rolled-up paper and she gets a satisfying start to fantasy—a fantasy that always stops short of inconveniencing Rocco. He gets a little inevitable grit in his windowsills, that's all. The firemen come at precisely the right moment. Her dream burns and smolders: all that remains is a small square box of debris upon the foundation.

She stretches the kinks out of her neck (careful to grind on vertebrae) and rolls off the bed. The successful daydream perks her up, almost makes up for the Victor setback. She grabs the portfolio and slips down the stairs without a sound, hand on thyroid. She scans hallways for unwelcome family members. Forget Holland. Victor could be under her nose. Her new relationship with electronics nudges her in a different direction: unless he has truly scraped the bottom of the barrel, he has a telephone! How many area codes can there be in the state, the country: couple of hundred? She manages to tiptoe across the lawn and shut her car door, unnoticed. The shades are pulled in Seamus's room.

She makes her way from her parents' Crocus Hill home to the bridge that links the city to her old neighborhood, a tiny isolated pocket along the river. Roaring across the uninspired yet aptly named High Bridge, she frightens the driver in front of her into picking up his pace. "Back Off" reads his bumper sticker. Leilani slams on the horn and carefully jerks her way within an inch of the slogan, gleeful for such a chance to disturb. Her mind keeps pace with the engine, racing: what if Victor Crea—alive and cogent, even mentally agile—has chosen to disappear? Perhaps he doesn't want to be found. He lives off record and grid, ties severed too effectively for Leilani's wit.

The minute the cars exit the bridge, Leilani roars past the elderly driver ahead, shaking her fist in outrage.

"Get your eyes checked," she screams. Her whole life, she's wanted to do that. She's rewarded by a small slice of adolescent jubilation.

Off the grid—the concept came to her attention when millennium fears introduced a survivalist mentality to previously ordinary people. One of her neighbors bred rabbits to insure a supply of protein for her two children. When March 2000 rolled around and the continent still stood, undisturbed, the woman found herself with a freezer full of rabbit, fifty live babies in the backyard, and not a single friend in the market for Thumper meat. Will, who laughed off Y2K as yet another made-for-TV drama, offered to steal a bunny for Holly. Leilani couldn't stand inviting a reminder of death into the house; one look at that fuzzy face, and she'd think of the dozens they didn't save. Survivalists sprang up everywhere. Living off the grid—without need for utilities or telephones or soft-water service—took on a rugged glamour. An aura of security hung around the phrase as if true independence were possible. The rest of the world could crumble and there you'd sit, smug as a bug in your dugout or armored truck, while nuclear waste or bombs or germs flew all around you. Yeah, that's security, joked Will. He took his chances, neglecting to fill the gas tank or buy batteries.

Victor Crea is off the grid. Leilani feels the truth in her bones. He's not dead. She'll never find him. He lives in a tin house, built by hand, and draws water from his own well. Victor reads by solar-generated light. Probably shoots and kills pheasants for food, tends a stupendous organic garden. No longer an emaciated drug addict, Victor glows good nutrition and homespun contentment. She sighs, more discouraged by this vision than by Victor eating out of garbage cans. A content man may be impossible to find. A man in need is malleable. A content man is not.

The car stops in front of her old house. Leilani rolls down the window and looks harder: two flapping shingles have been nailed down. The broken white metal gutter is gone, replaced by a green streamlined model that matches the flower boxes. The lawn has had the benefit of a first mowing. Rake lines are visible along the border garden! Someone has been planting and pruning, preparing for spring.

Outraged, she storms through their backyards to Rocco's kitchen door and pounds. Her body remembers the mechanics: the arc of a door, how far feet shuffle to stand inside. She walks in as he's entering the kitchen. Cecile never bothered with locks, either. Two feet away or upstairs, Cecile yelled 'come on in.' The words still echo. One more person lost to memory, thinks Leilani. Cecile will probably be extinct within, what—thirty years, if Rocco hangs on long?

Rocco strides toward her, alarmed. "You all right?" He's dressed for outdoor chores, crisp in clean, yet stained, olive pants and work shirt.

"I liked that cracked gutter. I wanted to keep those shingles, not some cheap replacements. Who said we needed to seed the border garden in front?" Leilani's voice shakes. Her degree of fury surprises them both.

Rocco quickly assesses and stands his ground. "Weather report says the first major rain is on the way. I was worried about drainage from the roof. I thought getting in early seeds might be worth the while, what with rain coming."

"That's my house. I don't want repairs and flowers."

He settles into a kitchen chair, gesturing for Leilani to do the same. She stays on her feet, arms folded. "I can't stand back and watch the place fall apart. A certain amount of maintenance is necessary—especially if you plan to sell," he adds, putting her on the spot. "House goes on the market this spring, right? Big home sales in the spring."

Two can play this game. Petulant, she wants to hurt him for no specific reason. Maybe in Victor's name. Who knew what drove the poor boy out.

She sits down. "What was I thinking? I have to get used to the idea of change, of improvements. Speaking of which," she says slowly, "my Dad is going to rip out the buckthorn. He's a zealot about erosion along the river, you know. He finally convinced me that a small fence would be better for the backyard."

Rocco doesn't look the least bit upset. He nods. "Good idea."

Leilani notices the dust. The room isn't grimy enough to repulse, just not tidy. A faint stale smell comes from dishes too long in the sink, garbage taken out at the last minute. The counter tops are cluttered. Cecile kept pale purple canisters of flower and sugar and salt on display. Seems as if Rocco uses the table to store old bills. Cecile used food as a centerpiece, cookies or apples or peanuts. Leilani hadn't known her well—they generally spoke of gardens, neighbors, and the irregularities of newspaper delivery, that sort of thing. Proximity, not temperament, made them intimates. No matter how casual, conversation took place in kitchens, porches, or backyards. They stood in bathrobes (and in Cecile's case, curlers twice a week) on Sunday mornings, chatting as they each retrieved morning papers.

"Ask him if he'll rip out mine, too," says Rocco suddenly. "As long as the bulldozer's here. We should keep things uniform. Run the fence along both backyards, the way the bush grows."

She's hurt and irritated. Didn't he offer to serve as guardian, to protect and maintain the home front? Where's his commitment to continuity?

"What would Cecile say," she wonders. The words burst out, unbidden. Yet she's glad to have the issue out in the open. She drew a line in the sand: here, shall we tread upon the graves that lie between us?

"She'd say go ahead. Time's come," he replies, without hesitation.

"I don't think so. She depended upon that bush for privacy. How can you be so sure?"

He shrugs, uncomfortable. "Guess I still try to predict her. Sort of helps me if I get into a sticky situation. I ask myself: what would Cecile say? After so many years, I generally know the answer."

"Oh." Her mood, always ungovernable, plummets. The most she thinks of Will is to wonder why she rarely thinks of Will. She resents his every breath. She hates him for the accident. She hates the way he held a steering wheel and was lax about checking the rearview mirror. How many times did she tell him not to change lanes without signaling? A more attentive driver may have swerved in the right direction.

More proof of her poor character, post-accident. Another mother and wife would be calling Sergeant Garcia every day, not once a month. Nobody is tracking that red pick-up, as far as she can tell. She'll never know whom to blame. Any activist worth her salt would be dialing up Mother Against Drunk Driving or scuttling to some legislative hearing about the way the road was paved or drafting a bill for a new speed limit. Once again, Anna's right. She's rotting away. Chalk one up for Will while the tally's being taken: isn't rotting the epitome of self-absorption? Forget how others feel, forget the good work one could do. Let's roll in the muck. Let the real Leilani step forward: the loser.

She fights back unexpected tears. She is the one who doesn't deserve to live. Not Holly, beautiful and innocent! A child's existence demands genuine altruism, the ability to love without expectation. Is this not the perfect life? She lays her head on the table.

Slightly horrified (although not entirely surprised), Rocco watches his houseguest lose herself. Where is her family! Those people should be trailing her in cars! They should be monitoring her every movement. That Carmen down the street finally stopped by, yesterday. More aware than he'd given her credit for, she explained she was keeping her distance. Her daughter made the situation difficult.

Rocco knows about reminders. Framed photographs fill the living room. A handful of pictures are too painful—not the public ones, weddings and anniversaries and such, but selections from early years when the camera captured something intimate, the Cecile he originally loved. Her eyes shine, vulnerable, confident of years ahead. He has been able to look at those pictures once, long enough to realize the magnitude of loss—not his, but Cecile's.

He sighs and stares into the top of Leilani's head. Home repair! Some help he's been. Her new nearly catatonic state reinforces his ineptitude. To live is to carry the greater burden.

He nearly jumps when she lifts her head. "Do you talk to Cecile?" she asks him, urgently.

Her left palm is bleeding. Rocco notices the red arc her fingernails have made, digging. He hadn't bargained on this when he opened his back door to the new young neighbors, six years earlier. Helped them plant trees and move furniture. Now he's in over his head. His arms begin to itch at the thought of discussing Cecile in more detail. Yet he can't stand back and lose another.

"I talk to her," he announces, awkwardly and too loudly. Despite himself, he checks the room for men in white coats holding hypodermics, bearing toward him.

Leilani nods, as if this was the most ordinary thing in the world. "Does she talk back," she asks, resignedly. She already knows the answer, is already disappointed.

"You could say so." He can't risk saying more. These days, Rocco opens his heart to Cecile in a way he was unable to when she slept beside him, breathing.

"I don't feel a thing," she says quietly. "I think about Holly all the time. Constantly. I never feel her. I never talk to either of them."

She puts her head down again and cries. She remembers: the left side of Holly's mouth curled up when she smiled, exactly the way Will's did. Her sobbing becomes rage. Who set up this system, where we all lose everybody we love, each last one?

Is crying good or bad, Rocco wonders, uncertain. Is he supposed to touch her? His hand hovers uselessly above her head.

When she finally looks up, Rocco freezes, unprepared for the hatred he finds in her face.

"I'm late," she sputters. "I have to go." She stands up and sprints, as if the past ten minutes—important developments to Rocco—had never occurred.

Confused, Rocco holds open the door behind her, watching her storm away. He stands there after she's gone, longer than he needs to.

Inside the car, Leilani kicks and pounds and cries, release of the thousand unbearable emotions that have come to define her. Spent, she finishes with her head on the steering wheel, red and wet.

Carmen watches from her driveway. She bets Leilani is taking up her daily station, spreading herself across that damn seat for the next four hours. Enough is enough. Carmen starts down the block.

Leilani's car screeches to a start and sails down the street—gone.

Tomorrow, Carmen will be ready. She will break a few emotional barriers of her own and wait for Leilani on the front steps or stage a backyard ambush, whatever is required. There is worse suffering! The thought steadies her. She resolves to watch the evening news and read the most wrenching articles in the paper. There is worse suffering: the starving scrape the ground for food before they squat in the same dirt to die, millions of them.

However, her own luck doesn't make her feel better—indeed, good fortune appears to be part of her problem.

Speeding toward Minneapolis, Leilani cries for Rocco, dully and steadily. Poor, sweet, old man! Deluded enough to believe he holds a connection to those who've gone. Maybe he secretly hopes Victor is alive. Does he talk to his son as he does his wife? Rocco lost exactly what she did: a spouse and a child. Who better than she to help him come to terms with reality? She will find Victor. Death records are public domain. She'll follow the lead of good-spirited (if simple, she can't decide) Mr. Van Eyck and search the past decade. Victor Crea is within driving distance. She can feel how close she is to answers.

Parked outside the Hennepin County Courthouse, Leilani attempts to reorganize her appearance into something resembling a solid citizen. Unfortunately, she sleeps in her clothes (pajamas are acquiescence to sleep). Spitting on her hands to wipe away wrinkles proves ineffective. A strained, gray face stares back from the rearview mirror: pass the death records, please. These eyes could attract attention. Fresh clothes and lipstick are her only hope.

Money simplifies matters. She leaves the lot for Marshall Fields. Striding in on all that life insurance, Leilani heads straight to the Oval Room, arena of personal shoppers and eager attendants. Half an hour later, she emerges linear and non-threatening in coordinated creams and pale blues. The salesperson couldn't get over her good fortune, a client who didn't look at a price tag and requested cosmetics to boot. First garbage can Leilani sees, she tosses the bag with her old clothes.

The courthouse is airy, a hundred feet of windows and rails and open spaces. Each floor rises up and around the park-like center at the bottom. An easy place to fall, observes Leilani. Administrative types buzz by above her, unaware of—or accustomed to—the fact that they're inches away from death. A pale freckled young woman leans on a rail and watches people below. She has strawberry blonde hair.

Leilani used to yank Holly away from the river bluff. She didn't let her daughter use the green stairs climbing the cliff. Holly begged to eat at the Carousel, a rotating restaurant on top of the Radisson Hotel. Leilani never took her. Holly asked to ride the Ferris wheel. When you're older, Leilani said. She looks back to her daughter's life and hears: no!

The girl on the railing has slanting cheekbones and slim elbows. She has been allowed to live to see twenty, maybe twenty-two, so far. Leilani estimates that she's spent that many years of her own life denying desires—hers and everyone else's.

How many times did Will put Holly to bed—even after he'd been with her nine hours—so that Leilani could get grading done by a decent hour? Holly fought for Leilani's presence. She didn't have to demand Will's, he was there without asking. Leilani handed over that role with relief. Children ask for more, regardless of how much they're given.

The young woman reluctantly releases herself from the railing, walking away and into an office. Leilani moves on, too.

After many false smiles, she finds herself in a brightly lit basement room, in front of an ancient computer. Nobody looked at her twice or batted an eye at her interest in Victor Crea. How we die, and when, is public information. A crabby clerical worker shoved instructions for the computer in her hand and unceremoniously ushered her to the appropriate machine.

Leilani braves a furtive low-lidded look at the other people huddled into screens, wondering what tragedy or job or prurient interest drew them. Half are well-dressed (like she is, she realizes with a start), reporters or government workers, commenting or keeping track. The rest wear jeans and less sanguine faces; these are comrades in a different search, she can feel it.

The man next to her gives his monitor a significant slap. Tall, with curly and possibly uncombed hair, youth allows him to wear the rumpled look she was forced to abandon. Momentarily envious, she remembers the sea of faces she's taught over the years. They were exactly like him—earnest and well-fed, casual in their confidence. Each poised to be crushed by life, harsh and efficient. Who would ask to live through that twice?

"You'd think they'd have upgraded beyond the late eighties," he says, politely apologetic after being caught banging official county property. "Bet city workers don't use these dinosaurs."

"Probably not," she replies noncommittally, imagining herself a news anchor forced to do her own grunt work, and therefore, put out on all levels. You walk a fine line with such celebrity: the unwashed masses must be simultaneously courted and kept at bay. Stolen identity appeals to her and shimmers through her thousand-dollar ensemble: I am prime time news. By the time she unravels the mysteries of her own machine, the young man has abandoned his for another. Precisely what stardom commands: contact, no matter how minimal, is the last thing she needs.

Within minutes, she learns that no death certificate for Victor Crea was ever issued—not a surprise. The John Does hold the key. She spends four unwavering hours in front of the snapping electric blue screen and ends up with results similar to Mr. Van Eyck's: a handful of men without identifying markers, without age. Victor could be one of six. While not particularly patriotic, she experiences a small surge of pride for her nation, letting a mere six slip by, as opposed to the greater number in Holland.

Still, she has six. Only one of the numbered Does could be Rocco's son. She sits quite still, listening to the lights buzz and contemplating the printout in her hand: John Doe Number Four. Rocco's? He was somebody's child, a portable pack of baby who morphed into a boy and died early. We lose each other in countless ways, daily. She looks up. The room is full of new people; a fresh frowning face has replaced the one formerly working counter. Plan B? She'll try Ramsey county, maybe Anoka. Call operators in each area code to inquire about listings for Crea. She realizes how much she'd been counting on Holland to do the job. The image of Victor as savvy enough to travel the world, only to die stupidly, held tremendous appeal.

Leilani uses the drive to Macalester to perfect fantasies of Victor's death. Today is a drug-induced haze and subsequent bathtub drowning, a spectacularly stupid demise. The image breaks new, more personal ground.

"Heroin," she say out loud, surprised. "Why didn't I think of that?"

Her own overdose would be tragic. Questions would fly. After all, one just doesn't become an addict overnight: her family would be second-guessing behavior that stemmed a decade past. Then they would be as busy as she is now.

Unfortunately, heroin has inherent problems, including the entire issue of locating and purchasing the drug. She has a hazy image of potential street corners and an even less unformed idea of how one actually gets to those corners, let alone signal (to whom, the man conveniently standing in the shadows?) that she's prepared to do bad. Pleasure is also a stumbling block. Heroin has its moments, or so she's gathered. Euphoria is not on her list of priorities.

Legal drugs, however dull, are more efficient. Certainly, there's a combination that will string her out in a terribly unpleasant way before killing? She hums. There are prescriptions in her purse for Buspar, Valium, Xanax, and Prozac, each given by doctors early on. Succumbing to the hospital chaplain's continuing concern and her mother's resolve, Leilani had found herself under the concurrent care of two doctors, in addition to her own family physician. Margaret pressed pills upon her—some herbal and others more potent, a mixture of mood soothers conveniently on hand, a fact that disturbed Leilani. At this very moment, Leilani has pills rolling around the bottom of her purse, yellows and pinks and oranges passed to her by well-meaning friends at the funeral and afterward: Mebaral, Nembutal, Halicon and more. Prescription drugs are not only effective—they are already quite convenient.

At the Macalester exhibit, she sets aside the question of her own demise and luxuriates in the actuality of others'. Leilani doesn't care that the paintings aren't necessarily of real people. The men hauling munitions, bodies, and tents are as real to her as anyone. She unobtrusively leans the portfolio against a low black bench and loses herself in the oceanic. Those Navy painters! A prolific bunch, they favored larger-than-life landscapes—replete with flames flying off ships and hundreds of men bobbing in the sea like clams, hard hats floating round and worthless as buttons. She can feel the chill in her own bones; smell the brine and blood and smoke. One more time she wonders: is this the noble death?

Tentatively, she touches Three Dead Chinese Soldiers, her favorite of those done by Ruben Kadish. The heavy frame shifts easily. She jiggles harder: the painting is barely fastened! A college student probably did the job. The girl sitting outside the gallery door is bent over a textbook. All involved are probably amateurs —a status she shares when it comes to stealing. The one other person in the room is a man taking copious notes in front of Tom Lea's famous painting, That 2,000 Yard Stare. The soldier's gaze is pop-eyed and fixed, the vacuous look of the traumatized. Well, don't we all know the feeling, thinks Leilani, suddenly irritated by the mountains of pity one anonymous man has warranted over the years.

She shimmies up to the wall for a look at the mounting. Convenience, not security, seems to have guided the curator's decisions. Simply lift the frame off the hooks? Could the job possibly be that easy? Her index finger slips behind the frame. Nobody notices her explorations. Standing squarely in front of Three Dead Chinese Soliders, she experiments with shifting the painting a hair. Heavier than anticipated, the glass square nonetheless wiggles side to side with ease. The man taking notes continues, moving to the next painting. Another man enters. She jumps from the wall to reclaim her spot in front of the Kerr Ebys.

By the time the exhibits closes, Leilani still hasn't decided.

Eby's perspective is gloomily authentic. His men are roped and sinewy, their limbs heavy and flat faces resigned. Kadish offers a colorful plum of a painting, thick Chinese men that look like babies, suspended outside of fight and feeling. She simply cannot pick. Both views are equally important; either one impossible to leave behind. In the end, she walks out, empty-handed—as usual.

The student at the desk waits for her to leave, jingling the keys more absent-mindedly than impatiently. Maybe Leilani's disappointment is visible: the young woman smiles politely and hands her last patron a pamphlet.

"I see you here a lot," she explains. "You might be interested in this."

Leilani is not pleased. Are all the student workers aware of her regular presence? Perhaps they consult. They know her habits. So much for invisibility. "Thank you," she mutters.

Ten feet down the hallway, the pamphlet is halfway into a garbage can when she notices the cover art—striking and sorrowful. A tiny Asian boy stands in a circle of squatting, screaming men. He holds a hatful of money as his elders cheer on two dying pit bulls, jaws locked around each other's necks. The men are steeped in rage and greed. The boy bears the heart of the painting. He takes up the burden of his fathers, young. Attention captured, she scans for the details: some newcomer named Yang Lee, at that pretentiously informal gallery downtown.

She slips the pamphlet into a pocket; the girl was right. She is interested.

11

DELPHI

Even though it's lounging time for the under-employed—a weekday afternoon during one of the warmest springs on record—Evelyn doesn't hesitate to close her café. She slaps a sign on the door the instant I arrive. We bring strong coffee and scones to a table, where we wait for stragglers to finish their croissants.

"Where's the dashing young man?" She holds her spoon as a professor holds a pointer. She spins the tool, appraising her pupil over the edges—except, instead of surveying me with the sour look favored by Gaines, she practically bobs out with enthusiasm.

In the reality of a brisk business-like Monday, she's too fairy-tale typecast to be true. The spun glass hair, the long white fingers, tulip sheen skin. She can't weigh more than a hundred pounds, soaking wet—quite a feat for somebody who slaves over baked goods all day. And dashing young man? Puh-leeze. Shock may have reduced me to putty that first afternoon. Maybe my attitude is adolescent, but today, I plan to call some shots. Not that I don't have questions—my stab at a séance illuminated a fair share of weak spots in my telepathic repertoire—but I think an agenda on my terms is required.

"Ian," I emphasize with authority, "is going to meet me here. We split the morning between courthouses, trying to find death records for that girl I told you about. He took Ramsey and Hennepin, I hit the suburbs."

"Find anything?"

"What do you think?" I ask, guardedly.

Evelyn puts down the spoon. "Honey, I know you're suspicious. The only way to find out whether or not I'm a fraud is to throw down the gauntlet and see if any heads roll. Jump in. I'd tell you to trust me, except you're light years away from that."

"I'm not exactly suspicious, I'm careful. After all, this is foreign territory—"

"—and you don't want to get burned." She nods sympathetically. "I promise to do my best. I was in your shoes once, you know."

"You were?"

"The circumstances were different. The uncertainty was the same. I was about your age when a friend brought me to an astrologer. The woman who did my chart told me that I had yet-to-be-developed psychic skills that should be put to good use."

"Were you surprised?"

"I was more excited than you are. I needed that astrologer to be right!" Evelyn laughs, ruefully. "Boy, did I have a romantic idea of the so-called psychic life."

I've harbored a few daydreams of my own. A small pleasant scenario has unfolded in my mind's eye: me wandering through a trim, lovely house to the spacious, and expensively furnished home office where I counsel clients with other-worldly advice. My fantasy feels placid, like landing the dream job at some unusually nice federal office: a steady income in comfortable digs.

Evelyn continues. "Hanging my shingle as a psychic was a stab at glamour. I wanted to hold all the cards, so to speak; to reign, to wield the power of knowledge!" She waves her arms expansively and kneels on her chair, the way children do. "Of course, this is five years of psychotherapy speaking. Like most people blessed with a little talent and even less self-discipline, I tried to create a larger-than-life persona as a way of escaping the realities of my own existence."

"A therapist? Here I thought shrinks were to be avoided at all costs—one word about communing with dead children and I'd be headed for shock therapy."

"True. Traditionally trained psychologists are dangerous enough to slap on a diagnosis and never think twice. That's their problem," she sniffs, pulling at her hair. "Those people are a singularly unimaginative group, assuming a science of the mind holds all answers. So yes, stay away—far, far away."

I'm confused. "What makes your doctor different?"

"Believe me, I didn't call the AMA for recommendations. I hooked up with a local who works in energy, oils, and soul. He started out as a Jungian and saw the light, thank God. He's a spiritual therapist. Last I heard he added gemology to his roster. Hardly your average shrink." She smiles.

"Hmm," I mutter noncommittally. Spiritual therapist? Tinkerbell travels in unique professional circles.

The lingering patrons finally wander toward the door, Evelyn close behind, keys jingling. She locks up and turns to me. "I wouldn't worry about therapy yet. You have a few more mistakes to make before you're ripe."

Well, that's reassuring.

"Plus, your unconscious impulses will be different. I craved center stage, adoration. You'll want something else. Let's hope that your subterranean desires attract less trouble."

"Any ideas what those desires might be?"

She winks. "That's where the surprises come in."

I hate it when people wink at me—especially in the course of a serious conversation, like one about my life! Time to reclaim control, set that agenda. "What if someone comes in and asks for an official reading. Aren't the hidden drives—life's larger meaning—exactly what you're supposed to discuss?"

"This is different." Her tone softens. "You've got to understand that you're wound up in my drama, now too. You're going to be a good psychic, exceptionally good. I'm mediocre. My job is to set you on the path and provide some basic guidelines."

"Might somebody else step in to offer me answers you can't?"

"Highly likely," she smiles.

I press in a different direction. "And how am I part of your story?"

Evelyn tosses those light lithe hands of hers, fairy-dust style. "You're sitting in part of my story, dear. I bought Crystal's when I downgraded my expectations. Clearly, I was a better realtor and bookstore owner than psychic—not only in financial terms, but psychologically. I'd be a wreck for a week before a big reading. Inevitably, I'd end up doing only half the job I should've done. I never let on—no, I billed myself as the Madame Curie of clairvoyance."

"For example?"

She rolls her eyes. "Heavens! Let's see if I can pick one that makes the necessary point." The way she stops to mull for a full minute makes me worry. Her list of errors is a tad too long. Finally, she pulls one out.

"I'm great at seeing occupations, which is why I nailed the realtor gig for myself. That's why I goaded one poor woman into medical school. I laid the hooey on thick, how being a doctor was her destiny. I was deluded enough to believe I had a grasp on the omnipotent thing. Did I bother to ask for her input? Of course not! I saw healer and went straight for the big guns. She suffered three years of anguish before calling it quits—newly saddled with a sense of herself as a failure. Then there's the guy who divorced his wife on my wise counsel. I was having a flip day, waxing philosophical. Told him that there was no such thing as soul mates and if there were, the wife would not be his. He went off the deep end. Not that I was wrong. He wasn't ready and I should've known."

She sighs, sets her pale pointed head in those icicle hands. "Those aren't the worst mistakes, just examples of harm rendered by a bit of knowledge and a boatload of ego."

Admittedly, I haven't yet contemplated the consequences of dishing out advice. Yet I'm instinctively annoyed with these people. Who in their right mind would forfeit thousands of dollars and years of life on the career advice of a single psychic? Where was this husband's free will?

"Caveat emptor," I argue. "Let the buyer beware. You offered advice. Nobody was forced to act upon that."

"You underestimate the power some people place in psychics—and the power I claimed to have. They believed me as wise as I thought myself. We were all wrong. That happened again and again."

"I'll write up some kind of disclaimer," I say, impulsively. "A legal way to get myself off the hook."

She shrugs. "The legal costs aren't the ones I'd worry about. There are more significant prices that most of us pay."

"What were the price tags on your fiascos?

"I sobered up. Got myself into AA and—don't look so horrified, please. There's no bottle hidden under the table. Alcoholism does not warrant that leper-like response firing up in your face. That's better, even if you're faking. Anyway, I sobered up and began the altogether unpleasant process of assessing my real strengths and weakness, without exaggeration or undue shame. I decided to cut back on craziness of all types. I trimmed my real estate goals, bought the café, and relinquished psychic consults to a pastime. Now I read for friends and acquaintances, take the occasional paying client that someone sends my way. I don't pretend to hold the key to anyone else's life."

"Except mine," I blurt out, unnerved by her various confessions.

"Yes," she says simply. "I have something more significant to offer you. Caveat Emptor."

Wound up with my own welfare, I don't tiptoe around her feeling. "Sounds like that astrologer steered you wrong when she waved her magic wand. You fell for the act and returned the favor to that doctor wannabe."

How many of Evelyn's life changing recommendations have crashed and burned? I'm supposed to have faith in somebody with half-baked gifts and a fully realized addiction?

"I prefer a more generous interpretation. The astrologer was right about my talents—they're here. However, I took her initial impressions and ran in a direction that wasn't necessarily right. My job here is to make sure that you don't do the same. Sometimes mistakes are preparation for a larger calling. Maybe you're mine."

Maybe. In my experience, people pay dearly for their mistakes, period. That whole silver lining concept is highly over-rated. I plan to avoid creating the muck in the first place.

Breezing past my stony face, she shifts into speed and air and elfin optimism again. "Let's get to work," she says happily, taking my hands in hers and squeezing. "Believe it or not, I do have a few things to teach you."

Guard a good deal higher, I turn myself over to her tutelage. After all, I'm here. Some dead kid is haunting me. Things are not normal and my options appear limited.

We spend nearly two hours steeped in things esoteric. The discussion ranges from life after death (in its various bizarre forms as outlined by Evelyn) to the practical problems raised by poltergeists ("Try concentrating with lamps flying straight for your forehead," is her cryptic comment) to relaxation tools valued by psychics the world over. Much to my surprise and discomfort, a fair amount of prayer pops up: pray for safety, for guidance, to serve the greater good, to retain integrity and seek truth. We discuss ominous figures, including the one I saw, and how to avoid them.

"Yell!" says Evelyn.

"Yell?"

"Sure. Stand your ground and holler: go away."

A general discussion of evil ensues. Evelyn sides with Meredith and Joshua. Evil exists in a more malicious form than my father maintains, yet is surprisingly easily banished. Once again, yelling comes in handy. Don't forget to bathe yourself in white light. Ride harmonic energy waves. No question, Evelyn is part of the 'love conquers all' school. She next shares tricks of the channeling trade, including the ups and downs of merging with spirits, which is what she thinks I did ("draining and not always necessary," is her assessment) and introduces me to the concept of spirit guides. She swears mine will become important.

"You'll talk to your guides as easily as you talk to me."

"Seems highly unlikely. I have no inkling such creatures exist."

She smiles knowingly. "What would you call the High Court? How about those girls from your childhood—Jane, right? Don't worry—your guides will take a more distinct and age appropriate shape, soon. You're still gelling!"

Involuntarily, I touch my hair and straighten my shirt to counteract my growing sense that, far from coming together, I'm falling apart. Poltergeists, spirit guides, and greeting committees for the dead? This is the framework in which I'm supposed to build a post-college career? To think last week I was aiming for any occupation more conventional than my father's.

Just as I think things couldn't get any weirder, Evelyn veers off into a short history of mediums, my new lineage. Not that anyone harbored much hope I'd be one of Daddy's dharma heirs— but this? Evelyn posits herself in a post-Spiritualist era, lecturing me on the debt we owe those great nineteenth-century mediums for popularizing (and somewhat legitimizing) communication with the dead.

"Of course the Spiritualists had their limitations," she says. "Hard to imagine any contemporary medium tolerating the whole ectoplasm issue."

"Ectoplasm?"

"Another word for slime, my dear. Slime that purportedly oozed out of a medium's orifices and hardened into the body parts of the spirits they were contacting. You'd get a random foot or hand, sometimes a head or whole body coming out of your nose or mouth or ear. The stuff smelled like ozone, or so they say." Evelyn wrinkles her nose.

I'm officially nauseous. And orifice? A bit too broad of a categorization for any acute imagination, thank you.

"Don't worry," she sympathizes. "Nobody's recorded any ecto-sightings in quite a while. Hot topic in the 1800s, though, when mediums relinquished control of their bodies to spirits. I think we're safe."

Possession is not part of any job description I plan to wittingly pursue.

"Okay then," Evelyn slaps the table and moves on. Her teaching style leaves little room for questions borne out of insecurity. "We've covered more territory than I'd hoped for in a first session! A final point and you should have enough time to make your shift at the gallery."

Suzanne's! Once again, practical concerns that used to consume me have vanished from my radar. I look at my watch. Where in the world is Ian? I can't imagine that searching two counties, even major metropolitan ones, could eat up an entire day.

She pauses to insure my attention. "Lesson to remember: a good psychic suspends her own needs in the service of others." She leans back and folds her arms, as if parting the Red Sea, for heaven's sake.

"That's all?" I ask, incredulous. "That's the day's major message?"

"Uh-huh—such sacrifice is much harder than would seem on the surface."

"Not if you were raised as a Buddhist," I smile, smug. "There is such a thing as selfless service, you know. Loving kindness and all that. We're trained to give, give, give."

"And do you?" she asks significantly.

I shrug. "Sure."

"Do feel free to interrogate that answer a bit, my dear. From what I understand, Buddhists—all the devoutly religious, for that matter—struggle mightily to balance the demands of the self against the needs of others. We succeed and fail, more and less, in cycles over again."

"Would you include psychics in your list of the devout?" Just my luck, to stumble on some quasi-religious order, when I can hardly wait to escape my own.

"The good ones." She doesn't miss a beat.

I sense another lecture brewing. We should all be Mother Theresa, blah, blah, blah. What a shame Evelyn brought up the time: must flee for the gallery.

"Okay, I won't forget—do good, vital lesson," I smile the edge off my impatience. "Evelyn, you're right about leaving. I have to drive through rush hour traffic. Amanda has a class on Monday nights, so I shouldn't be late."

She jumps up. "I expect to see you again on Thursday. I'll worry if I don't," she says gently.

We say good-bye on the sidewalk. Ms. Effervescent waves right up to the moment I shut the rustmobile's front door. A final glimpse out the rearview mirror catches her on the sidewalk, chatting with a passerby. Snaring a new one?

Maybe I'm schizophrenic after all: leery and enthused about the whole spirit quest. Sure, who wouldn't want a leg up on all sorts of information, from other people's secrets to what happens after we die? On the other hand, am I actually accepting advice from a self-proclaimed failure? She seems sober enough now (and I looked for evidence to the contrary), at least for someone pulling strangers off the street to discuss extrasensory powers. I wish Ian had been here. If I didn't know full well that Amanda's itching to leave, I'd wait for him. His absence better be a sign that he stumbled onto something vital, and not a more ominous note.

Traffic is horrible, stop and go the entire stretch between Uptown and St. Paul. The drive takes three times longer than usual. Amanda is probably furious. Turns out, she's gone. When I finally arrive, late, the reception desk is empty. Thankfully, there's only guy in the gallery, pacing and pulling at his watch—killing time before a date instead of enjoying the view, I'd guess. No sign of Dad, either. I fully expect him to pop in at some point since he smells trouble. Considering I haven't eaten dinner, I wouldn't mind to see him slinking around the corner with a tray tonight.

Amanda left me a pointed note: don't be late on Mondays. Okay, I'm sorry! I do feel badly. Not only did she gracefully take over weekend duties, I see a stack of books and magazines neatly marked for my attention. The gallery receives dozens of publications weekly. We even score gorgeous coffee table books in the hopes that Suzanne will toss them on her tables—or better yet, solicit work featured inside. Amanda and I preview material. She's prone to taping balloon commentary on the worst pages, a bubble critique of the terrible, trendy or pretentious. Even though Amanda's a little flighty (we've never been what I would call friends), I appreciate her sense of humor. I can't think of a better way to unwind than to entertain myself with a new set of books punctuated by her quirky worldview.

Half an hour, two guests and one phone call (to Meredith, who hasn't heard from Ian, either) later, I settle in for serious reading. Even though Meredith was unconcerned about Ian—he's notoriously unavailable, she says, whatever that means—I am.

All this discussion of death makes me morbid. Before I hit art literature, I leaf through the newspaper. Although I don't plan on reading the obituaries, I scrutinize each entry. Most of those listed died in their eighties, with a couple nineties tossed in. These people go in glory. They joyously meet their Savior, are happily Called Home. Look at the obit for the poor guy who keeled over at forty-two and the language differs: Thomas L. Kramer was taken. Snatched, I think. He left behind three young children. No glossy language about God here. I put the paper in my lap and imagine Kalya, Jack, and Kevin. Daddy has vanished into thin air. His wife's name is Belinda. Even in ten short lines, desperation seeps through Thomas L. Kramer's final paragraph. Will this be my future, the needy and bereaved? I see myself coddling an endless stream of seekers who can't say good-bye to what they've lost—not because they're necessarily weak, but the loss is truly too tragic to bear. Let's not forget Evelyn's examples: I can also fail at career and marriage counseling. I'm thoroughly depressing myself.

I turn toward the books and magazines. Don't fail me now, Amanda. I need a good laugh. Check my watch—nearly 7:00 and no Ian! A small group filters in: two thirty-something couples, confident and impeccably dressed. Potential buyers. I smile coolly before ignoring them, as any self-respecting gallery girl would.

One oversize book bears a post-it note with a smiley face and balloon message: see table of contents. The cover photo is a succulent pear, a lipstick-ringed bite in its round belly. The book is still prepublication, making the round for reader reviews. Food art. Even before I reach the table of contents, I guess why the book is tagged: Mom is one of the featured photographers. Her work pops up over the years, often in the best (in my humble opinion) publications.

This go-round, Mom focused on Indian street vendor fare, one of her favorite topics: mangos, coconuts, dahls and yogurt concoctions. She likes to capture delicacies in their demise, as they actually appear, rather than in the smooth studio state of staged, commercial work. Thrilled, I discover a photo of the artist herself! There's my Mom, smiling in a box at the bottom of her page with a tiny bio.

According to the blurb, Lisa Weisman is an artist and yogi best known for her presentation of Bombay's streets and their food, and for capturing the spiritual essence of asanas in black and white prints.

As the last lines come clear, my arms start to shake: "After nearly twenty years in India, Ms. Weisman has called a 1908 San Francisco brownstone home for the past two years. Her new challenge: to capture the culinary chaos of this great American city as beautifully as she's captured that of Bombay."

My heart pounds and shreds in disbelief. San Francisco!

I scroll the book jacket frantically for clues: the book focuses on Californian cuisine, with local artists taking the shots. Here she is: Lisa Weisman, a relatively recent and highly welcome addition to the West coast talent pool.

Is someone saying my name? Or am I about to faint? The walls—gorgeous slabs of color—twirl and lurch, Yang's children leer, monsters. This could be what death feels like, or a heart attack at least. Yes, I hear my name. I can't look up from this page. Must find the phone! The thought shakes my density and sickness. I knock through the stacked books to find the receiver. This cannot be happening. Her letters are postmarked Bombay. My mother writes about shopping at the bazaars of Mumbai. She jokes about the Aneja's, her next-door neighbors. She rides an orange bike through Bombay's loud, winding streets.

"Dephi!"

Ian hangs over the counter, face glassy with excitement. "Jesus, what's wrong? Delphi!" He waves a fistful of paper. "The girl! In the past three years there were five that fit the bill. I may have narrowed down enough to—Delphi! What's the matter?"

I pick up the telephone.

"Talk to me!" commands Ian.

"San Francisco," I dutifully respond to the computerized voice. "Lisa Weisman."

A real person comes on. "Here's your listing," he says, as if such a thing were not only possible, but oh so mundane—a listing for Lisa Weisman in San Francisco! I write down the number, her number, and then jab out the real numbers—without a plan, moving on shock and instinct.

And rage. Rage is what I feel when she answers. "Hello?"

Ian listens.

"Hello?"

I hate myself. I start to cry at the sound of the voice I've never heard. Warm rich voice, real body. My mother holds a phone that's not a three-day journey away, only a few hours. There's no doubt that this is my mother. I feel the truth this moment holds, as I did with the dead girl and her mother, dancing.

Music plays in the background. Lisa Weisman's voice, husky and confident, trails off as she disconnects. "Nobody," she says, against the arc of a question, a man's voice stirring behind. Someone is in her house. Or gallery? Is the man business or something else I don't know?

I hang up, unable to take my eyes off the telephone. What other secrets has she kept?

Ian moves to my side. "Hey, what's happening?" he asks, kindly, touching my hand.

Nobody—that's what she said. I'm nobody to her. Isn't the country you live in a sort of fundamental fact, information you'd offer to the most casual acquaintance or editor of some coffee table book?

I meet Ian's eyes and pull away my hand. I see the degree of concern in his face, a willingness to stand by my side that goes beyond being a good buddy. Well, we all get our hearts stomped on today, don't we? Without a word, I leave the gallery and walk down the hall to Moon.

Dad isn't in his office. I check the conference room. I peek through the square windows on the door to the Great Hall. My father and students share pillows on the floor, legs crossed and eyes closed. Even as a toddler, I knew the rule: no entering during zazen. You wait at the window until the bell rings.

I open the door, speaking loudly as I step inside. "Dad! I need to talk with you right now." I am not in the mood to mess with decorum. Breaking one boundary, formerly solid and indestructible, is my first step toward freedom.

The steadier students remain motionless; the distractible peek or jump outright. Daddy's eyes open. His response is instantaneous: one glance at me, and he folds upward to stride to my side, with whispered instructions a senior student. We step back through the door. I see Ian, waiting in a corner.

Daddy turns to me, a man who can sense when his child is in danger. "Tell me," he says quietly.

"Did you know that Mom's been living in San Francisco for two years," I ask, evenly, as much statement as question.

The surprise registers. "San Francisco? Are you sure . . . " he starts to say. As he looks at my face, the lines of his own transform with grief. "Oh baby. I am so sorry," he says, arms outstretched, the folds of his robe flowing like wings.

I snap out of reach. "I don't believe you!"

He stops, surprised.

"I don't believe you," I say, quietly, walking past him and Ian, up the stairs and toward the loft.

I do believe him. He didn't know.

He committed worse sins! I want him to suffer for taking me away in the first place—want them both to know that I'm not playing their parental game any longer, the way they set the rules and ran my life. I hate them both. I hate my life, the lies and the myth that somebody loves you when they don't.

I lock the door and slash the deadbolt, hard, to kept Daddy out. He and Ian, on my heels, are stopped in the hallway.

Daddy doesn't pound. He knocks as normal. "May I come

in?"

You two get to know one another, I think meanly: suffer. I throw clothes in a suitcase, march into the bathroom for essentials. I have a credit card for anything else. Better yet, I'll take one of Daddy's. Let him tally the costs. The thought of stealing pleases me. I go into his room and pluck out plastic from the wallet on the dresser. Now someone is pounding, not Daddy's style, even in a crisis. Knock till your knuckles bleed, Ian.

Back by my own bed, I hesitate. The letters.

I want to stomp away from them, too. I can't. Instead, I stoop down for the beautiful black box. The polished wood is smooth and cool, the single solid connection I have to my mother. I want to be angry enough to leave this behind or smash the box into a thousand jagged splinters. I'm incapable of such destruction. The box goes inside my suitcase.

Standing in front of the door, I listen to the subdued voices on the other side. Sounds as if the two are engaged in a steady exchange. What has Ian told Daddy? Nice to meet you, and by the way, your daughter's a voodoo queen. I don't think the Zen Master and New Age theory will mesh nicely. Doesn't matter. I don't particularly believe in either, anyway. How tapped into the Universal, or whatever trendy phrase Evelyn uses, can I be, strung along on a lie all these years? If there's one lie, about something so basic, there are others.

Is she remarried? Does she have other children? I know nothing about my mother. I've been in love with letters.

I take a fortifying breath before unbolting the deadlock for my exit.

"Leave me alone!" I hold out a hand against their movement.

Oh, they've filled each other in. I can tell by their faces, each fuller and wiser. Ian's earlier excitement over whatever he found has been replaced by worry.

Daddy takes the lead, completely calm as usual. "Fine. Any idea where you're going?"

God, I wish he would scream and rip off the robes! Something! Throw a fit or swear like the type of fathers my friends complain about. No, I get Mr. Sedate—monotone for a lifetime. Fine, he says. What secret has he been keeping? Let's not forget that he withheld the truth about their breakup for a decade. I can't trust either of them.

"No idea."

"Call and let me know where you are, please."

"Maybe," I say haughtily, moving unsteadily toward the elevator. I do feel decidedly unstable.

"If you don't call within twenty-four hours," he says, matter-of-factly, "I'll file a missing persons report. I will do my best to get your face in the newspaper and on television. You decide if that happens."

I hum to block out his voice and jab the elevator button furiously. Stupid, archaic machine!

Ian takes his turn. "Listen to me for a sec," he says, quickly. "I found a four-year old girl who died in October. Get this: her father's dead, too. They were killed in a car accident. Hennepin County was a bust, total drag with an ancient computer system that was practically garbage. I found records at Ramsey for three girls. I checked the weeks of each death in the newspapers. God, it was incredibly easy! Scoping the papers was a whim, a total whim, and there was a whole story about the accident! I have three possible names—and a really good feeling about the one. She was Holly and her father was Will Hibbon. Holly and Will Hibbon. What do you think? Ring a bell?"

When I find my own apartment, I will make sure the elevator operates efficiently before signing any lease. I refuse to so much as bat an eye at him.

He grabs my arm, much harder than he should. "Hey! You have something important you're supposed to be doing. You can't leave now."

The elevator opens. I look right at him. "Get a life, Ian. Stop hanging on mine." I heave my suitcase in and press another button. The metal doors close to cut us off.

"I don't care," I say to myself as the elevator drops silently, the words thudding against the small square box.

I get in the rustmobile and drive.

First, I torture myself by stopping at Ian's, sitting in my wreck of a car to stare at the warm mansion. Lights are on everywhere and the curtains already pulled. Meredith and Bill are probably helping kids with homework and filling brown bags for tomorrow's school lunch. I almost ring the bell, but think better. Meredith is exactly what I'm craving. She also too much to bear.

Wendy holds no appeal. She's hated her parents for years. I can't stand to hear her say, 'told you so.' Evelyn? A real friend would have given me warning. What was her big talk about responsibility—act in service of others? She failed miserably by her own standards or she had no idea what was ahead. She's either a hypocrite or a terrible seer, not just mediocre, as claimed. I add her to my list of people to loathe.

The phone number burns in my coat pocket. More torture: I

can't stop thinking about her voice. What has she been writing all these years? Listen and you'll find me at your side. Will she know me? I'm here, Mom, on the other end of the telephone—can you recognize me by listening to the silence we've been sharing all these years?

The thought circles and dances, then possesses me. Should I call her again?

I head to Grand Avenue and the pretty, well-lit night. The street is pleasantly full, people in bars and cafés and small shops, sharing spring's abundance. I should give her a chance! One chance. She can prove she didn't lie about listening. Walking up and down Grand, every pay phone is empty. I resist. I can't stand to call. Can't take the risk.

I dissolve shortly before 10:00 pm. The public phone in front of Café Latte is clean and well-contained. The paper shakes in my hands. Ringing. My throat catches.

Once again, the lyrical low voice. "Hello?"

At least I get this word, one round vowel sound, to remember. She's confused. "Is someone there?" she says, not unpleasantly.

Now I know what prayer is. I will myself across the wires, across the country, into her hands, eyes tearing with effort. Mommy: it's me, Delphi. I would give her another chance—if only she can take one step toward me, on her own. Please God. Anyone. Let her say my name.

"That's strange." She talks to someone in the background. The man? She hangs up.

The betrayal is sealed

No magical connection binds us. No instinct. I laugh out loud,

216

a stranger to myself.

A small boy on his way out of the café hears me, and moves closer to his own mother. Take what you can get, kiddo. Maybe she hits him.

Time for the bluff.

The Mississippi runs cold. Brisk air rises from the water. I walk on the west side, away from downtown and wanderers I might know. The buildings look fake, a bright theatre set. I'm high enough to be eye level with the bright banks of light and steel, directly across the river. Could I reach out and touch a window? Seems ten feet, not the wide waters, separates us.

Tomorrow the sun will rise on May Day, hoopla for socialists and ambitious mothers. I know a few of the latter from Moon. Forgoing the Christian menu, they greedily grab onto other, acceptable celebrations. Their offspring, budding Buddhists, will drop dainty May baskets on doorsteps tomorrow, full of candy and bubble gum and stickers and spring pink ribbons.

I've been the beneficiary of other children's overzealous mothers. I've collected my fair share of May baskets and other trinkets. There was always at least one woman at Moon—and the sanghas before—who recognized what the priest's daughter was missing. Each gave what she could while still running the course of her own life. A comfort, yet never enough: no, a woman stops herself, mid-stream, when she becomes a mother. She redirects and surfaces anew, guided by the currents of someone else's heart. The idea is miraculous, I realize, an abandonment of the self by anyone's standards, yet an act the world turns on every day. Removed from the cycle forever, I see both its gifts and perils.

Eventually, the night air whispers colder, darker secrets to me.

I watch the black river run. A sense of solitude forms a hard edge over my despair: yes, I know my place in the universe. I stand, alone, dirt and air and water around me, pretending I can see real starlight through the glare of the city.

Near midnight, I warm up for a few minutes in the car and turn on the radio to reinforce what I already know. Life buzzes around me, unaffected and unchanged. I even get the BBC, thanks to public radio. I listen to London's crisper pace for a few minutes before grabbing the lighter I picked up along the way. I sort through the suitcase for the black lacquer box and make my way back to the bluff's edge.

I burn her letters one by one. Surrounded by newly greening brush, I sit before my impromptu furnace and watch twenty years of ashes pile and cool. Now I have the strength I lacked earlier. I need no one. I'm more tired than I ever thought possible. My eyes flutter against their will.

The small fire warms my face. Do I see a child in the flames or am I facing the river? The world blurs and fades. Am I still awake? Girls rise up to wave hello. The shadows they cast aren't a consequence of sunshine, long gone. No, their losses have turned black, have been taped to their ankles and glued into the crooks of elbows. Each wave trails its lonely echo. My girl stands in the center, eyes green and hand open. Her sadness extends to me. Her presence is comfort. She asks nothing of me this time and I reach out, another child falling asleep along the river, a new shadow.

12
LEILANI

A red letter day! Real progress to mark on the calendar! First, Leilani stumbles upon a cache of pills, a veritable clinic—right in her parents' home. The few pills Margaret had forked over were the tip of the pharmaceutical iceberg. Leilani's best guess is that her hyper-vigilant mother is constitutionally incapable of tossing supplies. What if somebody needed penicillin on Christmas Eve? No need to fret or phone a physician, Margaret could march upstairs and save the day.

There are twenty years of remedies inside the upstairs hall closet, liquids and pills and lotions for high blood pressure, gum disease, constipation, diarrhea, sinus pain, strep throat, ear wax, insomnia, anxiety, depression, athlete's foot, acne and internal yeast. She finds steroids and blood thinners. A sharper, and somewhat unsettling, picture of her parents emerges. She had assumed that her father's stoicism and her mother's steel will extended to their internal organs; in fact, their arteries and airways and digestive tracks are clogged and caved. Knowledge is the price she pays for the Ziplock bag of pills, a potent variety of colors and shapes and sizes.

The second breakthrough comes in a parking lot. On her way into a pharmacy—her third, filling prescriptions—Leilani slams the car door on her fingers. However heroic, the damage was unintended. As the door swings, she has a split-second sensation of fingers wrongly placed and an instant in which to yank her hand to safety. She doesn't! For the first time, she's able to take advantage of random opportunity. Her eyes shut against the motion of the door, against metal's weight and pain.

Leilani smiles into the sound of steel meeting skin. Her daughter never, ever got her fingers chopped by such machinery. No—Leilani always pulled that tiny hand at the last minute. Holly knew the dangers of cars, parked or moving. Leilani smiles for the pale and pretty child who disembarked from a parked car with hands cautiously balled into her belly—a child who took her responsibilities seriously, no matter how small. Leilani laughs, low and lovingly, as pain rips through palm, up arm, and into shoulder.

Her injury draws the attention of the pharmacist, who insists on selling her an antibiotic cream. The two smallest fingers of her left hand are already hugely swollen and purple. The pinky droops to the side.

"You say that just happened?" the pharmacist clarifies.

"Uh huh," replies Leilani, still stunned. The thyroid! Talk about low expectations. Maiming gets the real results.

"Ma'am?" says the extraordinarily young pharmacist. She is a quirkily pretty woman, whose linear cat-eyed glasses (pink and jewel studded) and crisp hair hint at a life far more interesting than a bland white smock and cubicle of ointments and pills. Where does one purchase such eyewear? How can a woman this young—and wearing orange lipstick—command such authority?

"In the parking lot. I shut the door on my hand. Accidentally."

Competent and concerned, the woman peers through the boxed window. "One of those fingers could be broken. You popped some blood vessels, for sure. Right there." She points to the bulging sections of veins on two fingers, her own hands a rainbow of bold rings. "An x-ray couldn't hurt. Put your hand on ice for the night, take a couple of Tylenol and call your doctor in the morning." She nods and gives Leilani her Xanax, taking enough care to give real punch and drama to the standard speech on the drug's potential for abuse.

Leilani nods, taken with the quality of the throbbing in her hand, deep and bulbous and steady. Remarkable how much this hurts and how easily pain can be borne. She remains cogent enough for appropriate replies to the pharmacist. Leilani even follows the woman's instructions, obediently leaving with hand held upright. The younger woman's professional demeanor extends into the parking lot, where Leilani continues to walk as if under scrutiny. The pharmacist took her meager toehold on medicinal authority and ran with it, dishing out directions like a doctor. Leilani remembers similar performances in her classroom, when she was the picture of intellectual purpose. Was that an act, she wonders? Or did she believe what she was saying? She honestly can't remember.

Behind the wheel, she shakes her arm violently, teeth gritted against the shears of pain. She steers with one hand. Delight curls in her belly and lifts the corners of her mouth. A line has been crossed! New energy unleashed: finally, she feels pathology! An electrical system of crossfire and bad intentions ricochets across her muscle-skeletal system and severs nerves. Rules the rest of the world follows slip further away. Not only able to inflict pain—she surveys the thick, bent fingers—she is enjoying every second of the aftermath! The tautness of her abdomen means her kidneys are finally malfunctioning. The razor-like stab in her throat signals esophageal ulcers! Spontaneously, every fiber, each cell of Leilani's body reconstructs itself. You hear of mothers who lift cars to save children. That strength is hers now. She is capable of real harm!

Elated, she doesn't even mind the dearth of downtown parking. Every space within a block of the Suzanne Strauss Gallery is taken. No art gallery, no matter how prestigious, attracts such a crowd on Monday nights. The new coffee and wine place next door must reel them in. On her third swing around the block, a space opens up. Probably one of those Buddhists, she thinks, heading home early. Moon on Mountain Zen Center has been a downtown fixture for the past decade. Leilani can't think of a bunch of people she'd rather see less than the beatific. Hopefully, there's a night crowd to counteract goodwill—frat boys out drinking, single women in clusters at Spar, the young professionals whose wardrobes exceed their incomes. She'd take anything other than true believers.

There's no cause for concern. Spar and the Suzanne Strauss Gallery flank the first hallway of the huge warehouse. The Zen Center must be buried deep inside: not a single serene face in sight. Indeed, the elderly woman guarding the entrance to the gallery greets her with an expression that's nearly hostile. Gray-haired and grumpy, the woman thrusts a brochure at Leilani before trotting halfway down the hall to peer around a corner. This place should rethink its policy on senior citizens, Leilani decides, fully prepared to hate every second of her experience—until she sees the paintings.

She finds Holly in every frame.

Leilani sinks into the closest couch, derailed. She surveys the room in amazement. Who is this artist? A man to rival her war heroes, that much is certain. She glances at the brochure: Hmong? His look is the decidedly cautious Minnesotan hip, urban yet incredibly clean-cut. Handsome—and too young to understand, much less convey, such emotion! Yang Lee smiles in black and white from his back page photo, nobody special, a man she might stand next to at the grocery store.

You wouldn't say his paintings feature children. They're there, Asian and usually under ten, tucked into the sidelines. As such, they constitute the Greek Chorus rather than tragic hero, a mini-morality tale. Their bodies bear the brunt of the world adults create. In one, a girl assists a much older woman giving birth while a cluster of small children look on. Three men eat and drink in an adjoining kitchen. Eyes are initially drawn to the dichotomy between the laboring woman and laughing men. A harder look is required to truly see the children. Holding the baby's bloody head, the girl's eyes comprehend much: miracle of new life and what she will sacrifice, young.

The adults in the paintings pass time: they wait, resigned, at a pool table, for their dog to win, baby to be born, bus to arrive, groceries to be packed. The children are the ones living. Morning Egg reels in Leilani, hard. Set at the popular outdoor Farmer's Market, women haggle and gossip in groups, brightly woven baskets brim with vegetables, flowers, and herbs. Even the smooth-faced among them are maternal and tired. A pink sky signals that these are the vendors, at work by dawn. Hanging on a mother's skirt is a peanut of a girl, intelligent eyes full of freedom and hope. You can barely see the child. When you do, you know: this girl will go far. She is somebody! Miraculously, impossibly, generations of ambition and rage are visible in the tilt of her chin and cheek.

Leilani's general desire for destruction is replaced by a surge of admiration—pride not necessarily for this Yang Lee, who, alone, means nothing to her—but for the whole of humanity, the genius that is art. Reason enough to live, she wonders, caught in the memory of what used to move her: a lush Degas exhibit at the Met, that Bulgarian choir touring through Minneapolis, an Elizabeth Catlett sculpture. Maybe Leonard Cohen's Hallelujah? Sarah Vaughan, singing anything, doesn't matter what.

Yet her experience of the sublime rests upon the very relationships that torture her. Holly sat on her lap at the Bulgarian concert, mesmerized by the guttural harmonies and foreign chords. The glory of the music folded through mother and daughter, together. Will introduced her to Hallelujah one tipsy, candlelit evening early in their marriage, making her promise to play the song—sung only by Jeff Buckley—at his funeral. 'When I die at ninety-two,' he had quipped reassuringly, his fingers under her chin, their faces an inch apart. He'd been forty-four when the song brought two hundred people to tears at her parents' Catholic church. She can never again lose herself in the music her own life had unfolded upon.

The telephone brings the receptionist back into the gallery. Still spry, the woman half lays over the desk for the receiver and barks out a loud 'hello,' rather than the slick salutation Leilani would expect. She takes a second look at the woman's imperious expression and expensive casual clothing. Those shoes—in the air, as the woman is now sitting on the table—are pretty fancy footwear for a receptionist's salary. Understanding dawns: this is Suzanne Strauss, aging artist and gallery owner of considerable fame. Considering the sculptor's truly terrible manners (she glares under Leilani's scrutiny, pointedly plopping about on the table to turn her back), Leilani wonders if Ms. Strauss shouldn't rethink her hands-on office policy and banish herself to the studio.

Leilani speculates that if she had the wherewithal to create something—anything—she might find an urge to survive in that act. Such impulse died a long time ago. Looking back, she's not sure why. Ms. Strauss snorts into the phone and waves her arms. Listening in an offhand way, Leilani gets the drift: problem with the hired help. This may not be the artist's usual tour of duty.

Morning Egg! Leilani looks back into the girl's black eyes. She smiles at the curl of the child's fingers into her mother's skirt—the softness and vulnerability of that slim hand contradicting the command in her face. She loves this painting, even as she understands that bearing witness to someone else's vision will never be enough. Unbroken, the child in the painting throws out the challenge: do you have this kind of courage?

The phone slams down. Ms. Strauss pulls at a baggy pant leg and makes a beeline for the hall. Leilani walks cautiously to the doorway in time to see the artist turn a corner.

Heart rate accelerating, Leilani circles the gallery and waits. She leans back into the hall for another look. Finally, she walks the corridor, monitoring her watch and peering around the corner into a maze of more hallways. Signs direct visitors to various studios, businesses, and the Zen center. The one person Leilani sees is a plump teenager, scuttling from Spar to a photography studio. When six minutes pass, common sense sends Leilani back to position in front of a painting. What business owner leaves her wares unattended for more than five minutes?

A full nine minutes go by before Ms. Strauss pops her head in to check on tens of thousands of dollars of unguarded art.

She's gone again, that quickly.

Leilani calculates and projects. Ms. Strauss is not interested in reception duties. The water's been tested: her absence meant nothing. Confident, she can be gone longer and longer. There is a body in the shop, well dressed, middle-aged, and female—hardly a threat, indeed, a deterrent to crime. Only the boldest of thugs would steal with a credible witness milling about. Yes, Leilani will have more than nine minutes. Ten. Eleven, if she's lucky.

One last look down the hallway and she gently closes the door. She slides the lock. No bells or alarms. No patrons rush from Spar in a panic. Go for the purse, the miniature screwdriver and jackknife wrapped in plastic. Not much. What does dismantling a painting require? She'd selected the tools at a drugstore, anticipating the theft of Kerr Eby's darker work. But the curl of this girl's hand! This, she can't release.

Less than a minute and Leilani is busy with her screwdriver. Seems to be some type of permanent mounting on the walls? The trick is to ply off the painting, the secret in the sturdy wires on the back. She pries and pulls and tweaks, annoyed by a sweaty neck and shaky hands. Unable to move effectively, her injured fingers slow her down. She's clumsy. So much for assuming a cool, criminal stance.

Two minutes, three minutes, four. A final pull and the frame falls free! Success surprises her—she practically drops the massive painting as it slips downward. What a roll! What a day! Raw energy whips through her, pushing her onward without hesitation. She can do anything! Canvas and frame are incredibly heavy. She half carries, half shoves the thing to the door, which she unlocks, and pushes half an inch open. Not a soul!

Luck makes her giggle, giddy. She closes the door and, full of confidence and leisure, takes one full minute to straighten her hair and slow her pounding heart.

If she'd only brought the portfolio! Improvising, she gently drapes her coat on top of the large square painting and begins the journey to her car, lugging the canvas to the best of her ability. Thank God she doesn't believe in high heels. She wonders how Anna manages, stumbling around on stilts at work and continuing the torture on evening errands with tiny children in tow. Six minutes. The painting nearly tumbles down the four short steps at the front of the building. The swollen hand definitely hampers her progress.

"Need some help?" Two well-scrubbed young men—the air around them a veil of cologne and glycerin soap—stop on their way inside the building.

She hesitates. After all, she looked harmless, too.

"It's okay," reassures one, reading her silence. "We can pick that up and have it in your car in two minutes—if you're not parked too far," he adds, polite even in qualification.

Nobody rushes out the front door in search of a missing masterpiece.

She resigns herself to irony: allow the chivalrous to aid and abet.

"Right there," she smiles, pointing to her car halfway down the block.

Four uneventful minutes later, Leilani is driving down West Seventh Street, Yang's hard work wedged against back seat ceiling.

"Morning Egg," smiles Leilani, imagining the empty space above the painting's placard. She loves the sound of the two rotund words together, the way that description could fit any girl, fresh and whole in the world.

Deviance thrills. The internal force unleashed has left her pleasantly powerless, driven by urgency that borders on the hysterical. Now, now, now, wails the siren song, mysterious. In the past months, she has turned every corner and has found nothing to hold her. The sweat and heat of Suzanne's have not subsided. Veins bulge with blood's pressure and face flushes. Aberrant hormones, she hopes. Fingers and toes tap, tap, tap, body alive with energy. Yes, the tide has turned. One must bow to Fate.

She sings a lullaby Holly loved:

Tender Shepherd, Tender Shepherd, watching over all His sheep.
One, say your prayers and two, close your eyes. Three, safe and happily,
fall asleep.

Leilani's cello-like voice reverberates through the car, all butter and spice. Born to sing—that's what every choir teacher proclaimed, what Will had said in admiration, what the college theatre director maintained when he offered her every female musical lead. What a diaphragm! The high school choral conductor hated to see her graduate: colleges can pick their talent, the lower levels must pray for a miracle every year.

The car edges to a stop outside of her parents' house,

curbside. A miniature caterpillar bulldozer is parked in the driveway. Some job for her father, she thinks. Could be the fermenting buckthorn roots at her own house. She half regrets impulsively approving the job, then foisting the consequences on Rocco. Improvement is the last thing her property needs. The image of the entire lot overtaken, sinking downward in river muck or quicksand suits her.

When was the last time she sang? Having searched for countless 'lasts,' she can't remember tracking this one. Holly loved to dance. Only a four-year old girl in a tutu can turn commercial jingles into theatre. Her daughter understood music's call to movement and complied. Hum a little tune in the bathroom, the grocery store, the doctor's office and Holly's lips pursed like a rock star breaking for her dance sequence. All focus, she moved as space allowed, shimmying shoulders in an elevator and turning the jaunt up the school sidewalk into a two-step, hip hop on her face and in her heart.

The last song was in the kitchen. Some classics station on a Rolling Stones binge played Satisfaction. Unloading the dishwasher, Leilani sang along. Holly rushed from the living room to grab her mother's hands. They spun, feet bare on wood warmed by the afternoon sun. Maybe that song had a particular magic. More likely, Leilani was feeling benevolent—rare, by then, considering tensions with Will—but those were four good minutes, unmarked by anything other than pleasure with each other. After the song, Holly trotted back her dolls, sated. Leilani returned to the dishwasher. Strange how death molds memory: if Holly had lived, that afternoon would have died, one day lost among many. They didn't have countless days to accumulate after all, mother and daughter.

That was the last shared song.

"Eleven hundred and one," says Leilani softly to herself. Those are the days they were given. Her breath clouds the windshield.

As she exits the car, Seamus comes into her awareness. He's leaning behind the bulldozer, wineglass in hand. Now California-fragile, a sturdy cap and wool scarf compliment his spring jacket. Leilani smiles: the minute the thermometer climbs to forty-five, college campuses across the state fill with eighteen-year-olds playing Frisbee in shorts.

"Hey, you." Seamus stretches behind him for a second glass sitting on the engine. "Join me?"

She hesitates.

Feigning casualness, Seamus sips wine and pretends not to monitor his sister. He theorizes: her pause indicates that she understands his intent. After all, why would he possibly sit on this wretched piece of machinery in inclement weather (any day without sun qualifies), unless he's lying in wait for his sister, yearning for that heart-to-heart.

Leilani considers. Alcohol hasn't interested her much. Perhaps that's been part of her problem. Why not? Maybe she'll stop at a liquor store and grab her own bottle for later. She turns toward her brother.

Victory! Seamus smells progress. Tonight could be their breakthrough.

Leaning next to Seamus, Leilani forces herself to light a cigarette. Despite Surgeon Generals preaching for decades, Leilani could never quite get in the addictive swing of the things.

Seamus whistles. "How'd you get the Frankenstein fingers?"

"Car door. Accident. And no, rushing off to the E.R. isn't on my list of priorities."

Not one to rush to hospitals himself (he once broke an ankle and waited till the swelling scared Jim before consulting the doctor), Seamus nods.

"Nice outfit." Try a compliment.

She shrugs.

He toys with his wineglass; Leilani tastes. They stare into the slate gray sky. Dusk on a cloudy day doesn't bring spectacular sunsets, only cold. Night hisses at their ears, hinting of a season not long gone and certain to return. Seamus wonders why his sisters chose to remain in a climate defined by cold. Minnesotans gauge the rest of the weather against winter: therefore, every miserable rain-filled autumn or slushy spring can still be a winner. After all, the temperature's above zero!

Accustomed to disappointment, the raw weather calms Leilani. Her neck is cool—chilly even, with the wind—and her hands have stopped sweating. Half of her wine is already gone. The internal spin, the rush and shake of the past hour, has subsided. If she believed in symbols, or God, she would say that Seamus was placed here for some higher reason. Poor sweet Shay. He always holds someone's secrets. Everyone knows he remains his mother's confidant. Leilani is certain that this is as much burden as gift.

Seamus mulls over possible pathways into his sister's psyche: how are you doing, Lani? Or wait—how are you really doing, Lani? How are you doing? No, better to be direct: I'm worried about you, honey. Yes—an endearment is perfect. Of course he must use an 'I statement': I want to talk to you. He sighs, each sentence a vine butting against a brick wall, useless. Infiltration requires the durability of time. Jim arrives in two days. They leave two after. How can four days dent the lifetime of pain dished out to his sister, forty years too early?

Leilani solves the problem of approach. "Do you believe there's something out there for us after we die, Shay?" she asks, suddenly.

He's unprepared for such immediacy. What answer to soothe? How to convey his concern? Connect to Holly and Will? "If Catholicism is right, sure. Everybody's in Heaven or someplace less pleasant." He grimaces, unable to resist positing whole groups of evangelicals into the latter.

"That's not what I asked. What do you believe?"

"I asked Dad this question once, you know," remembers Seamus.

"You're kidding! Did he give you some version of St. Peter at the gate? When in the world did you ask him?"

Seamus laughs. "No, the eternal beauty of Heaven speech would be Mom's. Dad had a much darker view, which he was happy to offer. I asked him when I was about fifteen, pondering the big questions—before I came out, when Dad still felt his duty was to mold me into manhood. He has a dust-to-dust vision that does not include any soul soaring upward. We're mulch. Nothing more, nothing less."

"He was always looking for quality mulch," says Leilani, softly. "I can just hear him saying we're worm rot. Probably why I never asked him anything important. I was afraid of the answer."

"He's a realist."

"And you? Don't forget to answer my question: what do you think?" Maybe he can offer an advance description of her destination that she can finally believe.

"We continue. I don't know in what form, but the spirit goes on."

"Hope springs eternal in that heart of yours, Shay. How can you be sure—did catechism pay off or did you have some kind of awakening?"

"I didn't put much stock in the nuns and have never had any sort of spiritual awakening—the opposite, actually. My faith comes from confidence in intellect, I guess. Can centuries of great thinkers be wrong? Not just the theologians we know and love, Augustine and Martin Luther and that European bunch, but the shamans and monks and medicine men of the world. God is a bizarre concept to create out of the blue. Yet some of our best brainpower has chugged along in service of an idea, nothing concrete! What a tragic joke if all that labor was based on myth or psychological impulse. I'm a left brain believer, Lani, banking on my fellow man."

"Good. I was hoping for answer that moved beyond blind faith." She addresses her brother as a particularly bright student.

"What do you think?" Seamus is totally taken with the conversation, Leilani's plight momentarily suspended. His whole life, he's been unable to resist a curiosity or puzzle that's crossed his path—an endearing quality that somehow leaves Seamus, and the people around him, feeling better.

"Maybe five percent of the time, I believe in life after death—souls, Heaven, and all. The other ninety-five percent, I'm with Dad."

"No! Not mulch!" Seamus exaggerates a reaction to take the edge off his own pain. How she must suffer! Like most gay men, he knows his share of people left behind. He's seen the difference between those who believe the beloved lives on, and those who do not.

Leilani nods. "Annihilation. One minute you're more than alive—you're the center of the universe. Your own mind is the origin of all thought, emotion, physical sensation! Then nothing. I wouldn't even compare death to sleep. We're annihilated, gone. Eons of life continue, billions of years. You and I, the people that stand here and talk and think and feel—this is all we get, and it could be snatched from us any second. Sometimes I try to imagine not being, to prepare. Used to scare me into a near coma when I was a kid."

"You've felt this way since then?"

"Always."

Seamus takes one of her cigarettes. "That is spectacularly grim, sis."

"I know. You don't smoke."

They stop talking. Fears from adolescence rise quickly in Seamus, who, despite knowing better, vividly entertains the horrors of abrupt cessation.

Leilani realizes that liquor stores are either closed or will be soon. She'll have to raid her parents' supply. Good hosts, George and Margaret have a bit of everything on hand. No scotch or whisky for her, however. Her stomach clenches at the thought. In college, she'd played a game involving hard liquor and backgammon that forever soured her taste for both.

"I better get going," she says, tipping her glass for the last drop.

"Oh, don't! I really want to talk to you, Lani. I've been so worried!" There, the plea pours out of him spontaneously and truthful.

"That's nice!" Knowing Margaret sent Seamus, she appreciates hearing his own concern expressed with such feeling.

"Nice? Let me fill you in on your role at this moment. You are to acknowledge misery and outline specific steps we can take to lift you out of the morass; or, you assure me that you're rather mysteriously fine, and that massive depression and suicidal tendencies are actually average personality traits we've been misconstruing."

"No need to get testy."

"I'm not testy," he says firmly. If he doesn't stay sharp, he'll cry. "I'm worried and short on time."

"Aren't we all," she laughs.

"See? That's the type of caustic attitude that makes talking to you impossible—and scares the shit out of Mom."

"That's her problem. I don't set out to trigger particular emotions in people. I'm trying to figure out a way through each day."

"And doing a laudable job. How much sleep did you get last night?" He feels himself hammering now.

"I'm forty-three years old. I'm not going to answer that question."

Frustrated, Seamus barely catches himself from a knee-jerk retort. God, he's terrible at this. He takes a deep breath. "What can we talk about then? Can we talk about Holly and Will? I miss them too."

Distance, intractable and unforgiving, reshapes the contours of her eyes. The sound of their names hurts her physically. Cold floods her chest. Too tired to continue this game, she takes a full minute before answering.

"Maybe I should go home," she says slowly. She allows the rift between them to grow farther.

Seamus startles. Did he hit a nerve or do some good? He must proceed very, very carefully. "Okay," is the sole response that seems sufficiently non-threatening.

"I'd planned to be here tonight. Home would be better. I'm glad I thought of that." Her voice is stronger, more confident.

"Well, great!" Seamus is encouraged. "I'd love to keep you company! Please?"

"Oh, I can't," she says, somewhat distracted. "I need to be alone. Actually, I should go now. Are liquor stores still open?"

He checks his watch. "Nope."

"Let's go see what Mom and Dad won't miss."

They head to the small wine rack in the dining room. Seamus considers which wine would suit such melancholy. How frightening his own trim bungalow would be if Jim died! He pictures himself sitting on the floor amidst clothes and photos, nursing a cabernet, aged and throaty. Of course, his parents possess nothing near the quality.

Despite his prodding, Leilani picks up a non-descript chardonnay.

"You're joking!"

"White wine is easier to drink," she insists.

They part on pleasant, even hopeful, terms: Seamus gratified that his sister is at least taking significant action, even if confronting whatever demons await her at home was the last thing he expected her to grab for, so quickly. What progress! With

Leilani in the car, he taps the window of the Honda before it pulls from the curb.

"Call," he says loudly, an afterthought. "I'm sleeping by the telephone!"

She smiles. Seamus stands in the street and waves good-bye.

The accident site is her first stop. Yes, the grass continues to thicken and green. The guardrail shines, impenetrable. Not one stitch of evidence that two people died here. Parked on the shoulder, she treks to her spot and sits. She waits, as usual, for sign or apparition. As usual, none come. She listens beyond the city grind of cars and airplanes and sirens, in case the message is auditory. Nothing. She closes her eyes and tries to open her body to her daughter's spirit. She prays. She meditates. She begs: please. All she feels is a light breeze and chill. Every day, her father's perspective is confirmed: Holly no longer exists. She sings Holly's lullaby anyway, as a gift for what is now, for her, hallowed ground.

Fifteen minutes later, she pulls up to her old home. The house has totally absorbed the aura of abandonment. Not neglect—Rocco has seen to that—but emptiness. Not a single sign of day's spontaneity or life lies sleeping in the yard. From the sidewalk, the darkness behind the windows feels permanent. Leilani stands at the edge of her small, square front yard, wine (already opened and recorked) in hand, purse over her shoulder, and painting at her side.

The house isn't empty. Each room is stuffed with memory. Dishes are stacked in the kitchen. The pantry is full of stale food. There's a pretty green wool hook rug on the other side of that door. There are cheap homemade bead necklaces, sequined art projects, glue drawings, Barbie sleeping bags cut from worn out pajamas, a dead ladybug collection, non-toxic nail polish with a vegetable oil base, and alphabet flashcards with all the animal drawings on them cut out. There are three broken watches in the right hand dresser drawer, two Stephen King novels tucked next to the rose armchair, five overdue library books (history, politics, parenting), a package of new guitar strings, stacks of simple sheet music to seventies pop songs, binoculars for bird-watching, and coupons for money off countless items—all carefully clipped and filed in small (previously used) envelopes.

Leilani stands on the sidewalk, shaking. She may be hyperventilating—hard to tell, yet she's forced to consciously suck breath, slowly. Maybe lack of oxygen helps winnow her focus, maybe fate plays a hand—God? She is able to imagine their old bedroom as clearly as if she were inside. The amber comforter is freshly washed; her favorite turquoise earrings are on the nightstand. A lifeline, she refuses to look, to think, to feel beyond the bed. Get to that bed! She can cover herself with blankets that smell like Will and put her head on her own pillow to sleep without fear. The rest of the house disappears.

The front door unlocks easily. As she steps on the hook rug, the house roars to life, tempting: look here! See the photo on the mantel, the child-safe scissors in the kitchen, the blanket Margaret knit for your last birthday! The walls swell and scream. Breath and feet become anchors for her eyes, refusing, for her mind, locked on the bedroom. The heft of canvas and frame steady her. The painting demands attention and strength. She moves purposefully up the stairs, dragging Morning Egg, face straight ahead, inhaling and exhaling loudly. This is the rush of a hurricane, then—the terror of the gale that overtakes the senses. Ignoring the howl takes a kind of energy and pull that she didn't know she possessed. Panting, she is in Holly's room. The ratty pink cat blanket glows and beckons, the one item visible on her radar.

She starts to cry the minute she picks up the blanket. Edges frayed, cotton fingered thin, white kittens dingy. No! She can't afford to let the iron curtain fall, the focus fail her—not yet! Frantic against the storm, she uses her good hand to slide the wobbling frame on the wood floor, scraping down the hallway toward the master bedroom. Holly's blanket is on her aching arm.

She meets her goal—their room, her own room! The most peaceful place in the house, the calmest colors: pearls and creams and pale browns. The queen size bed, pillows neatly plumped, sits in the center of the room. She can hear the din in the distance, Holly and Will singing in the dining room as Daisy barks at the back door. With a grunt she hoists Morning Egg on the long dresser and falls onto the thick comforter, Holly's blanket balled into her belly. The room spins. The wine! Meeting the girl's gaze, unblinking, she drinks straight from the bottle and shakes open her purse. Thirty pills pool onto the bed. Getting them all into her mouth requires four handfuls and as many gulps of wine.

Leilani gasps and laughs, astonished. Terror flies through her for a few seconds: the death grip of the dreams, the sound of dirt sealing you in forever. As quickly, she finds relief. The battle is over! A luxurious calm descends, the peace of sound decisions. She has made the right choice. Gratitude allows her to take her eyes from the painting and notice the two shirts on the back of the armchair. Anna left the closet half open. Will's one working watch and a pile full of change sit beside Leilani's earrings on the dresser. A stack of magazines clutters the floor by the dresser. Everyone in the house tripped over that pile, daily.

She figures she has about thirty minutes. An hour? She smiles into the smell of Holly's blanket and settles in to enjoy her first sound sleep in months, a pure night, free from the fear of waking. A child's courage hangs on the wall beside her, and she follows.

13

DELPHI

Lisa Weisman has thick skin and no caller ID. She actually answers the phone to speak with 'nobody' four times before turning on the machine. I use an anonymous calling card rather than Dad's Visa. Not that I'm unwilling to rack up charges. I want to remain untraceable. Just like her. I stock up on fuel when I buy the card: Big Red gum, three Diet Mountain Dews, a pound of M & Ms, and a bag of potato chips—Ruffles, my favorite. Defiling my body seems superbly appropriate—besides, I could use the caffeine.

Her answering machine is perky and to the point: Hi! Lisa here. Leave a message.

I make sure to establish a solid connection and honor the tape with a few beats of dead Minnesota air. I hang up and check my watch. Nearly 3 a.m. Oh my – what was I thinking? Waking poor Lisa Weisman this way. If the soul is indeed reflected in the face, she needs every second of her beauty sleep.

I try to pretend I'm not freezing. Hop from foot to foot, then up and down on one to maintain circulation. Why couldn't Dad have fled to sunny California and let the fabulous Ms. Weisman call the hinterlands home?

A car drives up to the Blockbuster at which I'm positioned. A young woman, smoking a cigarette and a little shaky, slips a movie in the drop box and throws me a look that says I'm crazy. Well, yes, I am hopping. Plenty of harmless wackos roam Grand Avenue—enough that Dad has allotted them a category, complete with acronym: Grand Avenue Crazy, or GAC. Maybe I do fit right in. One wrinkled old man rides a highly decorated bicycle (Snoopy stickers, balloons, crepe paper, army banners) up and down Grand for hours, searching the gutters for cigarette butts and cans to recycle for cash. A thirty-ish woman hides a tiny terrier in her jacket as she moves from one pricey coffee bar to another. There's an underground culture among counter workers in this high-rent district. GACs are well fed. They have options for shelter in cold weather and hard rain.

I don't need anyone's pity or second glances. I set both feet solidly on the ground, picture of dignity and self-respect. The woman slams a car door shut, fast, as if I might make a move in her direction. Does returning videos in the middle of the night make her particularly sane?

Rain.

Perfect. Now I'm cold and wet, thanks to the lovely Lisa. Let's ring her again, shall we?

Ms. Weisman must be getting tired. The phone is off the hook.

Such self-restraint. Avoidance, even. Not once did Weisman scream or threaten. Maybe the yoga angle was true (yes, let's recategorize everything she's told me as angle, device against genuine interaction). Earlier, she called for peace into the quiet line.

She even said please. Once Billy Boy—that's what I call him—
answered. He picked up past midnight, California time. If this guy
is all about business, she must have an all-night occupation I never
suspected. Who knows how low she'll stoop.

Maybe I don't need those Dews after all. I am sooo wide
awake. My hands shake.

I walk to my car. The parking lot runs along an alley. Security
lights watch over the dumpsters and debris that cast squat
shadows. Where are the muggers when you're ready to take on
those that do harm? I wish I had a gun and justification. About a
year ago, I took a self-defense class. Don't get scared, the instructor
shouted at us. Get angry!! He hollered in our faces and called us
babes and twits. Anyone stupid enough to wear a ponytail got her
hair yanked, hard. Find a hat, he hollered. Long hair is the handle
they use to grab and pull you away.

Now I understand the order. Rage is raw, rich fuel. Rage feeds
every cell in your body and rewires the workings of the brain into a
more elemental machine. Mr. Karate shook his finger in my face
and predicted I'd crumble. I couldn't get riled up over some drill-
sergeant routine performed in the safety of a library basement. Too
bad he's not here to witness my transformation.

Driving is cathartic. The city moves differently at night. In
neighborhoods near the river, animals are out in full force: skunks
and raccoons and all their domestic brethren. I utilize streetlight to
study the architecture of each neighborhood, the density of trees,
and degree of income. I drink all three Mountain Dews, eat the
potato chips and polish off half the pound of M & M's. I sing
along with every song on the radio, even the ones I don't know. I
whistle. I make a conscious attempt to find drive-through root beer

joints. I spit on a Kleenex and clean the inside of my car while steering. Of course, there's chocolate in my spit, which smears the windshield. At red lights I recoat my fingernail polish and wonder why I remain stopped when there's not a single other car in sight.

Somehow I'm on Cleveland Avenue, in front of Daddy's favorite restaurant. Snuffy's serves fountain drinks and burgers. The place has orange leather stools and a counter restored from the fifties. A jukebox stands in the corner and a nickel bubble gum by the front door. My guilty pleasure, Dad would say. Three-hundred and sixty days a year, he's a vegetarian whose sugar high comes from rice soda. The other days he is ten years old. He orders a double bacon cheeseburger with fries and a hot fudge, caramel malt. He gets a salad on the side for the sole purpose of dipping the long, thick fries in dressing: first in Blue Cheese, then French. Dad, ask for only the condiments, I'd argue. He refuses. My father likes the onions on his burgers raw. He puts mustard on a top bun, never a bottom. He always plays the jukebox and hands me a round bubble gum on our way out.

I don't know a single detail like this about my mother.

Lisa Weisman.

How can I even call her Mom?

I'm driving. The off-and-on rain returns. The defroster in my car is cranked. Still, the windows steam and the world outside blurs. I open a window and realize that I'm crying, again. Who's to blame for saddling me with this wreck of a car? My life could be endangered, such poor visibility! Maybe that's what they both wanted. I can picture them now, plotting on some Nepali mountain peak: oh no, honey, you take care of the impoverishment angle and I'll feed her a lifetime of lies.

I'll show them. Not only will I be a success—but a secular one! Money will pave my way, thank you. I'd be a natural at sales. After all, ruthless manipulation is in my blood. When I win the awards for entrepreneur of the year, I'll make crystal clear that the sole person I need to thank is myself. The only charities I'll drop a dime into will feature orphans. Homeless children are my roots. Maybe I can pave my pockets doing something illicit and unsavory, to boot! Serve them both right, those proponents of peace and love who lie.

Back in the land of the loaded, Crocus Hill, I make a repeat loop down Goodrich, Lincoln, and Fairmount Avenues, analyzing architecture again. High style everywhere, from the Victorian painted ladies, to stone fortresses and all-American brick. My grandparents—Dad's side—live in a two-story colonial in Duluth. Somewhere on the planet, I should have another set. How come those people never looked me up? Where are the cousins and aunts and uncles? Lisa Weisman claimed general estrangement. She had that storyline down pat! Give the girl a Pulitzer. Oh, the hints of pain and complexities she'd share later. She's writer, actress and con artist wrapped up in one. Couldn't ask for a more perfect audience: me, the most pathetic, over-eager believer on the planet. I know whom to thank for that set-up. See what happens when you raise children to be pet-loving pacifists concerned with the integrity of all life? They get burned.

Driving down Fairmount, I start seeing beds instead of houses. Four-poster with canopies done in rose or lilac. For the son, buy bunk beds in the shape of ships. He can have sleepovers. Mom and Dad go for a contemporary king-size, done up in brass beautifully enough to fool the neighbors into thinking heirloom.

The pillows will be down and lush. I put myself in a red room, double bed with a pilgrim style headboard and four pillows. No futons, thank you, although I would settle for a waterbed at this point.

I am weak. I park the car in front of Ian's. Not that I plan to actually enter the estate. No, a ritzy residential street is simply the safest place to sleep in a car—and if that mugger does materialize, I'll have some help when I scream. Meredith and Bill would run out. The rest of the upper crust might very well mistake me for a GAC, ignoring the racket while I test out the karate teacher's theories.

I fall quickly, deeply—and very uncomfortably—asleep. My second to last thought is how amazingly little leg space was allocated in such a large car. My last thought: if there's a God, prove Yourself by letting me sleep without dreams.

My first waking thought: I am not committed to any bargain struck with entities. I didn't dream a bit.

Meredith is tapping on the window. She's not smiling. Groggy, I check my watch. Not even six a.m. She's already rounding up the homeless? If I had her bed—king-size with opulent linens—there's no way I'd roll out before eight.

I put my head in my hands and groan. Less than two hours of sleep. I need six, minimum, to feel sane.

"Delphi, unlock the door, please," she says firmly. Expecting compliance, she stops tapping and takes a step back.

This is my chance to accelerate and escape. After all, how many ties do I have to these people? If I never saw Ian, or his family again, we'd all be fine. We're talking less than a week out of our lives.

"Delphi," she says, plaintively. "Give me a break! I'm freezing."

Only then do I notice the sweatshirt and slippers. Her hair is tied back loosely, as if she just woke up. You'd think someone with five children and a mansion to maintain would look tired. Instead, she's bright with immediacy and ease. There's not a dishonest bone in this woman's body.

I start to cry.

Alarmed, she rattles the handle. "Sweetie, please open up."

I do. I open the door and am officially a-goner, practically falling into her kind, strong arms.

She sits right down in the driver's seat and takes command, stroking hair and rubbing my back as she mutters all the soothing, meaningless words of her profession.

"Everything's going to be fine, sweetie, fine," she croons.

I lose her and the rest of my bearings, as the world becomes my mother: liar, abandoner, betrayer and the one person I've craved—a physical, bone-dense yearning—my entire life. My eyes are tiny swollen slits when I'm finally done crying.

Timing impeccable, Meredith pulls away for a peek at my face. "Now," she says softly, "you need a hot bath."

Not an ounce of fight is left in my body. I let her steer me inside and up the shining stairs to the bedroom I used before. She sets me on the white straight-backed chair next to the tub and fills the enormous relic with hot water. I'm handed a towel, bathrobe, glass of water and instructions—soak.

"I'm checking on you every ten minutes," she warns as the door shuts.

In the tub with a washcloth over my eyes, I answer her—

fine—four times before I'm ready to stand up and look in the mirror.

Eventually, I'm able to pull myself together enough to put on the bathrobe. I fall back in the chair and listen, dull, to the morning sounds of the house, the hum and putter of preparations.

Meredith knocks and cracks the door an inch. "Kate and Josh are nearly ready for school. Ian was up half the night. I don't expect him to emerge till well past ten. You're safe to come down if you want." She winks encouragingly. "Bill makes a mean waffle."

I usually despise winking. On Meredith, it looks good.

The bathroom is a sauna. I open the window. A crisp new Jetta—driven by somebody barely old enough to baby-sit, let alone steer—pulls up and honks for Kate and Josh. Off they go, a gallop of smiles and backpacks and ironed clothing, two lifetimes of good nutrition. Steam clouds from the car, out of their mouths, and out of mine. I open the window farther and blow, hard. The gray puff floats and fades over the upper-class landscape. Such a tidy, domestic scene: every yard tidy and well-scrubbed, each life ordered.

Downstairs, I get my one shot at a grand entrance. Bill is wrestling with trendy kitchen equipment. Meredith savors the paper and a steaming cup of coffee—smells strong. Both stop at the sight of me waltzing into the kitchen.

"Waffle?" asks Bill, spoon in hand. Meredith sets down the paper.

I shake my head no and let Meredith hand me coffee. The solemn atmosphere tells me what I suspected: Dad spilled the full story to Ian, who did the same here. I pour a lot of sugar in my coffee. My eyes still sting. I sigh.

Meredith takes the plunge. She reaches for my hand across the cherry table.

"I'm sorry," she says.

Of course, I can't talk without blubbering all over again. I nod. Another minute drags past while I dredge up the courage to ask them the only question that matters.

"Why do you think she lied?"

Bill sets plates of hot egg waffles in front of Meredith and me. He returns to the counter for his own. Both appear uncertain, yet Bill emerges the braver of the two. "Well," he replies, slowly. "Why do you think she left, in the first place?"

Therein lies my answer. The two events come together, slowly, into an inseparable truth.

"For a long time, I thought she was like my father," I say quietly. "The same person, only female and invisible. A type of divinity, I guess. Then I found out that she moved to India because of another man." I pause and look up from the spot on the table into which I'd been speaking. "Did Ian tell you that?"

They shake their heads, no. Meredith sets down her coffee cup a little too loudly.

This is the easier half of the story, explanations I've analyzed for years. "After that, I saw her as a hopeless romantic. You know, swept off her feet and all. I felt sorry for her—poor mom, heart trampled. When I was in seventh grade, we learned about the Twelve Steps. I latched onto the addiction theory: my mom's hooked on love. You can't abandon somebody with a problem. My job was to support, not blame."

"Did she ask you for support?" wonders Bill. "Did she talk about tortured relationships?"

"No."

"Sort of strange for a love addict," observes Meredith gently.

"That harsh truth eventually landed on me, too. But the addict story got me through junior high."

Meredith speculates. "You made up explanatory stories. They changed with the information you had at hand—and as you got older."

"I never thought of it quite that way," I say, surprised. How obvious! How naïve! I should hate myself. "I always assumed I was progressing—making my way through layers to the real truth."

"And the next layer was?" asks Bill.

"Art." Which I'm now embarrassed to admit, thank you.

They smile and nod: ah, art—a word allowed to encompass endless transgressions.

"After all, she is a well-known photographer. She sculpts and paints. Dabbles, I guess. She owns a gallery in Bombay—I mean, that's what she said. But the photography's real," I add quickly. "I've seen dozens of books, actual physical evidence."

"Ever done other types of sleuthing?" asks Bill.

"Barely—I know that must seem strange. I can't explain it more than a fear of rocking the boat. I did do regular internet searches. Her home was always listed as Bombay."

"Does someone act as a middle-man for her, an attorney or agent?" asks Bill.

I nod. Her art dealer lived in London. Or so she said.

Bill contemplates. "Probably wouldn't be too tough for a professional to cover for her—fudge on her change of address, that sort of thing. Do you remember the dealer's name?"

"Nope. Is that important?"

"Probably not—although you never know." Bill hasn't touched a bite of breakfast. Nobody has. "Delphi, have you ever thought that maybe your mom's move doesn't reflect her feelings for you? She could have a legitimate reason to hide her locale—a reason strong enough to keep the truth from you?"

"Maybe she was running from a stalker and wanted to protect me? Or she had to leave the country for political reasons?" Not that I'm sure precisely what political reasons could have that effect. The idea sounds good. There's a solid sound to the word stalker!

Bill enthusiastically confirms that I'm on the right track. "We create all kinds of identities, one at work, another with friends, still another with family. You can construct yourself on-line and off. Your mother could be navigating who knows how many identities—maybe designed to protect or serve you, not harm."

Meredith interrupts. "This is not helping, Bill. You're creating the next layer—conjuncture to explain what we don't understand. According to Delphi, her mother's been a disciple, a co-dependent, and an artist. Now she's fugitive and chameleon? Doesn't this tell you both something?"

I shake my head. Bill's theory sounds plausible. Maybe I was too hard on her.

"The time has come to ask her certain direct questions," says Meredith.

"I can't," I blurt out without thinking.

"But why?" She's insistent. Bill lets her take the lead. "Sweetie, if you want a relationship with your mother—and I think you do—you should demand one that's honest."

Hating Lisa Weisman was easier. So were myths. I have no idea what to think. I put my head in my hands and groan. I do hate her. Maybe I shouldn't.

"I know you're afraid," says Meredith, gently, putting a hand on my arm.

"No, I'm not afraid," I snap back. "I'm angry."

Meredith sighs and doesn't remove her hand. I force my face into harder lines. Do not cry, I order myself, furiously. How could I be afraid of my own mother? Or of a stranger, which she also is.

"You don't have to forgive her, you know," says Bill quietly.

He has my attention. "I don't?"

"We put a lot of emphasis on forgive and forget, move on. I don't think you need to forgive off the bat. First, try to repair the damage. Acknowledge harm done and build from there. Imagine constructing a house on a fault line: living in the house doesn't mean you don't consider that tremor underneath, every single day. Your mother did wrong. She hurt you. In Judaism, this is a hole in the world: your mother is responsible for wrenching apart what should be together. Ask her if she is willing to acknowledge that hole and work toward its repair."

"I don't think I have ever forgiven her. Not for leaving in the first place—I don't think I ever will." I'm surprisingly freer for Bill's words. The tiniest shade of relief slips through me: I might not have to forgive the unforgivable? Responsibility is not solely on my shoulders?

"Maybe the next question," says Bill carefully, "is if you're ready to work with her to repair the hole."

"Not interested," I say firmly. "Not my damage to repair."

Meredith concentrates on her waffles.

Ian appears: sweat pants, rumpled t-shirt, and terrible hair. Obviously, he just woke up.

"I can't believe this," he moans when he sees me. He slumps in a spot at the table.

"Lovely way to greet a guest," says Bill.

I slurp coffee, guilty.

"I looked all over for you," complains Ian. "Your Dad was crazy with worry—so was half that wacky building you live in, not to mention your boss."

"Suzanne crawled out of her studio?" I say, surprised.

Ian shakes his head angrily. "What do you think? You storm off and nobody notices?"

I shrug, guilty and defensive. "I am an adult."

"Who could tell," snaps Ian.

"Ian," warns Meredith.

"I don't care, Mom. Everybody treats her like royalty, the novelty psychic act or stray cat for you and Bill to pamper, or who knows what. But if Delphi really is talking to this dead kid, she has a duty—a responsibility—to that girl and her family!"

Who is he to tell me where my duties lie? I turn the tables. "How'd that interview go? Wasn't that yesterday morning?"

Ian's ready for a fight. "Great," he barks. "The job is mine if I want." His words are more challenge than happy declaration.

Meredith's response is carefully drafted. "That's wonderful. I know you'll make the right decision."

Bill exhibits a tad bit more enthusiasm, even pride. "Well done, Ian. If anything, my presence was a discouraging factor: I hammered Phil about letting your work stand on its own. I happen to know that they saw nearly fifty portfolios."

Ian shrugs. He shifts the talk back in my direction. "Someone expected me. I showed up. Pretty simple. How about you,

Delphi?"

Meredith tries to lighten the tone. "You two must've been siblings in a past life," she jokes.

"I'm done with the psychic stuff, the entire era." There—I've made my own general career proclamation.

"When did this happen?" asks Meredith, surprised.

"Nothing happened—that's my point. Some ex-alcoholic—that's right—who now schleps coffee claims to be psychic and pegs me for her pupil. If she really knew anything, she would've given me some warning about my Mom. She even mentioned her! I didn't get a hint. Evelyn didn't know about the dead kid, either. How's that for magical powers? All this supernatural yatter has only distracted me from real life for a few days."

"And things fell apart while you weren't looking," theorizes Bill.

I can practically hear Ian thinking: good one! This whole family might be ten degrees too sane for my liking. Maybe my first impressions were right: they do belong on Nickelodeon. I've landed in the fifties, all happiness and joy, plus, a nineties ability to analyze.

"I think I should leave now." I stand up. "I have to go job and apartment hunting."

Ian remains seated. He folds his arms. "Truth hurts, huh?"

Meredith throws him a menacing look.

"What is this, an intervention?" I cry. "God! All I wanted last week, Ian, was a cup of coffee, not a shadow conscience. Thanks for the bath and breakfast, Meredith—and I really mean that," I add. I do. I leave the kitchen.

Bill and Ian stand. Meredith holds out her hand and says,

don't. She follows me into the hallway.

"I washed your clothes," she says. "They're in the dryer."

"Thank you," I say again. The day-old lump in my throat burns. Why am I always crying?

She puts her hands on my shoulders and brushes back my hair. "I trust you to do what's right—with everything," is all she says.

She's gone.

Tired, I sit down on the steps to wait. Maybe I shouldn't have shown up here. The entire episode has been thoroughly unnerving—and I was already walking quite the edge, thank you.

"Delphi?" Ian is a glutton for punishment. Hasn't he already suffered enough abuse? "Can we call a truce? I want to show you something, upstairs."

I hesitate, still hurt.

"Please?"

I'm obviously not in my right mind: every time I come to a crossroads with this family, a chance to disappear, I stay. "I'll give you the same ten minutes I gave Evelyn."

We wind through the heirlooms and cherry trim until we reach his bedroom. The door's closed, as it was on my initial tour. He tapped the door and said 'mine.' This time, he turns the handle and we walk in.

Every inch of wall is covered with black and white comics, Peanuts to Batman to The Simpsons and everything in between. At first, the scene creeps me out: Ian saved these clips from childhood and this is his big secret? He must've holed up in this room for years. I look closer. The strips aren't cut from newspapers at all. They're originals. I tour the room. The Charlie Brown Ian drew is the Charlie Brown—same with Spiderman, Calvin, Hobbes, Bugs Bunny, Captain Hook, Green Lantern and Elmer Fudd. He has penciled every animal, amphibian, and reptile. Half of an entire wall is devoted to Art Spiegelman's Maus.

"These are mine." He points to cutes Disney-like creatures, a mix of animal and elf. "And here." Superhero types, with a mythological twist—the broad foreheads and flowing robes of Athena, Zeus, and Poseidon.

"Did you draw all this?" My hand sweeps the room.

"Yup." He pulls a wheeled chair from a drafting table and sits, model of gloom.

"You told me you didn't have a talent. You specifically said you weren't an artist."

He shakes his head. "How can I call myself an artist? With a few pathetic exceptions, everything in this room is a reproduction of somebody else's creative juices. I copy. I'm a great copier." Here he allows himself a smile. "In fact, I spend most of my time copying other people's art. My favorites are comic book characters."

He stops to assess my reaction. As if I have any idea what's going on in that thick skull.

"You're a genius. You can draw anything. Why the doomsday look? You could be doing your own books or heading some big wig art division for Bill's firm."

"I can't!" He hits the desk. "I can't come up with a story or theme or connecting idea to save my life." He groans, head back.

He points to the animal-elf things. "I whipped up these stupid little creatures and waited for a story to appear—not to mention the month I was a hermit in front of the computer, trying to force the process. I thought: here's my crack at creating the next Peanuts crew! These guys could be as popular as Calvin and Hobbes. Except I can't even name them, much less make up stories about them!"

Ian's on a roll, pointing out shortcomings right and left. He drags out a black art portfolio, whipping through page after page of perfect pencil drawings, fast. "These are my samples for the job at Minehart and Meltzer. All replicas. All repeats of other people's work."

"So? You got the job, didn't you?"

He nods, miserable.

"You really think they offered you the position because of Bill? Last time I checked, the economy was in rough shape and nepotism was about as popular as Enron stock. Nobody's handing out sympathy employment, either. You're underestimating yourself. No—you're underestimating yourself incredibly. These drawings are amazing, every last one. They stand on their own. Of course, there's one way to find out."

"And that is?" he says with the resigned sigh of someone who already knows the answer.

"Call up that Phil or whoever, and ask if you got the job on the merits of your rather monumental artistic gift or because you're related to a name on the masthead."

He kicks the desk. "What if he gives the wrong answer?"

"You can turn down the job or take it. What do you want to do?" I'm starting to feel sorrier for Ian than for myself. He's miserable. Obviously, this dilemma is nothing new.

His voice drops, secretive. "Actually, I don't want to write books or create cartoons or dream up glitzy ad slogans. All I want to do is draw. I don't necessarily want to even think about drawing! I'd be happy copying logos or reproducing old calendar covers, eight hours a day, seven days a week. See the Roman Superheroes? A friend of mine wrote a play for his Classics seminar and I drew the pictures—he described each scene and character." He leans forward to conclude, dramatically. "I follow directions. I'm not creative. All I love is drawing. My ambition goes no further."

"You think you should have bigger goals—and the brains to generate original material."

He nods. "Whole thing was coming to a head with yesterday's interview: a job I half want and half don't, and was afraid I'd get because of Bill. In case you haven't noticed, lack of ambition is not my stepfather's defining personality trait—nor Mom's."

"Your real Dad?"

"Maybe that's where we're alike."

I see why Ian appeared to have no life of his own. He was actually happy to drop his problems and latch onto mine. Avoidance. So much for the magnetic pull I was beginning to assume I had.

"Why the biology major?"

"Science seemed certain—a healthy antidote to a skill as indeterminate as doodling. Plus, I enjoy biology." He grins. "You get to draw quite a bit if you play your cards right: bugs, plants, algae, and once, ozone. The last thing any professor wanted me doing was dreaming up a new species. Copy and label, that's all."

"Could you possibly just draw, draw, draw at Bill's firm?"

"Wouldn't say the job's entirely structured that way, although the bulk is artwork. I didn't delve into the sticky terrain of my preferences."

"Another question for Phil." Easy, dishing out life advice to anyone other than myself—and I'm not even dipping into the old spirit-world well. I'm on a roll. "This is a no-brainer, Ian. Whatever you find out, you need to follow your heart—follow this." We look around the room, wrapping paper tight in black and white sketches.

"I will if you will," he says.

"What's that supposed to mean?"

"Follow your heart. Find that kid's mother."

He's so serious, I wish I didn't have to disappoint him. "True confession time? I don't know what calls me. Finding out about my Mom—I mean, Lisa—threw me so much that I don't know which way is up. Ask me for a gut feeling and I can't give a clear answer. Everything I used to believe, whether I believed for two days or decades, seems suspect."

My turn to be miserable: must show on my face too. Ian gets off his high moral horse, momentarily.

"Let me give you the information. You decide." He reaches for crumpled pieces of papers on his desk. "Here are the names and addresses of all three girls. Holly Hibbon is starred. She's the one whose father died. Here's the newspaper article."

Holly. The name feels familiar. I'm impressed with Ian's investigative skills and tell him so. He brushes the compliment aside as somebody knocks on the door.

"You cannot believe how easy this was—which tells me that you're supposed to find her."

Meredith is at the door, a warm bundle in her hand. "Clothes?" she queries. She hands me mine with a wry smile. Ian and I look at each other uncertainly, attention drawn to my minimalist attire. I take the stack and nearly run to the guest room.

They're both waiting for me downstairs when I've finished.

"Still leaving?" asks Meredith. "Ian tells me you've straightened out some issues."

"Not entirely," he corrects. "Let's say things are now out in the open."

I'm antsy. Not quite 9:00 am and I already feel as if I'm two hours behind schedule. "I do have to go. There are some things I need to do. Alone," I add, anticipating Ian for once.

"No!" He's obviously disappointed. "I thought we were on speaking terms again."

"More than speaking. We're good. I just need to be alone. I have to start making my own decisions."

To his eternal credit, Ian doesn't try to sweet talk or coerce his way by my side. "Call me," he says, simply.

Meredith hugs me good-bye. "First, call your father," she whispers.

I don't want to lie to her. "I can't. I don't want anything to do with my parents. Is that so horrible? I want a fresh start—my own start."

She shakes her head. "Nobody gets to start from scratch, Delphi. History is part of the package we're handed at birth."

"Duly noted. Now I'm returning mine."

She looks at me critically. "You almost make me believe that's possible."

I'll take that as a compliment. We say good-bye and I promise to call Ian later. As I pull away in the rustmobile, he yells from the front door. "Talk to her! Do it!"

At least he didn't utter the word 'responsibility' again. The world is filled with people who shirk their obligations. My guess is that they're happier than I am.

I turn on the radio and wish for a more definitive plan. Apartment hunting? Job search? I haven't the faintest clue where to begin, particularly on two hours of sleep and a cup of coffee. Steer a few aimless corners. Where's the best beginning place, in this business of setting up a brand new life—my own?

Follow your heart, says Ian.

As if I knew.

Then follow somebody else's heart. The thought comes as both my own idea and singularly foreign, revelation dropped from the blue—or from the invisible girls of my past or the ones by the fire last night? Could be I'm suffering from lack of sleep or ordinary over-imagination, but I'm sure the dead girl spoke to me on the river bluff. Is her name Holly? I was so alone. She appeared and I wasn't lonely.

Time to return the favor?

Impulsively, I turn toward Minneapolis. I need Evelyn. Okay, she's wacky, loaded with baggage, and has made her fair share of mistakes. She's still my best option. She holds some key she's not sharing.

By the time I arrive at Crystal's, my expectations are high enough that Evelyn could solve almost any problem. Why, she might even have an apartment I can rent! Doesn't she employ people, too? Plus, she possesses (I hope) at least enough psychic skills to tell me if I'm obligated to return favors to the dead. Maybe she can offer advice on Lisa Weisman. World peace. Maybe today is the day she has the answers, for once.

Reality gets off to a bad start. Evelyn is not the person making cappuccinos. Oh God: Mr. Freak Show from The Curtain.

Paleface tells me that Evelyn isn't working.

"Where is she?"

"No idea," he whines. "Tuesdays are her day off." Everything about him looks unhelpful. He clanks two plates with scones onto a tray. "Do you want a coffee drink?"

No, you idiot, I want Evelyn. I dredge up my limited diplomatic skills and smile sweetly, lean across the counter. "I really need to talk to Evleyn. Very important. Do you have an address or phone number?"

Or a last name! I am at his mercy.

He points to the ceiling. "That would be her address. Last year, she renovated the entire upstairs into a three-bedroom apartment. She owns the building—and the one across the street. You can try calling. She's on the store speed dial, number one."

Talk about misreading a face! Thank you baby vampire man! I practically leap over the counter for the phone.

No answer! I cannot believe my rotten luck. I follow Bat Boy's instructions and make my way up the stairs, using a back entrance. The hallway is crisp like Crystal's. The real brass knocker seals the clean, middle-class feel to the entire second story.

I knock and knock and knock. "Evelyn! It's Delphi! I really need to see you!" I refuse to believe she's not here. The more I knock, the bigger my bubble of panic. She has to be here!

Twenty minutes and one trip to her building across the street later, I sit down on the curb and acknowledge the obvious: Evelyn is not home. I might start crying, again: a world record. Maybe I get to sob for twenty-four hours straight.

I look at my watch, inordinately anxious. No time like the present. No time to waste. Why do I feel as if the clock is ticking away? I should be in a hurry. My stomach growls from lack of food.

The papers Ian handed me are in my pocket. I skim the newspaper article: horrible car accident, father and daughter die, survived by a wife and mother named Leilani O'Brien. She lives on the West Side of St. Paul, less than four minutes away from Moon. Ian tracked down an address and phone number.

Presenting myself in person seems the only remotely possible option. Of course, there's the upcoming hurdle of initial introduction: Ma'am? I commune with your dead daughter. Too abrupt, or could shock be the easiest route? I'll cross that proverbial bridge when I come to it.

I look twice at Evelyn's upstairs windows. Was that shade up when I arrived? I watch a moment for shadow or movement I almost expect to see. No sign of life. I don't know what kind of car she drives or if she's off on a bike or by bus.

So much for tangible assistance—the kind offered by someone who actually breathes, thank you. I head back to St. Paul. Why not? I have no better plans. I'll follow somebody else's heart and see where she leads me.

14
LEILANI

Her sister's parked car and dark house leave Anna cheerful and self-congratulatory. This is exactly the type of situation at which she excels: crisis management. How Seamus allowed Leilani to traipse off with a bottle of wine and a morbid bent is beyond Anna, who is quite sure that their sister is currently drinking herself into a coma or has finally succumbed to hysteria. Either way, something about the situation struck Anna as odd when she called earlier.

Seamus picked up halfway through the first ring. He reported his great achievement.

"She hates the house." Anna was at the kitchen table. She put down the notes she was reviewing, protracted copyright case—a monstrosity she'll be pleased to plop on the desk of one of her more moronic colleagues when she leaves for New York.

"No, no," he protested. "She's ready to go back. She said she was glad she had the idea. Her idea, by the way, not mine."

Anna shook her head, thinking. "The day of the funeral, she swore she'd never enter that house again, not once. I distinctly remember believing her. There was something about the way she said it."

"Trust me to know when someone's lying. She's there. She took a bottle of wine."

"Wine?" Anna was standing by this point, packing up papers and pouring herself a cup of coffee for the car. Day or night, she drinks the stuff. Martin was in the study, working. She listened to Seamus while whispering to her husband, who raised his eyebrows and returned to his documents.

By the time Anna had coat on and keys in hand, a degree of her concern had rubbed off on Seamus.

"God, do you really think I've sent her off into the abyss? I'd feel terrible! Honestly, she seemed nearly normal for the first time since I've been here."

Anna convinced Seamus that his services were no longer needed (in friendlier words that nonetheless touched upon his incompetence) and promised to call once she had Leilani in the car, safe and sound, on the way back to their parents.

Always thinking ahead, Anna has keys to Leilani's house in her trunk, where she also stores a flashlight along with emergency supplies: animal crackers, aspirin, juice boxes, freeze-dried nuts, cotton swabs, Band-Aids, blankets, and latex gloves. Who better prepared to handle any situation? The house is stone still as she heads to the front door, key in hand and flashlight ready, just in case.

She didn't want Seamus for another reason. Tonight, she's not a messenger for her mother. The confrontation will be on Anna's terms. The complexities are practically addictive: simmering anger at her sister's capacity for self-pity (a lifelong problem, if you ask Anna); the bite of venturing out late; and the ache for her niece and brother-in-law combust with the underlying anxiety of her own life, to create an entirely heady, and not at all unpleasant, rush.

She opens the door. "Leilani?"

The windows let in the low glow of street and moon. Anna flicks the light switch, which works; as she suspected, Leilani has simply chosen to mope in the dark. The living room stands as always, Will's rag-tag thrift store taste evident in the antique stained glass lampshade standing next to a sleek seventies table that was supposedly designed by a Formica executive. Nothing matches, yet somehow the room pulls together—a colorful explosion of pieces from varying periods and trends. The effect is slightly disconcerting to Anna, whose own home is structured by one identifiable era and limited to seven contiguous colors.

She opens the refrigerator. Pickles, ketchup, horseradish relish, Tabasco sauce, rice. The canola oil has probably gone bad. Anna disposed of most perishables a few days after the funeral, when Leilani's intentions were clear. Not only was she not returning, her sister was abdicating all responsibility for the house. To this day, Anna pays the mortgage and utilities. However, when she slides her own bill under Leilani's bedroom door, that amount is routinely, quickly paid.

Now inside, Anna is less enthused about the crisis. The air is a bit too thick, the mood of the rooms, off. Will dumped Tabasco sauce on everything. She slams shut the refrigerator. Maybe Leilani has cause for concern. Maybe a house does hold its people when they die too early. She sighs, stiffening herself into a more commonsensical state. No need to succumb to superstition.

A dainty brass bell sits on the windowsill above the kitchen sink. Attracted, Anna blows off the dust before shaking the bell for its soft, airy ring. Through the window, she can see that weird old man next door doing a not-very-good job of spying from his own kitchen. Bemused, she waves. Startled, he waves back, less certain. The interaction heartens her. The neighbor is enjoying late night voyeurism and she's simply walking through rooms she's traveled a thousand times.

"Lani! It's me, Anna." She tours the rest of the downstairs and heads up, turning on lights as she goes.

"Good God, Lani," shouts Anna, at the top of the stairs. "Cut the crap and come here!"

A slow finger of fear taps on her belly. The whole house is a dark fairy tale. Something horrible is ready to leap: little piggy, let me in. She tries, more or less successfully, to stave off the worry. But she sucks in her breath as she checks the bathroom, half expecting to see Leilani with slit wrists on the tile floor. Empty! A porcelain clown smiles from the top of the white medicine cabinet. The room looks as it did weeks ago, untouched. Even so, Anna's heart races.

She skips Holly's room (last resort) and walks gingerly into the master bedroom. She flips a switch and a lamp on the nightstand flies on.

From the large bed, Leilani wiggles her fingers and grins, open bottle of wine by her side.

"Surprise!" Leilani giggles.

Relief nearly knocks Anna to her knees. She leans against the doorway, the simplest of fears confirmed and the worst unrealized.

"You're drunk," she announces the obvious. Her body—her exhausted, overwrought, lactating, pregnant body—fails her. Dizzy, she slumps against the wall to a sitting position. "I was right. Drunk. Thank God."

Leilani is unfazed by her sister's appearance. "Oh yea – drunk. Only I'm afraid I'll get a stomachache and throw up. I really don't want to do that. No, no, no."

Anna sighs, head in hands. "Maybe you should've thought of that before you started swigging alcohol."

"You're probably right, as usual," Leilani says, somberly.

Anna starts to cry.

"Whoa," says Leilani fuzzily, half sitting up. "I'm not dead yet." Curious in a strangely disembodied way—like entering a movie theatre high, as if you are both part of a movie and watching one—she watches Anna weep quietly, head in hands. Oh my: total collapse? How timely, thinks Leilani. The situation strikes her as inordinately funny. She should've saved Anna some pills. Hand over her mouth, Leilani stifles the urge to laugh.

"You think this is funny?" In her current condition, Anna's hallmark hiss turns into a moan.

Caught, Leilani shakes her head a wide, emphatic 'no,' eyes betraying her. The laugh turns into a half-cough. Ouch. Her stomach stretches and tromps, a small revolt. She hiccoughs and covers her mouth again.

Anger is Anna's knee-jerk response. Really, she would enjoy being angry—to throw a fabulous temper tantrum, maybe scream. She tries to pave the way for rage to emerge and only cries harder. The reserve she's diligently worked to maintain—strengthen, even, over the past week—crashes against the despair radiating through this room, the house. The mood is more powerful than she. Bleakness swallows her. She huddles against the wall, a low black ball.

"Aren't we pathetic," she sobs.

Not wanting to miss this, Leilani struggles to sharpen her senses. Did Anna say we?

"Look at you! You can't even walk down a hallway without some sort of psychological collapse. I mean, let's face facts," and here, Anna's fragile psyche snaps even farther, and she is the one to laugh outright, "your life totally sucks. You lose everything and go crazy to top it all off. God! Will and Holly, gone. Why even bother? What a mess, a complete, wretched mess. Why even try to repair yourself? What's the use?"

No news to her: Leilani sits straighter and nods in agreement, rabbit-like in her effort to stay attentive. Finally, someone is talking her language.

Anna continues, bitter and loud. "I don't even have your excuses—your very, very good excuses—yet I've managed to make a great, big mess out of my own life very well, thank you. Leaving all my friends, dumping my career, moving away from my family in service of my husband, as if I was living out some male fantasy from the fifties. Well, here's the reality: I'm going to be a stupid, fat housewife without friends or a job, rinsing out dirty diapers in some cramped but desirably zip-coded apartment for the next fucking decade, if things continue this smoothly."

Hard to imagine. Leilani yawns and shakes her head, no. Not Anna. "Oh no, honey," she says, fondly. A great sense of benevolence has begun to take hold of her. She steals a look at Morning Egg. Not long, now. She would like to go to sleep soon.

Ending what seems an eternity of self-control, Anna's just warming up. She looks directly at her sister. "I'm pregnant. Don't ask—this is not good news."

Shock and rage steady Leilani a bit. Anna gets a baby?

Another one? And she gets nothing. Zippo. All gone, dead, bye-bye: worse than never having one because you know precisely what you lost. Everything.

"Oh," Leilani manages.

"I think I'm going to have an abortion. I think I'm not going to tell Martin."

"Oh."

"Not that he particularly wants another baby. Not now. Maybe not at all—I'm not sure. I mean, we weren't sure if we wanted three. We thought, maybe—probably not, though. Three, now, is impossible." A few more short sobs and sighs escape. "I'm still breastfeeding! I hate babies—they're parasitical! Boring, boring, boring. Okay, you get about ten interesting minutes a day when they coo or something. Otherwise: ugh. Is there anything duller?"

Maybe Anna should've lost a child instead, thinks Leilani. She could just pop out replacements: boom, boom, boom.

"Well, lucky you," Leilani slurs, wryly.

Picking herself up, Anna sighs and sits next to her sister on the bed. "I don't blame you for hating me. Gets worse. Wanna hear?"

"Choices?"

"I was jealous of you, having Holly. If I already had a girl, I'd certainly opt for an abortion." Anna stares at Morning Egg without noticing the painting, eyes narrow. "If that is taking a life, I'd be willing to take a life to keep mine. But I don't have a daughter. Or do I? Holly's dead and Will is too. Here I sit, contemplating an end to what? Life, or its potential? Half the time I dread spending an afternoon with my own mother and here I am one myself? Having three children is somehow a personal affront. I'd love a daughter. I hate myself."

Leilani stares as Anna's flat stomach opens itself up. A strong-limbed girl unfolds. She crouches, stands and grows, face bright. Here is a young woman on the edge of becoming her stronger, more permanent self. The center of the universe stands and smiles before Leilani, a blaze of confidence and promise.

"You'll probably have a boy," announces Leilani weakly. Small yawn. "He could be your favorite."

"Yes," sighs Anna, who has thought of this and everything else. "And he could pave a path to peace in the Middle East, end terrorism and cure cancer. Human progress botched if I end this pregnancy."

"Don't do it," whispers Leilani. She means this. Anna cannot kill her daughter. She takes Anna's hand. "Don't. I'm begging you."

The touch of her sister's hand moves Anna beyond reason. Afraid to look at her sister's face, Anna stares at her hands and sniffles. The skin around each fingernail has been chewed to blood.

Suddenly, Leilani understands: this baby is why she lasted so long. She couldn't find Victor. She won't have another child. Anna should—not because of religious prescription or a misguided attempt to legislate morality—but because this, she knows, is Fate.

"You told me," says Leilani, "so I could stop you."

Unmoored, Anna sobs again. "I'm supposed to help you," she says, anger—at herself now—reasserting itself a little. "Some support system I am."

Leilani puts her arms around her sister until Anna has completed her cry, the good, hard cathartic kind that can right any situation. They lay together for a long time – so long that Leilani nearly drifts off. The urge to sleep swells and rolls, bad timing; this is a battle she's been fighting for months, certainly, she can last a few more minutes? Not much beyond, though. The gnawing in her stomach subsides as deeper exhaustion sets in. She closes her eyes.

"Lani?" Concern crawls through her sister's voice.

To be certain, Anna takes her hand out of Leilani's and scrutinizes her sister's fingers.

"What happened? I think your fingers are broken!"

Leilani grins. Broken! The pain is gone. Must've been a clean-cut, high-quality job. She moves away from Anna a bit in order to rest her head—very heavy now—on the pillow.

Awash in unaccustomed empathy and goodwill, Anna smiles at Leilani curled on the bed, eyes struggling to stay open. She pulls up a blanket and tucks in the edges. Setting the wine bottle on the nightstand, she sighs at how little alcohol her sister needed to get spectacularly drunk, how low her reserves and how high her willingness.

"Who can blame you?" she says, finishing her thought out loud.

Leilani's response is so low, so tiny—yet her tone is fierce. "They do," she says.

Anna shoots a hard look at her sister.

"They blame me," continues Leilani. She's given a small surge of energy that comes with compassion. Poor, unhappy Anna! Who knew! Her sister trusts her with a secret. Leilani urgently wants to give Anna something in return, a token of appreciation.

Floppily, she tries to explain. "They hate me. Will and Holly. I won't be getting any of those visits." She snaps her fingers, rolls her eyes. "Those la-la angel landings, you know, where somebody's soul zaps a butterfly on your shoulder or sends a secret message. No such signs for me," she sighs.

Anna picks up the wine bottle, puzzled. Two, three glasses at the most. Maybe Leilani is having some sort of psychotic break. About time the reserve snaps, thinks Anna, although she was hoping for something a little more cogent.

She takes Leilani's hand.

"Don't be silly. I'm sure they visit," she says firmly—the first lie she's told all evening.

Leilani speaks to the stolen painting. "I didn't love them enough. You know that. You feel the same. Try, try, try. Give, give, give. Then you give up. Everybody gives up. But Holly was so little!"

Anna tries to patch together some meaning. She follows her sister's gaze to the artwork and sucks in her breath at the expense—probably a pretty chunk of the insurance money—before returning her full attention to the bed.

"You're delirious," marvels Anna.

"Clear! I'm clear," whispers Leilani. She is. She can see her past self perfectly, every mistake she made, and is glad to step away. Leilani closes her eyes. Yes! She has earned this rest.

Somberly, Anna watches Leilani fall asleep. Or pass out? She isn't sure. She has an inkling of the burden her sister carries. Didn't love them enough? Impossible. But Anna understands. What mother isn't guilty, of sins real or imagined, no matter what choices she makes? Some of us will have tomorrow to try again. Some won't.

Anna checks her watch: past midnight. Her chest aches and her legs itch with exhaustion. She wonders what to do next. Spend the night on the couch, here? Leave Leilani and head home for a few hours? She calculates how—if—she'd be able to return before her sister wakes. As much as she doesn't want to abandon Leilani, she decidedly does not want to be the only conscious person in this house. Seamus can spend the night, she decides, wickedly. After all, he got the ball rolling.

She picks up the bedside phone and dials. Again, he answers quickly. Must be awake and waiting.

"Yes?"

"I was right, you dope. She passed out."

Seamus sighs into the phone. "Were you able to talk to her? Was she really suffering? I feel awful."

"We talked." Anna has a twinge of guilt, feeling herself the sole beneficiary. She changes the subject. "And of course, she's suffering: what do you think? Let's save the juicy details for tomorrow and address the immediate problem of who's going to spend a night babysitting. She's out, stone cold. I can't move her and I have an infant who will scream for a snack in an hour, not to mention a job in the morning."

"That pretty effectively narrows the field to me. Besides, I shouldn't have let her go."

"Right on both counts," says Anna, brightly, adjusting Leilani's blankets as she talks. "Move fast. This place gives me--"

Anna slowly sets down the receiver. Is Leilani drooling?

She gently touches her sister's cheek, gingerly tilts the chin up for a better view, a better sense of the situation. The head rolls easily. Yes, drool, yellow and pinkish, ropes out of Leilani's mouth and down the side of her jaw.

Leilani's lips are blue. Her skin is grayish. Purse on the bed, contents dumped. The wine! Only three glasses!

The world changes.

Gasping, Anna fumbles for the phone.

"Get off the fucking phone!" she screams into the receiver. "I have to call 911! Get off! Get off!"

"What? What?" Seamus screams too, although he has the good sense to hang up while doing so.

Anna tries to follow the dispatcher's instructions. Phone tucked under her chin, she cradles Leilani's head in her arms and checks the airway. No obstructions, she reports. Yes, she thinks there's a pulse.

"Barely," cries Anna into the phone. "Shit! I'm not sure. It's so tiny!"

"You can do this," says the dispatcher, his voice calm. "If there's no pulse, I'm going to walk you through CPR. Feel in her neck for a main artery. We're going to help your sister. What's your name, ma'am?"

"Anna." By now, Anna is weeping, completely gone. How could she not notice, let her sister die before her own eyes!

"You're doing great, Anna. How's that neck?"

She ends up learning CPR on the fly, the voice on the other end infinitely kind! So confident! Not to worry, Anna, he tells her: chances are you're only missing the pulse. Heartbeats are hard to pick up when they get this faint. He never fails to use her name. Anna, let's err on the safe side, okay? Here's how you do that first compression.

Sirens wail. Doors slam. Feet. Voices.

Here! Help us!

Paramedics storm up the stairs. They're in and out with

Leilani within minutes, a low, focused whirlwind of machines and movement and questions.

No, Anna can't tell them what her sister took. She performs better on other questions: allergies, age, illness. Yes, Anna's positive, one hundred percent certain. Suicide. A woman about her own age, a firefighter (they bring the whole team!) searches under the bed, in the nightstand, under each pillow. Experienced, the woman tugs through pockets of the purse, checks under the mattress and begins to open drawers.

"Where's the bathroom?" she asks Anna.

In the end, they bring along the empty Ziplock bag and a handful of tablets from the bathroom, nothing of particular import, no real clues.

Anna follows them outside, jogging to keep up.

The paramedic in charge would prefer that Anna drive, if she's able. Inside the ambulance, a blinking machine begins to whirr and the driver yells: let's go! Everyone bends over her sister.

"Call the rest of your family," is the last thing the paramedic shouts before the door closes.

Hand on her throat, Anna stands in the center of the street as the ambulance roars away. People watch from doorways and windows. Rocco is already dressed. He runs to Anna.

"Where did they take her?" His voice wavers.

"Regions Hospital."

He's off.

Anna moves toward her own car, ignoring the isolated voices: what happened? She okay? Was that Leilani? Her cell phone and purse are locked in the glove compartment. This is something she does every day—drive with one hand and dial with the other.

Numbly, she turns the lock while starting the ignition.

Her car isn't far behind Rocco's. She blinks and assembles her thoughts before making the first call. Her parents.

She starts to jab in numbers, then throws the phone down on the seat.

"Please, please, please!" Futilely, instinctively, Anna shakes her fist into the night light of the city sky. Her sobs are different than those of an hour ago, her own sense of self suspended in prayer for another. "Don't let her die, too. Don't let her die too."

The ambulance bumps and howls down streets and around corners. Inside, men and women paid to save lives earn their money on Leilani. They help her heart pump and make sure she's still breathing.

"Hang in there," whispers one.

Leilani can't hear them. She is alive. She isn't in the ambulance. She isn't fighting. She's most assuredly not pulling her weight—as far the medical team would be concerned—in the battle to keep the body breathing.

No, Leilani is at the midway marker of her journey. There are no pearls or angels. No great wise guides wait to usher her to the other side. She doesn't feel the heat of Hell, nor does she merge into an eternal oneness.

She stands by a river, shivering, as centuries of dead children rise up to meet her. The water foams with wispy cuts of baby hair, tiny toenails and teeth. Babies swarm and descend: locusts, greedy and unfed.

"Holly!" She plucks off the creatures that crawl up her belly, her thighs. She searches every face, only to discover that the mothers through time have lost the same child: each looks like the other, round and slightly brown with limpid black eyes.

"Holly!"

She trips and stumbles up, only to stagger again. Who could walk an inch? There are millions and millions of them. The toddling bodies on the bank thicken and pile. More emerge from the white river, endless.

Leilani gives in to the babies. She sits down so they can crawl all over, burrow her in. There's some comfort in this, she discovers. Babies! Meaty little packs of warm fat and skin, they claw their way higher and higher up her body until she nearly disappears. Fists, chunky thighs, a thunderous belly—the body parts obstruct her vision and limit her hearing to the swish and goo of newborns. Holly! No sound comes from her mouth, swollen with flesh and hair and fingers. The river is warm and smells like almonds, yarrow, and milled corn. The current calls and opens, folding her in as its own.

15
DELPHI

Okay, can I give up now? I've officially rang and pounded longer than my karma mandate. Nobody answers the door. If anyone even lives here—yes, I admit to peeking in a few windows. Not one newspaper on the floor, not a dish in the kitchen. Could be a model home, if the décor weren't so dicey.

The mailbox says 'Hibbon/O'Brien.' She didn't change her name. She didn't change the mailbox, either. Yet.

You can almost imagine this house feeling homey. The backyard has a snug quality, squared off and surrounded by bushes and fence. Somebody was a gardener—not the big-time fancy sort, a naturalist with an eye for prairie grass and daisies. The tall stalks left over from last year stand brown and dry; green nubs grow around their bottoms.

I check my watch—not that I have anywhere to go. I have precisely the opposite problem, yet still feel time racing. Mid-morning. Let's use good old reason, for once. This neighborhood does not house the upper crust. Ms. O'Brien is undoubtedly employed. She's sitting at some desk stamping 'denied' on loan applications or firing up asthma medication for long lines of the sickly in an elementary school.

If I were truly skilled at this psychic thing, I'd know what she did for a living—maybe even where. Instead, I'm stuck with a vague sense that she's an energetic reader. Good going, Delphi: that narrows down the field. Energetic! That tells me exactly nothing. I could be referring to fossil fuels or her state of being. Yes, generally safe to say that I have no idea what I'm referring to at all. I'm going to be a great big bundle of help when I finally find Leilani O'Brien.

Look at the time! Way, way too late. Could I blame this whole fiasco on Evelyn? She should have been home.

I scan for clues to this woman's whereabouts. The Hibbon/O'Brien homestead is one of three solid stuccos in a row—working class fare from the early twentieth century, if Daddy's impromptu architectural lectures are right. He claimed you could mail order a kit from Sears and bingo: boxed-up house bits were deployed, upon a train, across country. All the homeowner required was a toolbox.

The southernmost house stands out with a bit of flair. The roof and trimmings are an unusual shade of green, bright almost to the point of garish—but not quite. A pathway of mismatched tiles winds from the front porch to the backyard's elaborate garden: slates of marble, tiny fountains, and stone benches abound. Looks as if there's very little in the way of standard Minnesotan scenery— no prudish petunias, begonias or other annual affairs. The back door is old and intricately carved. The whole set-up is so inviting that I debate knocking on that nice door to inquire about Leilani O'Brien. What could I possibly say? Delphi here: I've been chatting with your neighbor kid. Know where the grieving widow works?

Maybe I was wrong: I do qualify as a GAC! In fact, I can picture myself running amuck down the street, screaming and shedding my life. I hate my choices: which doorbell to ring, what stranger to confront, what stories to share and which to hide?

What if my mother was tucked inside that green-roofed stucco? She could have selected those terra cotta tiles, going to great length to insure that handcrafted stones looked like treasures mined from rubble. The walls inside Lisa Weisman's house are a uniform white. She presents her paintings the traditional way. Every morning, my mother drinks strong oolong tea with a trace of milk and honey. She listens to campy show tunes from the thirties and forties—Broadway hits and lesser fare.

How do you knock on the door of an already-ordered life? Do I say: hi Mom, it's me, Delphi? By the way, why did you leave me and spend the next decades lying? Who created that hole in the world? Does Lisa Weisman lay awake and worry about how to repair the damage she's done?

I sit down on the cold front steps and cover my eyes with my hands. My morning is rounding itself off nicely with a headache. Either I'm overly tired, coming off an M & M high, caffeine deprived, or about to receive another visitation. I jump on the caffeine theory. I saw a coffee shop two blocks down. If only I'd let Bat Boy give me that espresso, I wouldn't have to haul myself in front of humanity once more. I am so not in the mood for company, other than this O'Brien woman.

Bad luck keeps giving and giving. Someone heads in my direction—pretty, Hispanic, and parental. She has a small girl in tow, a child unfortunate enough to inherit the other parent's features: Daddy is not as pretty as Mom. Or maybe I'm tired, bone tired, of small children and their problems. Could be all the creatures will appear peaked and pinched to me today.

The girl trails a few feet after the woman. They walk up the sidewalk toward me.

"Can I help you?" Her voice is cool: who are you and what do you want, would be her subtext.

Moment of truth! What would Miss Manners say? There must be a delicate way to introduce the topic of clairvoyance. I want to giggle and cry at the same time. The past twenty-four hours could very well catch up with me at this moment. Now, that would leave an impression!

"I'm—I mean, I'm looking for Ms. O'Brien. My name's Delphi Sandquist." I hold out my hand with what I hope is polite enthusiasm.

She shakes my hand cautiously. "I'm Carmen Castillos. This is my daughter, Isabel."

"Hi Isabel." I wiggle my fingers, feigning sunshine and good cheer I don't feel.

The girl smiles tentatively. Ouch: I was wrong about sharing her father's appearance. She looks more like a poached egg. I smile back.

"Ms. O'Brien isn't home. Perhaps I can take her a message?" So reserved! Her excess caution is alarming. I wonder if others have been here before me? Is the kid sending off some psychic beacon for hundreds to catch?

"Oh, is she at work, then?" Come on! Point me in the right direction.

Carmen smiles, a pro, patient and undefeatable. "Maybe I can help you. What would you like to see Ms. O'Brien about?"

I flounder. Without a plan or easily available lie, I toy with the truth. I must look as torn as I feel because Ice Queen softens enough to encourage.

"Are you a student of hers? Could the college help you instead?"

Aha! College! How to reply: "Uh—not really."

God, that was brilliant. I scan through my short list of options. How would my student stance fare if my next question is: what college? I don't think she teaches at Macalester. The name doesn't ring a bell.

"Well," she begins, "I can take your name and number. Waiting here probably won't—."

The urge to glance at my watch, undoubtedly rude, is irresistible. Nearly 11:00! I feel as if I've been punched in the stomach. "I really need to see Ms. O'Brien as soon as possible. It's urgent. Terribly urgent." Please! Can't one moment of my day be easy?

"That's impossible. Leilani—Ms. O'Brien isn't available."

Better judgment tells me to shut up and cut my losses. I let desperation drive me. "I know this is going to sound strange—and believe me, the situation still seems bizarre to me." Here, of course, I'm condemned to nervous laughter and jitters, all of which combine with what's coming out of my mouth to securely drive that wedge in between us. No, not wedge: think Berlin Wall. I see the barrier rise and plow forward anyway.

"I have a message from her daughter. Holly. I guess you could say that I'm psychic, I think—I mean, sort of—well, I do need to talk to Ms. O'Brien. I might be able to help."

I smile. She does not.

"That's sick," she snaps. "Coming here today. Who are you, really?" Isabel stares.

"Ms. O'Brien doesn't know me. My name really is Delphi Sandquist. I'm a senior at Macalester. I can show you a driver's license. I live a few minutes away, downtown. My Dad's a priest, the Buddhist kind. I promise you: I would never do anything to harm your friend. I need to talk to her." My Dad's a priest? Those are my best credentials?

"You should leave before I call the police." Carmen stretches an arm in the direction of my exit.

Well, now we all know what a successful first impression I make. "I'm sorry," I say, sincerely. I pause, in case apology earns me points.

"You're trespassing."

Staying another second is only going to make her angrier. I take two tentative steps away. Carmilla the Hun, I think, angrily: I'm a tad bit tired of people acting as if I'm the only one who is straightjacket material.

Then I remember the coffee shop. Of course! Someone there will know Leilani O'Brien. Big tragedy in a house two blocks away: she'll still be the talk of the locals. Why didn't I think of that before?

Carmen waits to ensure my complete departure. Isabel makes her break.

"Isa!"

The kid runs right up to me, intent and efficient. "She's in the hospital," she whispers, quickly, even as she pivots back to her mother.

"Isabel!" reprimands Carmen. She steers the child in the opposite direction. "Go away, please," she calls to me over her shoulder.

Isabel turns around, too. She waves. I wave back: thank you! Then Carmilla the Hun reads her the riot act. Poor kid.

Hospital? Leilani O'Brien is making me incredibly anxious. I nearly run to my car.

Why didn't I take our cell phone? That would be far handier than the Visa. Of course, I may think differently while charging a first month's rent and deposit. I look for yet another public phone. Not the corner café, no need to get bogged down by inquisitive neighbors now that I have information. Besides, Carmen's hearty embrace has clued me in: must not alert the troops to my presence.

I pull into one of those archaic drive-up telephones in the parking lot of Sammy's—a beat-up convenience store whose diverse clientele looks a little rough around their inner-city edges. One of the jumpier, sniffier white boys hanging on the sidewalk jams his hands in his fatigues and watches me closely for a sign. Buyer from the burbs?

Not on your life, loser.

Thankfully, my stay under watchful eyes is short: two calls to major hospitals and I have Leilani's O'Brien's room number and phone. The operator at Regions asked if I want to be patched through—to a nurses' station, not the room.

I stare at my scribbles on the paper. Regions Hospital, room 410. She wants to die. She probably tried. I feel the event—not the idea or intent but a series of actions that have occurred—although I can't articulate how she did the deed.

A low glow of excitement refuels my spirit.

Unexpectedly, I think of Yang. Once, I asked him why he painted. He described the push of each particular painting, the drive to capture an exact emotion or scene. You lose yourself in the impulse, he had stated. The life of the painting takes over and you comply. Whatever my response had been, Yang had thought me funny: he laughed. Don't worry, he had told me, painting is the greatest thrill I get.

I think I cracked a joke: you need more excitement. Now I see differently. Maybe I understand what he meant, about finding your calling. The joy is in the answer.

I hear you, Holly. I'm coming

The hospital is downtown, streets I could navigate with eyes shut. I should prepare. What did Evelyn advise? Deep breathing, visualization, forehead massages and peppermint tea. Forgo pills when you can't sleep and take Valerian root instead. Use beeswax balm on the dry skin of your elbows and keep a journal of your dreams. Pray. Drop essential oils in hot bathwater. Incense? Bah— a bad habit. Toss rose petals in water or boil apple skins till the house smells like summertime and pie. She rambled through dozens of things, each useless: never pack more than a day before a journey and never, ever underestimate the power of a good luck charm.

The closest thing I have to a charm is the jade necklace Daddy gave me on my eighteenth birthday—a stunning stone spinning in diamonds on a delicate gold chain. Probably set him back a month's salary. I rarely dare put the thing on, out of fear of losing or breaking something so gorgeous. He knew how well he had chosen. The celebrations of my childhood were markedly spare, the greater wants of the suffering world duly noted, emphasized even, in the midst of already minimalist hoopla. To mark my adulthood, he handed me the slim silver box: I want you to have something incredibly expensive, he said.

Better to have brought that box, than the one with the letters. My mistake.

Oh, that reminds me: must build own life. I'm whiling away an afternoon on behalf of somebody else's life because I don't have one of my own? Well, compared to my own problems, soothing the suicidal sounds like fun.

Until I find myself inside Regions Hospital, in front of room 402. Leilani O'Brien may be eight doors down. The nurses' station is right next to me. Where's the hustle and bustle I see on TV? Other than a portly middle-aged man in salmon scrubs—bad color with his complexion, let's hope the women do better—the place is empty. The man mutters into the phone, taking notes.

Down the hall, two women mill outside of a room. Visitors, not dressed for any job here. Lots of tension in that body language, especially the thin, younger woman—she paces and circles while the older slumps against the wall. The grandmotherly type rests her face in her hands. I count the doorways and estimate. Could be her room. Impossible to be certain unless I check. Why wouldn't I? This is an unlocked facility. I'm free to walk up and down a hall. Nobody will even notice.

"Excuse me," the lone nurse taps my arm. "Are you here for someone?" He holds a clipboard helpfully.

I plant a smile on my face, eager to appear benign, harbinger of good intentions. Harmless: that's me. Think fast! No use getting kicked out within three minutes of arriving.

"Thank you!" Good start! Polite, ordinary. "Actually, I might be early. My aunt is probably still in the emergency room. They told me she'd go to this floor. I thought I'd wait." Hey, I sound fabulous, slick and unrehearsed! Please, please, let that work for a few minutes!

The nurse nods sympathetically. "No orders from the ER have come up yet. When they do, I'll let you know where she'll be and how long till she gets there. What's her name?"

"Wendy Katz."

"I'll keep an eye out. You could be in for a wait, dear. The paperwork generally appears long before the patient." He points past the women. "Family room right down there. You could be looking at a good hour or more," he warns.

"I don't mind," I say soberly. "I'm just grateful Aunt Wendy's still with us."

"Oh yes," he clucks automatically and gives my shoulder a small soothing pat.

Another nurse emerges out of someone's room. Thank God: her smock is a royal blue that sets off her coppery skin. My nurse leaves me to consult on a more pressing issue with his colleague. I feel sorry for the poor guy. Possibly, he picked that hideous color himself?

More pressing matters: I've bought some time, yet hurdles remain. The two women continue to pace. I try to appear appropriately bereaved: devoted niece, anxious for auntie, grateful the news thus far has been good. There's my story, if anyone asks. Keep your lies simple. Can't remember where I read that advice, which certainly makes a dubious sort of sense. I wrinkle my face into a preoccupied position, take a deep breath, and trek down the hall.

I walk as slowly as possible. That's logical, me being weighed down with filial worry and all. The women are standing outside of room 410. My heart pounds as I pass them, inexplicably guilty. Avoiding their faces, I focus on cramming in what I can of the room while creeping by: bed, window, man. Go any slower and I'll be at a complete halt.

She's here. She's alive. I'm freezing. Millions of tiny goose bumps erupt over my arms. My mind shimmers into a new direction: Leilani! I want to say her first name out loud, feel the word move through tongue and teeth.

Her daughter stands at the end of the hallway. She wiggles and glows. First time I've seen the kid happy! She claps her hands with excitement. I can't help myself: I nearly laugh with joy, caught up in her. Me too! I can't wait either, Holly. I know your name. My back is toward the nurses' station and Leilani's room. Nobody can see my face as I walk into the waiting area, an idiot beaming into an empty spot on the floor.

She disappears. I'm left with the familiar message: hurry! I assumed the need for speed was Leilani's. However, she's flat on her back, as good as jailed as far as suicide goes, hospitalized and monitored and labeled all around risk.

Maybe Holly is in a hurry? Great—with my luck, she's poised to disappear forever if I don't get my butt in gear. I'll have to pry Evelyn on the time constraints of ghosts, if I decide to grace her café with my presence again.

The women reconfigure themselves, alert, as two men come down the hallway. They're about the same age—one is dark, Spanish? The other walks right up to Grandma and puts his arm around her.

The thin woman looks my way.

I smile weakly, caught. Shit! Sit down, hard, pick up a magazine, and look at my watch. Remember the poor aunt. Kidney failure. I sigh broadly in case sound carries that far, and stare out the window, suffering. Hope she's watching. In a few carefully timed minutes (grief makes me easily distractible), I open the magazine. A few more minutes later, I finally risk a peek from the pages.

Nobody is interested in me at all. They're focused on what a nurse is saying—not my Mr. Salmon but the African-American woman with better taste.

I'm practically sick with relief. Every muscle in my body is tense, breath barely getting past the ribs. Quite the stress level involved with this vocation. Too bad nobody includes psychics on various annual lists of high risk, high stress jobs. Maybe I can be the one to put us on the map.

The nurse gestures and—to my joyful shock—begins to lead away the whole huddle! They traipse to the nurses' station and continue down the hallway beyond. Mr. Salmon darts out of a room, grabs a box from a closet and strides into a different doorway. He notices me and tosses an encouraging smile.

Long wait, my dour face acknowledges. Poor Aunt Wendy.

The hall is empty.

Don't think! Can't hesitate! I stand up, quickly, a fog of fear and excitement. My feet hurry in her direction. I take another look toward the nurses' station. Nothing. Now. I'm outside room 410. I take a deep breath. What am I afraid of? Somebody will yell at me again? Kick me out? Worse things can, and have, happened. Stop thinking. Open the door and go in!

I do.

The woman on the bed turns to me. Her hands are tied to the guardrail. She might've been pretty before. On technical terms, she's alive. The eyes that follow me are empty. The loneliness I felt last night returns. All those years listening to Daddy and only now do I know what he means by compassion.

I'm calm. I'm shaking. I'm a wreck and know I should be here, and nowhere else on earth. I have the urge to close my eyes and to look out the window. I do both. I feel the blood rush of recognition again, certain of what I am required to say. I sit in the chair next to her bed and give my mind over to both of them—Holly and her mother—without fear.

We have all the time in the world and nothing to lose.

16
LEILANI

Does this young woman have her painting? Leilani is confused. She keeps falling asleep and coming to, over and over. The waking is ordinary but unexpected. Every time she falls again, she thinks: now! Her mouth is unbearably dry and her throat, raw. There should be water in that river. And why can't her hands move anymore? Yes, if the river had water she would cup her hands for a drink. Maybe this person hid the painting. Leilani tries to talk as the room comes into focus. The sensation of falling returns. She stumbles up again, in a hospital with bound hands and an acidic stomach.

This woman—with a face too clear to know real trouble—is probably an assigned psychiatrist. She must confront youth, punishment for failing! As if waking wasn't enough. At least she's not tormented by the memory's return. She thinks about them even while asleep now, or in the state mimicking sleep—a restless, dreamy condition halfway between a dozen different worlds at once. Maybe they gave her drugs. If so, she'll remember the benefits of their appropriate use. She'll stash the rest and be more cautious next time. Goddamn Anna.

Leilani resolves, getting sharper every second, to tell Martin about the abortion. The pregnancy is a secondary point. Anna's arrogance is the issue. Who is she to make decisions as if paternity no longer mattered? Of course, that's how some women get babies in the first place. A little slip of the pill: you beg forgetfulness, get off the hook, and make some man a Daddy. God knows, she's toyed with that plan herself the past few months. Not some stranger in a bar. No, she wants one of the decent men. That very qualification complicates matters. Maybe the husband of the woman Will was in love with? People recently betrayed do unpredictable things.

She's right back where she started: simultaneously dead and alive. Leilani puffs air out of her stale, painful mouth and stares at the ceiling.

Anna trusted her enough to talk. Maybe she won't exactly tell Martin. Could there be a way to cast broad hints?

The next time she decides to die, Leilani resolves to fly to another city.

Even though the young woman appears poised, relaxed even, inexperience is written all over her face. If Leilani weren't supremely tired, she would give the poor girl a break and start the conversation herself. One would probably begin with statistical information: name, address, phone number, and insurance.

Speech is surprisingly difficult. By the time her jaw is oiled enough for use, Leilani can think of one thing: "Could you please get me some water?"

The demands of the body, back so soon!

The psychiatrist leaps for the sink. She hesitates, unsure of medical restrictions for those with recently pumped stomachs.

Common courtesy rules. She stops again, cup hovering above Leilani. Both women look at Leilani's bound hands.

"My name is Delphi." She pulls off the ties and raises the bed to let Leilani sit.

Leilani drinks. The water simultaneously scalds and soothes her scratchy throat. Her eyes ache. How in the world is she going to muster up the energy to start the process again—the drive toward sickness and mayhem? She is far, far too tired for the energy her own death requires. You hear about people who simply lie down and die. Why can't she have that sort of droopy constitution? Instead, she has to come from stable stock, capable of real endurance.

"Don't bother," Leilani tells the young woman, between slurps. There simply is not enough water in the world to satisfy.

Delphi fills the cup again. "Last time. You could get sick."

"Finally."

"Don't bother with what?" wonders Delphi.

"A cure. Help. Anything remotely therapeutic. I'd accept pharmaceutical assistance, although I'm probably no longer a viable candidate by your standards."

"My standards," Delphi repeats. She sneaks a peek at the door. Too bad there's no lock. Anyone can interrupt.

Leilani wonders why the shades are open. Far too much sunlight is allowed to enter. If this person is not prepared to write a prescription for narcotics, she should go away. Now, please. Did the words come out of her mouth? She can't always tell. Her eyes shut again. The drift of strange sleep washes over her.

"Leilani? I know what I'm about to say will sound strange. Okay, bizarre. Listen with an open mind for a couple of minutes.

What's that literary term—suspend your disbelief? Do that. Try not to get too upset."

Leilani cracks an eye. This girl could be one of her students, tossing out a stock phrase from drama class. Oddly, the concept used to be among Leilani's favorites, sound advice, versatile enough for a surprising number of non-literary situations: imagine that you do believe and you might! The familiarity of the words momentarily eases her aversion to psychiatry. Maybe the drugs this woman will prescribe are even more marvelous than the ones she's currently experiencing. Maybe if she listens up, a good girl, she'll earn more water.

"Here comes the strange truth. I'm psychic—I mean, I'm new at being psychic. The whole thing started with your daughter, Holly. She wanted me to come to you."

Now, hasn't Leilani been awake? She has to think hard about this. She feels awake. In fact, her body is tense, every nerve poised for flight. Someone sees Holly? Here she is on what should've been her deathbed and this person, barely out of the teenie-bopper stage, claims to have a message from Holly? This had better be part of the strange sleep—drug-induced, no doubt. She blinks her eyes again as test. They're open. She certainly seems conscious, to herself.

Her confusion is almost funny. She's experiencing the dilemma behind Alice's tumble down that rabbit hole: dream or reality or drugs? Asleep or not, she takes a more critical look at this doctor. How to assess such a claim? Perhaps she is not supposed to assess. Perhaps what remains of her life has permanently fallen into the realm of the ridiculous.

"Well, good for you," says Leilani lightly. "Let's at least hope for longevity in your relationship."

Delphi decides her duty is to ignore sarcasm and despair. "I think this is a short term thing for me," she answers politely.

Leilani realizes that this is not a conversation she cares to have. Hearing someone else—especially a stranger who looks so free—talk about her daughter is unbearable. If this is how therapy is conducted nowadays, with talks of psychics and visions, she swears to become an even more ardent anti-Freudian.

"I'm really not up to this. Could we ring for a nurse please? There's a distinct possibility that you're a hallucination. I may need new medication."

Delphi doesn't answer. She listens. She hears the words she needs. "Cricket," she says confidently. "Your nickname for her was Cricket."

Leilani believes that if she moves as much as a muscle—twitches an eye—she breaks the spell and the witch doctor vanishes. This is a cruel, cruel trick. Where did this person get her information? The stability of her life wavers, suddenly on a fault line.

"You don't think Holly's with you. She is, every day. She says thank you for the lullaby. She misses your singing and wants you to know that she still dances."

Leilani begins to cry, her life broken anew. This is too much—torture to be suddenly pushed this close yet remain so infinitely far away. She cannot bear to hear this sort of talk! More than anything, she wants more! She bites the inside of her cheek, hard. Blood. She is awake. Here is real pain. Here is torture.

Intent on accurate reporting, Delphi barely registers Leilani's reaction. Her gaze drops down near the floor as she concentrates.

No voices, no drama of the chorus or High Court—as in the beginning, she thinks someone else's thoughts. Holly's thoughts—and they're gorgeously, magnificently clear.

"You still aren't sure. Ask for another detail."

Leilani wavers, instantly without details. Relinquish passivity and she's complicit in the hoax or dream or strange New Age moment. For months, she's wanted nothing other than to talk to Holly. Here someone else has been offered her heart's desire. No words come out of her mouth.

"Okay," says Delphi, resolutely. "Her favorite blanket was pink with kittens.

She took the tag with her."

Leilani starts to shake. How dare she evoke that image? In her nightmares, Leilani sees Holly's face—not the warm, moist face that cried and kissed, with its slightly pointed chin and bright, liquid eyes—no, her dreams are of the new face, the putrid mass buried underneath the ground, bones hollowing out and flesh fallen away. Roaches and worms wander across cheekbones, into eye sockets. The new hands flake and mold; they smell like rot. In between two decomposing fingers lies the tag Margaret had sewn onto Holly's cherished, well-worn, blanket: Made with Love by Mama Meg. That unimportant, filthy, tag will hold together longer than her daughter. The unbearable fact—unbearable—is that this is not a dream, but reality. Holly will never hold anything. Her decomposing corpse clutches half a blanket. The other half is on Leilani's bed—or the floor, tossed aside in the fray of her so-called rescue.

Leilani hides her face in the thin hospital sheets, where she can weep in peace. Consciousness vanishes. The biology of pain takes over. She is propelled into the experience of loss all over again, into the desperation of watching your child disappear, forever. The questions of who Leilani is or what she may or may not believe is meaningless: the raw present tense of emotion structures the world.

Panic grips Delphi. Such grief makes her feel a million years old. As quickly, she's a child again, out of her league and stumbling toward lives larger than her own. Yet there's no time for self-doubt or hesitation. In an instant, that door could open to a crowd. She can't waste Holly's hard, hard work, getting everyone to this point.

"Leilani," begins Delphi. Her voice catches. She feels herself filled with the love she's supposed to convey, the urgency of the message. Her own need disappears.

Hearing the difference, Leilani lifts her head.

"Holly has one important message. She forgives you. She forgives you for every mistake and the ones you think you made, but didn't. Her life was perfect. You did love her enough. You did. You loved her more than enough, more."

More than enough, more than enough, more: the room dims for both women as Delphi loses herself in the rhythm of words, reaching for Leilani as part of her own body, repeating: you loved her more than enough, more than enough, more. Rules of time and space slip away. Leilani is granted the one wish of her lifetime: she feels Holly again. The grace of forgiveness falls over her and Leilani recognizes—with the clarity of her own breath and bones— her daughter's presence. At the same time, she will never be certain of breath nor bones again, of the terms of her own existence.

Eventually, Leilani is able to breath enough to notice that she has fallen onto the psychiatrist's lap, rocked and soothed and spoken to like a baby. She sits up straighter to look at this woman who shakes the world open. She cannot wait to hear more, more, more! Can she ask Holly anything? She needs to tell Holly how much she misses her, how hard she tried. Her own life pales in comparison to even the memory, the scent or hint, of her daughter. Holly was reason enough for the world to keep spinning.

She grabs Delphi's arm and tries to speak.

"I know! She loves you like that, too," says Delphi, who is hardly the picture of self-containment herself. Yes, she decides: this is the world record for weeping.

Leilani's heart may not be able to handle the shock of the next sentence that comes out of this person's mouth. Yesterday, she would've welcomed that sensation. Today, she wants the strength to tolerate ten more minutes if those minutes are spent discussing Holly.

Delphi is silent. Holly remains nearby, waiting. Both are content, their separate responsibilities met. A new sense of serenity slips over Delphi, softening her smile and her stance in the world.

Slowly reviving, yet spent, Leilani laughs out loud. "Something tells me that your services aren't covered by my insurance policy."

Delphi slaps a hand over her mouth to cover her own giggles. "If anyone here knows, I'm history. Your neighbor nearly threw me to the cops."

Who can sustain such a peak of emotion? They relax enough to exchange the slimmest of stories: who are you again, really, and how did this unfold? After what they already know, intimacy is spectacularly simple: Delphi plops on the bed, slumber-party style. They put their heads together. Leilani tries to imprint every word in her memory. The back of the mind hums: this is my miracle, this!

Knowing that nothing she can say will ever be enough, Delphi recounts every last detail of Holly's appearances, beginning with the window walks in physics. She describes the dress.

"The yellow dress! We had to bribe her to wear others. She even slept in it a few times."

The dress still hangs in Holly's closet. She was buried in velvet. Anna thought the heavier material more appropriate for winter. Leilani agreed, considering all the cold seasons ahead.

Delphi takes care to recount each movement, every nuance. She doesn't mince words. She describes the precise curl of Holly's hair and the sadness of her eyes.

"A serious human being, my daughter" says Leilani. "Holly should've lived to be a theatre critic." Her small laugh grows too loud, an edge of hysteria audible. Delphi smiles politely, uncertain.

Leilani grabs Delphi's hands. "Thank you." She whispers.

For years, Delphi has been imagining her perfect adult life. In the fantasy, she is an executive in the making, emerging from an upscale and well-ordered apartment to hail a cab (life always took place on a coast, east or west, according to mood and desire for warm weather). Not only does she appear chic, urban, organized, and unshakable—she is all of those qualities, to her core. Her daytime duties are to tick off tasks; evenings are spent in isolation or with the one or two equally insulated friends she'll make. There will eventually be a boyfriend, a fiancé, and later perhaps, a husband—although the last step isn't required. Never a child, never a mess or fuss or headache she won't be able to handle. A dutiful daughter, she'll visit her father and write her mother until she dies. Delphi envisions a stock portfolio, faithful partner, and a stable physical environment to compliment the core of serenity that is her birthright, daughter of a priest and yogi.

Instead, strung out from lack of food and sleep, she is tangled on a bed with a strange woman twice her age. She is without home or family. Her college degree hangs in jeopardy. She has neither job nor significant money in the bank. Yet she's happy. Serenity and security are nowhere in sight. She has never been so uncertain of her next move. She sits on the bed with Leilani's arms in hers, talking to and about a dead four-year old, and is shamelessly, inexplicably, happy.

Leilani has another urgent question. "You said Holly was here every day. I've never felt her. How will I know?"

"You never felt her?" Nearly impossible for Delphi to imagine! She senses Holly strongly, listens for the child's imprints upon her psyche, footprints Leilani is to follow. "You could have. You will. 'She'll be in every perfect song?' Those are the exact words."

Leilani struggles against another wave of pain. "You know the perfect song? Turn on the radio and bingo: the song you were wishing for plays, or one that exactly suits your mood? One of us would yell—the perfect song! The other two would come running. You'd have to explain why the music fit the moment. Will said there were no accidents, no matter how small the synchronicity."

"She'll be in each perfect song. She always has been."

Leilani imagines being surprised by Holly again—music in the doctor's office, in the car, on the stereo—the way Holly slipped her hand into hers, out of the blue, or emerged from a doorway all sneak and smiles. For the first time, the emotions her imagination evokes are not wholly unpleasant. Terrible, but not completely unpleasant.

"It won't be easy," says Delphi somberly. "You can call me if you want," she adds, without forethought. Would Evelyn recommend such a move?

"Obsessively," jokes Leilani. As soon as the words come out of her mouth, she realizes she's more serious than presentation may imply.

"Hopefully not. No, I think not." Delphi smiles. "Start over. Don't take anything for granted, good or bad."

Leilani doesn't want to ask; she must, as punishment. "What about Will?"

"He's with Holly. Every second."

"I'm so sorry," chokes out Leilani, bile and grief arising simultaneously. "I've been blaming him—for everything."

"Especially the accident."

Leilani can only nod.

"The crash wasn't his fault. You know that—another car hit theirs. Even so, they died when they were meant to. Nothing could have changed that."

Leilani is too afraid to ask more: afraid of abandoning anger, afraid of finding that Will is angry, too.

"You were the defining love in his life. He wants you to have a better memory—that's what he says. Have a better memory. You'll find your answers about Will there. They won't be all that bad," Delphi adds, kindly.

"I hate to admit this--" Leilani is unable to complete the confession.

"You hardly miss him," finishes Delphi, carefully. "You think you hate him."

Once again, Leilani falls away. She wipes her eyes. Will she ever be able to move beyond her current psychological condition, breaking down every forty-five seconds?

"You're a little, just a little, relieved that the problems were solved," continues Delphi.

The sludge of her psyche, aired like a weather report! The words sound worse than Leilani had imagined. Sick! More than selfish, she is repulsive.

Delphi concludes: "Relief makes you guilty and guilt is the great brick wall. You can't miss him. You won't let yourself remember how you loved him. Missing Will would be too much, on top of Holly. Better to have righteousness than only pain."

Leilani steadies herself with the guardrail. Remember Will? Remember: midnights with a bottle of wine and a telescope; four hours to pick their first shared mattress (queen size, his requirement); finding Daisy, the gem, in the melee of the local pound; in the library, passing notes like school children while they worked—or pretended to—on their dissertations. They held Holly for the first time, together, on a hospital bed like this one, and cried.

She was not interested in having a child. Will was: one, he promised. He courted and cajoled and flirted for a year before she tossed aside the diaphragm, neither opposed nor excited, but committed to the realization of both their life dreams—and having a child was Will's. She had Holly for him. Then she fell in love with both of them, again and again, every day. He stands at the center of everything she loved and lost.

Leilani covers her face. She can't look at another person, even this one.

"I hate him for giving me everything and taking it away. I

hate him for every stupid thing, leaving coffee cup rings on tables or forgetting to lock the front door. I'm evil."

Since her hands are visible, Delphi relies on a back up: she crosses her toes. Too late, she sees the value in a good luck charm. Please, don't let her blow this! One wrong word, and Leilani will be lost. Her only hope is to ignore her own voice and listen to others.

"You're not evil. You're tardy. These are conflicts you were supposed to deal with while Will was alive, and didn't. Those dynamics didn't die with him. You're doing the same thing now you did then: seeing part of the picture. Selective vision. This may sound harsh, but half the truth is a lie."

"He never did have an affair, you know," announces Leilani abruptly. "Nothing happened, yet."

Half of her statement is an attempt at confirmation. This young woman appears to be a seemingly effortless and endless source of previously inaccessible information. The things Leilani doesn't know, and wants to, are countless.

"There's the beginning of the truth. You were married. You and Will had problems and he did not have an affair. What makes that such a betrayal?"

"We were drifting. He was infatuated with someone."

"Memory. You're in possession of the answers, always have been."

Distractions, Leilani thinks. Her life had been a series of distractions. Were the past five months any different? She's surprised by the revelation, but probably shouldn't be: her worldview has shifted half a dozen times in the past twenty minutes.

"You know those women consumed with emotional work?

The person at the office who remembers every birthday, or the friend who calls because she noticed you looked tired or trampled on or something subtle? I mean the mothers who analyze their children's interior lives, looking for clues into what makes the kids tick. Mostly, they're women—the ones who ask you how you're feeling and then go away and act on what they heard."

Delphi is reminded of the women who tried—other people's mothers who handed her boxes on her birthday or, better yet, those who dragged her from the Zen Center to share hot chocolate on otherwise ordinary afternoons. These women pried her open and made her life shine in a different light, reflected from their eyes. Did those women make a difference? They meant everything, even as they failed. Delphi nods. Yes, she understands the value of such labor.

Leilani shakes her head. "I had no time for those women. I had no time for the emotional work of my own life, let alone attending to others."

"You got more than you bargained for. You have to catch up on work left undone."

"Does neglect catch up with everyone?" wonders Leilani. "Is that part of fate?"

Delphi wishes she knew these larger answers—not simply the details, intimate and ordinary, of another family's life.

"Wait—there is Victor," muses Leilani. "I really do want to know what happened to him, for Rocco, as much as myself. I think. That's legitimate emotional work?" Or is it? Objectivity is not one of her current strong points.

"Victor?" Delphi looks at the goose bumps sprouting over her arms. She starts to feel cold.

"My neighbor's son. He disappeared years ago. Rocco, my neighbor, has no idea where he is or if he's even alive." Leilani's excitement skyrockets. "You could tell me! You could tell both of us!"

A sickening sensation closes in on Delphi. "Does Rocco live in the house next to yours, the one with the green roof?"

"Yes! See! You know something already."

"I liked that house," says Delphi softly. "Something special about that house. Let me see about Victor."

She knows there is nothing left to see but closes her eyes anyway. The decay is there—darkness that comes from within, whether the body breathes or not. Victor Crea was a bad man. His death, painful and unpleasant, served the world well—even his father.

Delphi opens her eyes to Leilani's waiting face, newly lit and fragile. She hesitates.

"I'm sorry. I don't know a thing about Victor. I draw a complete blank."

Leilani whole body drops a notch in disappointment. "Too bad!" she cries. "I was sure you would know. I could tell Rocco."

"Maybe Rocco holds the clues to Victor, the way you do to Will. Ask him to tell you about his son."

Talk to Rocco in direct terms rather than skirting around their respective ghosts? Agitated, Leilani's body aches from upheaval and abuse. The work ahead, on all fronts, is overwhelming. So is the path she had been diligently forging, the one toward her own demise. Sleep could be an acceptable middle ground. Perhaps she can be unconscious for a couple of years, then decide? Leilani does not want the witch doctor to leave. Entirely over-stimulated and ready for immediate collapse, Leilani wants the conversation to continue as much as she needs a short nap.

"Please leave me a phone number," says Leilani.

Delphi wishes she had one. She writes down Ian's. "I'm apartment hunting. My friend will know where I am. You should sleep again. I better leave before somebody shows up."

"All my well-wishers," moans Leilani, fear and melancholy arching their ugly snake fingers. She closes her eyes, a hand on her forehead. "Don't go. I'm not ready." I'll never be ready, she thinks.

Having never received instruction on the timing of exits and wise parting words (or much of anything else, for that matter), Delphi briefly considers remaining by Leilani's side, indefinitely. She could serve as general interpreter, a freelance gig. She would mediate between Holly and Leilani, between Leilani and the greater world. Such a task could take up—and over—entire lifetimes, hers and Leilani's.

Instead, she gathers what remains of her courage and moves toward the door. The back of a dead child is not the best vantage point from which to build a future. Wasn't that one of the mistakes Leilani already made for her? Delphi tries to formulate a good-bye in the face of such need—tremendous need!

Leilani is crying again.

The door opens. Instead of a crowd, there's Anna. "Hello!"

Anna immediately focuses on Delphi, whom she logically believes to be here on business. "I'm the patient's sister, Anna O'Brien."

Delphi shakes Anna's hand and struggles with self-presentation. That student thing worked with Carmen.

Leilani barks from the bed. "Don't talk about me in the third person, please. Remember, I didn't die? Anna, meet Dr. Sandquist. Psych resident on duty. She tours the rooms of the suicidal."

Anna blinks. "The adage is true: you know you're getting older when everyone else seems impossibly young. Can I talk to you, alone, for a few minutes?" She begins to politely steer Delphi outside.

Just as politely, Delphi declines. What she wants to do is drop to the floor and giggle, and eat a good lunch. Even the idea of crawling into bed for a nap alongside Leilani is appealing. Instead, she pretends to be a psychiatrist.

"I'm not actually assigned. I'm floating, you know, making rounds? The official psychiatrist will be here soon. We chatted." Anna's attentiveness is an opportunity Delphi cannot resist. "Wait—there's one thing. Your sister needs a lot of help—I mean a lot. Rally around her, stuff like that. Make her go to movies, call up old friends. Spend an afternoon with her. Be inventive."

"Oh." Anna crosses her arms. She was definitely thinking more along the lines of heavy medication. This does make a certain kind of sense: take the down-to-earth approach, the old-fashioned route, that sort of thing. If the commonsensical approach proves too time-consuming, there are, of course, second opinions.

"Buy her silk pajamas," continues Delphi. "Blue. Silk has a soothing quality. Get her back on whole grains and vegetables instead of the feast or famine routine. Every room she is in should have flowers."

The patient laughs.

Delphi shakes a serious finger at Leilani. "I hope you're listening. Think expensive flowers—everything exotic and out of season. Pamper yourself beyond reason. A weekly massage is not out of the question. I'd recommend regular facials and pedicures. That dog you have—get her back. Buy every new bestselling book, hardcover."

"Music," adds Anna.

Delphi and Leilani stop giggling, surprised.

"She used to listen all the time. She needs music in every room, too."

"That's a wonderful idea," says Delphi earnestly. "You're on the right track." She looks at her watch. "Oh, those appointments," she exclaims, brightly. "Gotta go! Hang onto that phone number, Leilani. Meeting you was an incredible pleasure."

"Amazing," agrees Leilani. "Thank you."

Anna appraises the strange change in Leilani, no longer presenting herself as an advertisement for successful lobotomies.

By the door, Delphi waves her arms and mouths, "Girl," behind Anna's back several times, jabbing at Anna and her own belly.

"Oh my God," blurts out Leilani.

"What?" Anna spins around only to see Delphi's final, cheery good-bye. The door closes. She turns back to her sister, who is indeed minimally lifelike again.

"Are you all right?" she asks suspiciously, knowing the question is innately impossible.

"Of course not," says Leilani, with complete seriousness. "I'm horrible. You?"

"I haven't recently attempted to kill myself—and potentially take along my aging parents while I'm at it. Please think about them the next time you're uncorking bottles. Lie down! You look as if you're going to fall off that bed any second. You should be sleeping."

Anna puffs pillows and reorganizes Leilani to her own satisfaction. "Do you think that psychiatrist skipped elementary school? She seemed painfully young. Or I'm painfully old."

Leilani props herself up on an elbow. "Have you decided what to do about the baby?"

"Oh, you mean in the vast amount of private reflection time I've had since discovering that you weren't drunk, but nearly dead?" Anna bites her lip. The other doctor—the more seasoned one with glasses and age spots and the whole nine yards—had cautioned against lashing out. You'll want to hurt her for hurting you, he had warned. Be gentle. Anna does not feel gentle. Nor does she want to be the one to push Leilani over another edge.

"Okay, okay," she relents. "I told Martin. Call me weak: here we are, the whole family waiting in the E.R. on pins and needles—you without heartbeat or brainwave as far as we know, and I'm the one doing the deathbed confession. I couldn't keep the secret. I told him."

"And?"

"He's horrified. Repelled." Anna sits down wearily, pillow in hand. "Ecstatic. Maybe some machismo thing, pride in his ability to create progeny. You should hear him: three boys and he'll have half of some sports team or other. If he gets a girl, she's an instant princess, complete with adoring court. Either way, he's rightfully scared out of his skull and halfway to the cigar shop, waving a banner."

Leilani listens, nearly asleep. Perhaps she can reside on middle ground? Not happy and not dead either. She peers at Anna through half-closed eyes. Anna smiles, drifting into her future. Her sister has perfected the ability to be simultaneously miserable and content. A girl! So many secrets hide inside of us. Leilani's eyes close completely. She wonders if she will ever trust time again. Minutes, hours, and days tick by—and for what? Tomorrow guarantees only pain or miracle, as if the distinction is possible.

17
DELPHI

Since I'm traveling light these days, I could take a cab to the airport. Ian insists on giving me a ride.

"I'm afraid you'll change your mind," he says over the phone.

What mind? In the past twenty-four hours I appear to have lost mine. I went right from the hospital to the Midway Sheraton where I slept away the remainder of the day—and topped that off with a good eight hours of regular nighttime snooze.

The minute I wake up, I call the airline. No, I repeat to the reservation clerk: no need to delay for reduced fare. I hang up with a ticket to San Francisco on a flight that leaves later today.

Next call, Ian. To say he's thrilled—on all fronts—would be an understatement.

"Wait, describe that again! Carmilla the Hun, huh? Did you mention her to the kid's mom? You're joking about the shrink thing. You are definitely not doctor material."

"Hey! Maybe I'm considering medical school? We can toss Evelyn another fiasco." I offer up every detail he requests, and more. After all, he's equally responsible for hooking up mother and daughter—maybe more.

Ian keeps returning to the question of guilt. "Did Leilani do something horrible?" he presses. "I don't get it. She's driven to suicide, over what—gainful employment? A rocky marriage?"

"That was the worst, Ian. Nothing out of the ordinary happened. She did the best she could and wishes she'd done better. The small mistakes, totaled, were killing her."

"That's scarier than if she'd committed some crime. Hate to think of all my mistakes. No doubt, I've stomped on my parents' feeling a zillion times. God knows what I've done to Kate and Joshua. And I'm barely getting started—haven't even graduated from college. Yet."

"Physics!"

"Don't worry. Our project is nearly complete. I'll give you the scoop when I see you, which will be in about an hour."

"An hour? My plane doesn't leave until two. And I owe you, big time, for the physics thing."

Airport security: he mimics a bullhorn. "Really—I'd want to make one stop. Consider that payback for all the grinding library research you didn't do."

"As long as it's not my father."

He promises and puts Meredith on the line. Seems that she's been the source of the impatient background noises.

"I'm so proud of you," she says.

"Me too," I admit, although I'm not sure if she's talking about the Leilani trip or the one to Lisa Weisman.

"Are you nervous about meeting your mother?"

I can't answer. I nod, which would be more helpful if videophones were indeed a reality among the masses.

"Delphi? Would you like me to come with you?"

I close my eyes. Could she be any kinder? Meredith offers to put a hold on her own life in order to help sort out mine. Without question, best offer I've had.

"That's so sweet of you," I eventually choke. "But no thanks. I should go alone."

"You're sure?"

"Positive."

"If you change your mind?"

"I'll call."

We hang up. I realize why I didn't leave at those earlier crossroads, my chances to flee Ian and his family: Meredith isn't offering an isolated hand or helping some motherless child out of duty. I've made a lifelong friend—a good one.

The one person I don't call is Daddy. Not that I'm quite as angry as I was before. I'm simply less clear on the legitimacy of my emotions: is he somebody I'm supposed to blame? Mother Weisman may have that answer, too.

I write him a letter. Let him know where I'll be so he won't worry. I make sure he has Ian's phone number and ask him to call Wendy and other friends who've fallen by the wayside. My burgeoning career as a psychic gets a paragraph. Don't worry, I conclude. I'll be fine.

Within the hour Ian allotted me, the letter has been handed off to overnight express. On the sidewalk in front of the hotel, I scope the street for a maroon mini-van.

This time when I hop from foot to foot, I'm not cold. I am incredibly, fantastically nervous. So anxious about meeting my mother after all these years that I cannot make myself stand still and actually have to run back inside to use the lobby bathroom—

twice.

The mini-van moves as if driven by a middle-aged matron. I swear, Ian can't take a risk. He motions for every possible pedestrian to pass in front of him. He forgoes his own turn at the stop sign.

"Living on an edge, huh?" I joke, climbing in. "The speed limit in the parking lot is 20. Throw caution to the wind. Try 10."

To my total shock, he hooks an arm around me and squeezes me into his side, effectively immobilizing me in a grip stronger than Edgar's. He accelerates at the precise moment he takes the other hand off the wheel to turn my face toward his and hit me with a big fat celebratory smooch on the cheek—which would be more effective if I wasn't starting to scream. The van veers.

"Ian!" I disentangle myself. "What are you doing?"

He laughs. "Trying 20." Fist in the air, he gives a scream. "I am totally psyched! We did it!"

We look at each other and smile.

"We did," I agree.

For a few quiet, happy moments, Leilani and Holly sit between us. Their presence isn't mysterious or spooky, but the most natural thing in the world.

The mini-van maneuvers on the freeway. I ask Ian if he's planning yet another obscure career. "Private investigator? Seriously, you did a great job. I wouldn't have had the foggiest notion where to start—not in the real world, anyway."

He laughs. "Tell you what: consider me on permanent retainer. If you ever need gumshoe-type assistance, I'm your man."

Ian's smile is suspiciously lighter. Yes, his mood is so very good the cause may go beyond solving somebody else's problems.

"Let me guess. The job offer was legit. You said no anyway."

He launches into a mock eerie chant. "Ooh, the great psychic has spoken."

"Please! Will we ever be able to have a conversation that doesn't touch on my so-called powers of precognition?"

"I've actually given that some thought. Any relationship you have will be, by nature, freaky. Fundamentally, we have an imbalance. You might know my future plans before I make them—not to mention current motives and past sins. Definitely will take some adjustment on my part."

Freaky? I'm not sure I like either the description or the implications. Or the fact that he could be right. Who will ever come to me for a normal heart-to-heart again? Takes the give-and-take—and fun—out of the very type of conversations that Ian and I have had from the get-go.

Ian continues. "Tricky? Sure. Insurmountable. No way. Don't worry. I'll read up on mind blocks. I've reconsidered my earlier offer as guinea pig. I think I'll keep my psyche to myself—mostly."

"When we were talking jobs and art yesterday, did that feel—oh, to put this delicately—freaky? Or earth level?"

"Definite earth," he grins, reassuringly. "Don't get defensive. Hanging with a psychic is a new to me."

"So is being one."

"Does this mean you're official? You'll put out the psychic shingle?"

I sigh. "God, I have no idea. I mean, I think so. Probably, yes. How's that for self-assurance?"

"On par with mine. Yes, I got the job on the merits of my amazing ability to copy anything ever created in pencil or ink.

Unfortunately, the job does entail more than drawing in isolation for hours on end." He puff and bellows, drill sergeant-style. "Employee must attend meetings. Brainstorm. Newly hired peon, in particular, is required to multi-task and share toys with others. Prostrate self to project manager. Be team player."

I laugh. "You're not?"

"Not this team. Too much huddling for my reclusive tastes."

"Have any alternatives?"

"A surprising amount. Once I decided to go with drawing—"

"You did? For sure?" I'm so excited for him! "Why?"

His own nature forces him to forge the straight-up honest path, even when that proves embarrassing—to both of us. "You. Not the lame advice you dished out yesterday—yeah, don't look so shocked. I didn't expect a forecast of the future, okay? You pretty much echoed eighteen points I'd already made in my own head, thank you. No, I mean what you're doing."

"If there's praise ahead, I could use some. What am I doing? I'm a complete wreck."

"Exactly. Instead of sticking to the safe route, you're chasing the 'follow your dreams' crowd. Why can't I?"

"Follow my dreams?" I laugh. "Ian, you are so wrong. I am way too cautious to follow dreams, or for that matter, to follow your advice on the topic. You were the one urging the very route you're now taking."

He's confused. "You're not going to find your mother? You didn't play guru the past few days?"

"How to put this? Fear drives me, not dreams. Fear of regret, of the big mistakes you look back on when you're forty and say: if only. I've seen so many people like that! They come to the Moon because they lost or forgot, or have never seen, what's essential to their lives. They want a second shot at happiness. They want suffering to end."

"Does it?"

"Sometimes. If not, they tried—which means they've learned that they can try and try again. I don't want to end up with all the 'if only's.' Holly asked me for a favor. Imagine how denying that could've haunted me in a hundred different ways."

He whistles. "I see your point. Is this why you're off to San Fran, too?"

"I'll kick myself for a century if I don't try to get some answers from my mother. Here's the shocker. Her lies weren't the wake-up call. Leilani was. She taught me that words left unspoken are the ones that stay with you forever. The thought of having the conversation I need to have with Lisa Weisman hanging over my head an entire lifetime—and maybe beyond—is too much. I need to know the past to build my future. Am I Jewish? Buddhist? Is there a line of psychics in the family? Let's not forget certain tiny details like why she left me and who she really is." Saying the list out loud overwhelms. I sigh.

"God, I wish I could help you," he says earnestly. "Tough trip, huh?"

"Tough trip."

"So much for caution. Your version of self-protection sends you hurtling off on the riskiest paths."

"Could be everyone else misinterprets caution, its appropriate use and direction. We're protecting ourselves from the wrong things. Remember who's psychic," I smile.

"See," he teases. "You brought up the topic. On the tips of

our tongues at all times, I swear."

"Guess you're right. We both better get used to the uncanny between us."

We're laying permanent groundwork here. Getting used to anything, as a unit, carries a sense of commitment—who knows what kind. We don't talk for a couple of miles, content. Then, the fact that we're in Uptown dawns on me.

"Evelyn?" I groan. "Tell me you're kidding."

"Stay in the car if you want. I'm spilling my guts."

Not that I mind seeing Evelyn. I did survive without her expertise, and don't plan on holding her absence against her—much. I'm simply too preoccupied with the visit ahead.

"Let's wait until I get back," I offer.

"And if you don't?"

"Don't what?"

"Come back." He doesn't take his eyes off the road.

"Don't be silly," I moan, guiltily. The thought has crossed my mind. What if San Francisco screams: home! What if Lisa Weisman convinces me of the same? The mood in the car takes a bit of downturn. So much for permanent ground.

Ian shrugs. "I like to think you'll be back. I hope so. Just in case, here's one less regret: we're paying a courtesy call."

"Can't hurt, I suppose," I offer, relenting.

"Can't hurt. Plus, you owe me. Remember the Tao and the atom? Your good friend Gaines?"

"Promise me you'll never tally all my debts, Ian. I mean that."

Still steering, he twists to grab a folder from the backseat, which he deposits in my lap. Inside are three copies of a bound comic book. A quick flip through the pages and I see: Ian documented our journey. A young man and woman, college-age, search for a spirit's mother. What is spirit, or consciousness for that matter, the narrator asks on the first page. The drawings are intricate, detailed. Perfect.

"Seems the names and faces have been changed to protect the innocent." I joke to hide how oddly pleased I am by his effort.

"Do you like it?" he asks, anxiously. "You're not mad? One of the copies is for you to take on the plane."

"And study! In case Gaines asks me a question about 'my' work. Seriously, Ian, I love this. It's beautiful—and brilliant! I can't wait to read the whole thing."

He beams. "Hey, my pleasure. I got to draw without inventing a single creative detail. Right up my alley. I did pound some pages at the library, though. Tried to toss in some discussion of molecules, although the thing does read more poetic than atomic."

I flip through a few more pages. My character is not too bad-looking. Maybe I am leaving the city with a good luck charm, after all.

Ian parks next to another mini-van within two blocks of Crystal's. We walk the distance in silence. As always, I'm struck by how many apparently employable people populate these streets as if they've nothing better to do than lounge—or spend money. I think of the woman in the green slip dress. Flimsy attire this time of year, even for those born and bred here. I scan the street. I wish I would see her.

Of course, Ian holds open the door for me. I nearly step smack into Evelyn, who is two feet away. Waiting?

"Ian! Delphi! What a wonderful surprise," she exclaims, arms in the air for emphasis.

"Surprise?" My skepticism shows. Can't help myself.

"Well, maybe." She grins and wags a finger, which we follow.

Crystal's is packed. Mid-morning, the café has a handful of mothers, fathers, and a smattering of less attentive types who I peg for nannies—all with children, of course. For the first time, I notice that a corner of the café contains toys and pillows. The customers who sit by themselves seem not to mind the occasional tantrum. An elderly couple talks, heads bent, by the window.

"The restaurant business treats you well," observes Ian.

"I'm nearly always busy, mid-morning. Families with young children come out before naptime, looking for a place that meets everybody's needs. Toss the toddlers a few toys and bingo: you're family friendly. People think I'm politick. Actually, I'm calculating every penny." She laughs lightly.

Now, here's an attitude that garners my respect. Hope I can put my talents to profitable use, as much as for that greater-good loophole.

Ian jumps in. "We found her," he announces, excitedly.

Evelyn apparently hasn't been on the edge of her seat about the whole issue. She takes a few seconds to come round. "Oh! The little mystery girl! Yes, tell me."

He tells the story.

Clearly, Evelyn is pleased for us. Less clear, again, is her degree of surprise. No regrets, I remind myself. I ask her flat out if she's been withholding.

"Ever since we met, I feel as if you've known stuff you weren't telling. Maybe about Holly? Whether we'd find her mother, or how?"

"No," she says sincerely. "I was in the dark. Completely."

I frown. "I had such a strong sense that you were keeping something from me! Especially the day I came and you weren't here. I really could've used some advice, you know," I conclude, accusingly.

"This reframes the question. No: I had no information about Holly. Yes: I knew a few facts about you."

Ian breaks in. "I spend half of my conversations with the two of you thoroughly confused."

I'm annoyed—and vindicated. "Tell me!"

"Don't think that I'm here solely for your benefit—or yours, young man. Remember, you're both equally a part of my saga. Delphi, you were an obvious crisis in the making. Disintegration was written all over you, plain as the headline of a newspaper. I knew the fallout was near."

"Why didn't you tell me?" I wail. "That's so unfair!"

"Really?" She smiles and folds hands in lap. "I didn't know details, honey. Remember me: famous for half the story? Time and again, I've been presented with the choice to tip people off or not. One wrong word from me, and disaster strikes. Taking care of myself means backing off from a crisis. That's been my life lesson."

"You were avoiding me on Tuesday," I blurt out. "That's not a guess, either."

She laughs lightly. "I knew you'd knock on my door, early. Made myself scarce. Don't worry. I had plenty of errands to do, business at the bank. Hiding didn't inconvenience me at all."

"I wasn't worried about that," I reply, coolly. "I was pretty disappointed."

Ian chimes in. "I'm glad Evelyn didn't help you, Delph."

"You don't understand, Ian. Evelyn was the one person who

could've helped me—and she jumped ship. I understand the rationale better now," I add hurriedly. "But then, I was devastated."

"And alone," he concludes. "You figured out, the hard way, that you were capable of the right decision. Nobody pointed you in the perfect direction and said: go. You did that."

Just when I'm feeling a bit better about how events unfolded, Evelyn is compelled to ruin my good mood once again.

"You're partly right," she says to him. "Ask yourself how Delphi got to my doorstep in the first place. She had a lot of help getting that far."

"Mom," he muses.

"You," I add. "And Holly."

"And Heaven knows who else," finishes Evelyn. "Nobody's an independent player, kids. We're all tangled in the same web, constantly in motion and largely invisible. Even by removing myself, I pulled a string."

"I have a headache," I announce abruptly. "Too much analysis after so much trauma—okay?"

Evelyn appraises me, finger on chin. "I see a double cappuccino in your future. With a dollop of cream—perfect antidote to head pain."

"And a sprinkle of cocoa," I add, meekly.

We concentrate on selecting refined sugars and caffeine. I need the respite. Evelyn's meta-theorizing brought home one huge point: I am not out of the woods, by a long shot. My crisis has barely begun, what with visiting my mother and the rest of my unformed, newly tumultuous life, ahead.

Still, I'm glad Ian brought us here, especially after I've downed my particularly tasty coffee confection. Fate continues to smile on me—Ian and Evelyn are merciful. The visit winds up softly, conversation light.

"You look tired," comments Evelyn as we walk to the door.

I pat my puffy, sore eyes. "Too much crying followed by twenty-four hours of sleep! They'll be swollen for a week."

"Take care of yourself," she says cheerfully, hands on my shoulders as she studies my face. "This won't be easy. You know that."

"Hey, even I know that," jokes Ian.

"Any other words of wisdom? Can't hurt to ask," I tease her.

"I dished mine all out already. You'll remember them as you need to. Good luck, Delphi. I hope you find what you're looking for."

"Me too," I say soberly. I can barely think about meeting Lisa Weisman without getting an immediate stomachache and itchy skin. My luck, I'll probably break out in psychosomatic hives mid-flight.

I can't resist a final question. "Evelyn, was your absence entirely self-interest? Or were you thinking along Ian's lines, leaving me to my own devices as a lesson?"

"Self-interest? I didn't use that word at all. You'll see." She squeezes my shoulders. "Call in a week with a full report," she orders.

Evelyn's cheery good-bye waves ushers us down the block.

Ian and I are talked out. Or maybe just the opposite—the questions that loom ahead make conversation daunting. We listen to his Nora Jones CD most of the way to the airport. She reminds me of my father because he listens to hers.

We slide into a space near the airport's entry. A security guard takes note. We'll have about forty seconds before Ian's shooed on his way. Other cars pause and passengers disembark, quickly.

He hands me a small box. I'm floored. "A present!"

"Absolute self-interest. Go ahead."

I rip open the box: a tiny silver cell phone, one of those new, compact kinds.

"Programmed and ready to go. My number is three on the speed dial."

I joke. "Way down low at three, huh?"

"I figure you should put your parents on one and two, current situation considered. After that, well, you may be free to reprioritize." He gives me a wicked grin.

"I am going to miss you so much! Thank you, Ian. For everything."

The minute I step on that sidewalk, I'll have only my own strength to rely on. I've gotten used to his. When we put our arms around each other to say good-bye, I close my eyes and imagine his good grace and sweet spirit rubbing off on me. Sort of a loan.

Mr. Security tosses a meaningful look in our direction. Poor guy. The bulk of his day must be spent breaking up good-byes.

I step out and twirl the phone, a trophy. "I'll be in touch."

"No matter how she actually acts, Delph, your mom should drop to her knees and thank her lucky stars that you're her daughter. Remember that."

After he drives away, I really, really want to sit on the cement and stay there a long time. Instead, I grab my bag and force myself through the revolving doors. The security guard throws me a sympathetic smile.

Despite all the warnings and regulatory hoopla, I glide through screeners and scans in no time flat. At my departure gate, I scrutinize my ticket as the pleasant official airport voice booms: Northwest Flight 359, Minneapolis to San Francisco, boards from Gate 28 in fifteen minutes.

Confirmation is good. A new believer in cosmic mistakes, I can't quite shake the fear that I've accidentally booked myself into Alaska.

Final point of business: reading material for the flight ahead. Could peruse Ian's comic, although I may need to save that as some sort of reward for the trials ahead. A juicy paperback novel is just what the doctor ordered, pure fantasy. Magazines are out. I think I sorted through every issue on the stands during my earlier reading jag.

I turn around for one of those tiny bookstores that line the corridor.

Daddy stands about four feet away, watching me. He's wearing street clothes—his civvies, I joke. An ancient carry-on garment bag hangs over his shoulder. He waves a ticket.

"What a coincidence. I'm on the same flight."

Words are still coming out of his mouth as I hurl myself toward him for my final, complete collapse. I have never been so happy to see anyone in my life—and don't think I ever will be again.

I never want to lift my head out of his warm wool jacket. One of his solid hands smoothes my hair and the other is on my back, wrapping me in the way he used to, when my biggest injuries were skinned knees and hurt feelings.

"I'm so sorry," I finally manage to say.

"I'm fine. Don't worry."

I lift my face toward his. "No irreparable damage done?"

He smiles. "Never. Not between us. And I have a few things to be sorry for, myself."

Relief nearly knocks me off my feet. Dad motions me toward a chair and I obey, grateful. I grab his ticket. He is on the same flight.

"How did you know?"

"Your new friends. Meredith called me, one concerned parent to another. She knew far more details of your travel plans that I did—or indeed, that you were traveling at all." He laughs, wryly.

"You'll know tomorrow. Overnight mail."

"Well, that makes me feel so much better. A letter, just your style, and safely after the fact."

My guard wants to go up, but can't. He's right. He's here! He's exactly what I need. The entire trip—plunking myself in the danger zone, within arm's reach of my mother's skin, her eyes, her smell—is no longer as frightening.

Dad taps his ticket against his leg, nervous. "I want to set one thing straight. We should be on the same wavelength. Ready?"

His somber tone piques my curiosity. "Sure."

"Okay." He takes a deep breath, visibly composing himself. Now I'm not only curious, I'm afraid. Dad is never ruffled.

"I'm making this trip for myself, Delphi. I have questions for her, too."

Never once did I imagine he had unfinished business. I actually have to remind myself to close my mouth, fallen open.

"I'm angry. All these years, and I'm still mad. Believe me, I thought I'd moved beyond anger—built an entire life on moving beyond anger, actually. Your pain led me back to my own, again. I need to talk to her."

"You seemed so content! I assumed you had some secret story between the two of you that made sense—that neatly tied up ends I couldn't see."

"Sure, there's more of a story than you know—only not much. Not enough. In all honesty, Delphi, I've never entirely understood her decision. I walked away when she did, no questions asked—because I was too hurt."

My heart is in my throat. "You don't really know why she left us?"

He shakes his head, no.

I lean back in the chair and cover my face with my hands.

"You okay?" he asks in a few minutes.

The airport voice soars overhead: Northwest Flight 359. Now boarding the young, the old, and the needy.

My fingers slip away. "I'm unbelievably relieved," I admit.

Now it's his turn to look surprised. "Relieved?"

"All this time, I thought you had an answer—some magical pearl of wisdom—that you had simply decided never to share with me."

He's stricken. "I'd never do that to you!"

The look on his face cracks me up—oh, now I know what else is ahead, something predictable, for once! "Let's have the 'how could you think I would let you down this way' conversation on the plane or at the hotel or something. I promise. Right now, I'm simply spectacularly glad I was wrong! I'm so afraid to ask Mom to give me anything—answers or even a warm welcome. She might slam the door in my face for all I know. I'm glad I won't be asking alone."

He nods. "Me, too."

We watch the first rows of passengers shuffle into line.

"Shall we?" Daddy stands up and holds out an arm, old-fashioned.

I accept. "You should really be demonstrating such chivalry to Edgar," I advise. "When we get back."

We board the plane, together.

18
HOLLY

We watch them. Watching isn't what you'd expect, the way earth uses eyes and ears. Mama and the old man aren't happy. They spend a lot of time together. They sit in chairs outside and talk about stars. They talk about Holly and some other little boy we don't know. They clean Holly's room. They walk the dog. Daisy follows Mama everywhere, and that makes her feel better. The old man is her friend now, and that helps, too. Mama will find a new house. We're told not to worry about her. We do. Some people don't get to be happy.

Now we are air and water and music and paint! We slip into the world a million ways. Some people see us. Most don't. We are the babies that stopped breathing. We are each lost child, the ones who fell, burned, bled, drowned, sickened, seized—were crumpled and crushed and trampled and buried. We are the children of the famine, the car crash, the bomb. History's sorrow trails behind us, centuries of stories and songs. That's our gift to the people who lose us.

Mama knows Holly through music. We send her songs. By earth's measure, we send millions of messages every second! One of the younger women needs a ladybug without spots. Another will find a lost wallet to return. This lady gets a Van Gogh—sunflowers already famous will be new to her. Here, a woman uncovers her son's Christmas wish list in the bottom of a drawer she uses every day. The messages must be precise and come at only one moment—the moment.

Yet time is nothing we know here. Earth is marked by hours, a burial ground for people and dreams. Mama sits with the old man on his orange lawn chair, looking at stars with Daisy. She waits until darkness to cry. Mama walks to the thick, buggy river every night; she draws water for the morning meal and weeps the long walk home. Mama sews a wool cap for brother, back turned so he can't see her tears. Mama lives in an apartment high above the city. She stands on the marble balcony at night and wonders how long the fall will be. Mama wakes before the sun. She feeds the chickens and milks the cows. Animals understand why she cries. Mama uses a gourd to grind corn, the salt of tears serve as flavor and protection for the girls she can still touch.

We lose her skin and blood and bones. We miss her. We lose everyone. We're sad about them all for a while, but she is the one we watch over. She is the one we will miss, as long as the children keep coming. They will. We are the bridge, the universe's center. Find the pulse of a painting or song or someone else's skin, and you will see Holly. You'll see us all. We're waiting.

ABOUT THE AUTHOR

Mary Petrie, Ph.D., teaches English and Gender Studies at Inver Hills Community College. She's the recipient of a number of writing awards, including a Loft McKnight, Minnesota State Arts Board Grant, and Loft Mentor Series; her nonfiction has appeared in The Rake and The New York Times. She lives in St. Paul, Minnesota, with her husband and three children.

marypetrie.com

CPSIA information can be obtained at www.ICGtesting.com
Printed in the USA
LVOW10s1843150914

404140LV00008B/1093/P